UNRELENTING LOVE

BLACK SWAN BOOK ONE

KALYN COOPER

Unrelenting Love

KaLyn Cooper

Cover Artist: Drue Hoffman

Editors: Devin Govaere, Marci Boudreaux Clark, Trenda London, Rebecca Hodgkins

Published 2016, 2020

ISBN: 978-1-970145-05-2

Published 2020 by Black Swan Publishing, LLC

Printed in the United States of America

This is a work of fiction. The characters, incidents and dialogues in this book are of the author's imagination and are not to be construed as real. Any resemblance to actual events or persons, living or dead, is completely coincidental.

Dear Reader,

If you are new to my books…Welcome!

If you are already a reader of my books… Thank You!

A stand-alone story, **Unrelenting Love** is a contemporary / romantic suspense novel that is the first of many adventures the Ladies of Black Swan undertake.

Team leader, Katlin Callahan is reunited with her old high school friend, Alex Wolf. Look for more of their on-going relationship in almost every Black Swan book.

Thank you for purchasing **Unrelenting Love.** If you enjoy this book, consider purchasing the other books in the Black Swan series as well as the related Guardian Security series.

Always,

KaLyn Cooper

DEDICATION

I dedicate this book to the women who have fought for our country, for their battle is on many fronts, their challenges often unimaginable. Many leave their children and families to work and train side-by-side with men who all too often do not see them as equals. These are some of the strongest women in the world.

ACKNOWLEDGMENTS

I'd like to thank my critique partners: contemporary and historical author Vikki Vaught, contemporary author Deborah Grace Staley, and romantic suspense author Monette Michaels for all your guidance and plotting assistance. My thanks to Drue Hoffman for this stunning cover, formatting and the many things she does for my career. Thank you, Devin Govaere for seeing this book from another perspective and forcing me to make it better. My sincere thanks to Laura Perkins for sharing insights into the Navy. Last, but not least, I thank my husband who helps add colorful language, realistic scenes and demonstrates Alpha male characteristics every day.

Rara avis in terris is Latin for "a rare bird in the lands."

In the ancient world, it was believed that the landing of a single black swan created a change that would affect the entire world.

Fact: A woman can get a man alone within hours…and kill him in seconds.

Fact: Men always underestimate beautiful women.

Fact: The military doesn't do anything without years of successful training, most often completed in secret.

Fact: In February 2013 the United States military opened combat roles to women, but no woman has "officially" been trained in military Special Operations.

CHAPTER 1

"Operations Control." The man's voice was expectant, ready to handle anything she threw at him.

"Lady Hawk confirming extraction site," Katlin Callahan spoke quietly into the tiny headset attached to the encrypted satellite phone clipped on her duty belt. She glanced up and down the nearly empty city street, alert to the armed men she and her team passed who might be listening. She was going to get pissed if Homeland Security had changed their exit plans…again.

The Iraqi afternoon heat baked her body under the mandatory *abaya* that covered her, shoulders to toes, in black cotton, but it also conveniently hid her weapons and survival gear. The *niqab* covered her long blonde hair, and its thick veil screened her alabaster face and blue eyes. It was a great disguise since it allowed her team of five American women to move freely within the warring country—as freely as a group of women could move in any Muslim-controlled region.

"I have you at one click out, moving west toward the Marine encampment." The man's voice in her ear bud brought her back to the current situation. "No change in plans at this time. Base commander has been informed and is expecting you. Proceed as ordered."

Thank God for small favors. She was about to close the conversation when he continued. "Hold for Director of Ops."

What the fuck does he want?

Dread piled onto her tired body as the tech threw more on her insurmountable load. She released a long sigh. She could handle her boss.

Katlin glanced at the other four women on her team who literally surrounded her. She smiled. As always, they had her back. They waited on a street corner while a caravan of allied troops in Hummers passed then scurried across the rutted Fallujah street. She glanced down the row of sun-bleached shops that struggled daily to provide goods and services to people tired of decades of war.

As her team strode past a recently bombed building, she watched a pre-teen boy scavenge for blocks that remained somewhat rectangle. He'd take them to his parents' home to replace ones falling apart from too many bullet holes, or if he was homeless like thousands of other children, he'd sell the formed concrete to someone for scraps of food. At least he'd eat today.

The physical and emotional devastation tore at her soul. She was glad her own country had never known the perils of war. She was in the Middle East to be sure no one would bring this unrest to the United States, as their target had threatened.

"Report," Jack Ashworth's baritone voice commanded. Katlin could picture him sitting straight-backed behind his immaculately clean, hand-carved mahogany desk at Section 7 in D.C.—in cool air conditioning—as he controlled agents all over the world.

She looked down at her dusty military boots and the bottom eighteen inches of her robe, which was covered in the gray powder that permeated every surface in that part of the world. She yearned for a long hot shower, followed by hours of sleep that wasn't interrupted by gunfire or bombs. Soon, she promised herself.

"Mission accomplished. Target eliminated. You already have the video feed. I'll upload the after action report on the way home." She didn't try to hide the pride in her gravelly voice.

"Great work, Lady Hawk. Get some well-deserved rest then get Black Swan in the sky tonight," he ordered, referring to their sleek black Gulfstream 550 jet.

"Yes, sir." Her team chatted in Arabic to cover her conversation with headquarters as the five women rounded the next corner.

"I'll see you in the morning." Jack's voice held a hint of excitement.

Damn it.

"No, sir." Her boss was the last person she wanted to see after this mission, or ever. "We're not headed to D.C. We're slated for five days off, and I have plans in Miami. The whole team has decided to stay there for a few days." She knew that would piss him off, but tough. He was the main reason she avoided her office. The fact that Washington, D.C. was filled with too many personal ghosts was another.

"Fine." The word was gruff, almost childish in its indignant tone. She heard a few clicks over the secured line and wondered if they had company on this call or if Jack was up to something.

"Private conversation, please, Kat."

Christ no. Not here. Not now.

Then she realized what he'd called her. Katlin never permitted anyone to call her by a pet name, least of all Jack ass. There were only two men she had ever allowed to shorten her name, her father and her best friend since high school. Her father had passed away three years ago, and she hadn't spoken to Alejandro Lobo since he'd handed her the flag that had draped her husband's coffin.

No. Don't go there. She had to shove all thoughts of Alejandro and the cheating bastard she'd married, Tyler Malone, into a box and never open it again. Okay, that was impossible, but she could at least seal it up for now.

"Katlin...you still there?" Jack asked impatiently.

Damn it, yes. Of course she was still there. Section 7 had all the best and newest toys available to international operatives like her. Dropped calls never happened to them because they had priority use of satellites.

She squinted and clenched her jaw, fearing their next conversation would not only be private, but personal. There were dozens of things to do before she could get her team out of Iraq. She didn't have time for this conversation.

But he was her boss. At least for another two years, she was committed to serving the United States government as a Navy officer. She had to go where they sent her and do whatever they asked of her. She would do her duty and not complain. Katlin Callahan was no quitter. That was evidenced by her success as the top graduate of the secret special operations training she and her team had endured. As for Jack, she could handle him.

"Yes, sir, private." The rest of her team couldn't hear him through her ear bud, and it didn't matter. She shared everything with the four women who had become the sisters she'd never had...almost everything. Some secrets could never be told.

"Kat," he said in a warm seductive voice, "when you get back to D.C., I need some time alone with you. We need to talk about us."

"Jack," she said firmly as she tamped down her anger, "you are *never* to call me Kat. Do you understand? No one calls me by that nickname." *Well, no one these days.* "You may address me as Ms. Callahan, Katlin, or my code name, Lady

Hawk. That's it. And there *is no us*, so there's nothing to talk about. You're my boss, which makes it inappropriate for us to be having this conversation."

"You were my wife—"

"Pretend wife," she interrupted, "during an operation." An undercover op she'd regret the rest of her life.

"Yes, during an op, but you felt the connection we made. We're good together." His voice became tender. "I understand you and what you need. We belong together."

No. None of that was true for her. "Well, obviously, if my acting abilities were good enough to fool you, it's no wonder the bad guys fell for it." She trailed her teammates around the next corner and down a mobbed street filled with cart-pushing vendors who called out to anyone passing their makeshift store.

"Skip Miami and come home to D.C. so we can talk about this," he asked, somewhere between a command and a plea.

No fucking way.

The last time they'd been alone together, he'd almost…*No.*

She didn't have time to think about that dreadful evening.

Then a flash ran through her analytical brain. Was this a test? Was some Section 7 shrink listening in on this conversation, trying to determine if she could handle the personal pressure added onto the professional shit she was trying to accomplish? That would be just like them.

Concentrate on getting the hell out of here.

As the women broke though the crowded marketplace, Katlin scolded, "Jack, this is neither the time nor place to have this discussion." That was professional, in case someone else was listening. "We're still in a hostile situation and a mile from a safe base." She took a deep breath and told Jack honestly, "Besides, it's a family thing I have to do in Miami, and I'm looking forward to it." She wasn't going to explain that it was her goddaughter's birthday and she'd missed too much of the little girl's life already. He could use that personal information against her someday, and knowing him, he would.

Lady Harrier grabbed her hand and squeezed it hard.

What the hell? Women holding hands in this country was not unusual, actually, it was a highly acceptable practice, but her teammate holding her hand…in public…never.

In an Iraqi dialect of Arabic, Lady Kite started talking loudly about babies and giving birth, as though she'd pushed out a few. Then Katlin saw the two local policemen moving closer to them. Machine-guns crossed their bodies, one hand rested on the grip, index finger extended down the action, only millimeters from the trigger. The men had taken a great deal of interest in her team.

"Trouble. Lady Hawk out." She disconnected the signal as much to end their on-going personal battle as to discontinue the current conversation.

In the local language, Katlin added to the conversation. "Oh, when I had Bizhan, he was such a big baby. I was in labor for hours." Saying those words hurt to her very soul because she would never know what it felt like to carry a child within her body.

She kept her gaze cast downward, not only because eye contact with men was forbidden but she was afraid they might catch a glimmer of her blue eyes through the veil. The brown contacts had irritated in the desert dust so she'd removed them hours ago. That might have been a bad decision since the streets were filled with men and women hurrying to reach home before sunset.

As they passed the uniformed officers, she watched the younger one scan her body as though he could see through her abaya. He couldn't, but she slid her gloved hand into the side slit and rested it on her holstered Smith and Wesson Shield. She glanced around, planning an exit strategy in case they were stopped.

"As your midwife, your delivery wasn't bad," Lady

Harrier, the team medic, extolled, "but there was a lot more anionic fluid and blood than we expected. You really should have emptied your bowels when you first started your contractions. Feces is common during delivery, but you had more than normal."

Katlin watched the two men turn away with pinched faces. It took every ounce of waning strength she had to withhold the burst of laughter that tried to escape. Damn, she loved these women. Leave it to Lady Harrier to play on a man's aversion to the maladies of womanhood.

The five women slipped easily through the darkening streets to the U.S. Marine Corps camp. As they approached the outer guard post, Katlin spoke loudly in English when the young Marine brought an M4 rifle to his shoulder.

"Captain Calloway and team returning," she announced using her cover name for this op. She lowered her niqab so he could see her white face as she dug handfuls of hair from under the abaya and flipped thick golden strands over the traditional Iraqi outer dress. Her teammates followed her lead, exposing their faces and hair, an act local women would never dare. They would be killed for it.

"Ma'am, may I see some ID, please?" He then spoke quietly into his communication system.

"Certainly"—she looked to his rank then embroidered name over his pocket as she held her hands out where he could see them—"Lance Corporal Framer. I'm going to reach into my pocket and get it."

"Yes, ma'am."

She produced the ID created for that mission and held it out to him as he was joined by another Marine, whose gun also pointed at the women. She was fine with this. It was standard operating procedure for this war-torn area, one of the few Muslim countries that understood women could be as deadly as men, a hard-learned lesson for American troops.

Two up-armored Hummers with remote weapon systems

perched atop roared to the gate. Four Marines in full battle dress jumped out and took up defensive positions while a lieutenant colonel strode to the guards.

"Quickly, inside ladies." He jerked a thumb toward the vehicles. "And get out of those things." He didn't have to say it twice. All five women hurriedly flipped the black mantles over their heads and wrapped them into a ball. She knew her team had looked fat and moved awkwardly, but the packs they carried in front of their bodies made it difficult to maneuver with any amount of grace. The disguise had worked flawlessly.

The men's eyes widened as the women shrugged the packs off their chests. Desert camouflaged uniforms now revealed the curves of every member of her team. The women shook off the weight of all they'd carried for days.

She rubbed her scalp with glee, lifting her heavy hair, allowing the slight breeze to cool her sweat-dampened head. Not for the first time, she considered getting her hair cut short, the way she'd worn it while in the Navy before being selected for the top-secret test group. She quickly rejected the idea. She spent weeks at a time Stateside and loved her long hair that fell below her bra strap in the back.

The mid-forties man before her took a deep breath before he spoke. Katlin knew the effect her team had on men, especially those who hadn't seen a woman this close in months. She checked out the nametag above his pocket then offered, "Thank you, Lieutenant Colonel Rogers." She gestured to her team, who moved in closer to her back. "We really appreciate your hospitality."

The senior officer nodded in acknowledgement. "Let's get a move on. You're on a tight schedule." Katlin smiled inwardly at his roughened voice. A glance toward the other women confirmed that they too had noticed. Blending in on an all-male Marine base was impossible, but she was confident their cover would hold.

The Ladies of Black Swan team had been created to stand out when necessary, or disappear in the shadows. None were movie-star beautiful, or truly ugly. They were chameleons, thanks to the makeup tricks taught at the C.I.A. From Katlin's blonde hair and blue eyes, to Tori's chocolate brown complexion and nearly-black eyes, at least one of them had the physical attributes to morph into whatever was needed for the mission. Each woman could get a man alone in hours…and kill him within seconds.

But LtCol Rogers wasn't their target. That ISIS fucker had already been eliminated. This wonderful man beside them was their host in the next stage toward home. As ordered, Katlin jumped into the Hummer. They sped through the inner checkpoint and stopped in front of the mess tent.

"Join me for supper," LtCol Rogers ordered as he led the way in.

CHAPTER 2

Food. American food. Just the smell of cooked meat made Katlin's stomach growl with anticipation. They'd eaten MREs, the military's packaged Meals Ready to Eat, for two weeks, and the thought of real food made her mouth water.

The murmur of deep voices fell silent when the five women stepped in. All eyes fixed on them.

"You see nothing." The base commander's booming voice left no room for questions. "Carry on."

When her team glanced at her, Katlin nodded toward the chow line, and Lady Kite picked up a tray. If it weren't for the desert digital uniforms, the mess hall would look like any cafeteria found in an all-boys high school, down to the young male faces.

Long tables stretched from one end to the other. Most enlisted men ate wherever there was an open seat, but ranks seldom mixed, especially in the Marine Corps. Katlin's team was guided to a far corner where other officers sat speaking in low tones. When the men noticed the base CO approach with five women, they all started to stand. Women were few and far between in theater and even less common on the Marine Corps forward base.

"Seats." Katlin and their host spoke at once. He looked at her and smiled.

"Not my first dance." She shrugged and set her tray on the well-used table that gleamed with cleanliness. It certainly wasn't her first meal at a table filled with Marine officers. Her father had reached the rank of major general in the Marines before he'd died suddenly behind his Pentagon desk. It had been a horrific end to the worst year of her life.

When Katlin sat down, she immediately bowed her head and prayed for the meal to nourish her body. She added on a prayer for her team and all the men in the tent to safely reach home. She crossed herself before she looked up. The women ignored her ritual, but the men seemed relieved as she reached for her fork.

"I take it, Capt. Calloway, that your mission was successful? I hope you got some good Intel for us. Anything you can share?" The man, about ten years older than she, sounded hopeful as he cut a piece of mystery meat smothered in brown gravy.

Those who needed to know anything about their mission were told that the five women had infiltrated the local community and were tasked for HUMINT, human intelligence purposes. Their real mission had been the same as always, find and eliminate a designated man. In this case, he'd been miles away from the civilities found in a modern, albeit war-ravaged, city.

"I'm sorry, but we really didn't learn much." It was the truth.

"We heard a rumor that Nassar al-Jamil was killed, but he's way up north near Mosul." The major's west Texas accent was undeniable.

Damn, word has gotten there already. It probably hit the Internet before we'd escaped down the Tigris River. Katlin shuddered as she remembered the overland trek in the back of a rickety truck in the middle of the night. She wasn't sure if she should damn the CIA for their lowlife contacts or bless them for getting her team safely to Fallujah in the wee hours of the morning.

"He has ties to this area. Did you hear anything about it?" The handsome captain beside him sipped coffee and bit off chunks of a thin cake. "

She walked a fine line here, but Katlin wanted to reassure the men that the small villages their Marines patrolled were safe now from that murderous ISIS leader.

"We heard about that," she admitted then hid her satisfied smile behind a long drink of water.

Her teammates remained silent as they devoured the hot meal, concealing their own gratification for a job well done. They were all tired and hungry. This hot meal took care of half the problem. They'd sleep before they flew seven thousand miles to the U.S.A, hiding within the night sky over the Atlantic Ocean. They were headed home, unlike most of the young men in the canvas tent.

"I'm sure the women were talking about him." The captain glanced to each team member looking for an answer. "He'd taken a few lessons straight from the Taliban book of horrors and was trying to bring back fundamentalist views on women."

Actually, al-Jamil had written a few new chapters of his own, especially where it came to the role of women in the fundamentalist Muslim community. That might have been why Section 7 had targeted him. The reason didn't matter to Katlin, although she knew how Iraqi women had fought their way back into politics and professional jobs since the war had begun over a decade before. She was proud of how fast and far the women in this country had come. With the elimination of this terrorist, hopefully they'd continue toward equality.

For Katlin, this was her job, and she was obligated by sworn oath to follow orders and use her skills to accomplish the goals set by her superiors. Her profession was more specific than any of the Marine officers at the table, but at its core, it was the same. They all fought for the United States of America, and the friends of their country, to maintain freedom.

Returning to the conversation, she told the anxious men, "Yes, we heard those same rumors." They'd started a few of their own. Dis-information was as important as information. But she and her team knew it was more than wives' tales.

When they'd finished all the food on their plates, and even had seconds of cake, Katlin couldn't stifle her yawn. She'd barely slept in the past week. "Sir, we need to sleep for a few hours."

"You can sleep with me," the captain offered with a sultry smile. He was handsome in that Alpha Marine way, but there was no zing.

She hadn't felt the indefinable instant chemistry in years. The last man to charge her body with jolts of interest hadn't been her husband, no matter how hard she'd tried. Katlin had loved Ty, but their relationship had been a cycle of his cheating and her forgiveness. It never had the constant flow of electricity. A lot of sex, yes, and it had been really good sex, especially make up sex of which there had been plenty. Their on-again, off-again relationship throughout college had allowed Katlin to date other men, and she'd experienced real zing.

Alejandro Lobo was walking Zing with a capital Z.

Maybe it was being on a Marine base again that brought the clear picture of her good friend in dress blues, rows of colorful ribbons filling the left side of his chest, his whiskey brown eyes with gold flecks that turned molten chocolate when he was aroused. Just the thought of him made tingles run from her heart to that special spot between her legs. Thinking about the long hours of making love with him in her college dorm made her smile.

"You're considering it," the captain encouraged. "I can see it in your eyes."

"That's a sweet offer, but—" She started to let him down gently.

"It would be very sweet, darling." His smile was seductive.

Maybe if it were some other time, and definitely some other place, she'd take him up on his offer. Who was she kidding? She'd never done a one-night stand in her life, and it'd been way too long since she'd allowed a man in her bed. Once back in the States, maybe she'd rescind her self-imposed celibacy. It was time.

"Tempting, but we need to sleep." She gestured to the other four women as they all rose from the table.

As the tempting captain opened his mouth to speak again, the lieutenant colonel shot him a reproachful glance before turning his intense gaze to her. "I've made arrangements for your team to sleep until oh-two-hundred hours. Your plane will be fueled and ready to roll at oh-three-hundred."

"Thank you, sir." Katlin was so grateful to be headed home. This mission had taken much longer than expected because Nassar al-Jamil rarely slept in the same place twice and always moved at night, often into caves rather than homes.

She and her team followed LtCol Rogers out of the testosterone-filled mess hall, and he walked them to their tent, pointing out the showers on the way. She'd get five good hours sleep before they left. Katlin could function well on that until they reached Miami, and then she'd crash for a few days.

The other women entered the tent after thanking the senior officer. Katlin held back. "Private conversation, sir?"

He nodded, and they walked to the end of the row of personnel tents.

"What can I do for you, Captain Calloway?" By the look

on his face, he was expecting a request that he'd have difficulty filling.

"Sir, it's what I can do for you." Katlin smiled. "I can confirm that Nassar al-Jamil is dead."

"How the hell can you do that, Captain?" he sneered. She was accustomed to the way men doubted her abilities. Some believed women shouldn't even be in the military. Even more doubted the sanity of those who placed women in combat, and almost all military men believed females should be never be in special operations. Her team was living proof they were all wrong.

The Ladies of Black Swan had been part of a top-secret test program. They'd been trained exactly like Navy SEALs, Army Special Forces, and Marine Corps Special Operations. Once they'd successfully completed that training, they could never return to their respective services so they'd been assigned to Section 7 of Homeland Security.

Katlin stared into the doubtful eyes of the man who'd seen years of war, heard thousands of hopeful lies, and probably thought she was a waste of good Marine Corps money that should have been spent on his men.

"You can trust me on this fact." She pulled a satellite phone from her side pocket and punched in a series of numbers. With a snick, the phone mechanically unfolded revealing a six inch square screen.

"Cool toy," LtCol Rogers commented as he glanced away from the blank display to meet her eyes.

"We're testing it." That's all she'd admit as she touched the corners of the screen in a precise order. A stilled picture of Nassar al-Jamil filled the display. With the press of a side button, a video showed the terrorist leader walking through a well-known village Marines patrolled daily. A blur flipped across the screen a millisecond before the extremist slumped toward the ground, and then his body jerked and spun before it hit the unpaved street. Two shots.

"Captain, where did you get this?" The man sounded angry.

She said nothing.

The angle pulled back as it widened. Two shooters lay on the ground, with small waists and full hips. The woman on the left wore a long blonde braid down her back, and the spotter had loops of jet-black hair tied at her nape. Wild, curly red hair lay across the shoulders of the second shooter.

The field grade officer's gaze shot to Katlin. She nodded toward the small screen where her face turned toward the camera and mouthed, "Did you get it?" The spotter's fine-boned Asian face looked into the camera seconds before the redhead's green eyes flashed up. All three women smiled and high-fived each other. In the distance, the video showed men in desert utilities surround a downed and bloody body.

"You?" the older Marine managed.

"Yes. I wanted you to know what your men will, and won't, be facing in the northern areas." She shook her head. "But we both know someone else will fill his vacated spot. My guess is his brother, Khalid Junayd, will take over, but he has over a dozen immediate brothers not counting any of the half siblings by his father's other wives." She pressed the button on the side of her phone, and the screen went blank before it slowly folded in on itself. She slid it into her cammies. "You never saw this video because we were never here. A HUMINT team of women spent a few hours in your camp." That was all she was willing to explain to him.

He stared at her for a long time before he admitted, "Yes, a team of extraordinary women spent a few hours in my camp. Thank you, Captain." For a few seconds he stared at the black double bars she wore on the front of her utilities. "Are you really a Marine captain?"

Katlin smiled as she walked away. "I am today."

CHAPTER 3

Alex Wolf thrashed side to side in the king-sized bed as the dream repeated the worst night of his life.

Red streaks lit the shallow ravine that seemed to extend into hell. The smell of gunpowder and dust choked the air. Screams of dying men echoed under the report of machine guns.

The dream jumped back in time.

"Drinks on me when this is over, Lobo. You've got my back, old friend." Tyler Malone's voice and brilliant smile cut through the thick night air just before he and his SEAL team blended into the darkness and the sandy foothills to secure the perimeter.

The nightmare leapt forward this time.

Rapid-firing bullets. Red tracers. Men in turbans with dark stains on their digitized camouflage lay screaming in pain in several languages.

Sweat seeped from every pore in Alex's body as the dream dragged him through it all again.

"Alpha and Delta, left flank, come around them from the back. Bravo and Charlie, right flank. Clean sweep. Echo, with me." Alex had called out orders through his helmet mic in the blackness of the Afghan mountains to his company of Special Operations Marines.

"I'm hit." Muffled cries from American boys pierced by enemy fire seeped through his comm unit.

He felt the ancient-packed sandy soil shift under his desert boots as his legs peddled in the soft tan sheets of the huge bed.

Three-shot bursts of gunfire mixed with machine guns on squirt. Men in light brown camouflage lay beside American Navy SEALs, dark spots on every man that lay on the ground. The screams. Oh God, the screams.

"Medic, forward," Alex ordered. "Comm, we need medevac ASAP. Get some choppers in here now."

He ran as fast as he could. Alex checked every SEAL looking for Ty. Looking for his best friend.

Finally, Ty's face.

He'd found him. There was blood everywhere.

Alex placed his fingers on Ty's throat to find a pulse, but it wasn't there.

His throat wasn't there.

Alex looked at the blood on his hand illuminated by the red tracer bullets that flew around him Then, he looked into the empty eyes of his best friend.

No. No. No.

"No!" Alex awoke to his own screams. He sat up, heart pounding. He was alone in the king-sized bed in the quiet penthouse apartment at the New York City location of Guardian Security, Inc. As he glanced around the barely lit room, he reassured himself that it had been only a dream.

It was *the* dream. Again.

He lifted the sheet and wiped the sweat off his face while he controlled his breathing to bring his pounding heart rate down. A glance at the clock revealed that it was only three thirty in the morning. He didn't have to be at JFK International Airport until nine o'clock.

He raked all ten fingers through his long damp hair. "Christ!" he said on an exhale. It had been nearly three years since he'd left a combat zone. He'd led Marines on top-secret black ops missions all over the globe. He'd seen plenty of death before, and after, he'd held Ty's bullet-riddled body in that ravine in Afghanistan. He thought he'd left all that behind him when he'd resigned his commission as a Marine Corps captain and said goodbye to his Special Operations company on Onslow Beach at Camp Lejeune, North Carolina.

More sleep would be impossible.

Alex threw off the clammy sheets and padded naked to the gigantic marble shower where he turned on all eight body jets and both showerheads, hot and full blast.

As water pummeled his body in the bright lights of the bathroom, it rinsed away the darkness of the dream and the pain of a lost friend. He shoved his head under the stream of wet heat, and when he surfaced, she was there.

She was always in his subconscious, but after the dream, she would come to him. He couldn't think about Ty without thinking of Katlin Callahan. Vivid memories of her pale face draped in golden hair, lips reddened and swollen from their potent kisses. His cock grew as hard as a rifle barrel and trigger-finger ready. His mind showed him her infectious smile, looking down at him as she rode him hard. Those blue-within-blue eyes captured and held him until she took both of them into orgasmic bliss.

Then she was gone. Just as she had disappeared from his life three years ago.

"Fuck." It was a whispered oath as he glanced at his throbbing erection. That was what he needed, though, a good hard fuck. A whole night of fucking. Maybe he'd troll a few bars in Miami with Griffin, his manager there. Over the past few years, their relationship had grown into good friends, so more than boss and employee.

Or maybe he'd visit the Chicago Center after Miami and

see Aleta. She was the absolute opposite of Katlin Callahan. Aleta's dark brown skin under him as he pumped into her was the solution. After a nice dinner and great conversation, she always invited him back to her condo, and the sex was good. Not mind blowing, but really good.

He hadn't had mind blowing in years…since college…since Kat.

God dammit, quit thinking about her. He hadn't seen her since the funeral, and she hadn't spoken a word to him since. Why then couldn't he exorcise himself from their past? From her?

Alex looked at his long, hard cock and knew his erection wouldn't go away while memories of her lingered. He soaped his hand then leaned his forehead against the cool rock of the shower. Closing his eyes, it was her face, smiling down at him, he saw as he sought the much-needed release.

Christ. Will I never find peace?

Ten minutes later, Alex forced his focus to his workday as he pulled on a Guardian Security, Inc. polo shirt over sore shoulder muscles. At thirty years old, with a more sedentary job than he'd ever had in his life, he now worshiped at the altar of weight benches, ran at least five miles, and ate "clean" every day. No love handles for him.

He'd abused his body in the company gym yesterday for over an hour then taught a hand-to-hand refresher class to his men. They'd all wanted to prove how tough they were to the boss so he'd taken a beating on the mats. It was a pack thing. In the end he'd proven he was still the alpha. But damn, he would pay for it today, especially after being cramped on an airplane for hours. Even in first class, his long legs didn't fit well under the seat in front of him.

He pulled on khaki slacks and grimaced as his right knee reminded him of the lack of cartilage under his kneecap thanks to too many ugly jumps out of perfectly good aircraft. His bad knee would ache all fucking day.

He finished packing, excited, yet apprehensive, to see his daughter in Miami. She was growing up so fast.

Six hours later, Alex strode into the Miami Center manager's office. He'd lucked into an earlier flight and arrived several hours prior than planned. A Guardian limousine had been waiting for him at baggage, enabling him to check in with several of his other centers during the ride.

"Can you believe this shit?" Parker "Griffin" Mitchell III asked in his slow Georgia drawl without glancing up from the computer screen.

"What shit is that?" Alex lowered his aching body as casually as he could into the guest chair across the tidy desk from his friend. He held his face passive when he really wanted to wince at that one spot where his knee pinched, reminding him to spend some extra time in the next few weeks building up the muscles around the kneecap so it didn't slip.

"The media is making such a big deal out of a girl passing Ranger School." Griffin shrugged. "Rangers aren't all that tough."

Alex extended his legs with a satisfying stretch and crossed them at the ankles just above his Italian loafers. He'd have to change into boots and cargo pants, the official Guardian uniform of the day, before he inspected the facility. The building and records would be in perfect shape, but he had to go through the routine. Griffin ran a tight ship.

After considering the former SEAL's remark for a moment, Alex commented, "Most of the women I knew in the Marine Corps would sail through Ranger School. It's little more than what every Marine goes through in boot camp."

"Hell, it can't be that hard." Griffin grinned. "Seems like half the Army has a Ranger patch."

Alex chuckled. "Every Army vet I've ever met claimed he was a Ranger."

"Yeah, until you ask him if he knows any of our men, who

were certifiable Rangers before they went into Special Forces." Griffin returned to reading the screen. "This just pisses me off. Next thing you know, they'll try to put women into Special Operations."

"No fucking way." Alex's dream slammed through his mind. Bullets flying all around. Dead bodies everywhere. And the screams. Trepidation seized his whole body before he regained control and cleared his brain clean like wipers on a windshield. "They couldn't handle it."

"Could you see some little woman trying to carry me a mile?" Griffin laughed. "Or you?"

Both men were over six feet tall. Griffin had played football for the University of Georgia while Alex had been a wrestler at George Washington University. They were big men, muscled and deadly.

The idea of a woman carrying him brought a flash of memory. Katlin had picked him up in a fireman's carry once and walked around the huge recreation room in her parents' basement. She'd surprised him more than once with her strength and dexterity.

Since Katlin had grown up in Third World embassies, her father had his Marines teach her how to defend herself, and she was very good at it. It was no wonder she'd been grabbed up by the Office of Naval Intelligence right out of college. If Ty was to be believed during one of his many drunken stupors, she'd gone to work for Naval Special Warfare, which provided intelligence for SEALs and Marine SpecOps.

For the first time, Alex wondered if Griffin had ever worked with Kat. Then it hit him and knocked him back into every mission he'd carried out... Had she supported him with Intel? For a nanosecond, he wondered if she still worked there. Or was still in the Navy.

"After all the affairs I saw on rotation in Afghanistan and Iraq, I'm surprised they still allow women in theater."

Griffin's comment brought Alex out of the past and away from thoughts of a woman he hadn't seen in years.

"Not all are like that," Alex defended. "I worked with some very professional women over there. They were attached to our task force and went into the towns with us. They actually provided good HUMINT."

"Sounds more like you were their bodyguards," Griffin replied.

Alex had to admit, during that mission he was often overprotective of the women. "Yeah. That and more." He then remembered Butter. Shit, what was her real name? Betty? Betsy? Cute little blonde and she knew it. During the day she'd dug in and did her job without a word, and damn the woman could shoot. But at night, she wanted a man in her bed. She'd been aptly code named. She'd spread her thighs for several of his team members and the situation had nearly become disastrous for the cohesion of his team. After discussing it with his female counterpart, they'd agreed to send her back on the next supply flight. "Sometimes women are more problems than they're worth."

"Next thing you know we'll have women applying for jobs here," Griffin teased. "You ready to hire a woman as personal protection for our clients?"

"Never going to happen," Alex reassured his friend. "Not on my watch."

CHAPTER 4

Katlin Callahan awakened instantly when the apartment door opened. She breathed deeply as though she were still asleep–the way she'd been trained–while she listened carefully and fought her way awake. Some part of her brain knew she wasn't in theater and registered that she was safe, but the covert agent in her knew something was wrong.

Target or friendly? Fight or flight?

Unknown.

From the middle of the massive four-poster bed, she considered the solid oak dressers that could be used as a barricade if necessary. They also hid additional weapons in secret compartments that opened with a touch. Like everything in her life, the furniture in this bedroom had a dual purpose.

An untrained eye would see forest green walls that set off the fancy quarter-sawn wood in a typically decorated, perhaps male oriented, executive bedroom. For Katlin, it instilled comfort, safety, the feeling of home that always seemed to elude her.

She was in the owners' apartment at Guardian Security and had every right to be there since she owned the company.

Secretly. Only Barry Howell, who was her friend, personal attorney and the Chief Financial Officer for Guardian, knew she was the silent partner, and was under her strict orders never to reveal that information to anyone, especially Alex Wolf.

But in which city, she wasn't sure. All ten were exactly alike. Her eyes shot to a framed poster between the bathroom door and a walk-in dressing room. *Welcome to Miami* was written in script above the familiar cityscape.

Snippets of the mission in Iraq flooded her brain. She'd piloted Black Swan the entire flight back to the U.S.A., pushing the Rolls Royce engines so she'd make it to her goddaughter's birthday…in Miami. The sleep haze was clearing.

Soft footsteps fell on the foyer tile as the intruder entered, throwing her out of her recollections.

Damn it. Move.

Katlin slipped her hand under her pillow and grabbed the .40 caliber Smith & Wesson pistol that had become an extension of her body in the past six years as a Naval officer and as an agent for Homeland Security.

The familiar weight of her gun, its roughened grip against her palm and fingertips, soothed the growing fear. She could defend herself with something other than her trained hands and feet. Fight or flight, she was ready.

Soundlessly, she slid out of the warm king-sized bed, and her bare feet sank into thick-padded carpet. She glanced at the cheval mirror angled to see into the adjoining living room through the open door. Butter-soft leather couches connected in an L by an oversized lamp table, and an ottoman big enough to sleep on sat empty, but inviting.

This apartment was her refuge, a sanctuary that had now been invaded.

Why, and by whom, she intended to find out right now.

From the rhythm of the footfalls and their slap on the

imported African marble, she determined it was a man in leather shoes.

Trouble. Everyone who worked at Guardian wore the same uniform; grey polo shirt, black cargo pants, and soft-soled military-style black boots…not leather shoes.

Target.

Has he come to kill me? A second shot of adrenalin coursed through her body.

He certainly wasn't trying to be silent.

A soft thud told her he'd just dropped something cloth sided and heavy on the foyer floor.

Frozen beside the bed, she forced control of her breathing until it was slow and silent. She caught the slight scent of masculine sweat and expensive aftershave. Both were hours old. His breathing was normal, almost calm.

One clink, then a second, as metal touched the long glass table just inside the door that held a dozen fresh, long-stem yellow roses placed there especially for her by the staff whenever she was in residence. Bright as a Miami afternoon and saturated with fragrance, the buds always warmed her hardened soul and reassured her of the earth's beauty, literally forcing her stop to smell the roses.

Rattle. Clunk. Keys dropped onto the silver platter next to the cut-crystal vase.

He began to move so she used his footsteps to cover her own. In two long strides, Katlin slid behind the bedroom door and peered through the crack between the hinges to see a tall man with broad shoulders in the apartment kitchen. She estimated his height at over six feet. probably close to six two, about 185 pounds of hardened muscle. His full dark brown hair was tied in a ponytail that fell just below the collar of a light blue oxford shirt.

She didn't recognize him, but he could be any one of a dozen men hunting her. Lady Hawk had become a target of hit men worldwide as her confirmed kill list grew. Her team of five women was one hundred per cent successful; they'd never failed to eliminate a target who could cause a Black Swan event, one that could drastically change the future of the entire world.

Again, she chanced a glance through the crack. A custom-made, black web, two-gun holster stretched across his expansive back that tapered into tailored khaki slacks, resting low on narrow hips. They were just tight enough that she could see the well-toned muscles of his butt ripple as he moved around the kitchen, opened cabinet doors, and reached for filters before he moved to the fridge for the coffee.

Really? He's making coffee? Damn, he seems so at home.
Friendly.

There was something about the way he moved, but she couldn't place him. Hell, she'd just awakened from a deep sleep. In self-protection mode, she'd question everyone, even her own teammates.

His body was similar to most of the men who worked at Guardian Security. They were all former military, gym-toned, and fast with their feet and fists when needed.

For a nanosecond, she thought it might be Alex Wolf, the managing partner, but he wasn't supposed to be there until Thursday. She was in residence, and no one was allowed in the apartment while she was there, unless she invited him. She'd never invited a man into the penthouse.

Katlin stole another look. She'd taken down bigger men than him. She was strong and agile. She knew all the weaknesses of the human male from the body to the brain.

Since she'd just awoken, she hoped she wouldn't need those skills now because she wasn't at her best. As her teammates could attest, Katlin wasn't a morning person. A grunt of acknowledgement was all anyone could expect from her until she'd seen the bottom of her second cup of extremely strong coffee, black of course. Sometimes it took three. Until she'd reached that moment of ideal morning, she could be as mean as a wet lioness and as fierce as a hellcat reacting with pure muscle memory and barely controlled temper. Not good for a trained assassin. Not good at all for the intruder.

Katlin stretched her fingers and readjusted her hold on the gun grips then checked the safety. On. *Damn.* She knew she should have switched to her new Glock with the silent grip safety. This one would make noise. Nothing she could do about that now.

He unbuttoned the long sleeves of the expensive dress shirt and rolled them to just below his elbows, revealing brown skin. It wasn't golden like the usual Miami tan or a light black. This was naturally light brown skin. South American, probably, but it was dangerous to assume.

The silver Rolex glinted in the recessed lighting of the kitchen.

She was pretty sure he didn't know she was there when he turned on the water in the sink and began filling the glass coffee pot.

Katlin used the noise to cover her footsteps onto the Brazilian cherry floor of the ultra-modern living room. Her eyes, sighted over the gun, swept the room from right to left. Nothing there but sleek chrome-and-glass furniture, modern art, and the magnificent view of Miami through the ivory sheers, which held back the heat of the day's sun.

Sun. The word niggled at the back of her brain as though a whole thought centered on that one word was out of focus. She ignored it.

Tango at fifteen feet.

The man had folded a navy-blue silk suit jacket and carefully placed it on the back of the dark brown microfiber living room chair. He knew good quality and took care of his belongings. He also had money. Although valuable information, it didn't change the situation.

Katlin pointed the gun at the man in the kitchen who was

busy with coffee preparation. With great care, she looked at the foyer while listening to the pot fill with water.

A slightly worn black and gray duffel bag sat on the tile in the foyer. It was the standard Guardian travel bag, so he was an employee. And, yes, two guns lay on the glass foyer table.

The niggle had become a squiggle in the depths of her brain, but in survival mode=, Katlin's total focus was on her target.

Checking him again from his long brown hair to his hand-stitched shoes, she still couldn't tell if he had an ankle holster with another weapon.

As he turned off the water, Katlin spoke in Spanish. "Don't move!" Her command helped to cover the noise as she clicked off the safety on the gun.

The man froze with his back to her, still facing the sink.

Again, in Spanish, Katlin asked, "What language do you prefer to speak? Spanish? Portuguese? Or English?"

"English," was all he said, but he'd obviously understood the Spanish she'd spoken. He tilted his head as if considering something.

"Excellent," Katlin replied in English. Her voice was low and scratchy from hours of sleep but steady and sure. "Now, very slowly, move your hands straight out to your sides then to the back of your head. Interlock your fingers."

He complied. She watched his body language. He'd already rolled to the balls of his feet, bent his knees slightly, and centered his weight into a professional defensive stance taught to military and government agents and police.

He was a pro.

His forearm muscles rolled just beneath the surface of his smooth skin as he flexed manicured fingers before he spread and interlocked them.

There it was again, at the back of her brain. She recognized that movement.

"I'm looking forward to the frisking," he said. "I can't wait to have your hands roam all over me. You know you can have my body anytime you want…Kat."

She knew that teasing voice.

"Goddamn it, Alejandro." Katlin seethed as she called him by his given Spanish name, the one she'd used since she was fourteen years old. She knew he'd changed his name to Alex Wolf, but to her, he'd always be Alejandro Lobo.

"What the hell are you doing here?" she asked. "You weren't expected in Miami until Thursday."

He held his pose, fingers laced on the back of his head.

"Do you still have a gun pointed at my back?" He didn't sound worried, but he hadn't moved.

"No." She lowered the gun to make her statement true. "You can turn around now. And, for chrissake, put your hands down."

Alex Wolf turned to face her and dropped his hands to his sides. The chiseled features of his Latin heritage were irresistible to most women, and she was no exception. Serious brown eyes flecked with gold missed nothing. It was obvious that his nose had been broken more than once and had a slight bump but fit the hard lines of his caramel-brown face. That square jaw and strong chin made him look like the billboard-perfect Marine, a face that demanded attention, which he got from both men and women.

Her gaze finally landed on his full lips that begged to be kissed. She'd felt the warmth of those soft lips as he'd discovered every inch of her body. The memories of what he'd done to her with that mouth sent a zing through her, hardening her nipples, and awoke places she was sure had died years ago.

"Hello, Kat." Those two words, soft and seductive, hit her like a jet blast, searing and overpowering.

She wanted to run to him and have him hold her like he should have done when they buried Ty.

She wanted to smack the shit out him because he hadn't been there when she needed him most.

She wanted to cry in his arms and have him comfort her.

She wanted to cut him to the core with her words and actions, making him hurt as much as he'd hurt her.

In the wave of reactions, Katlin realized that she had overwhelming emotions for the first time in three years. She felt...something...everything...as sensation poured into the void that had been left cold and empty far too long. Since the day they had stood in Arlington Cemetery and said goodbye to the man who had been best friend to both of them. The man she had loved, and trusted, longer than the cheating bastard had deserved.

She should have known Alejandro's mere presence would do that to her. Standing casually before her was the only man who could infuriate her to violence one second and stir her passion to the edge of orgasm in the next.

Stunned by internal war, she stood motionless.

Her heart pounded, yet she could barely breathe.

She was speechless.

And naked.

CHAPTER 5

Training mandated that Alex first look for weapons. She held a pistol next to her long, muscled thigh, pointed at the ground. As he looked at it, she clicked on the safety. He bit back a smile.

That's my girl. But, no, she isn't mine. She never has been, not really. His heart clenched at that last thought.

Experience told him the next step was to look into the eyes of his captor to see if she would indeed shoot him. He saw blue eyes very capable of death. She'd killed before, according to her father's often-regaled story of how Kat had defended embassy children during a Panamanian coup. And she would kill again if necessary. She was a trained Navy officer. He wondered if she was still in the military or, like him, she had left the service for a better life.

He was supposed to look for "telling" body language, but when he saw the honey-blonde hair that framed her porcelain face, he paused. Memories flashed of running his fingers through the silky strands then pulling her head to him, followed by passionate kisses. His cock stirred.

Her blue-on-blue eyes were the color of a cool, crisp fall sky speckled with silver clouds, surrounded by a deep blue ring that increased their intensity exponentially. He remembered the power of those eyes ten years ago when he'd told her, "Look at me. I want you to know who's inside you. I want you to know *I'm* the man making you feel this way. I want you to know it's me making love to you." *I want you to love me the way I love you* went unsaid that night, or any other time.

His attention dropped to her tightened lips, visibly trying to hold in words, but he recalled them reddened and puffy from his kisses. Hidden behind them were straight white teeth that had scraped his shoulder just before she fell apart in his arms screaming his name in ecstasy.

The pink tip of Katlin's tongue dashed out and licked her bottom lip. Breath gushed from his lungs, releasing… something…that plummeted from his chest to his growing erection. That pink tongue had licked every part of his body, just as he'd explored every inch of hers.

Alex sucked in his breath when his gaze dropped lower.

She was naked.

High, rounded breasts tipped by light pink nipples peeked out from thick blonde hair that fell halfway to her waist. He wanted to tease those nipples, roll them between his thumb and fingers, then worship them with his tongue once again. Long-forgotten passion ripped through his core and straight to his cock, which stood at attention.

He skimmed over toned abs and stuttered to a stop at her navel. One of his favorite memories surfaced, licking champagne from her innie after one of her sorority parties. Although he'd had the opportunity with many other women, he'd never repeated the act. The memory was sacred.

A smile tugged at the corners of his mouth as his eyes fell just a few inches to the strip of light blonde hair he'd nuzzled into before he had licked her softness and savored her unique taste. His smile broadened as he remembered just how much she liked that.

Alex shifted his hips to release the growing pressure from behind his zipper.

He appraised her well-developed legs, which he knew had unbelievable flexibility and strength. The two of them had laughed and play-wrestled on the thick carpet in her parents' rec room dozens of times in high school and college. He also remembered those legs wrapped around his waist, pulling him so deep into her.

"Yes, Alejandro," she'd whispered, her hot breath saturating his ear, her words fulfilling his hopes.

Stop. Don't go there. She's not yours and never can be.

The Katlin of his youth hadn't been his lover in ten years. She'd married his best friend, Ty Malone, while his own wife and baby watched a few pews away.

Alex was sure she hated him…with good reason. He was none too happy with her either. She had held him at gunpoint mere minutes ago.

His smile faded.

Alex dragged his gaze back to Katlin's intense eyes.

"You're naked." His voice sounded raw, even to him.

"I'm not naked. I have a gun," she stated, as though that explained everything.

But then he caught it. Just a whiff.

His nostrils flared as he breathed in her feminine scent. Although it'd been many, many years, it was hers and hers alone. He'd never forget the unique scent of Kat…aroused.

Well, damn! She was as turned on as him. He shifted his hips again. Sure, it'd been several weeks since he'd slept with a woman, but he hadn't been this quick off the go since… college, the last time he'd been intimate with Kat. Inside Kat. Exploding with her underneath him, on top of him, behind her.

Stop it, damn it. He took a shallow breath because a deep one was simply out of the question. He shoved his hands into the pockets of his pants before he did something stupid with them, like reach out and grab her, pull her to him, and kiss her senseless. She was naked, and he was a man.

"Okay then, why don't you have on any clothes?" So she wanted to play semantics.

"You've obviously forgotten I sleep naked."

Fuck. Kat. Naked. Asleep in my bed. Alex wasn't sure if he should go caveman and drag her back to his bed, or be pissed as hell, since he hadn't seen or heard from her since Ty's funeral. Anger had simmered for years so he went with that emotion. It was one he could hold in check, or so he hoped.

"After three years without a word—not a letter, a call, or even a fucking Christmas card—you decide to say hello to me by getting naked in my bed? Or was it at gunpoint you wanted me?"

"No!" she said without hesitation. "You weren't supposed to be here until Thursday. I'd planned to be long gone before you claimed your baggage at the airport."

She sounded indignant.

How could she dare be annoyed because I walked into my apartment? Then it hit him.

"Babe, it *is* Thursday."

"If you hadn't come here early, I'd be long gone and you'd never have known—" She tilted her head as if she'd just heard what he'd said. "It's Thursday? What happened to Wednesday?" She sighed. "Did I sleep through the entire day?"

He almost laughed. She looked confused, an expression he'd rarely seen in their fifteen years of friendship, or should it be counted as twelve since they hadn't spoken in the last three? He should be more upset about that time span, but it'd been his choice too, and he'd stayed far away for good reason.

"I have no idea how long you slept. When did you get here?" His eyes swept the length of her soft curves again. He couldn't help it. She was naked, and he'd been hungry for that body since they were teenagers. Even while they had been lovers, he could never seem to get enough of her.

"Around two on Tuesday night, actually, that would be Wednesday morning. I pulled down the blackout shades and crawled into bed. I remember getting up a few times, but other than that, I guess I slept for over thirty hours straight."

Katlin looked at him, and damn it, she'd caught him checking out her body, again. What the hell could she expect? She was naked, and he was only a mere man.

She rolled her eyes.

"You've seen me naked before, many times." She tried to make it sound off-handed, but there was a tinge of red on her cheeks. Was that a flash of anger he'd seen in her eyes? It was true. They'd been lovers, on and off, the first two years in college.

"Yes," Alex admitted. "But not in the past ten years. You've changed. I've never seen *that* body naked." She'd filled out, womanly curves that, on any other female, would look soft, yet there was harder side to her now than he'd ever seen before. Maybe it was Ty's death. It didn't matter. Katlin was naked and standing ten feet away.

He took a step closer to her. The things he'd like to do with that body. He'd start by kissing his way down it, mapping her luscious curves with his hands and lips. His arousal was nearing painful.

"Well, now you have. Don't expect to see it again any time soon." Her tone was sharp.

Pounding came from the apartment door.

"Miss Katlin. Are you all right?" Griffin's deep voice and usually slow Southern drawl was as insistent as the knocking. "Katlin, please answer the door."

CHAPTER 6

Katlin took a deep breath to get her voice, if not her emotions, under control. Without moving, she looked directly into Alex's beautiful brown eyes then loudly called to the door, "I'm fine."

"Miss Katlin, please answer the door. Eyes on," Griffin demanded. "Alex is here, and I want to be sure you're all right."

Griffin wouldn't stop until he saw she was as good as she claimed. Sometimes men could be so overprotective. The man had no idea what she did for a living. She could more than handle herself. She turned away from Alex and headed to the door.

"Kat." At Alex's use of her pet name, she stopped and glanced over her shoulder at him. His appreciative smile told her he'd been checking out her ass. He quickly frowned. "Are you going to answer the door naked?"

Damn. He's right.

She deliberately turned and strode back to him. She tugged his shirttails from his pants.

Bam. Bam. Bam.

"Although I really like the direction this is headed," Alex

noted, a smile teasing his lips, "in a minute Griffin is going to break down that door."

She slid the shirt over his head then, in one continuous motion, over hers. As she slipped her arms into the sleeves, which even rolled up fell to her wrists, she vaguely realized it was inside out and left Alex bare-chested.

"Better?" she said, glancing over her shoulder as she moved to the apartment door.

"No, I liked you better naked."

Of course he did.

Katlin opened the door to Griffin. She trusted him to guard her life while in Miami so she could let loose and be a twenty-eight-year-old single woman for a few hours. But should it all go to hell in an instant, she would be the one to protect him. Did the brawny man really think she was in danger from Alex? Probably, because the party-girl portion of her real personality was all she'd ever allowed him to see. She'd have to play this out.

She forced a smile then said, "See. I'm fine."

Katlin felt Alex step up behind her, but he didn't touch her. She still held the gun in her right hand, now hidden in the small of her back where Griffin couldn't see it.

The Miami manager's eyes flicked between hers and Alex. She was sure the fact that Alex was shirtless, and Katlin now wore the blue oxford he'd arrived in, wasn't missed by the other man as concerned eyes returned to hers.

"I'm so sorry, Miss Katlin. I didn't know you were in house." Griffin apologized then explained, "I was off Tuesday night when you arrived, and again on Wednesday. I just now checked the log and saw that you were in residence."

"That's okay." She glanced over her shoulder at a scowling Alex. "As you can see, everything is fine." *Damn, couldn't I come up with another word other than fine?* She wasn't fine, but she wasn't about to tell either of these hulks that she was so far off her game all she wanted to do was escape. And she would. She put on what she hoped to be a reassuring smile and added, "I was just about to leave."

Griffin gave Alex a long hard glare before returning his gaze to her, softening his hazel eyes. "I'll have a car ready to take you. Ten minutes give you enough time?"

"That would be wonderful." Yes. Perfect in fact. "Thank you."

"I saw you had scheduled a driver and guard tonight. Will there be five as usual?" Griffin was back to business.

"Yes. We're doing dinner and definitely dancing, so set me up with a night crawler."

Griffin nodded. "Yes, ma'am."

Katlin shifted her weight and breathed in a scent so familiar. Alex. She glanced down at the shirt that dwarfed her body, and realization slammed through her. She was naked under his shirt, talking to the facility manager. She needed to send Griffin away and to jump into the shower. Then she'd get the hell out of there.

"Everything is fine, Griffin." She lightly touched his muscled bicep, which automatically flexed.

"You know I would have been up here and gotten you out before he arrived had I known you were here." He hurried his Southern drawl to ask forgiveness. "I know how things can be between..." He let the phrase hang as he shifted his eyes from her to Alex.

Katlin lifted a brow and slowly turned her head toward Alex. This should be interesting. She waited for Alex to answer and internally smirked. He had no idea she had every right to be in the owner's suite. She owned as much of the business as he did, although the man who stood behind her, emanating waves of heat, was clueless to that fact that she had provided the money to make his dream come true.

Alex stared back at her expectantly.

Well, if he wasn't going to handle it, she would. She ignored the question and took control. "Griffin, thank you for your concern. As you can see, Mr. Wolf is now in residence, and I shall be leaving shortly. Please have Sara come up and freshen the room in an hour. If you'll now return to your office to confirm my plans for this evening, perhaps I'll see you tonight, if you place yourself on personal protection duty." It was as much an order as any she'd given during her years as a Navy officer, and she was sure Griffin had received her message. Katlin turned in a dismissive gesture and walked away, leaving Griffin and Alex face to face.

"My office, fifteen minutes." The command in Alex's voice couldn't be missed.

Oh, to be a fly on the wall for that conversation. Katlin was sure Griffin wouldn't give away any of her secrets because he didn't know any.

With a long, slow, deep breath, she internally shrugged. She'd put off this day for too many years. Time to pull up her proverbial big girl panties and face the many things she'd done in her past that had affected the lives of the two men in the room, and so many others.

Katlin felt their gazes on her back and hoped the shirttails didn't reveal too much of her ass to them. She wasn't worried so much about Alex. He'd seen it, and a whole lot more, just five minutes ago. Griffin, on the other hand, had seen her in her tiniest bikini, but she still felt exposed.

"Aye-aye, sir," was Griffin's reply, followed by footsteps. She heard the apartment door close.

"Kat." Alex's voice was a demand. She kept walking toward the bedroom. He was behind her in an instant and grabbed her shoulders.

She froze. No, he wouldn't hurt her. Physically. Emotionally was a whole different animal. He was probably the only person alive who could. Or would.

She spun around to face him. "What." It was an ultimatum, not a question.

"How long have you been sleeping with my Miami manager?" Alex accused.

Katlin hurriedly assessed the situation and understood how he could come to that conclusion.

Damn. Did he have it wrong.

Katlin gave him a what-the-fuck look then answered. "I pay the Guardian men to protect me and my team while we let loose on leave. Griffin is very defensive of me, but I assure you, I don't sleep with the hired help." Mumbling, she added, "I don't sleep with anyone."

She tried to twist away, but Alex held her shoulders tight. She could easily break the hold, but the heat that emanated from his hands and traveled throughout her body held her in place. Part of her wanted to step into him so he'd wrap his arms around her, pull her to his bare chest, and make her feel like a woman, the real Katlin Callahan, once again. Another part of her wanted to break his arm for touching her.

Defiantly, she lifted her chin and captured his gaze. "I'm not sleeping with Griffin, nor have I ever. Just because I occasionally sleep in this room doesn't mean I'm fucking someone. I have permission to stay here, and at any Guardian Center, whenever I wish, as long as you are not there or expected."

Alex's brows drew together. "Who gave you permission?"

Her inner smirk was back. He'd find out that little secret when she was damn good and ready, but for now, all she'd admit was, "Your business partners."

His jaw dropped slightly and white surrounded his milk chocolate brown eyes. "You know them?"

She used the opportunity to extract herself from his grasp. "Yes." To distract him as she moved away, she added, "I really need to leave, Alex. I'm obviously not supposed to be here."

Her eyes traveled to the glass pot filled with water sitting on the counter. Damn, she needed caffeine. "Why don't you finish making the coffee. I'd love a cup on my way out." She smiled and turned toward the bedroom. "I'll be out of here within ten minutes."

Katlin stifled the urge to run.

She had to get away from Alejandro—no, he now called himself Alex. She'd have to get used to that because the man she'd faced moments ago was no longer her high school best friend. He was now different, as was she. He'd always had an overpowering presence, but seeing him again was just too much. She didn't really care that she'd been naked. It was the way he affected her that she couldn't handle. She never could.

As with every threatening situation in her life, it came down to fight or flight; fight the feelings he brought to her or take flight and run away. Flight won out almost every time when it came to Alejandro Lobo. Obviously, she had the same reaction to Alex Wolf. Wasn't that interesting?

Katlin closed the bedroom door behind her and locked it. Not that it would stop him if he really wanted to get in there. She considered the click of the lock a statement.

Damn it, damn it, damn it. How was it that she could work side by side, as an equal of any Army Special Forces, Navy SEAL, Marine SpecOps, undercover CIA agent, and live and work in a man's world, yet not know what to do when someone with a Y-chromosome flirted with her...the real her. And Alex *had* flirted with her.

Oh, her Lady Hawk persona would know exactly what to do, depending on her role in that particular mission. She would do whatever it took for the operation to succeed.

Damn, she still loved the way he pronounced *Kat,* containing just a hint of his innate Spanish accent, tempting her with a single word. But had it been her old friend Alejandro flirting with his friend Kat?

Or had it been Alex Wolf seducing the woman he'd discovered naked in his apartment?

Why had she run away? That wasn't like her. What had

happened to that emboldened young girl who'd accepted anyone's dare with flare and flourish then proved she was just as good as any boy? She could climb as high, jump down as far, shoot as well as they could. Somewhere along the way, had she lost the personal female part of the real Katlin Callahan who was female? Now, her confidence in her femininity became apparent only when required during a mission.

But she hadn't been Katlin Callahan Malone, wife and lover, in over three years. That woman had disappeared with her screamed words of of abhorrence and repugnance the night before her husband left for his last Middle East mission.

For the past few years, she'd sat in front of a mirror and applied the appropriate makeup as she transformed into whatever woman was necessary. Totally shoving Katlin Callahan aside, she'd emerge as a prostitute, or a regal socialite, or a soccer mom. As she pulled up pantyhose with purposeful runs or attached a red garter to silk hose, she became that person and held in character until the mission had been successfully completed.

She was the best actress in the world. She had to be. Her life, and the lives of the women on her team, depended on it.

But she didn't know who, or what, to be with Alex. She had no mission that involved him, no defined role to play. They'd been good friends once…best friends.

Then Ty had died.

Seeing Alex again released the pain that, three years ago, she'd stuffed into a box, bound it with hate and disappointment, then shoved it into the darkest corner of her mind that she could find. The next day, she'd gotten up as usual and gone to work, just like any other day. That was the way she'd lived her life for the past three years. Emotionless.

As soon as Katlin passed through the bathroom doorway, she released the breath she didn't know she was holding.

With it went the wall of silence she'd constructed the day she and Alex had buried Ty. The day Alex had left her life.

She, and the man she'd left standing in the other room, needed to talk about so many things, but, most importantly, where they would go from there.

Not ready for any conversation with him, least of all while she was naked and he was fully clothed, she twisted on the hot water and adjusted the dial so the body jets accompanied the dual showerheads. Not that her body needed additional stimulation. Just seeing Alex was enough to make every pore open to absorb his very essence.

While Alex had been her lover, they'd been combustible. Their lovemaking had been so intense at times she was sure her college dorm room would catch fire. And other times, Alex had been so sweet and gentle she'd felt cherished in his arms. But it never lasted. Alex would eventually distance himself, emotionally pushing her away until she'd fled from his overpowering ways back into the safety of Ty's embrace.

Her relationship with Ty had more twists and turns than the best roller coaster on the planet, but she and Ty always ended up back together, often because Alex reattached those broken bonds for them. He was their best friend and seemed to want to keep her and Ty together.

The afternoon they had buried Ty, Alex had left her holding a triangular-folded American flag and memories. Nothing else. His last words to her had been the scripted "On behalf of the President of the United States, a grateful nation, and a proud Navy, this flag is presented as a token of our appreciation for the honorable and faithful service...."

Damn, she hated those words. She'd heard them three times in her life while she held a heavy flag of stars and stripes in shaking hands.

They were the last words Alex had spoken to her until five minutes ago. The same number of years she'd held her silence about the terrible thing she'd done.

It was time to tell the truth.

Katlin stepped into the steamy shower, arms outstretched with fingertips inches from the two showerheads allowing the body jets to pelt her sore back and abdominal muscles.

He may already know it was my fault that all those Navy SEALs were killed along with Ty. Maybe that's why he's kept his distance from me all this time.

She lathered with her favorite perfume-scented body wash as she considered her situation. She'd purposely avoided Alex, true, but the phone rang on her end too, so he'd avoided her for that same time. Now she had to face him, her past, and the consequences.

Katlin closed her eyes. She felt the intensity of his gaze as he'd looked her up and down minutes ago like the rivulets of water streaming their way from her face, down her breasts, and dripping from nipples peaked with desire. Body jets pulsed against her stomach the way his words had hit her, relentless, tingling, yet unsatisfying.

She liked his long hair, although it hadn't softened the chiseled planes of his face. She'd last seen him with a Marine buzz cut, spit and polished in his Dress Blues, two gleaming gold bars on each shoulder as he led the pallbearers sent from SEAL Team Four. A Marine ordering around Navy men, just one more thing that had made Ty's funeral unusual.

She'd never been able to hide from his penetrating gaze, which could be as hard as the Marine he was to his core. What was the saying? Once a Marine, always a Marine. It was certainly true for Alex. He was still granite at the core, but she'd seen the gold in his eyes spark with his deep laughter and turn nearly black with desire.

Water ran over her flat stomach and down her back, creating a warm river between her slightly spread legs. She remembered Alex's hands as they'd made love in the shower. He'd used his palm to run down her belly and cup her mound, teasing her with the tip of one finger as he rocked into her from behind.

Damn. She was so turned on all it'd take was a water pulse in the right spot or a brush of her own hand to throw her over the edge. His mere proximity had always been able to do that to her.

She'd missed him. But at the same time, she was so angry with him. Disappointed. He'd left her when she needed him the most, and she'd been all alone for the past three years. She had managed because she always did what had to be done. She'd been strong, held it all in, bearing the weight alone. It was the only way she knew how to handle the pain...since Alex hadn't been there to share the burden.

Katlin shifted the nozzle, shutting off the jets and turning on the waterfall faucet. She worked in shampoo as she cleansed her mind, washed away the post-adrenaline sexual need, and prepared for the battle ahead.

It would be one hell of a fight, her soul to be won or lost, her heart to be shattered or healed.

Everything depended on the man in the kitchen.

Alex had watched the swish right and left of his shirttail an inch below Kat's tightly toned butt as she walked into his bedroom. He wanted to follow her in there, throw her on his giant bed, and keep her there for hours–maybe even days—as they made love and slept in each other's arms.

He could have her for a while, but he could never keep her. He wasn't sure any man could ever hold on to Katlin Callahan. She was bigger than life itself. He knew he couldn't possess her, make her his own forever. He'd realized that when he was fifteen years old. He'd been nothing more than a bad boy from the dark side of D.C., a peasant in the presence of royalty.

He'd met some of her childhood friends while they'd dated in college…real princes, sons and daughters of diplomats, heads of state, and more senior military officers than he'd known existed before he'd joined Marine Corps ROTC. She'd grown up in embassies all over the world, and he'd lived in the same dilapidated bungalow with a dirt front yard all his life.

Sure, he'd recently made a few million dollars, but that didn't mean he was the right man for her. He never had been.

But if he were lucky, he'd get to play with her for a while and warm his empty heart with the blazing bonfire that was Kat. He'd known that, too, from the moment he'd met her.

Fifteen years ago he'd joined a neighborhood gang in D.C., but when his mother found out, she'd shipped him off to live with Nana Rosa in Little Havana so he'd be sure to finish high school. He'd sauntered into the Miami Magnet School as the cocky new kid. Except for Alex's latte-colored skin, his outer armor had been stripped that morning. Nana Rosa had forced him to remove the eyebrow piercing, nose ring, and ear studs before she'd let him out of the house.

By third period biology lab, Alex had realized that he might be the only Cuban-American in the whole high school for gifted and advanced students. He'd been born in the nation's capital, and the U.S.A. was his home, but when it suited him, he used his heritage to intimidate. The teacher had looked him up and down, worry painted on his wrinkled face.

Alex had cautiously glanced around the high granite tables for an empty seat...and then he'd seen her. The sun had shone through the big windows of the century-old school and backlit her honey-blonde hair, forming an aura around her pale face. He remembered looking into her blue-on-blue eyes and everything in the classroom disappeared, except the two of them.

"Angel," escaped in a whisper of Spanish.

Her smile flashed two rows of bright white teeth, and sapphire eyes sparkled as she answered in Spanish. "There's an empty seat here. Come sit beside me." It didn't take him long to understand Katlin Callahan was no angel. She was his personal demon.

When the biology teacher heard them conversing in Spanish, he immediately assigned Alex to be Kat's lab partner. They were the only two permitted to talk during class.

It had been weeks before the bio teacher realized that Alex spoke perfect English. In the meantime, he'd gotten to know Kat very well. He'd discovered that she, too, was good friends with Ty Malone, who'd become his best friend. Oh, damn, the trouble the three of them had gotten into. His lips stretched into a grin.

She radiated fun, danger, and living life to its fullest. He and Ty had been absorbed in her light it had gotten them suspended from school more than once. They'd come so damn close to getting arrested more times than he could count. But she'd always had an exit plan, which, to his and Ty's amazement, worked every time.

Her smile could still light up a room…and spark passion within him. Their last encounter, when he'd brought her Ty's body in a casket, hadn't gone the way he'd intended. He'd wanted to be there to ease the pain of loss for her, and let her comfort him. They'd both loved Ty, she as his wife and he as his best friend. Alex had imagined them suffering the loss together, healing together, as good friends helping each other through a bad time.

But that hadn't happened.

Alex checked the dripping coffee. Almost done. His gaze wandered to the locked bedroom door. The right side of his grin kicked up. Her message had been received loud and clear. No trespassing. But Katlin was naked in there. And Christ had his body noticed every change in hers.

The coffeemaker gurgled, interrupting any trip down that road. He'd pour her a cup and make her sit and eat breakfast as they talked like friends are supposed to do. He'd ordered food for her from the company cook.

Alex would be happy with Kat as a friend again. He could handle that. Friends with benefits would be even better. He'd definitely like that.

They needed to talk first. So much had gone unsaid three years ago and every day of their silence since. He'd eventually tell her about the night Ty died. Maybe she would forgive him for not saving her husband's life.

Maybe then he could forgive himself.

He heard the shower stop at the same time a light knock sounded on the apartment door.

Sara brought in a tray of assorted fruit, eggs Benedict, a grilled turkey panini, orange juice, vegetable chips, a Greek salad, and Pepsi. It looked wonderful and smelled even better. The cook knew how to throw together a small brunch while prepping to feed twenty men lunch in less than an hour. He really had wonderful people working for him.

Alex didn't realize just how hungry he was until he saw the food. He had grabbed a banana on his way out of the New York City Center very early that morning, a cup of coffee in his other hand.

He'd wanted to get to Miami as soon as possible so he could finish reviewing the Center's accounts and spend some time with his daughter. Jenny's ninth birthday was Saturday, and he had her for a few hours on Friday afternoon. What the hell they were going to do, he didn't know.

He'd never known what to do with his little girl, not that he'd ever had much of a chance to find out. Within months of their move to Marine Corps Base Camp Lejeune in North Carolina, Rachelle had taken their two-year-old to visit her parents in Florida. His wife and daughter had never left Miami, although they'd moved from her parents' home into Ted's house in the suburbs. That was four years ago. No, maybe it was five. Their two boys were—

"Good morning, Alex." Sara's cheeks rounded with her cheery smile, interrupting his mental mathematics. "Did you have a good flight?" The mid-forties woman went to the drawer in the kitchen closest to the dining room and took out two placemats with coordinating napkins.

"Yes. I caught an earlier flight, so that was good." Very

good. He got to see Kat naked. The image was seared into his brain forever.

"So how was everything in…?" She waited for him to fill in the blank as she set the thick glass dining table.

"I was at the New York Center."

"Bet it was cooler up there. We've had a blistering heat wave." She kept up a casual conversation over the clink of ice from the fridge door as she filled heavily leaded crystal glasses and placed them on the table. The matching diamond-cut pitcher sprayed tiny rainbows throughout the kitchen as she lowered it from the cabinet before she filled it with ice and water.

Alex strode to the closed bedroom door and knocked. "Kat, Sara's here with food. Come eat while it's still hot."

He turned back to the conversation with his Miami Center cook. "The city was blistering hot. I swear there was no fresh air. Must be all that hot air from those financial types and international politicians. At least here we get a breeze from the ocean."

Sara giggled. "Downtown Miami can get the same way. May I ask, how's Jonathan? We were real sorry to lose him to the Dallas office. He was a charmer, that one, but I knew he was going places in this company. We were all so proud you picked him as an assistant manager. Is he doing okay over there in that new office?"

"Yes. He's a real asset to the Dallas Center." She didn't need to know the details that Alex had put three managers—ones he'd inherited with the purchase—under arrest. He'd moved Quinlan Barrister from the L.A. Center to become the manager and Jonathan as one of three to assist him at the company's newest Texas center.

When he'd bought the well-established Dallas security company two months ago, he'd reviewed their financials and known he could improve its profitability. It didn't take long until Barry Howell, Guardian's CFO, had discovered why the numbers looked off to Alex. The upper management had been skimming funds for years, to the tune of $750,000, so far as they could prove. Since most of that was under the previous ownership, Alex was helping them, and the district attorney, establish a firm case against those thieves.

Sara stepped back to survey her work once finished setting the table. She turned toward Alex.

"Sir, will there—" Her whole face lit up.

He followed her gaze and spotted Kat as she emerged from the bedroom. Scrubbed clean and still pink from her hot shower, she was the most beautiful woman he'd seen in years. The Hollywood divas that paid for their personal protection services looked like painted dolls compared to Kat's natural beauty. Her long blonde hair was obviously still wet and braided down her back. Slung over one shoulder was a large black duffel bag.

She was on her way out. He needed to work fast but was interrupted before he could say a word.

"Ms. Katlin, good morning." Sara's glance bounced nervously from Alex to Kat, to Alex, and back to Katlin.

"Good morning, Sara." Kat surveyed the food. "Mmmm. It smells heavenly." Kat hugged the motherly woman.

When they separated, Sara kept hold of Kat's forearm and pointed to a spider web of fine pink lines on her bicep. "It's healed nicely."

"Yeah." Kat smiled. "Nita has real talent for stitching, but the bullet was a through and through. I'm just thankful it missed the bone. That's my shooting arm."

Katlin had been shot? Alex wanted to jump up and examine every inch of the scar then go kill the son of a bitch who'd dared shoot at her. And where had she been with live fire? That kind of training was limited to combat roles. What the hell was she doing to get herself shot?

"At least you got him," Sara stated.

Kat's smile said more than her words. "That I did. And all his bad-ass buddies."

"Good. That's one less drug runner to poison our children." Sara grabbed the coffee pot and poured into the china cups she'd placed on the table.

Drugs? Was Katlin now working for DEA? Or Border Patrol? Or was she a cop?

The image of Katlin decked in tactical gear was hot. Guns strapped to her long thighs, duty belt resting on the curve of her hips with extra magazines and a backup holster, knee-high boots protecting her calves, and a tight black tank top under a black shirt. Carrying an M4. Fuck yes.

Alex sat down at the table while he tried to get his hormones, and hardening erection, under control. He thought he was past instant reactions to the presence of a beautiful woman. His responses to Kat had always been stronger, direct, instant.

He shouldn't be thinking about his friend that way. Hell. Maybe she'd remarried. It had been three years. He glanced at her hands. Long fingers were free of rings and showed no sign of indentation, which could mean nothing, or everything.

Alex added that to the growing list of things he needed to find out.

Katlin's stomach growled, and both women laughed.

In unison, they glanced toward the table laden with food. He could tell the moment they remembered they were not alone.

Sara gave Katlin a worried look.

"This all looks wonderful, Sara, but I was on my out." Kat's response was quick and a bit harsh. It hit Alex like a spear, deflating his mounting hope. "Unfortunately, I overslept and didn't get out before Mr. Wolf arrived this morning."

Katlin grabbed the panini from the platter mid-table and

wrapped a napkin around it. She swiped the coffee cup from the place setting obviously set for her and downed half of it. The bliss that melted over her face reminded Alex what she looked like after sex. And damn, there was his cock again.

Kat filled the cup again. "Hey, Sara, before I forget, you have a special anniversary later this week, don't you?"

"Yes, our twenty-fifth. How did you know?"

Katlin just smiled as she walked back to Sara. "Well, Saturday is my treat. I've arranged a spa day for you with the works, even a new hairstyle." Kat ran her hands through Sara's shoulder-length silvering hair. "Later, the limo will take you and Larry to Chez Louis. Don't worry about anything. I'll cook for the Guardian men."

Alex thought he saw tears in Sara's eyes as she choked out, "Thank you, Katlin." She threw her arms around the younger woman then hurriedly left the apartment. Alex didn't know it was their anniversary. The couple had worked for him since he'd opened the company, Sara cooking for his men and Larry meticulously caring for the building. They lived on the fourth floor, along with several of his men, except their apartment was much larger.

Kat walked over to what should have been her place at the table and stood behind the chair. She emptied the second cup of coffee and set it down. "Aleja-, Alex, it was good seeing you again. Take care of yourself." She spun and strode toward the door.

Oh, no. She wasn't leaving without a conversation. He stood. "Kat." Alex glanced at the table. "Come sit and have some breakfast. You must be starving."

She rounded the wall to the foyer. "Sorry, Alex. I have a car waiting for me."

Damn, she was fast. He ran to stop her.

He heard the door open.

At the elevator, he caught up with her. "Please, Kat. We need to talk." He heard the hum of the elevator approach.

She looked away. "Yes, we do. But not right now. I have to—"

"Three years, Kat. We're long overdue," he protested.

The elevator doors opened. With one arm he held the doors in place and the other came around Kat's small waist. He pulled her to him in a hug he hoped was friendly yet conveyed more. He inhaled the scent of her shampoo and clean woman, and Kat. He whispered the truth in her ear. "I've missed you."

To his surprise, she threw her arms around his neck. "I've missed my best friend, too." She kissed his cheek and quickly stepped away. Her eyes were bright as she rolled her lips into a fine line and stepped into the elevator. As he released the doors, she called out, "I'm in town for a few days. I'll call you."

Alex doubted she would. But he'd call her. He turned and jogged down the stairs to the Control Room so he could watch her leave.

And get some answers.

CHAPTER 8

Katlin stepped out of the SUV and immediately scanned her surroundings. Nothing looked out of place behind the gated driveway. She stretched as she looked up at the white stucco building she owned on Miami Beach. Her teammates were probably sunning themselves on the roof outside the top floor condo she shared with them. The other apartments were rented to executives she'd vetted through Guardian Security. Under her company's constant eyes, the building was certainly secure, but had never given her the same feeling of safe—and, yes, if she admitted it to herself…home—that she had in the penthouse at the Miami Guardian Center.

"May I carry your bags in for you, Miss Katlin?" Dave asked as he easily lifted her heavy duffel bags from the back of the black Mercedes G63 with the discrete gray Guardian logos on each side.

"Thanks, but I've got them." Katlin hoisted one bag over her shoulder as Grace and Nita walked up, sweaty from their run on the beach. She bit back a smile as Dave's eyes ran over her friends in tiny running shorts and cropped tops that put their toned bodies and feminine curves on display.

"Hello, Grace, Nita," Dave finally managed to say with a

nod to each woman. Over the past year, he'd been their bodyguard a few times and, like several other men at Guardian Security, had joined the ladies for drinks once they were off duty.

"I got this," Grace said and shrugged into a bag, backpack style.

"Christ, Katlin, how much gear do you have in this son of a bitch?" Nita complained as she pretended to struggle with the last bag. It contained a sniper rifle and ammo, along with survival essentials, and weighed exactly the same as Nita's own bag with the same contents. What the hell? Did she really want to appear weak to Dave?

"Here, let me help you with that," Dave immediately offered and effortlessly lifted the bag off the ground and placed the long strap over her head. As the webbing crossed her breasts, Nita fake-stumbled under the supposed weight, and all but fell into Dave, his hand brushing her breasts.

All three women heard his quiet gasp, and Katlin saw satisfaction paint Nita's face.

Grace slid Katlin a look that silently said "can you believe her" just before Grace rolled her emerald green eyes. Her red ponytail swished as she shook her head in disgust.

"Let me carry that upstairs for you, Nita." Dave had begun to take the bag off Katlin's friend when Katlin cleared her throat.

Nita flashed her a smile, and Katlin shook her head. The condo was off-limits to men. After the second time Katlin had walked out of her bedroom—barely covered in a short robe, and thankful she'd bothered with that much—she'd pulled a gun on the strange man sitting at her table drinking coffee and eating breakfast. Katlin had made the executive decision that her friends were welcome to crash there, but no men. Ever.

"Thank you, Dave," Nita said in a throaty voice, "but I've got it now." She petted his sizable bicep and added, "I like strong men. Are you going to be our…personal protection tonight?"

"No, ma'am. I'm off duty tonight."

"Too bad. I could use a little personal"—and she stepped close to him and nearly whispered—"protection tonight."

Dave was so stunned he didn't move. Katlin wasn't sure the man was breathing. She enjoyed watching her friends and teammates in action. They turned men into blubbering idiots in minutes. It was their job, but Katlin wasn't sure what game Nita was playing, teasing Dave this way. Maybe she just wanted a man to take care of her *personal* needs tonight.

"As I said, I'm off tonight. We could get together for supper, then…maybe some dancing." Dave was in the game, finally. Katlin crossed her arms and watched as Nita reeled him in.

"I'm sorry, but I already have supper plans." Nita gave him a penitent grimace. "We're taking our friend—you remember Lei Lu, don't you?" When he nodded like a bobble head, she continued, "It's her birthday, and we're taking her out to celebrate. But if you want to join us later, we'll head out to a few clubs afterward. Check with Guardian's operations center. They'll know where we are."

"I'll do that," Dave promised. He lifted her hand from his arm and kissed her palm.

She closed her fingers over the spot and, in a husky voice, promised, "Until tonight then."

Nita joined Katlin and Grace as Dave moved toward the driver's side of the SUV. "I'll wait until you ladies get into the building. Mr. Mitchell would have my ass if anything happened to you."

At Griffin Mitchell's name, Grace shifted her stance. Out of the corner of her eye, Katlin watched a small smile play at the edges of Grace's lips and a blush add to her already reddened cheeks. Katlin wondered when Griffin and Grace would start to play the game seriously, given the way they'd danced around their attraction for almost a year.

"Thanks for the ride, Dave," Katlin called and moved to the secure door to her beach condo. Nita and Grace followed silently.

As soon as the elevator doors closed, Grace started in, "What was that all about, Nita?"

"That, my dear friend, was all about sex. It's been four weeks, five days, seven hours and"—she looked at her watch, which was yellow today to match her outfit—"fifty-two minutes since I had sex with a man. If all goes according to my plan, within the next twelve hours, I'll be in bed with Dave. Do you think his pubic hair is as blonde as the hair on his head?"

Aghast, Grace said, "Nita, I…I…I really don't want to know."

The door opened on the top floor, and all three women turned to the only apartment there.

"Well, Katlin is a natural blonde and hers is, but I've noticed in men that sometimes it's more red than blonde. We didn't really cover that in med school."

Grace and Nita slid Katlin's bags onto her shelf in the large cabinet next to the door, joining eight other identical bags. The Ladies of Black Swan had to be ready to move out with a phone call. Katlin took her bag of clothes to the laundry room and started a load.

When she emerged, Grace handed her a glass of wine, pointed toward the living room, and ordered, "Sit. You look rested, but tense. What's up?"

Even though her body had just consumed breakfast, it was well past noon and Katlin appreciated the wine. She needed a drink and Grace knew it. She couldn't hide her uproarious emotions from her friend. They'd bonded the first day of their secret training. With Grace's husband at Navy flight school in Pensacola, Florida, and Katlin's at SEAL training in

Coronado, California, neither woman had much in common with the ninety-eight single women selected for the program. They'd spent many long hours together, first as recruits and now as members of the elite team of women known only to a select few as the Ladies of Black Swan. They couldn't read each other's minds but were definitely attuned to the other's emotions.

"Alejandro, I mean Alex, caught me in the penthouse this morning." Katlin curled her legs under her and nestled in a corner of the huge L-shaped sectional in the bright, airy living room.

Grace stretched out on the chaise portion and lay on her side, head propped on her hand. She set the wine glass on the tile floor in front of her, almost dropping it at Katlin's confession. "What happened?"

"I heard a man come in and thought he was after me. I held the intruder at gunpoint until I figured out it was Alex." Short and concise. That covered most of it.

"I was wondering where you were yesterday, but it's no wonder you crashed." Grace adjusted a pillow. "You should have let me fly home, at least part of the way."

"You all needed your sleep. It was an easy op on me, this time." Katlin had gotten several hours of good sleep in the Marine camp before they'd left Iraq and had felt great.

Grace stopped and seemed to consider for a moment before she noted, "Katlin, you sleep…uhm—"

"Yep. I was naked." She could still see the look on Alex's face when he'd turned around. Reality and disbelief, desire and confusion all had mixed in his intense brown eyes.

Grace buried her face in throw pillows in shared embarrassment. "Oh my gosh. He saw you naked? What did he say?"

"He who? Who saw Katlin naked?" Nita asked as she wandered into the living room with a sandwich plate and glass of milk.

"An old friend of mine." Katlin tried to brush it off, knowing Nita would be like a dog with bone and gnaw at it forever. "After I figured out that I'd slept for over thirty hours, and it was indeed Thursday, not Wednesday as I'd thought, I took a shower and left."

"Who did you sleep with? Tell me. Tell me." Nita bounced as she set her lunch on the small stand next to the overstuffed chair facing both of them.

"I didn't sleep *with* anyone." Katlin needed to be sure she got that point across. "I just overslept, and when my old friend came in—it's his apartment—I thought he was an assassin after me and held him at gunpoint."

"Did you shoot him?" Nita asked nonchalantly and took a bite of her ham and cheese.

"No, I didn't shoot anyone…today…so far." But there were several hours left in the day.

"So then you got naked with your old friend and that's why you're late getting here? Good, 'bout time you got laid." Nita had summed it up…wrong.

"No, no, no." Katlin shook her head, and Grace laughed into the pillows. "I didn't wake up until a few hours ago. I'd been asleep since an hour after we landed."

"Holy shit. Are you sick? Should I get my bag?" Nita sounded concerned, morphing into team doc mode. She started to get up.

"Damn it, I'm not sick. Sit down and eat your lunch." Something clicked in the back of Katlin's brain. She looked around. "Where's Damnit? Where's our puppy?"

"He's still at school," Grace explained, catching her breath. "Tanner wanted to wait until we were all here so he could train *us*. Seems Damnit now has some new commands, and I guess he picked up a few bad habits hanging with us last time we were home, so be prepared for Tanner's lecture."

With their work demands and constant travel, Katlin worried that a dog had been a bad decision, but she loved that pup, and so did her whole team. She'd sent him to training school during their last mission but was more than ready to see her little boy and cuddle him. He was the only male constant in her life now, and that was fine with her.

"So did you sleep with the guy or not?" Nita pointed at Katlin with her sandwich.

"No. I didn't sleep with him," Katlin insisted.

"Of course Katlin didn't sleep with him," Tori said from the kitchen doorway, reaching into a bag of vinegar and sea salt chips. "She doesn't sleep with anyone. Hell, she doesn't even date."

"Why not? You were naked in his bed, right?" Nita quizzed.

"Katlin was naked in a man's bed and didn't do the deed?" Tori looked at Katlin. "Why not?" Those two words seemed to bounce off the floor-to-ceiling windows that overlooked the Atlantic Ocean, just like they ricocheted around Katlin's mind. Why hadn't she just grabbed Alex and dragged his tight little ass into the bed where she'd slept for too many hours? Why hadn't she pulled his face to hers and kissed him the way she'd wanted to?

Because we are nothing more than old friends, at best. That's why.

"I couldn't sleep with Alex. We're just friends." Katlin really didn't want to explain their whole relationship. She wasn't sure she could. It was so complicated. She knew these women too well, and circuitous interrogation was their forte. She prepared herself for the truth, should they press her.

"You need to start dating," Grace encouraged Katlin. "It's been nearly four years since Ty died. That's more than long enough to grieve."

Katlin didn't still mourn Ty's death. Besides, she'd dated. "I went out with that Air Force major the last time we were in D.C." She thought it was the last time they were there. Maybe it was the time before.

"Yeah, but you didn't even let him walk you to the door," Tori pointed out.

"It was cold outside." No, it was before Christmas. She remembered gazing at the twinkling lights in her condo windows from the front seat of his minivan. "Besides, I'd already told him goodnight. We both knew it'd never go anywhere." He definitely wasn't her type. He shared two small children with his ex, and she was all he'd talked about through the excruciating long meal at a chain restaurant. As far as first dates went, it had sucked.

"What about John Dolen, the senator's grandson?" Nita suggested. "You could give him a call next week when we're back in D.C." Nita's snicker gave her away. She didn't mean it.

Katlin scrunched up her face. "That weasel with those thin little snake lips that he pulled back over small teeth? He didn't smile, he sneered. All during dinner he never looked me in the eyes. He couldn't drag his eyes away from my boobs." When he'd walked her to the door, she'd put the key in the lock and turned around to shake his hand, but he'd invaded her personal space. "He was disgusting…wet kisses, slobbering all over my face. I wanted to shove him on his ass and slam the door. As soon as I got away and into my apartment, I ran to the bathroom and washed my face…three times…with lots of soap."

"Well, what about Hernandez?" Tori asked about the man their D.C. neighbor, Harper, had introduced to her. "My God, he's such a hunk and an ATF agent." Tori sat on the couch and crossed the long, shapely legs that had strutted down runways around the world and her body parts, especially her gorgeous legs and long-fingered hands, had been featured in hundreds of magazines. She'd never reached super model status because there was nothing unique about her, except for her ability to become African, Middle Eastern, or Native American with the right brush strokes and foundation. She was perfect for the Black Swan team.

"He was interesting," Katlin admitted. "We got into some really stimulating conversations about new weapons and explosives. When we went jogging…that sweaty body of his was magnificent. I'm positive he took off his shirt to let me know what he had to offer." She questioned herself about her decision not to see him again then admitted, "But you know, it just wasn't there. No sizzle, not even a spark. No magical connection. No zing."

"You don't have to have sizzle." Nita waved her hand in the air. "What happened to just having sex for the sake of getting off? Two consenting adults scratching a coital itch?"

"I can't do that." Katlin had often wondered if something was wrong with her. Men and women all around her did exactly that, a one-night stand for the sake of physical pleasure. Some of her teammates changed men after every mission, rarely keeping the man a second night, say nothing about a whole week.

Except Grace. She'd dated more in the past two years, since her husband's plane crash, and kept the men around for a few months, but she dumped them in the end. Griffin had tempted her in the background for nearly a year, but Katlin was sure Grace hadn't even kissed him, yet.

Katlin tried to explain. "There has to more to it, at least for me, than insert tab A into slot B. I need to feel some kind of connection."

"What you need, Katlin, is an introduction-to-dating guy." Grace shot up to a sitting position, almost knocking over the wine glass as her feet touched the floor.

"Yeah, somebody who will take you to bed, fuck your brains out, reintroduce you to the stars above," Nita suggested. "And, since you seem to need it, cuddle you until he's ready to do it all again."

"Yes, that's it," Tori agreed. "She needs someone to get her back in the game. Someone who knows up front that it's not going to last. Hell, Katlin, you're a man's dream woman."

"Yeah, right," Katlin retorted. "If I'm such a dream woman, why did my son of a bitch husband cheat on me?" Damn. She hadn't meant to say that. What the hell was wrong with her? She didn't want to talk about Ty. He was her past, and it was high time she moved on.

"Any man will want you if he knows up front that you're not interested in the long term or the R word," Nita reiterated.

"R word?" Grace asked.

"Relationship," the others sang in chorus.

"Well, I don't want a relationship, that's for damn sure." Katlin wasn't sure she'd ever want another man in her life permanently. "I don't have time for that. I can't be bothered with a man's demands right now."

Grace asked, "What kind of lover was Alex before?"

"We were young." Katlin smiled and shook her head slightly. "Fumbling. Exploring our bodies and needs. You know…teenagers. In college, he was very passionate, very slow-handed—not a grab and squeeze guy—and very focused. He was intent on giving me anything I needed, and less concerned with his own needs until I was ready for him."

"Wow, to have a guy like that. And you gave him up?" Tori chided.

"Not exactly." Katlin hated to admit it, even to her good friends…he'd pushed her away, once again.

Nita encouraged, "So what happened between the two of you?"

"I'm not sure." Katlin glanced to Grace, who knew the whole story. She just shrugged. Katlin figured the rest of the team should know, too. There was a chance they might meet Alex while in Miami this trip. "It seemed to me that, every time Ty would dump me, I went running to Alex. He was my best friend. I didn't have girlfriends back then. He listened, gave me advice, and for years, encouraged me to work it out with Ty. There was never anything sexual between me and Alex until late senior year, when I'd reached my limit of other girls bragging about sleeping with my boyfriend. Then I asked Alex to take me to the prom. We were only together for a few weeks. After graduation, we all went our separate ways. Daddy was stationed at the Pentagon so I went to D.C. and college at Georgetown, Ty left for the Naval Academy and Alex went to George Washington University with an ROTC scholarship."

Katlin looked at each woman and gave them a warm smile. "Where were girls like you in high school? All the ones I'd met were such backstabbing bitches. Maybe it's because I didn't grow up in public schools, surrounded by cliques, so I didn't know how to handle them."

"Where did you go to school?" Nita, the newest member of their team, asked.

"I was raised in embassies all over the world, so I had English-speaking tutors for most subjects. Sometimes I attended the small schools created for kids stationed overseas." Katlin sipped her wine before she went on to explain. "Most parents who worked in embassies sent their children to private schools, where they lived full time and just visited their parents on holiday. Mom and Daddy didn't want that for me. I think, after all her miscarriages, Mom wanted to keep me close to her. I always thought they'd send me away to school when I got older, like they did my brother Daniel, but that never happened."

"So you never went to a real school until high school?" Nita clarified and downed the last of her milk.

"Yes. Actually, it was just my last three years. They tested me when we moved to Miami and wanted to put me in a magnet school as a senior, but I protested. So we agreed I'd be a sophomore, just a year younger than the others in grade ten."

"I hated fuckin' high school," Nita piped in.

"I left for the Army the day after graduation," Tori told the group. "I couldn't get out of there fast enough."

Grace said on a sigh, "I loved high school."

"Bet you were the prom queen," Tori said and crumpled the now empty chip bag.

Grace raised her chin and said, "And homecoming queen and pork queen."

They all stared at her.

Tori tried to hold back a laugh but failed. "Pork Queen? Really?"

Grace looked indignant. "In Iowa, Miss Pork Queen is a very important position."

Nita rolled her hazel eyes and vowed, "I don't even want to know."

Tori shot in, "And let me guess, your future husband was king to all those queen crowns you wore."

Grace blushed. "Yes, except there was no pork king."

Nita raised her hands toward the ceiling and said, "Thank God for small favors."

The edges of Grace's smile tipped downward.

Katlin quickly said, "I'm sorry, Grace. We didn't mean to remind you of Kevin."

"I know," Grace said. "In high school, he was my best friend. Kind of like you and Alex, except I had girlfriends, too."

"I never did," Katlin said. "I only had guy friends, most of my life. Alex and I just connected on a level that I'd never had before, or since. You ladies come close, though. I've cried in Alex's arms more times than I can count."

They all looked at her, wide-eyed.

"What?" Katlin probed.

Silence.

"You cried?" Nita finally asked.

CHAPTER 9

"Yeah, I cry on occasion." Katlin looked at the shocked faces of her friends and teammates.

Tori spoke up. "I've known you for two years, and we've been through hell and back together. I've never seen you tear up or blink away leaky eyes, say nothing about an all-out cry."

"We're not talking false tears to get some tango to do what you want. I'm talking about bawling your fucking heart out." Leave it to Nita to lay it all out there.

"I've cried, just not often in the past few years." Katlin didn't want to admit that she hadn't had the emotion in her to cry. Not in years.

They all shook their heads, even Grace who knew all about Ty's infidelity and Katlin's less-than-perfect marriage.

"No, I don't see that in your personality," Nita claimed. "You're hard as nails, the toughest woman I know with the most resolve of anyone I've ever known, male or female. If you were a man, your balls would be made of brass and as big as a bull's. And you'd have the biggest cock in D.C., but since you're a woman, most men think you're a bitch."

Was she really that much of a hardass? Insensitive? "But

I'm not like that. I'm fully female. Breasts. Vagina. Clitoris. I've got all the right girl parts." Well, not all.

She had ovaries; they just didn't work. She knew she was damaged as a woman, and maybe that had changed her hormones. Perhaps she had more testosterone than most women, and that made her personality…manly?

She competed in a man's world, successfully. She jumped out of airplanes into the darkness of night, swam in the depths of the ocean, and was an expert shot with any gun. Admittedly, she wasn't as strong as a man, but she could carry her own teammates away from danger. She'd been trained since childhood how to think through a problem, take control of the situation and resolve it while keeping innocents safe— just in a female body. Emotions had no place in the middle of a crisis. Crying never helped any situation unless it was intended to manipulate men. Damn, she was really fucked up, wasn't she?

No, she was a woman through every cell in her overly curvaceous body. She was sure of it, deep within. And a few hours ago Alex had reminded her precisely how much of a woman she was. She'd ached for his hands on her breasts, and for him to touch her in that sensitive spot that had come to life after years of dormancy when she first saw his familiar face. To have him lick, kiss…hell no. She was all woman.

"Yeah, but that's not what you show the world." Tori might be right. "We've had conversations where we end up crying in each other's arms…well…everybody but you. You're the one holding us, telling us to let it all out. You never give yourself that permission."

"When was the last time you cried? When Ty died?" Grace asked with reverence.

"No." Katlin's confession was barely a whisper. With more fervor, she added, "I wouldn't shed a tear for that bastard."

"So, when was it? Your dad's funeral?" Grace pressed.

"No. I loved him. But I couldn't cry. I had to be strong."

Katlin had loved her father with all her heart. "It was just another funeral." Another procession through Arlington. One more time when everyone tried to say the right words and no one knew how to ease the pain. "No, I couldn't cry for Daddy, but it was the total opposite of why I couldn't cry for Ty."

She looked at the women who were her best friends, her sisters of the heart, and told them what she'd just realized herself. "For Ty, I had no feelings left whatsoever. For me, he died—along with anything I'd ever felt for him—when I saw the video of him banging his Lieutenant JG's wife. Every ounce of love I'd ever felt for him had completely vanished. All I wanted at that point was to be free. Free of him. Free of his lies. Free of his infidelities. How could he tell me the night before that he loved me and sixteen hours later he's deep inside another woman?"

She shuddered as she remembered his lie. *Katlin, I swear that's not me. I didn't sleep with her.* Yeah, like she didn't have eyes and hadn't seen that sexy grin of his as he walked naked to the bitch's bed, the same way he'd strutted toward her a hundred times, so proud of his toned and ready SEAL body. She used to love his I-want-you smile and how his eyes hooded with lust. The entire video was forever seared into her memory like a porn flick she couldn't forget.

Katlin took a deep breath and glanced at her friends' reactions. Pity. Understanding. Contempt for Ty.

Nita left the colorful chair and sat beside Katlin then slid an arm around her. "So every time you broke up with Ty—"

"No. I never broke up with him. He always broke up with me. He'd tell me he needed space, and I was willing to give him that. We were still in school and I knew he'd come back to me. He always did. Deep down he loved me and I loved him. I believed that old adage, if you love something enough let it go free. If it comes back, it's yours. If it doesn't, it never was." Katlin shrugged. "Ty was mine and I was his." The she corrected, "Until I asked him for a divorce."

"Fine, every time Ty broke it off with you, you went running to Alex? Right?" Nita corrected her statement.

"Yes, that pretty much sums up my high school years and the first two years in college." Katlin still felt every stab of pain Ty had inflicted over the years, but when Nita had described her relationship, it sounded so simple.

"Why the hell did you marry this asshole?" Nita's question had a simple answer.

"Because I loved him." The reason behind it was complicated. Katlin took in deep breath and tried to explain. "I believed that charismatic son-of-a-bitch when he claimed he loved me enough to stay true to only me. I gave him my virginity and I'd been brought up to believe that's the one thing a woman can only give to the man she loves. When I allowed him into my body, I vowed to love him forever, marry him and be true to only him until death do us part. I'd made a choice that night that Ty was the one man for me, forever." She shook her head. "Wasn't I the fool? We were just naive high school kids. What did we know about love back then? Other than raging hormones that begged for physical satisfaction. "

She had loved Ty and had given him everything from her virginity to her heart. She was sure that he was finished with his wandering ways and would settle down to become the loving husband he'd promised in front of God and a cathedral filled with family and friends. Katlin had thought since Alex had become a great husband and wonderful father, so could…would…Ty. She'd been wrong, and her heart paid the price for his deception.

"But what happened with you and Alex? You got together in college, right?" Tori prodded.

"Yes." She caught the smile about to burst over her face. Those were good times. "Ty couldn't get off the academy grounds much that first year, but Alex and I often met up and walked the Smithsonian together. We'd eat in little hole-in-the-wall delis, visit the National Zoo, then fuck like bunnies in my dorm room all night." This time she did smile, but it soon dropped. "One Sunday shortly after Easter, Ty showed up at my parents' house in his Midshipman's uniform and asked permission to talk with me. We sat on the porch swing and he begged my forgiveness..." She lowered her voice an octave. "You know I love you. Those other women, it was just sex. It didn't mean anything. You're the only one I've ever loved." She returned to her normal tone. "We all know the lines. But I couldn't go back to Ty. I was seeing Alex. I think Ty knew that. I agreed we could be friends."

Katlin filled her mouth with wine and swished it around, as though to rid herself of a bad taste. "About that same time, Alex seemed to distance himself. He and I would argue and we finally agreed to take a break. Before I knew it, the three of us had fallen back into what it was our norm...best friends."

Nita raised her eyebrows and asked with a grin, "A threesome? Did you ever have both of them at the same time?"

"No, I couldn't do that." Hell. She couldn't keep one man happy in bed; two would be impossible.

Tori and Nita looked at each other and bit back smiles. Nita finally spoke, "You don't know what you're missing."

Grace's eyes danced between the two guilty women. "We'll talk later. I have to hear about this, but please tell me it was two men."

"Oh, yeah, and they were twins," Nita confessed. "They seemed to read each other's mind, and mine."

"I had romance novel cover models," Tori announced. "We'd been on a photo shoot all day together starting with Elizabethan costumes and ended nearly naked and greased up for BDSM covers. We were all so turned on...well, we didn't want to waste all that baby oil." She closed her eyes and smiled as if she'd tasted the sweetest dessert.

Katlin didn't think she could ever be naked with two men

at once. If it could have happened, it would have been with Ty and Alex, but thankfully, they'd never wanted to go there. One man in bed at a time was obviously more than she could handle. Why else had Ty strayed? It was obvious to her that she just wasn't enough woman for him in bed and he'd needed more than she could give him. Not that she was prudish. Hell, she'd searched several sites on sex for their first anniversary and each night was a different experience. None of it had kept Ty faithful.

Katlin didn't want to hear any more about her friends' success with multiple partners, so she went back to her story. "Eventually, Ty crawled back into my heart…and my bed. Alex got Rachelle pregnant our second year in college and married her. Ty and I were married the day after he graduated from the Naval Academy."

"Nice story, but ancient history. Bottom line"—once again, Nita pulled it all together— "Ty's dead, and Alex is divorced, right?"

"Yes, but—" Before Katlin could finish, Nita charged in.

"So you and Alex are both unattached. There's really no reason the two of you can't get it on."

"That's not the kind of relationship we had—"

"Not true. You were lovers once and can be again. He's perfect as your re-introductory guy." Nita finished her milk, and the glass clinked as she set it on the coffee table.

Sex with Alex. At least she'd been there before and knew what to expect. She was comfortable with him. Maybe he was the perfect man to help her transition into the dating world.

Grace offered, "They're right. Alex is the perfect choice for you. Shoot, Kevin's been gone four years. I listened to their advice, and I'm dating now."

"Mister Tall, Dark, and Handsome from the church you go to in D.C.?" Nita threw in. "I thought you ditched him."

"I did. He was a terrible lover," Grace told them. "I thought he'd have a heart attack when I rolled on top of him and took over. Missionary was the only position he wanted, and that wasn't doing it for me."

"Hey, I offered her my bag of toys," Tori interjected.

"What goes on in the bedroom should be private," Grace reprimanded them. "It's between a man and woman."

They all looked at each other and burst out laughing. These women were never private. They told each other everything. Almost everything. Katlin was sure each woman in that room held deep, dark personal secrets.

Tori brought everyone back to the original topic as she scooted in next to Katlin's other side. "So, why don't you use Alex? You feel emotionally safe with him, don't you?"

"Of course. He'd never hurt me." Of that, Katlin was sure.

Nita grinned. "Just think of everything he's learned in ten years. I doubt he fumbles anymore."

"Make sure he knows up front that it's temporary and be sure that's all you want," Grace warned. "He could break your heart if you give it to him."

Damn Grace. She knew too much. Alex already had part of her heart as her friend. Could she resist giving it all to him when he touched her with such tenderness? Held her and made her feel safe with him?

"So don't give him your heart, just your body...as often as possible," Nita said with a hug.

Lei Lu yawned and stretched as she emerged from her bedroom. "Who's giving their body to whom this time? What'd I miss?"

"I'll fill you in later," Tori promised. "But Katlin has decided to start dating."

"Yeah, dating Bob doesn't do it as well for me either. Sometimes you need a *real* man." All eyes turned to Lei Lu as she brought a glass of juice in from the kitchen.

"Who's this Bob you've been dating?" Nita asked.

Lei Lu rolled her almond-shaped dark eyes and said, "Bob, Battery Operated Boyfriend. I actually call mine

Channing." She sat on the beige couch next to Nita and effortlessly slipped into the lotus position. As though she realized everyone was staring at her, she added, "A woman can dream."

"I channel Daniel Sunjata," Tori admitted. "He's so fucking hot. I'd do him."

"I don't want to play Who Would You Do," Grace said and hid her scarlet face behind a purple pillow.

"Afraid a certain Guardian manager's name would come up?" Nita taunted.

Lei Lu asked the group, "Do we have someone in mind as a hook up for Katlin, or are we going to sign her up for online dating?"

"Ooo. That could be fun." Tori bounced in excitement. "We'd have to run him through Section 7's search programs first."

"Then we could follow him to make sure he wasn't really married," Grace suggested. "That happened to a friend of mine back home. She met and dated this guy for weeks—"

Nita cut her off. "Don't care. We won't let that happen to Katlin. She deserves someone great."

"Hold up." At Katlin's voice, everyone shut up. "No online jerks. I'll work things out with Alex. He can be my reintroduction back into the dating world."

"Who's Alex?" Lei Lu asked then finished the juice.

"Katlin's old lover who saw her naked this morning." Once again, Nita did her thing and brought Katlin's whole morning together in one sentence.

"I want to check this guy out." Lei Lu pulled her enhanced tablet off the sofa table where it'd been charging and laid her hand on the screen for scanning.

"Alejandro Lobo." Grace offered the name Alex was given at birth, knowing Section 7's search engine would have more under that name.

"Here, I've got him," Lei Lu announced.

"I'm starved," Tori said as she headed to the kitchen. "Read it to me. I'm making a cheese and fruit plate for all of us. I need real food."

"In that case, you'd better bring chocolate, too," Nita suggested.

Lei Lu read aloud. "Ah, a Marine. Ooooh, Special Operations Group. After The Basic School in Quantico, he went to Reconnaissance School, SERE—"

Nita broke in, "Hey, we all went to SERE school; Survival, Evasion, Resistance, Escape training. I ate snake for the first time there." She was proud of the last fact.

Lei Lu continued. "Combat Diver Course, Airborne then Jump Master school–"

"Been there, done that, too," Tori called from the kitchen. "Well, I'm not a Jump Master, but I've done my share of jumping out of perfectly good airplanes. Personally, I don't need to do a night jump again, but I'm sure we will."

Unrelenting, Lei Lu read on. "High Risk Personnel class, Mountain Leader Course, Sniper School, the list goes on and on."

"We've been to some of those schools," Nita bragged. "Hell, Grace, you and I went through Sniper School together. I swear that women are natural shots. We did better than almost all of the men."

"Do you still have your HOG tooth?" Tori asked from the kitchen. "I do, but I never wear it. That bullet gets cold between my boobs."

"You don't have boobs," Nita gibed. "You could wear Band-Aids over your nipples and call it a bra. Now, Katlin has boobs. Her HOG tooth would get lost in the cleavage."

"I'm with Tori on that one," Katlin piped in. "Who would believe that two inches of brass bullet could get so damn cold. Mine sits in my jewelry box."

"Yeah, next to the two-carat diamond you no longer wear," Nita threw at her.

"Which is attached to the diamond-encrusted wedding band I no longer wear," Katlin volleyed back. Her friends knew that the brass bullet on her dog tag chain meant more to her than either lavish ring.

Lei Lu clicked to the next page that listed the missions and the larger operations that Alex had been involved in or led.

"Damn," Lei Lu scanned the screen then read aloud the long list of black ops that spanned every continent. Some were simply reconnaissance. There were a couple of kidnap rescues, most in South American countries and several in Africa. A few missions were assassinations of lesser politicians and middle management drug cartel and gunrunners. One involved a large team that had wiped out an entire group of guerillas in Guatemala just before they were to overthrow the current government.

"This guy is one badass dude. I like him. He can date Katlin," Nita nodded in approval.

"But everything for Alejandro Lobo ends over two years ago," Lei Lu noted. "What's he doing now?"

Grace told her to enter the name Alex Wolf. "He left the Marine Corps and changed his name."

Lei Lu stared at the screen a minute. "Oh, I get it. Alejandro is like Alexander in English, thus Alex. Lobo is Spanish for wolf. He Americanized his name. I've considered doing that."

"Is he working for the government?" Nita prodded.

"No," Katlin said and watched her team do what they did best, investigate a man's entire life. Look for his weaknesses and strengths and figure out a way to utilize both.

"Damn, Katlin." Lei Lu's voice sounded accusatory. "He's the managing partner of Guardian Security, ten offices and millions of dollars in revenue. Is he why we always have a bodyguard from there?"

"No, not exactly." Katlin wasn't ready to tell them about her connection with Guardian Security. "We're not truly safe even on U.S. soil, but we need to relax. Our personal protection is essential." They seemed to accept the answer without comment but Katlin caught the furtive looks her friends exchanged.

"I like the long hair," Nita said. "Is it as soft as it looks?"

"I wouldn't know." Although Katlin hoped to find out, maybe soon.

"Is he cute?" Tori asked and popped her head out of the kitchen.

"There's nothing cute about this man," Nita answered

"If you don't want him, introduce me. I can handle a man like him." Lei Lu could handle Alex the way she handled all men. Katlin had seen men all but fall at her friend's small feet and beg for her attention. Lei Lu's fine Asian bone structure and delicate Chinese features belied the strong woman underneath.

"With a name like Alejandro, is he a Latin lover?" Tori said as she brought a huge plate laden with various fruits, vegetables, dips, and cheeses and set it on the oversized ottoman. "I had one of those a few years ago. Once those guys set you as a target they're so smooth you don't even realize they're chasing you. You become their total focus, and they don't even see other women as potential lovers. Ricardo was a great lover."

"No, Alex was born and raised in D.C.," Katlin told them. "He has very modern pursuit techniques. He's several generations away from that."

"So, when do we get to meet this Alex Wolf, a.k.a Alejandro Lobo?" Lei Lu's eyes pinned Katlin.

"I don't know." Suddenly Katlin wasn't sure this was a good idea. But then again…maybe this was the perfect time. "When I left him, I told him I'd be in town for a few days and that I'd call. But I have a pretty busy schedule with Jenny's birthday, the opera—"

"Excuses," Nita accused.

"Invite him to join us for supper. He can help me celebrate my birthday, tonight," Lei Lu suggested.

Tori agreed. "The sooner we meet this man, the sooner you get our approval and have an affair with him. Then you can move on with the rest of your life."

Katlin could do this. Her friends had convinced her that Alex was her next step to moving on with her life. She was looking forward to this portion of the plan. She couldn't wait for Alex's hands on her body as they danced, his lips on her as he kissed every inch of skin while he slowly stripped her out of her dress. His hands on her breasts, flicking her nipples with his tongue. Oh, yes. She was ready for the seduction to begin.

"What the fuck are you waiting for?" Nita elbowed her. "Call the man."

"And while you're on the phone with him, ask if it's okay that I come over and use the range," Tori added. "I need to push a few hundred rounds through my new Smith and Wesson Shield. The action is stiff, and I could use the range time."

"Let's go," Katlin suggested and stood up. She was always up for shooting the hell out of something and target practice right now sounded like the best idea all day. "We can use the range anytime we want."

"And while you're there," Nita proposed, "hunt up that muscled Marine and ask him to join us tonight. In person, you can watch his reactions."

Her friend was right. Face-to-face, Katlin would be able to tell if he was lying or if he was at all interested in her. Sure, she'd seen his erection that morning but she'd been naked. Any man would react the same way. Alex had to be a willing participant in order for this plan to work. And damn, she wanted it to work with Alex.

CHAPTER 10

Alex approached the control room door as Dave strode in from the other side, grinning ear to ear. "Log me back in. Ms. Callahan has been delivered to her condo safe and sound."

"Done." Rick glanced away from the wall of flat screens monitoring various properties under Guardian's protection to take in Dave. "What the fuck are you smiling about? Don't tell me Ms. Callahan asked for you to be put on her personal protection duty tonight because Griffin already set the schedule."

Alex slid inside the darkened room and stood in the shadows, hoping Dave would speak freely, mentally noting that Katlin's condo was close because it hadn't taken her driver long to get there and return.

Dave cocked his head and gave his friend a shit-eating grin. "Better. I got invited to join the women tonight when they go clubbing."

Jealousy and resentment coursed through every muscle in Alex's body.

Then he saw the shock on Rick's face as the man asked, "Miss Katlin asked you to join them?"

"Hell no." Dave looked down at Rick with incredulity. "I can't even imagine her dating…well…dating a man."

"You know, I've wondered that too," Rick interjected, "if she doesn't play for the other team. I've never seen her interested in a man."

"Me neither, but she and her friends sure hug and touch a lot," Dave noted.

Alex didn't know what to think about that. He was elated that they hadn't seen her with other men, but then again, why would they have known? Unless it was someone who worked there and he'd already dismissed that idea.

Had she become a lesbian? No way. He remembered her aroused scent from an hour ago. At least he turned her on. Memories of their nights together flashed through his mind. The way she'd responded to his every touch. But Ty had hurt her so many times, she may have lost confidence in men and turned to women for comfort. She certainly hadn't turned to him.

"Yeah. I've had fantasies about that." Rick scanned the ever-changing screens then returned his gaze to Dave. "Can you picture a little girl-on-girl action with those women?"

"Fuck yes," Dave admitted. "They are so fucking hot, all five of them." Smugly he added, "And I get to play with them tonight."

"So if it wasn't Miss Katlin who invited you?" Rick queried.

"Nita." Dave waggled his eyebrows. "She and Grace had been running on the beach and saw me bring Miss Katlin home so they came to help with her bags." Dave leaned in. "They were all hot and sweaty in running shorts and those little tops that barely covered their breasts. Fuck. I popped a chubby just looking at them."

"You'd better not make a move on Grace," Rick warned and perused the screens again. "Griffin's been sniffing after that tail for a year."

Alex made another mental note of that tidbit.

"No worries," Dave said. "I'll have my hands full with Nita. I think she has a wild side."

"Have fun. But I hope it doesn't get weird," Rick cautioned. "I've never seen any of them with the same man twice, and with Miss Katlin knowing the owners and all…"

"She wouldn't get me fired for fucking Nita…do ya think?" Dave sounded slightly concerned.

Alex wouldn't let that happen. He was the one who made final hiring and firing decisions for all his operations. But it reminded him that Katlin did have some connection with this business partners. He needed to find out about that connection.

"Nah." Rick's gaze held on one screen. He zoomed the external warehouse camera in on a bum approaching the door. Without looking up, he offered, "Miss Katlin is nice and seems…professional, not vindictive. Besides, you're two consenting adults."

"Yeah," Dave agreed. "She can be…I don't know…distant. She doesn't act better than any of us, just conservative. I can't imagine her letting loose like the other women. She's a little uptight. I don't think I've ever seen her drunk. Always in control."

Rick zoomed in on the bum's face and clicked several pictures of the man as his gloved hand rattled the doorknob. "Like I said, professional. She reminds me of the women officers I knew in the Army."

Alex chuckled to himself. If they only knew how close they were to being correct. Once again, he wondered if she was still in the Navy.

Griffin strode into the control room and Alex stepped from the shadows to stand beside him.

During an inspection, Alex had developed a fresh-eyes methodology where he looked at everything as though he'd never observed the scene before. What he saw before him were two large, well-muscled men sitting before computer keyboards with tiny headsets, the kind used by SWAT and covert teams, but these were the very latest technology. Doug and Rick scanned pictures on the large LCD screens that covered the wall in front of them.

Doug clicked his mouse and one live shot filled six of the twelve screens. Alex and Griffin watched in real time as two teenagers walked past the door to a warehouse that had been converted to upscale loft apartments.

"Third pass for these bozos," Doug said disgustedly as the boys looked around for cameras. "That's right, you little street urchins, take a good look at that light." Still photographs of their faces appeared on another screen, just taken by the hidden camera.

"What the hell is up today?" Rick commented and continued to scan the remaining screens. "That's the third B and E attempt."

"Here we go," Doug announced. Alex watched as one of the boys opened a set of lock picks and kneeled at the door.

"Damn kids." Doug cursed as he hit a red button on a panel in front of him and spoke into his headset. "This is Guardian Security. I have a 459 Alpha in progress at…"

Alex shook his head at the audacity of the two young boys who should be in school. They'd be in jail within an hour.

With a nod, he and Griffin stepped into the next room of glassed offices for salesmen and computer techs who checked backgrounds for corporate clients. With a quick look, Alex could see exactly what each man was doing because all screens faced the center manager's office.

Everyone wore a standard uniform provided by Guardian. The flat black high-tech cargo pants were extremely comfortable and made no noise when the staff walked in them. The sturdy black web belt held a gun holster at either side or in the back, depending on the man's preference. A utility belt with all the latest "toys" could be worn comfortably over top. Those were stored, fully ready, in the cabinet next to the control room beside the gun safe that remained unlocked.

Gray golf shirts with the dark gray Guardian logo embroidered on the left pocket covered toned and fit bodies. Each man wore his last name embroidered in matching dark gray on a removable Velcro strip. Crepe-soled military-style boots of breathable Denier 600 assured their footsteps were quiet on the highly polished tile floors. Lightweight jackets hung nearby to hide weapons while in public because it was mandatory that every employee have a concealed weapon permit and carry a gun, even when off duty.

Alex was pleased with his Miami Center. This was his company. He knew every man by name, by sight, and knew his background. They were former military, Navy SEALs, Marine Special Operations, Air Force Special Tactics, and Army Special Forces, all with several combat tours in their past.

No, not all, he reminded himself. Breton Reed in the D.C. Center had never been in the military, but he'd earned his badass rep in a federal prison for breaking into the FBI data base. Alex was sure Bret had also seen the inside of many other federal agency computer systems, just for the fun of it. The man knew satellites inside and out and could write code faster than he could speak. Someday, those skills would come in handy.

They took the elevator to the bottom floor to begin his stringent inspection of the facilities, as he always did upon arrival at a Guardian Center. He believed it was essential to provide a healthy working environment and was adamant about cleanliness.

Together, he and Griffin examined the building from the street, where Guardian Security looked like any other boring white office building centrally located in Miami.

Excellent, exactly as I expected. It shouldn't attract attention.

Larry, Sara's husband, was this center's maintenance man and kept the outside clean enough to be good neighbors but never overdone. With the expensive electronic equipment inside, and personal security of each and every client at stake, Guardian couldn't be too careful. They needed to blend.

The business door faced the street next to a small gray and black plaque with the Guardian logo and address, daunting with the first floor devoid of windows. Known only to a few, the small horizontal windows on the second floor were fakes.

"Everything looks good here." Alex nodded to the men in the control room through the hidden camera before he used his master key to electronically unlock the door.

His gaze swept the brightly lit reception area. Seldom did any client come to the office, but those who did were greeted in an open area that offered overstuffed living room furniture in front of a huge flat-screen TV. Clients were never kept long before they were met in the small, conservative conference room to the far side.

Alex didn't bother with the secure parking in the covered garage that took up the remainder of the first floor and housed the fleet of upgraded Land Rovers and Mercedes, the corporate limousines, and protected employees' vehicles from the beastly Miami sun. He'd checked that area when he'd arrived a few hours earlier.

They passed the elevator and took the steps to the second floor, where Alex stuck his head into the world-class gym. A blond man watched himself in the floor-length mirrors as he finished a set of bicep curls in the free weight area that would be the envy of any fitness center. Two men sweated to music, only they heard through their ear buds while pushing their bodies on the best cardio equipment available. The mats for hand-to-hand combat training were empty, but men could often be found sparring at any time of the day or night. Everything at Guardian ran twenty-four hours a day, 365 days a year.

When they turned the corner, Alex heard the muffled sounds of gunshots. The two men grabbed sound suppressors hanging on pegs outside the five-station private range.

He opened the door, and his heart stopped.

Kat was there.

With a loaded gun in her hand.

CHAPTER 11

"Go," Nate shouted, and Katlin turned, quickly scanning the six life-sized pictures for the greatest threat. This time, they were set in a zigzag across the range, some very close and others almost to the back wall. Decisions made, she put bullets through the foreheads of six bad guys then ejected the magazine and cleared the chamber. In less than five seconds, it was over and her gun was safe.

"Pull them in," Katlin ordered as she laid her Kimber Solo on the carpet-covered bench in front of her and pulled out her custom-made earplugs. She hit the button for the pulley to retrieve the target in her lane.

"Awesome shooting, Miss Katlin," Nate complimented and slid his ear protection to his neck.

She wasn't so sure. The sights may have been off just a little…or she was. Seconds before she'd turned to shoot, her whole body had lit up like it did when danger was near. It had snatched a corner of her focus.

Their last mission in Iraq had been a big one, and she'd actually expected retribution from al-Jamil's family. There was no way they could know who she and her team were, and even if they had been discovered, the fundamentalist

Muslims would never believe that a woman could take out their leader. Besides, USSOCOM had given credit for the kill to an Army Special Forces Alpha Team in an attempt to take some of the heat off Navy SEALs, who each had a ten thousand dollar bounty on their head just for wearing the trident.

She grabbed the paper from her lane as Nate, Tori, Rob, and Johnathan brought the others over to her. The sheets were littered with holes surrounded by geometric symbols. She drew a triangle around each of her shots then evaluated them carefully. "I was off here, almost an inch." She pointed to the hole above the eyebrow on the lane four target. "My third shot," she noted.

"Your fourth was dead center," Tori noted. "And this mofo would have spattered brain tissue all over the ditsy chick he was holding hostage."

"I should have shot her." Katlin tried to lighten her mood. "That's the stupidest expression I've ever seen." She raised her voice to a squeaky falsetto and mimicked the model's face perfectly, "Oh. Help me. I'm so scared."

"Somebody should eliminate that bitch from the gene pool," Tori agreed.

"We're not in the business of killing innocent civilians." Alex's voice from behind her shot tingles up Katlin's spine.

She turned in unison with the other shooters as Alex and Griffin emerged from the shadows in the back of the gallery.

Damn he looked delicious. He'd changed into the Guardian uniform of gray polo shirt which showed off his well-developed biceps. Even under the black cargo pants, that body was drool-worthy. Griffin stood beside him, equally as fit, but Katlin's zing factor was pinging on his boss.

She smiled at Alex's comment then glanced to Tori. "Neither are we, but we have to be prepared to take out the guilty ones."

With a raised eyebrow, Tori silently asked Katlin if Alex

knew about the Ladies of Black Swan. The women had worked together so tightly for the past two years, it seemed her team could almost read each other's minds at times. She replied with an almost unnoticeable shake of her head. Although she would trust her life to any man in that room, she didn't dare trust them with her team's secret. Maybe someday she and Alex would reach that point, but it wasn't today.

"Interesting game." Alex's gaze swept over the five shooters.

"Yes, sir," Rob explained. "The training is very realistic since we use photographs depicting human targets, hostages and innocents rather than black and white outlines. Speed and accuracy are as essential as judgment, discerning who should be shot and who should be saved."

"Nice to see you again, Mr. Wolf. Hope you're finding our center satisfactory," Nate said with a broad smile across his ruddy face. The big man moved like a lion, despite his size, hand outstretched toward Alex.

"Nate, it looks like you've made training fun," Alex said to the Miami Center's assistant manager as he shook his hand.

"Miss Katlin taught us several shooting games." Nate gave her a dazzling smile. "We like this one best."

Alex glanced to Kat as Rob stepped up to him. "It's good to see you, sir." Jonathan followed, greeting Alex with a brief handshake and acknowledged Griffin with a nod.

Katlin figured she was next. "Alex, I'd like you to meet my friend and teammate, Tori Snyder." She turned slightly and gestured to Alex. "Tori, this is Alex Wolf, the managing partner of Guardian Security."

In the deep seductive voice Katlin had heard Tori use on targets, her friend captured his hand in a warm yet firm shake. "This is certainly an unexpected pleasure." She held his gaze, the way they'd been taught in CIA school.

Katlin wondered if Alex would prefer Tori's tall, model-thin stature to her rounded curves. Or her friend's dark brown skin to hers, which remained almost white as paper or pink when she spent time in the sun. A twinge of green ran through her but dissipated almost instantly. If he wanted Tori, Katlin would do what she could to make that happen. She had always wanted Alex to be happy, no matter what toll it took on her.

"It's nice to meet one of Kat's friends." Alex removed his hand from Tori's and stepped into Katlin's personal space.

He claimed her hand but faced the others. "Finish your game," he ordered. "I need to talk to Kat for a few minutes." He turned to Griffin and suggested, "Why don't you fill in Kat's slot. I believe she was at shooting station three."

Alex pulled Katlin to the back of the room where benches sat in the dark for spectators to watch while waiting their turn to enter the live shooting area. It was one of the many safety features designed into all Guardian ranges. He sat down and dragged her next to him, close.

"I didn't expect to find you here." His dark eyes were barely visible, too difficult to read.

"I have permission to use the range," she told him as she tried to extricate her hand. He gripped it tighter. Fine. If he wanted the contact, she'd allow it. It was rather nice, actually. She couldn't remember when a man had held her hand last. "I logged us in with the control room."

"I don't care that you use the range or any of the other facilities." His voice was low, but with the others using ear protection, she doubted they could hear anyway. "I wish you would have called and let me know you were here. I would have shot with you."

She shrugged. "It was kind of a last-minute decision."

They both glanced at the live range as Rob razzed Jonathan, who had finished his turn.

Katlin wasn't sure what this conversation in the dark was

all about, but it was the perfect opportunity to move forward with her plan. "If you're not busy tonight"—she hesitated as he turned to look at her then continued—"would you like to join us for dinner and dancing?"

"You mean club hopping where the music is so loud the next day my ears still ring and I feel like I've been at the range all day without ear protection?" He shook his head, and her heart dropped to her feet. "I'm not much for dancing."

She squeezed his hand, which still held hers. "You used to go dancing with me. Remember sneaking out late at night and going to the salsa clubs in Little Havana?" She remembered all too well. She'd taught him Latin dancing, and he'd held her as they moved their bodies in sync, rubbing against each other from shoulders to knees. She shivered at the memory.

"That was a long time ago." He gave her a small smile. "These days the women dance with each other, and all they do is bump and grind their hips and wave their hands in the air."

"You've been spending too much time in strip clubs if that's the kind of dancing you're talking about. I really don't want to know when was the last time you got a lap dance," Katlin said with an air of faked disgust.

He glanced back at the shooters.

Shit. She'd fucked up. He was probably involved with someone, and taking her out would be cheating. Being the other woman was the last thing she would ever do. "I'm sorry. You're probably seeing someone." She turned away as she erased the disappointment from her face. But she needed to see his face, read the truth or lie, so she returned her gaze to him. "Hell, for all I know, you may have a live-in girlfriend or at least someone special in your life. You aren't married, again, are you?"

He gave her a long, hard unreadable look before he said,

"I'm not married. And yes, I'll go to supper and dancing with you."

Relief washed through her whole body, and excitement followed in the next wave.

"Wonderful." Katlin had to hold back the huge smile. She wasn't sure she wanted him to know just how thrilled she was at his answer. "You might want to let Griffin know that you'll be joining us. It may make a difference as to who he schedules as personal protection for us."

"Us being you and Tori?" Alex asked and nodded toward her friend, whose back was to the range, gun pointed up, ready to shoot next.

"No. Well, yes," she explained, "Tori will be there, but there will be five women."

"I understand the need for a limousine, but why do you need a bodyguard?"

This was one of many questions she wasn't about to answer. Six shots filled the air from Tori's gun, giving Katlin an excuse not to talk.

She stood up but couldn't move very far. They were still connected, her hand in his. "Your turn to shoot, Alex." She tugged, and he begrudgingly rose to his feet.

Twenty minutes later, as they all reloaded bullets into their magazines, Rob asked, "Tori, from a woman's perspective, what do you think about those two women who just graduated from Ranger School,"

Katlin doubted anyone but her noticed Tori's split-second hesitation. Their whole team had attended the graduation, each wearing the uniform of their respective services. Tori, an Army captain, was most proud of her sisters in green. She had told them so in the private meeting they'd had over breakfast with the four female general officers who had created the top secret program the Ladies of Black Swan had completed nearly three years earlier. The very public graduation was another step in the plan to allow women in military special operations. Legally.

"I'm so fucking proud of those two women I could burst." Tori tucked a full clip into an empty slot in the foam of the protective gun case and grabbed the next empty one.

"Do you really think women can compete on the same level as men?" Incredulity laced Griffin's voice.

Katlin burst out laughing. "We just did. And beat all four of you, shot for shot." She pointed to the trashcan where the evidence lay then high-fived Tori. The two women had mentally slid into competitive mode and beat the men, fair and square.

"Sure, *you* two can shoot—" Nate started.

"And very well," Alex interjected as he re-holstered his guns.

"But you're the exception," Nate finished.

"So you are agreeing that the two female Army officers who just graduated are exceptional," Katlin smiled. "Thanks for admitting that, Nate." She shoved another bullet into the magazine.

"Yes, in that sense, they are," Nate conceded. "But I don't believe women have any place on the front lines, and behind them in bad guy country, which is required of a Ranger. I've been there, and it's dangerous."

"So you're okay with the helpless women in the rear with the gear?" Tori asked and then facetiously added, "Doing admin for the CO? Typing correspondence to the Pentagon on a base protected by double walls and armed gate guards?"

"There are other jobs women can do besides be a secretary," Rob reasoned. "In Afghanistan, we had an awesome girl running supply. All we needed to do was call her and she'd find us almost anything and get it to us no matter where we were."

"Again," Katlin noted, "far behind the lines." This whole protective attitude pissed her off, but she had fought it her entire life. Thankfully, her father had not adhered to that archaic philosophy and made sure she learned everything her older brother did, from weapons to martial arts. Her personal attitude must have slipped into her voice because Alex gave her a cautious glance.

With his beautiful Southern inflection, Griffin commented, "I knew a lot of women in the Navy who were hard as nails, but I prefer mine soft and sweet. It's my job to protect them. Keep them safe." He looked at Alex and added, "That's why I love this job. Guarding all those socialites and celebrities with their amazing bodies."

"Well, Katlin," Tori sneered, "aren't you glad they lower themselves to protect us?"

"Oh. No, Miss Tori." Griffin faced her. "I most definitely count you and all your friends among those beautiful women. You need my protection, even though you can outshoot me on the range. In real life, shooting someone is different than slinging lead at a piece of paper."

Katlin watched Tori's hackles rise. Her friend had a higher kill count than the man belittling her skills, but he had no idea how many men she'd sent to meet their maker. Tori had taken out six last week when their initial extraction zone became overrun by tangoes while waiting for the choppers. The attack had forced them on to Fallujah to the Marine base.

To diffuse the bomb that Tori was about to explode, Katlin touched her friend's arm and spoke to all the men. "I, for one, am so glad you gentlemen protect me and my friends while we're in Miami. You allow us to let our guard down for a few hours and truly relax."

"What is it that you ladies do?" Jonathan asked innocently.

By rote, Katlin answered, "We work for the government."

Rob picked up the questioning. "What department?" He glanced at all the men before returning his gaze to the women. "We were all in the military."

"Us too," Tori revealed. "I am a captain in the Army. Katlin is a Navy Lieutenant Commander."

Katlin watched Alex's eyebrows raise. "We're TDY to Homeland Security." She figured it was okay for them to know they were temporarily working outside the purview of the military. That line of questioning would naturally lead to who they worked for, where they were stationed, and a long attempt to find common acquaintances, especially since Griffin was a former SEAL and both Jonathan and Rob were Army Special Forces. Before she could re-direct the questioning, Alex beat her to the end game.

"Tucked safe and sound behind a desk in Washington," Alex added with a gratified smile. "No way in hell would I want you, or any female friend of mine, anywhere near the sandbox."

Tori tossed a knowing look to Katlin. Four days ago they'd been crushing regimes who'd built castles in the sand deep behind enemy lines. These men were clueless. And as far as Katlin was concerned, they could stay that way. Alex had made his viewpoint clear. Women were to be weak and helpless so big, strong men could protect them.

Well, Katlin didn't need a man to protect her. She needed one to fuck her senseless, give her multiple orgasms, and remind her why men had those penises they were so proud of. She inwardly smiled, remembering Nita's recent comment. *"I don't need a penis. Then I'd only have one. With this vagina, I can have all the dicks I want, then send them away so I can get the real work done."*

Damn she loved the women on her team.

"Just because those two passed the Ranger course doesn't mean they'll serve with the Rangers," Nate pointed out. "Putting a woman in with all those guys would be a disaster."

"I have to agree," Katlin told the men as she put boxes of bullets into a plastic carrying case. "Even deep in a mission, if a woman gets hurt, five men will rush to help her, but if a man gets hurt, one guy takes care of him and the others move on. Sometimes I think there's a gene attached to the Y chromosome for protecting women."

The men's heads all bobbed in agreement.

Homeland Security had proven this theory. Jack had assigned a woman to each of the existing teams when Katlin and her friends had arrived at Section 7. After one mission, he was ready to scrap the whole project. Thankfully, after she and her friends debriefed with the women generals who had created the secret program, they were allowed to form the Ladies of Black Swan. Their team's success was indisputable.

"Then there is the testosterone spike that follows an adrenaline rush," Tori added. "It's human nature to want to reproduce after a life-threatening event. One woman surrounded by a team of horny men isn't a good place to be."

Tori would know. The team of Alphas she'd been placed on for her first operation with Section 7 were total asses to her the entire flight home from their South American mission. According to her report, they were completely unprofessional with lewd sexual invitations and comments when she politely refused their advances. Thank God the generals had gotten involved and straightened Jack out. Although the men on that team weren't written up, as they should have been, the Ladies of Black Swan got their revenge. They knocked that team out of the first place standing in mission success.

"Another dangerous situation I wouldn't want my friends in." Alex stared directly at Katlin. "Some men just don't understand the word no."

Definitely oblivious. And he would stay that way. She could never see herself long term with a man who believed women didn't belong in the middle of the action. Katlin gathered her guns and ammunition and stuffed them in her black duffel. Slinging the bag over her shoulder, she asked,

"Griffin, will you log us out, please? Tori and I need to head home."

"My pleasure, ma'am." He glanced at their heavy bags. "Do you need help to your car?"

"Thanks, but we've got this." Tori strode to the range door. "Not all women are helpless Southern belles. Save your strength for those socialite beauty queens you prefer to guard." She opened the door and never looked back.

Katlin glanced over her shoulder at the four men. "Thanks, guys. It was fun." She gave them what she hoped was an apologetic smile.

Alex caught up with her in the hallway. "Are we still on for tonight?"

"Of course." Katlin wondered if he was going to back out. To be sure he was on board, she grabbed the front of his shirt and pulled him to her. Going up on tiptoes, she brushed her lips over his in a teasing move they'd been taught at Langley. Just above a whisper, she said, "I'm looking forward to it." She pressed her breasts into his chest in a move made to signal the man she wanted his body. "I hope you are too."

Stepping away, she spun around and headed for the stairs…adding a little more sway in her hips.

She'd been taught by the best how to seduce a man.

Hot guilt coursed through her cold veins as she stepped into the garage.

But this was Alex she was playing with, and he deserved better.

So did she.

CHAPTER 12

Alex stepped back into the range as Rob commented, "I hope she brings some new guns for us to try next time she's in town."

"Yeah, me too," Jonathan agreed. "Whoever designed that last piece of shit was never in combat. It was the most awkward rifle I'd ever shot."

"Those Israeli semi-autos she let us test were sweet, though," Rob said.

"Hooyah," Jonathan, a former SEAL, cried out. "I wonder how soon they'll be in production? I'd buy one."

Alex knew his face had given away his lack of knowledge when Nate said, "Miss Katlin sometimes gets prototypes to test, and she lets us shoot them."

"So," Alex asked the group of men, "you all know Kat rather well?" He could tell by their faces they'd caught her nickname.

"Yes, sir. I've shot with her several times. She's fast," Rob said with admiration.

"I've shot with her. And I've sparred with her in the gym, but I'll never make that mistake again." Jonathan looked at his feet.

"Knocked you on your ass, did she?" Nate said and slapped Jonathan on the back.

"Holy fuck. With her skills, I'm not really sure why she needs a bodyguard, but I'm there for her." At Jonathan's words, a flash of envy ran through Alex.

"So you have guarded her, Jonathan?" Alex had to know more.

Griffin nodded to his boss. "Yes, sir. I rotate the women's protection so no one becomes too comfortable with them. Especially with those women, it's very easy to become part of the fun rather than focusing on their personal safety."

"Guarding Miss Katlin and her friends is no hardship, that's for damn sure," Rob agreed. "And the sexy way they dance."

Jonathan let out a long, slow breath. "Fucking hot."

"They're all so goddamn beautiful with bodies to die for," Nate added.

"Yes, and that's your job when you're her personal protection. Just remember that." Griffin's stern admonishment brought the conversation back around. "And that's exactly why I rotate their bodyguards."

"Good shooting, men." Alex had enjoyed testing his own skills against those of his men and the women. He loved the feel of his Kimber 1911 pistols, but they were his personal weapons. Guardian provided guns and ammunition to employees, and every man who worked for the company was expected to be an expert shot with every weapon the company provided, from submachine guns to pistols of every caliber, from high-powered rifles to shotguns. Constant training was essential. Lives depended on it.

"Even though the women kicked our asses," Jonathan complained.

"Miss Katlin always kicks our ass," Nate noted.

"Yeah, but it was embarrassing to have both of them beat us," Rob added.

"That just means all of us need to take advantage of the range more often," Griffin suggested. "Shooting is a learned skill and improves with practice."

Alex had bested the other four men, but he knew he wasn't the best shot in the company. Wondering who was the most accurate, he decided to find out. "What do you think about an inner company competition with each center sending its best shooter to one site for a final creative competition, as realistic as possible?"

"That would be awesome," Rob enthused.

"The winner would get an additional week of paid vacation." Carrying the thought further, Alex suggested, "Maybe we'd send the man and his family on a cruise."

"Excellent idea," Griffin agreed. "The end result would be great training for everyone, especially considering how competitive all the men are." His pager buzzed. He glanced at the screen and said, "Catch up with you later, Alex. I need to talk with a client." Turning to his employees, he complimented them. "Men, good shooting. Miami needs to win that competition."

Alex thanked the men before he left. Shooting that way had been fun. He smiled at just what fierce contestants Katlin and Tori had become.

Alone, Alex finished his inspection. As he passed the Miami manager's office, Griffin looked up and smiled. Alex opened the door and asked, "Got a few minutes? No rush."

Griffin dropped his pen and left the report he was working on. He rose quickly and stepped around the highly organized desk. "Certainly, sir. I hope you found my Center satisfactory." His Georgian drawl stretched out the words.

Alex led the way to the corner office, Griffin at his side. He closed the large oak door behind him and sealed the two men into the soundproof room, away from the eyes of all the Miami employees. Griffin took one of the two dark brown leather chairs in front of the massive oak desk from Alex.

"How long has Katlin Callahan been sleeping in the penthouse?" Alex slipped into the burgundy leather executive chair and winced inwardly as sore muscles rebelled. Time for more ibuprofen. He rested his long, lean frame into its tall back and steepled his fingers.

"I apologize, sir. She's usually gone before you arrive. It will never happen again, I assure you." Contrite didn't look good on the former linebacker's hard face.

"That wasn't my question." Alex dropped his hands to the desktop.

"Since a few months after we opened. We were told Miss Katlin had permission to stay in the apartment whenever she wished." Griffin explained in his slow Southern way. Alex liked the way the men there had given her the genteel title of Miss and was sure the man across his desk was the reason why.

"Who told you that?" Alex held his astonishment in check.

"We got an email from Barry several years ago. I still have it in the manager's file on the computer if you'd like to see it," Griffin answered with confidence. "It's in the center manager's Manual."

Barry and Alex had gone to high school together, but it was pretty bold of the company CFO to keep a secret like this from him. Another list of questions formed in his mind, this time for Barry.

"Go on," Alex ordered.

"About a week after the email, Miss Katlin showed up. She had an electronic master key for the garage and had already parked her Lamborghini there."

At the mention of the car, Alex's eyebrows rose slightly.

Griffin smiled. "Yes, it's a sweet ride." He knew Griffin was talking about the car, not Kat, but the desire in the man's voice couldn't be missed.

At an unhurried pace, Griffin continued. "I brought her to the control room, and she signed in. I escorted her up the elevator to the apartment where her master key beeped her in." Griffin stopped and regarded Alex as if waiting for directions. Alex simply nodded.

"She comes in about every six weeks, sometimes it's four, sometimes it's eight, stays for a few days, then leaves. While she's in Miami, we provide bodyguards for her whenever she leaves the building."

"Free?" The businessman in Alex slipped out.

"No, sir," Griffin explained with fervor. "The first time she was here she gave us billing information, and we send a bill when she leaves. We don't charge for the apartment. Barry said not to, but she pays for every hour of limo and protection services. She pays immediately, too. She's considered a Prime Client," he said, referring to the highest level of their clientele scale.

"Where does she go?" Alex felt just a little guilty checking up on Kat, but he had three empty years to fill. *She'd been so close, yet so far away. Without a single fucking word to me.*

"She jogs at least five miles." With a smile, Griffin added, "And runs our men into the ground for being such a little thing. She takes the limo, and they pick up her girlfriends, and then they all go clubbing a lot. Sometimes they party afterwards at one of the really upscale hotels." Griffin paused again, as though wondering if he should go on. Alex waited him out. It was such a successful interrogation technique, even with Griffin, who'd been trained to withstand brutal grilling.

"Oh," Griffin popped in. "She takes the little girl, Jenny, to museums, the ballet, operas, and usually out to dinner. Sometimes Jenny stays in the apartment with her."

What the fuck? Jenny? His Jenny? Stays in his apartment? He'd never brought his daughter there, say nothing about spending the night. Maybe it wasn't his daughter. Perhaps it was some other child. Did Kat have a child?

"Describe Jenny, please." He had to be sure.

The leather seat moaned as Griffin shifted. "About seven or eight, long dark hair, a pretty face and eyes…" He looked at Alex then said, "Brown, kind of like yours."

Alex reached into his back pocket and pulled out his wallet. He rifled through until he found her school picture then handed it over to Griffin. "Is this her?"

Griffin smiled. "Yeah, that's her, a couple of years ago."

Alex cringed when Griffin handed it back to him. He needed a newer picture. Returning it to his wallet, he caught the questioning look from Griffin. "Jenny is my daughter."

"Then is Miss Katlin…was she your wife?" It was almost humorous to watch Griffin try to piece together the puzzle. "Or your sister-in-law?" He hurried on to explain. "When we pick Jenny up, we often see her mother, who looks just like Katlin, blonde, about the same height, not as athletically built as Katlin, but she works out a lot. Similar facial features, though, and blue eyes."

Alex was thrown by that. Did his ex-wife, Rachelle, and Kat look that much alike? Yes, they both had blonde hair and blue eyes, but that was it. Wasn't it? He hadn't seen the two of them together in over seven years. He'd never thought they looked enough alike to be sisters, but Griffin thought they did, and he was trained to see patterns. His life had depended on it.

"Tell me more," Alex ordered.

"Well, sir," Griffin hesitated then continued, "she usually knows when you're coming and clears out before you arrive. When she logs in, she'll always ask if you're expected, just in case your plans had changed. She's adamant about being gone before you get here."

Alex could picture her leaving as he was arriving, yet she never bothered to talk to him. Three goddamned years. She'd been right there all the time, avoiding him.

Alex decided to tell his Miami manager the truth. "To set the record straight, Kat and I have been friends since high school. She married my best friend, who was killed in Afghanistan three years ago." As an afterthought, he added, "He was SEAL, like you."

"Callahan. I didn't know any Callahans while I was in the Teams."

Alex deliberately looked at his desk. He didn't want Griffin to see the pain he was sure his eyes would reveal. "His name wasn't Callahan. It was Malone. Ty Malone."

He forced his gaze across the desk. Recognition flashed in Griffin's eyes. Every man in military special operations units knew that name and the op. It'd become the unspoken horror story that had affected joint operations since that night.

"*He* was Miss Katlin's husband?"

Alex couldn't speak. His throat was clamped tight. He only nodded.

"And your friend?" Griffin quickly added, "I'm so sorry, sir. I didn't know."

"Kat and I haven't seen each other since his funeral." Wanting to move on, Alex said, "Jenny is *my* daughter, and Kat is her godmother, a role she takes seriously. Kat and Jenny's mother are not related, but they are friends."

Griffin's brows knitted together as he seemed to absorb all he'd been told. "So, it's okay for Miss Katlin to stay here?"

"Definitely."

"And she can use all the facilities, right?"

"Sure." Alex was curious at this point. "I know she uses the range. What else has she used in the past?"

"She works out in the gym every day for an hour or more. Sometimes she'll spar with one of us, hand-to-hand work, you know the drill, but she's so flexible the men end up on their backs quite often. And it's not because we're holding back. She'd never stand for that. She's tough."

"You've sparred with her?"

"Yes, sir. Often. It's a great workout." Griffin's smile filled his face. "If you're going to take her on, beware. She fights dirty. And when you do, I want to watch."

Alex grinned, remembering how Kat's years as a gymnast had made her strong and flexible. He'd wrestled 152 in high school before he'd hit his growth spurt, and she could take him down. That'd been a lot of fun wrestling on the floor of what her family called the playroom. His grin widened at the other things they'd done in that aptly named room.

He caught himself and continued the questioning. "Why does she always have a bodyguard?" This one bothered him. She was a trained military officer, so why did she need personal protection?

"I'm not sure, sir. When she jogs, I imagine it's because there's nowhere in her cute little shorts and sports bra to put a gun so her bodyguard has to carry it, and his of course." His Miami manager had certainly noticed her body and had seen her often in the past few years.

Griffin continued, "When she goes out to dinner, she treats us almost like a date rather than her personal protection. I used to think it was just for the company, but more than once I've got the feeling–you know the one—like she was being watched, stalked. I'm not so sure the threat isn't real. She's never said though, nor been specific as to what danger threatened her."

Oh, yeah, I know that feeling. The tingling that starts at the back your neck and clenches your balls as it yells at you to pay attention. It's the sixth sense that had kept him alive more than once.

As though he suddenly remembered, Griffin added, "And she cooks for the men, giving Sara a day off. She's a good cook. She makes all these international dishes that always taste great. Some of the men were leery at first, but after she made them take a teaspoon sample, now, they'll try anything she cooks."

Alex grinned at all the tiny teaspoons he'd sampled of her mother's cuisine.

"Sounds like the men really like her."

"Yes, sir. Every one of them would kill for her, take a bullet for her. She's friendly, but not flirtatious like some women are with their bodyguards. She's respectful, but knows them all, right down to their families, pets, and hobbies. James made her a pen out of some fancy wood. And Sam's wife made this necklace out of a green rock Katlin brought back from Africa, malachite I think, then Miss Katlin gave her a big piece to keep."

"So do you guard her on dates?" Alex tried to ask without inflection in his voice. This was what he really wanted to know.

Griffin seemed to think about his answer before he said, "No, sir…she doesn't… date…the way you'd think." He hesitated and took a deep breath before he blurted out, "I'm not sure she likes men."

There it was again. Alex had started to wonder if Ty's frequent infidelity could have turned her away from men. But she'd asked him out, and they were going dancing tonight.

Griffin seemed to have regained his reporting stature. "She goes out to dinner and dancing with women. She'll dance with men at the clubs, but I think they're gay. She parties with her girlfriends a lot, and there's always men around them. Sometimes, a few of our men and I will meet them all for drinks, and some even go dancing with them, but Miss Katlin is never *with* anyone. It's more of a group thing." Alex watched a small smile cross Griffin's face.

Was that a smile remembering a private time with Kat? Damn it, he hoped not. "I take it you enjoy their company?"

"Yes, sir. They're all gorgeous." He dragged the last word

out with Southern intonations. "And it's fun to be around them."

"Good to know. I look forward to meeting all of them." Alex was more excited about tonight than he'd let on. Dancing meant Kat in his arms.

CHAPTER 13

Alex stepped into the apartment around six thirty that evening and immediately felt the emptiness. He entered the bedroom suite. The bed was made with fresh sheets, and the bathroom door was open. It smelled of cleaners rather than Kat. Fresh towels now hung on the bars. A glance into the dressing room closet confirmed that it was devoid of her clothes.

Kat was gone. Every trace of her had been wiped clean.

For a fleeting second, he wondered if she'd been real, or if he'd dreamed her naked in front of him that morning.

No. She was in Miami, and they had a date. He was supposed to pick them up at seven.

He lifted the house phone next to the bed and called the control room to see when he needed to leave.

"Yes, sir. The limo is ready when you are. You have dinner reservations at seven thirty at Chef Allen's. James is your driver tonight. Mr. Mitchell has her bodyguard duty until nine. Manuel will join you for the clubbing, relieving Mr. Mitchell when he's had enough." Alex looked at his Rolex and knew he'd better get a move on.

"Tell James I'll be down in ten minutes. Does he know

where Kat's condo is?"

"Yes, sir, it's on the beach. Mr. Mitchell is on his way in, so there's only one pickup. James will call Miss Katlin just before he pulls up to the front door, like usual. Take your time, sir, it's only a few minutes' drive from here."

Alex felt as nervous as a teenager on his first real date.

When he came downstairs to the Guardian parking decks, Griffin stood next to the black limousine, dark blue suit jacket carefully folded over his arm, chatting with James. The Miami Center manager wore Guardian's personal protection uniform of a crisp white dress shirt with navy blue tie and pleated gray dress slacks. His holstered gun was under his right arm, since he was left-handed.

Alex noticed an empty holster at his back. "Where's your backup gun?"

"On my ankle. That one's for Miss Katlin's. She prefers I wear it there," Griffin explained as he slid his arms into the suit jacket.

"She doesn't carry it herself?"

Griffin smiled. "Sir, there's no way her dress could ever conceal it, and all she ever carries is a tiny purse. Nights like this, her bodyguard carries her weapon."

Irked, Alex sniped, "And you've seen all her dresses?"

"I doubt it, but I've seen the way she dresses for clubbing. There is no place for a forty-caliber handgun. You'll see what I mean in just a few minutes." Griffin got into the back seat.

Alex wondered if he should offer to carry Kat's gun. He didn't want her reaching around Griffin's waist for her weapon, but hell, if she needed a gun, he'd have his own drawn, shooting whoever threatened her life.

Alex donned his custom-cut jacket, which allowed for his double holster to fit comfortably without printing the guns, making their outline visible. Although trained as a bodyguard, he left that duty to his men. But he always wore weapons. Always.

As soon as the limo stopped, Griffin emerged from the back door, unfolding his large six-foot four-inch frame. His hazel eyes swept the entire area behind mirrored aviator sunglasses as he took in everything. He was in bodyguard mode, feet shoulder-width apart, balanced on his toes. Ready. For anything.

Alex stepped out of the limo and took a similar, yet slightly more relaxed, stance beside him.

Kat emerged arm-in-arm with a small-boned Asian woman. Although they were the same height, they were a study in dark and light.

Kat's curve-hugging black dress shimmered as she moved toward the car. The low-cut V neckline revealed several inches of enticing cleavage. Long blonde hair flowed in waves over her lightly tanned, nearly bare shoulders. Though the dress stopped mid-thigh, exposing long, athletic legs, it was the three-inch high heels tied on with black ribbons that crisscrossed up her well-developed calves that made Alex slowly force air into his lungs.

The other woman floated in cream-colored chiffon that lifted on the ocean breeze to reveal a golden form-fitting dress underneath. The empire waist accented her small breasts. She tossed back her perfectly straight, jet-black hair that shined as it poured down her back and stopped at the hem of the dress, about two inches below her perfectly curved ass.

The two women laughed and giggled as they crossed to the limo.

"Beautiful, aren't they?" Griffin quietly acknowledged as he surveyed the area once again.

"I, of course, know Kat. Who is that with her?" Alex said with a slight nod of his head.

"That's Lei Lu."

A look of approving hunger swept across the tiny Chinese woman's face as the two approached the limo. "Damn, Katlin. He's delicious." Alex felt Lei Lu's nearly black eyes rake over every inch of his body, undressing him as though he were a male stripper and supposed to give her a show. There had been a time, not so long ago, when he'd gladly oblige her and give her exactly what she desired. Lei Lu was extremely beautiful, like a panther crouched, patiently waiting under the disciplined façade.

"Won't you share tonight?" Lei Lu begged. "It's my very first birthday party."

Share? As in a threesome? Alex ventured if Kat was into that. He'd had his share of ménages, but the mere idea of sharing Kat with anyone in bed, even another woman, stirred a possessiveness he hadn't felt in years.

Katlin bit the side of her bottom lip and looked back and forth between Lei Lu and him several times before she looked into Alex's eyes then said to Lei Lu, "No. He's mine tonight. We'll find someone else for you to play with."

Their brazen conversation had him shaking his head in disbelief. Didn't they know picking up strange men for the night was extremely dangerous?

Lei Lu's red lips curved upward. "Promise?"

"Absolutely. If that's what you want," Katlin promised.

Alex released a slow silent breath he didn't know he'd been holding as relief rose from deep inside. He didn't want to share Kat tonight, but he would have done almost anything just to get her into his bed.

Griffin held out his hand and assisted Lei Lu into the car.

All eyes turned toward the condo lobby doors as three more women emerged. The edges of Griffin's mouth twitched upward when the woman with auburn hair looked at him. Her sultry smile slowly revealed white teeth and suppressed obvious desire for the man next to him.

She had to be Grace. When she licked her lips, Griffin let out a small, barely audible groan. Alex thought his friend was going to lose it right then, but all he did was shift his stance and cross his hands in front of his zipper. Her forest green dress matched her eyes, which glimmered with craving. She swung her hips just a little more as she lengthened her stride and headed toward the limo.

"Grace is on the left," Katlin said as she stepped beside Alex, "and Nita is in the middle."

Dark curls bounced off the girl-next-door face as she shook her head. Hidden beneath hazel eyes and playful personality was intelligence. The pleats on her red dress had a sassy swing when she gave her hips a little more action as she strode across the pavement.

"And that's Tori on the right."

Model tall at over five ten, she strutted with bold confidence toward them. Her runway walk made Alex look twice at the golden-clad woman with skin slightly darker than his own. She looked like a man-eating tiger, and until this morning, he'd have enjoyed being the focus of her attention. Tall, dark, and strikingly beautiful had been his type for the past several years.

His eyes were irresistibly drawn to the stunning blonde at his side. Katlin had always been his type, and he'd fooled himself for too many years lately. In college, when she'd gone back to Ty, he'd loved blondes, as many as possible. Rachelle had been included in that number, but once they were married, he'd never strayed. After their divorce, he'd preferred dark hair and skin at least as dark as his own. Katlin looked up at him and smiled. He knew in that instance that it hadn't been Rachelle's blue eyes and ivory skin he'd run from. It had been Kat.

It had always been Kat.

Grace, Nita, and Tori each took Griffin's hand in turn and ducked into the car, followed by Katlin. Alex bowed deeply as he followed her magnificent derriere inside. He wanted to see it naked and in front of him as he pushed into her from behind. They'd both enjoyed it that way; he'd made sure. As if she could read his thoughts, she glanced over her shoulder at him. The corner of her mouth kicked up, and he swore her eyes twinkled. *Damn. She remembered, too.*

Griffin was last to fold himself into the back seat of the bulletproof car. Protocol demanded that Griffin sit next to Katlin, to protect her body with his, but Alex had taken the seat next to her.

"Griffin, slide over there next to Grace, would you please?" Katlin ordered as much as she'd asked. She reached into her black, gem-studded purse and extracted her gun, dropped the magazine, pulled back the slide to check the chamber, and slid the magazine back in. She handed it, grip first, to Griffin, who checked it himself before he slipped it into the holster at the small of his back. He settled into the soft leather seat across from them. None of the other women had paid attention to the weapon exchange; they were too busy chatting.

"Ladies, as you can see, we have a guest tonight, so play nice," Katlin warned. "I'd like you all to meet Alex Wolf, an old friend of mine. Alex, this is Grace, Nita, Tori, and Lei Lu." She pointed to each woman as she said their name. They seemed to consider him with intensity, as though his every move was being judged. He wondered what Kat had told them about him and their relationship.

"Also," Katlin continued, "Griffin is our bodyguard, at least through dinner. Manuel will go clubbing with us, though."

"Hot damn, lots of men tonight," Nita proclaimed. "Dave might join us at the club, too. Alex, I understand that you dance. I call at least one."

Oh hell. He'd planned on spending all his time with Kat. He looked at her, and she shrugged. "It's up to you. I usually don't share but—"

"Fuck that, Katlin, you usually don't have a man to share," Nita pinned her. That hadn't surprised Alex since Griffin had told him earlier that Kat didn't go on dates as far as he knew. Good. Nita's confirmation gave Alex satisfaction, although he wasn't sure why it pleased him knowing she hadn't dated much.

"Hey, I'm the birthday girl. I get one dance, too," Lei Lu piped in.

"We'll see," Alex answered without commitment.

"We need to decide which club we're going to first." Katlin turned the conversation in another direction for the remainder of the ride. He was content to listen and watch the interaction of the women. It was evident that they were good friends and extremely comfortable, touching often, laughing at inside jokes. But he didn't miss the glances his way. They were checking him out, watching his reactions. Interesting. They were protective of Kat.

Twenty minutes later, they pulled up to the door at Chef Allen's, one of the best restaurants in Miami. Per protocol, Griffin emerged first and blocked the door until his visual sweep of the surroundings was completed. Through the darkened windows, Alex scanned the rooftops for possible threats. The crowded sidewalk overflowed with well-dressed couples of all ages, awaiting their turn to enter the busy restaurant.

Griffin reached into the car and took Grace's hand. As soon as her long legs came into view, the men in line took notice, even though their dates were right beside them.

The five gorgeous women, dressed to attract the attention of any Y-chromosome within sight, strode confidently to the door. Women watched appraisingly, sizing up the competition. When Alex stepped out last, he felt all eyes on him and overheard quiet speculation.

"Who are they?"

"Is that…?" suggesting some rising starlet.

"He must be a drug lord. This *is* Miami."

"I think I recognize…"

CHAPTER 14

Alex smiled as though all the women were his and followed last as Griffin led them through the oversized carved-wood doors. No waiting in long lines for this party of seven.

Inside the well-appointed restaurant, they were immediately escorted to the round table at the back of the room. Katlin seated herself between Griffin and Alex, their backs to the wall with a clear view of every seat in the house as well as the front, back, and kitchen doors. Their drink orders were taken immediately, but before they were served, Chef Allen, in white high-collared chef attire and puffed hat, gregariously approached the table.

"Katlin, ladies"—he looked surprised at Alex and added with a nod—"gentlemen, it's so wonderful of you to visit my humble restaurant." The thirty-something owner had a broad smile and eyes that sparkled.

"Humble?" Katlin noted. "Where did you get that line from?"

"Do you think it's too much?" Chef Allen asked sincerely in a quiet voice.

"You might want to tone it down a little," Tori suggested. "All this success is going to your head."

"Yeah, I'm beginning to think I liked you better when you had that little hole-in-the-wall downtown," Nita taunted.

"So what are you going to feed us tonight, Al?" Katlin quizzed with a warm smile. The executive chef explained every dish from appetizers through dessert. Many were Lei Lu's favorites, and she shrieked with delight several times.

Chef Allen looked at Katlin and said, "Only the best for my partner." Then he disappeared into the kitchen.

Several bottles of wine arrived immediately; their origin was explained in detail as a stout man in a tuxedo opened each bottle. The sommelier should have given the tasting to the man of the table, but he obviously knew Katlin, so all samples went to her.

"Partner?" Alex asked, leaning close to Katlin as he refilled her glass with French Vouvray.

"Al was a great cook but a terrible businessman. I found him a manager, rented him this place, and gave him a few bucks to get started. Barry handles all the money, and this restaurant is hopping every night. The food is great," Katlin explained.

Her business acumen surprised him, but her generosity hadn't. He wondered what other ways she'd changed. Her body had rounded into womanly curves that had warmed his entire right side during the ride. Every time she'd leaned forward, he'd gotten to see more of her high, smooth breasts. He wanted to fill his hands, run his tongue over their curves, taste them once again. But they were friends, a word she'd made sure to use. He'd let her set the pace and hoped she'd change the rules, soon.

With five women at the table, conversation never stopped. The ladies quizzed Alex on his business then turned on both him and Kat and circled their prey.

"So the two of you went to high school together," Tori stated. "I hear you were anything but angels."

What? Had Kat talked about all the trouble they'd gotten

into in school? Sure she had. These women were her friends. Even guys talked about the shit they'd pulled and gotten away with in high school.

"I checked your school records," Lei Lu announced with a Cheshire-Cat grin. "You were suspended several times, together, but the report didn't give details."

"Give it up," Nita ordered. "We want all the deets."

"How dare you hack into my school files," Katlin scolded.

"Hey, just doing my job. I had to check Alex out, and your name popped up numerous times," Lei Lu defended.

"Quit the diversionary tactic. We fuckin' want specifics," Nita chided.

"Let's start with the lab explosion," Tori suggested.

Katlin looked to Alex and burst out laughing. She signaled for him to go ahead.

"Kat and I were chemistry lab partners, and we were supposed to make a miniscule reaction with three elements," Alex began.

"You were admitted to a Miami magnet school as a certified science genius, right?" Lei Lu added. Well, damn, she had checked him out, a deep investigation.

"Yes, science was one of my subjects, and I was pretty good at it. You had to excel in at least two areas to get in," he casually stated before he went on with the story. "So, I knew how to make a big fizzle and watched several other students overflow containers with bubbles. But we wanted to make a bang. So I mixed a few choice elements together, and when it was hit, it popped. So we made more and put some on a cube of sugar. The school was old and always had flies."

"You didn't," Tori accused.

"Oh, yes we did," Katlin retorted. "It blew the wings off the fly. So we made an even bigger batch." Katlin hid her face behind her hand, and her shoulders shook in suppressed laughter.

Alex picked the story back up. "We painted Chase

Bartholomew's lab chair with some of it."

"He was a real dickweed," Katlin explained. "Thought he knew everything and lived off his father's legend as the richest asshole to graduate from our magnet school."

Alex resumed. "When he sat down, it made a bigger bang."

The table erupted in laughter.

"It didn't hurt him," Katlin reassured everyone, "but it literally scared the shit out of him. He had to change into his gym clothes for the rest of the day."

Another round of laughter filled the corner of the crowded restaurant.

"We got sent to the principal's office and scolded," Alex explained.

"The hardest thing was trying to keep a straight face when confessing," Katlin added.

Alex continued. "After a half-hour lecture about how dangerous that was, we got after-school suspension and told we had to do the experiment right."

"Well, Ty was in a different chem class but was still serving after-school suspension for groping a cheerleader in the janitor's closet, so he joined us in the lab to help us perform the experiment correctly." Katlin made air quotes around the last word before dropping her hand lightly on Alex's forearm.

He lost his train of thought when the jolt flashed through him. Just her touch could light him up and ignite passions buried so deeply he hadn't felt them in years. Thank God Kat kept the story going.

"So we decided to make even more while Ty combined the chemicals for the assigned experiment," Katlin clarified.

Alex caught up and jumped in. "We had this gallon of liquid that was inert in that state, but when it dried, it was explosive. Then the instructor walked over to watch us complete the assigned experiment."

"Oh shit," Nita declared.

"Yeah, we were in deep shit," Katlin agreed.

"The guy grabbed the gallon of liquid, threw it under the blast shield, and turned on the heater. Fucking idiot," Alex said. "The man who should have been smarter than that."

"He pushed us all out of the room and called the bomb squad." Tears leaked from Kat's pretty blue eyes as she used her napkin to dab away the moisture.

"I think I just peed, just a little bit," Nita confessed as her whole body shook with laughter.

When Katlin regained some of her composure, she admitted, "Well, the police chief, the SWAT team, the bomb disposal guys, and the school board wanted us in jail, and the FBI wanted the formula."

Alex told the end. "The FBI got the formula, and the three of us were suspended from school for a week, which we spent on the beach and in the Callahan's boat."

"Daddy didn't think we should be punished since the real danger was the instructor's fault, not ours. In the end, the instructor got reprimanded for not keeping track of his students' experiments and told"—she lowered her voice—"you are working with geniuses. You need to expect creative thinking."

Their food arrived as the story ended and everyone except Katlin immediately dug in. With a forkful halfway to his mouth, out of the corner of his eye, Alex caught Katlin crossing herself. It seemed like forever since he'd prayed over a meal…or prayed period. Not since he'd held Ty's lifeless body in his arms in fucking Afghanistan. He now sat beside his friend's widow, enjoying her company more than he should.

Wasn't he a terrible friend? He'd made a promise to Ty years ago and hadn't kept it until today. Alex would be a much better friend to Katlin now that she was back in his life.

She looked at him. "Are you okay? Is there something wrong?"

"I'm fine." He was better than fine. "Everything in the world is right, now."

Laughter, good people, and great food made the perfect recipe for building friendships. Alex liked these women even more with every barb they exchanged, every story they told and hug they gave each other.

They ate until they couldn't take another forkful. Then Chef Allen emerged from the kitchen pushing a cart laden with a chocolate and strawberry layer cake that stood a foot tall and was at least three feet long. Everyone in the restaurant sang Happy Birthday to Lei Lu as she blew out twenty-eight candles. With a bright smile and a thank you, Lei Lu personally delivered a slice to each person in the whole restaurant.

After a second helping of birthday cake, Lei Lu came around the table, shoved Griffin out of the way, and sat down in Katlin's lap.

"Thank you!" She hugged her friend fiercely then kissed her on each cheek before she gave her a smacking kiss on the lips. Alex looked around, but none of the women seemed surprised or offended by this overt girl-on-girl public display of affection. "This has been the best birthday dinner ever."

"Well, that wasn't too hard considering it's the first one you've ever had," Katlin said.

Had Lei Lu led a deprived childhood? He couldn't imagine a year without birthdays as a child. Hell, his whole family, all his friends, practically the whole neighborhood showed up for birthday parties at his house. Kat's birthday parties had been legendary in Miami, pool parties, beach parties, and often a hundred guests. But to reach twenty-eight without celebrating? He'd ask Kat about it later.

Practically bouncing on Katlin's lap, Lei Lu begged, "Now where are we going dancing?"

"La Marea Turbulenta is playing at that great place we like in Little Havana," Tori announced.

Nita jumped in. "Damn, I love them."

"We have to go," Grace agreed. "They're the best salsa band in Miami." She danced her shoulders, and Alex watched Griffin's eyes grow dark and heated. Yes, just as he'd thought.

"I like Club 21," Nita said.

"Oh, yeah," Grace agreed. "And I want to try that new one down on the beach. Oh, heck, I can't remember the name of it now. It used to be the Sand Bar." She waved her hands as if she could stir up the name.

"That place was a fucking dive," Nita flung at her. "They should have named it the Sandy Bottom because it was just a bunch of skanks getting nailed on the beach by greasy losers."

"They cleaned it up, and now it's an upscale club with dancing on the beach," Grace explained.

"I hope they poured gallons of bleach over the sand. I'd be afraid to get an STD from dancing barefoot," Nita shot back.

A heated discussion ensued about the newest clubs, the best clubs, and their favorite clubs. In the end Lei Lu picked one, but she never left Katlin's lap until the decision was made.

As the seven got up to leave, Alex reached for his wallet since no bill had arrived. Katlin gently touched his arm, shook her head slightly, and softly said, "Al knows where to send the bill, and Barry will include a generous tip."

"Guardian is paying for this?" Shit. He hadn't meant to say that out loud. His managing partner brain, always cognizant of costs and the P&L bottom line, had pushed forward and blurted out his thoughts. Katlin stepped back, her expression abhorrent.

"Certainly not. Barry may be the C.F.O. for Guardian, but he's also my attorney and handles all my personal financial transactions. Tonight is my treat. The whole night." She turned and headed toward the door.

Damn. He'd screwed up. But he'd learned a few things too. Kat was very sensitive when it came to money matters.

Lei Lu had Katlin by the hand and excitedly pulled her toward the door. Once outside, she propelled Katlin to the awaiting limo. Nita and Tori were arm in arm as Grace kept pace beside them, bending in and laughing. These women sure seemed to touch a lot.

In the car, Katlin sat beside Alex with Lei Lu on her other side. Griffin was again beside Grace, opposite them.

"My friends really like you," Katlin said, leaning in close to Alex. "They want to know if I'm going to share you tonight." *Share?* Alex shot her a worried look, yet he was slightly intrigued.

He'd done a few threesomes with Ty the summer between freshman and sophomore year in college. Ty was doing his Naval Academy Summer Cruise and Alex's Marine Corps ROTC summer duty was with the same Amphibious Task Force in the Mediterranean Sea. Both single and unattached at the time, they'd enjoyed the European women individually and together for those six weeks. But there'd always been an unspoken rule that it would never happen with Kat, even though each had been intimate with her. She was too special to both of them.

"Don't worry. I told them no." Katlin brought him back to present. "You're my date. Even though I love these ladies, we don't share everything. Maybe I'll let you dance with them, if you want. I'm feeling rather possessive at the moment, though."

"It looks to me like Lei Lu is your date," he said, nodding at their intertwined fingers.

"She's never really celebrated her birthday, so this is a very special night for her. We're like family, very openly affectionate. It works for us."

"Like the Callahans?" Alex had spent enough time with Kat's family to know they hugged a lot, kissed often, and played hard. The first time he'd eaten at her house, he'd gone to shake her mother's hand and thank her but had been embraced instead. It took some getting used to, but he liked it after a while. His family was deeply rooted in Cuban propriety, and although they hugged, it wasn't the all-out physicality of the Callahan home.

"Yes, exactly." Katlin's smile surrounded his heart with happiness. Damn it was good to be with her again.

Changing the subject, Alex asked, "Never had a birthday party?"

"Never. She's led a different life than most people, but that's hers to tell if she chooses for you to know." Several ideas ran through his mind, but he let them go. Kat was his interest, not Lei Lu.

Alex changed the subject again. "You know you didn't have to leave this morning." He'd hoped she would stay.

"It's your apartment, and there's only one bed," Katlin replied.

"That never used to be a problem," Alex said as he looked at her in the subdued lighting of the dark car. The shadows made her cheekbones look even higher, her smooth alabaster skin almost ghostly under streetlights that tried to penetrate the tinted windows.

"We're not the same people we were back then." Her gaze held his. "We need to get to know each other again. That's what we're doing tonight. I'm showing you one part of my life, letting you get to know the people I spend my time with when we're not working."

Her eyes dropped. "I know you have questions. So do I. And we'll get to them." She took his hand in hers. As heat rushed to his cock, she added, "Let's just enjoy each other tonight."

Alex wondered just how much enjoyment she meant to have. He'd be happy to make her scream his name as she came.

CHAPTER 15

The limo pulled to the curb in front of Club 21. Hundreds of women in shiny low-cut miniskirts and young men in dress slacks and collared shirts filled the sidewalk all the way down the block. All faces turned to get a glimpse of the celebrity inside the arriving limousine.

Alex glanced around the car, but Kat and her friends seemed accustomed to this reaction and ignored the activity outside. Or so it seemed. The women maintained a high level of vigilance, an awareness of their surroundings that he hadn't seen in years. They were good. The furtive sweeps of the area as they turned to one another to chat, broad smiles and body language that projected a casual demeanor, yet hid a readiness to act, would be overlooked by an untrained observer. Alex felt the underlying tension. That mysterious energy that ramped up just before his SpecOps team entered a hostile situation.

The women portrayed, to the unknowing eye, that they were merely socialites out for a good time at a popular club, but in truth, they acted like trained operatives. He was positive he could ask any one of them how many people were in line, the height of each building, and the best positions for a sniper and they'd accurately rattle off the details.

He'd accompanied several starlets to events, both as a date and personal protection, but no matter which, he automatically slid into defensive mode when the vehicle stopped.

A surge of need to safeguard these women swelled within Alex. He wondered what their actual threat level was. As Griffin had indicated earlier, there was more than a possible stalker. His need to keep them safe, shield them from danger, amped up.

Tonight, he was along as Kat's friend, but in that moment, he knew he'd take a bullet for any one of these women and die protecting them.

Griffin stepped out first, again. He held the door partially closed until he'd checked the area and assessed every possible threat to the ladies. Manuel strode out of the Club, spoke into the bouncer's ear, then nodded toward the car. The bouncer smiled and unhooked the velvet rope that prohibited the long line from entry.

With Griffin on watch, Manuel fully opened the limo's back door and reached for the first of the women. Whistles and catcalls shrilled from the men in the waiting line as women, hopeful to get close to a celebrity, probed their A-list.

"Who are they?"

"Who's that?"

"Is she..?"

"Is he..?" Per Guardian protocol, the four men quickly herded inside the blackened doors. Griffin entered last, leaving the club's hulk as he clipped the velvet rope closed.

Woofers pounded a deafening beat as Manuel led the group through the darkened club, lit only by flashing purple and white neon. On the balcony level, their reserved VIP seating area had three purple and gray couches in a U shape with a low table in front. Buckets of iced Red Bull and bottled water filled the corners. Wavy smoked glass changed color from gray to purple, which offered the only light and separated them from other VIPs. The private bar that contained top-shelf liquor was accessed by servers clad in skin-tight gray and purple spandex minidresses that showed every female curve.

Demetri announced that he'd been personally selected by the club's owner to serve their party. Appreciative, very female gazes raked over the skintight Club 21 t-shirt that showed off his excellent six-pack abs and cut biceps. He genuinely smiled at the five women and flashed very bright white, mostly-straight teeth. As soon as orders were taken, all the women headed to the dance floor below.

Alex sat back as he sipped his eighteen-year-old scotch and watched as the ladies found a place on one side of the gyrating crowd and caught the beat of the music. Several men approached them and tried to dance in, but they closed ranks, ignoring most of them.

Two men, obviously regulars and excellent dancers, seemed to know the women and were allowed to join the group. The men danced very close, grinding hip to hip, with several of Kat's friends, who smiled and laughed.

Now that Griffin was officially off duty, he sipped a fine Kentucky bourbon and made small-talk with Alex until Katlin and Grace returned after a few songs.

"You ready to dance with me?" Katlin asked as she glided onto the couch very close to Alex.

"Who were the two guys you shared down there?" Alex asked, nodding toward the dance floor.

She gave him a long gaze before she answered. "They dance with touring pop stars. We first met them in Rio when they were with Lady GaGa. They're great guys, a lot of fun and fantastic dancers."

Alex was a little miffed. He didn't usually share his dates with anyone, but he'd shared Kat with Lei Lu most of the evening, and he wasn't sure if this was a real date. He wasn't sure exactly what it was other than an opportunity to meet her friends.

"They're gay, and we've checked them out," Kat tried to assure him.

Alex relaxed a little.

She picked up her drink and downed it. Before she could set it on the table, Demetri materialized, looked at Katlin, who nodded then added, "Make it a double, please."

She leaned across Alex to reach the tub of ice filled with water bottles and grabbed one. He felt her breast brush against his arm. As she pulled back across, her nipple had hardened. He took in a slow, deep breath. Her heat warmed his side from his shoulder to his thigh, everywhere she was pressed against him. He wanted her, not just because she was a beautiful woman but because she was his Kat, and she was now back in his life. Or was she? She was practically in his lap at the moment.

She rolled the chilled bottle across her chest and up her neck. "Were you jealous?"

Alex watched as a drop of water ran from Katlin's jaw line down her neck headed for her cleavage. Without thinking he bent and licked the line of water. He heard her gasp, and then she held her breath the closer he came to her dress's neckline. She moaned as she arched and offered his tongue the swell of her exposed breasts.

He raised his head to look at her then licked his lips.

"Salty," he said and moved in slowly to kiss her. A fraction of an inch away, he stopped to give her a chance to say no.

With only the tip of her soft pink tongue, she leisurely licked his top lip. Her teeth captured his bottom lip and held it captive while she ran her tongue from one side to the other.

Katlin released his lip then whispered, "Yes."

～

Confirmed. The seduction was working, on Alex as well as on her. The dress had done its duty, and she'd thought her casual touches during supper had been perfect. If he'd been a tango, he was taking the bait, hook, line, and sinker.

But this was Alex, not an assignment. He was her friend. Yes, they'd been lovers ten years ago, but she certainly wasn't that teenage girl anymore, and he wasn't the same inexperienced guy.

Katlin wanted to forget most of the past, especially the last three years, and kiss Alex, everywhere. Maybe it was the wine at dinner, maybe it was the drink she'd already downed. No, it was the man beside her. He'd always been able to crumble her strongest defenses. And damn it, she wanted him. Yes, she needed a transitional sexual relationship and he was perfect, but she also needed Alex to remain her friend.

She could do this. She had to do this. The need to move on with her life as she pushed hard at thirty pressed on her soul. She wanted more out of life than the next mission. She wanted what her parents had shown her every day of their lives. A relationship of give and take where the crevasses were filled with love that moved with every shift the world threw at them.

When Alex had touched her that morning, he'd opened the door to a large, empty space deep within. She'd lied to herself that she didn't need a man to fill the void in her life, a place she'd packed with work, friendship, and exhaustion. She wanted Alex, not just for sex and to hone her rusted dating skills. She wanted him to fill that room, wall to wall.

It was a crazy thought. She'd fallen into old habits, expecting Alex to pick up the pieces and help her rebuild the broken parts of her life.

She had felt his erection as she'd purposefully slid across him. She was already seducing his body. Settling beside him, she cracked open the plastic bottle top. She chugged nearly half of it before placing it on the table. She then turned and faced Alex. His dark brown eyes were filled with so much passion she just wanted to kiss him for hours then make love with him until the sun interrupted them. *He's still so handsome. And all male, "a man's man," as Daddy would say. It's been so long since anyone looked at me that way. The real me.*

She placed her hands on his broad chest and felt his well-developed muscles tighten at her touch. She ran both hands up to his cheeks, dragging her manicured nails slowly over his neck.

He closed his eyes as if to concentrate on the heightened nerves she brought to life with every touch. Slipping his arms around to her back, he massaged her spine as one hand moved up to her neck and the other to the small of her back.

Katlin ran her hands over his bound hair and pulled the ponytail loose. "That's better," she said and ran her fingers through his long, silky hair. He closed his eyes and made a deep purring hum when her nails scraped over his scalp. With her hands woven deep in his hair, she pulled his head down.

Against his lips, Katlin whispered, "I've missed this," and captured his mouth. She opened immediately, and he swept in. He tasted of fine whiskey and Alex as she tangled her tongue with his. The explosion that erupted within her was familiar yet long forgotten. It was the flavor of Alex. Passion took an awakening breath. It had been sealed with all the lies and betrayals under six feet of dirt, compressed with three years of overbearing silence.

Katlin had been emotionally numb since the night before Ty left for Afghanistan, the night she'd asked for a divorce. She'd left him sitting at the dining table, the video of his most recent infidelity playing on the flat screen at the other end of the great room.

She'd thrown herself into her work, which sustained her even through the news of his death. When she buried Ty, she'd hoped for the comfort of Alex's arms, his soft words, as they both mourned the loss of their best friend. But she never saw him after he handed her the folded flag. The weight of that rejection had piled onto her suppressed emotions.

In his arms was where she should have been hours after they returned from Arlington National Cemetery. Now, years later, it wasn't comfort from Ty's death she sought. It was a need to end the loneliness.

She'd tried to date, more so in the last few months. Some of the men who'd asked her out were everything most women would want, drop-dead-gorgeous, rich, intelligent, and, in many cases, powerful. But it was easy to say no. From their initial conversations, the spark, the chemistry, the knowing it was right–or even right for now– just wasn't there.

But damn, it was exploding all around and within her now. After the silence of celibacy, the onslaught of emotions was more than she could handle. At the same time, she wanted more. She wanted to attack Alex right there, assured he'd satisfy her every need. Just as he had so many years ago. Before. Before Rachelle. Before Jenny. Before Ty. She had to forget everything that had happened before and concentrate on now.

Alex pressed his whole body against her and took her mouth with commitment. It was too much. She hadn't been kissed like that in...years. She slowly pulled back and gentled the kiss.

When they came up for air, he hugged her tightly as they both caught their breath. He ran his hand up and down her back.

"Christ, I've missed you," he said into her ear and squeezed her even tighter.

Tori and Nita walked into their VIP seating area and grabbed their drinks. Nita swatted Katlin's outstretched legs and said, "Get a room, bitch, or share." Katlin untangled herself from Alex and gave him a passing kiss as she sat upright on the couch. Nita fell into the space beside her. Tori threw her endless legs onto the third couch and stretched as everyone ignored Grace, who was having a private conversation with Griffin.

"Where's our birthday girl?" Tori asked, looking around.

"I thought she was with you," Katlin said.

Manuel, standing at the railing to watch the dancing mob, announced, "She's on the floor with both the pro dancers. She's having a good time. She's on her third shot, though."

"She's an adult, and besides, it's her birthday." Nita shrugged as she licked the last drop of her pink drink. "She can deal with it."

"She'll just sleep in tomorrow, and we'll be expected to drag her sorry ass out of bed sometime after noon," Tori reasoned.

"I'll whip up my hangover cure, and she'll be fine within a few hours," Nita offered.

Katlin finished her double, a needed alcoholic reinforcement. She looked at Alex and said, "Let's go dance." She took his hand and pulled him off the couch toward the floor of bouncing bodies. As they found space amidst the dancers, a Latin pop song started.

Katlin draped her hands loosely on Alex's shoulders as her whole body moved to the music. He placed his hands to her hips, and they moved together as though they had been professional Salsa dancing partners for years.

"Remember sneaking out to the clubs on Calle Ocho in Little Havana? We'd dance for hours." Growing up in several Latin American countries, Katlin had learned her dance style from the streets and clubs as a child and loved the sexy music.

"You once told me that Latin dancing was public vertical movement to music of what you wanted to do privately and horizontally." Alex pulled her hips into his, and she couldn't miss the bulge in his slacks. That part hadn't changed since their teenage years. She loved to tease Alex with the sensuous motions of heated dance.

But he was no longer Alejandro, and she was a very different woman than that young, carefree girl. She rocked her hips to the beat and felt him grow harder, longer. This was what she wanted now. Needed now. She was a woman, and he was helping her find that feminine inner self she'd lost. The plan was working.

As the next song started, her friends surrounded them and began to dance in a group. Griffin had joined them on the floor. The men danced with each of her friends. When Dave showed up, he was immediately included.

It didn't take Nita a full hour before she and Dave left after hugging Lei Lu as they wished her one last Happy Birthday before they left together, hand in hand. Griffin used their exodus to call it a night, to Grace's fallen hopes. But she rallied on in celebration.

Two more clubs, four hours of dancing, and too many drinks to count, Lei Lu declared that she'd had the best birthday of her life and was ready to sleep. In the limo on the way to the condo, she fell asleep as she leaned on Tori.

"Thank you so much for coming out with us tonight," Katlin told Alex as they pulled into the circular drive of her condominium. "Would you like to come up for a nightcap or cup of coffee?" Katlin knew this broke her rule, but it was her rule and her condo.

"Just a quick one," Alex agreed and smiled. The hunger in his eyes melted something deep inside her and pooled in her panties.

A quick one? Not if she had anything to say about it. Katlin couldn't hold in her smile, or her hope.

Katlin, Grace, and Tori struggled to get a sleepy, drunk Lei Lu out of the car. Alex leaned in and plucked the birthday girl from the seat.

"I've got her," he said with a grin. With a nod of his head, he dismissed Manuel and the limo for the night. Katlin opened the glass door to the building, and Tori pressed the button for the elevator, which opened immediately. Upstairs, Grace swiped her card for the electronic door.

Nails scratched on hardwood floors, and heavy paws thumped. A deep "woof" followed.

"Damnit," Tori and Katlin called in unison as one hundred pounds of Rottweiler mixed with English Labrador charged toward the open door. Still a puppy at heart, he greeted them with slobbering licks. His thick tail stopped whacking the open door when he looked up at Lei Lu, who was cuddled into Alex's broad chest. He whimpered.

"She's fine, boy, just drunk." Katlin petted his head. Damnit nudged Lei Lu's butt with his head.

"Awk." Lei Lu's eyes flew open, and she stared at Alex. "Ooooh. Hello."

Damnit poked her again with his nose.

"It's not me." Alex sounded sheepish. Just then Damnit barked.

"I can walk." Lei Lu slid out of Alex's arms and gingerly tested her legs when her bare feet touched the cherry floor. She reached down and ruffled Damnit's head. "Better now, big boy?"

"Alex, I hope you're not afraid of dogs." Katlin grabbed the wide dog collar. "Meet Damnit. Hold out the back of your hand so he can sniff it. Otherwise, he'll head for your crotch."

Alex did as ordered. "Thanks for the warning."

"Damnit, Alex is a friend." Katlin emphasized the last word then repeated it. "Friend." The dog seemed to accept the newcomer and finally licked his hand.

Tori and Grace managed to get Lei Lu to her bedroom, nearly stumbling over the rambunctious pup that insisted on circling them every step.

"I'll take him outside," Tori offered as she grabbed his long leash. "Come on, Damnit, let's go." Before he'd leave, he gave Katlin another doggy kiss. He hesitated when he reached Alex, sniffed his hand, and regarded Katlin as if she'd betrayed him. Finally, he tentatively licked Alex's hand before bounding out the door toward the staircase.

"I'm off to bed," Grace announced with a yawn. "Nice to meet you, Alex." She waved as she sauntered down the hallway to the bedrooms.

"Your dog's name is Damnit?" Alex asked as he followed her to the living room.

"Yeah, more by default than anything else," she admitted. "When I brought him home from the pound, we found ourselves saying 'no, damn it,' 'come here, damn it,' 'oh, damn it.' The next thing we knew, he answered to Damnit. It stuck."

Katlin still wasn't sure what had driven her to walk into the Miami animal shelter several months ago, but she knew the moment Damnit leapt to the cage door as she approached and looked at her with his hopeful hazel puppy eyes that he'd be going home with her. He was the first male she'd taken home in more than three years. Alex was now the second. This was proof she was ready to move ahead with her life. Right?

Katlin went into the open kitchen that covered one whole wall behind a long breakfast bar that seated six. She was nervous but managed to ask as she opened the refrigerator, "Beer, wine, coffee, soda?"

"Coffee would be great," Alex replied as he climbed onto a striped bar stool. While Katlin assembled the coffee, filter, and water and set the pot to drip, she watched Alex take in the condo. When he came to the smoky glass of the twelve-foot windows that faced the City of Miami, he stopped and stared.

"Let's go out on the terrace while it drips. It's an incredible view." Katlin opened the sliding glass doors. Alex followed her through to a breathtaking view of the Miami skyline at night, lit by the glow of city lights.

She took his hand and said, "Come on, up here." They climbed the six steps to the Penthouse deck, where a small pool was surrounded with an outdoor kitchen and groupings of chairs. She led him to a double chaise lounge and stretched out.

"This is the best way to take it all in." Katlin encouraged him down.

"I've never seen Miami like this before. It's an awesome view and a fantastic place." Alex lay on his side, his head propped in one hand and looked down at her. "Thanks for inviting me tonight."

The nightly ocean wind blew a strand of hair across her face before he gently slid it over, tucked it behind her ear, and tenderly followed its outer curves. His touch sent heat coursing through her veins and warmed her to her toes. Her nipples hardened when he left his palm on her cheek and he bent down and kissed her. It was slow at first, but as she kissed him back, the intensity grew. Her whole body seemed to buzz.

No, she felt something vibrating on her hip. It was her damn cell phone. *Who the hell could that be?* Since their bedroom door was closed, she knew Nita was home in her own bed. Tori was out with the dog. Maybe she'd had a problem with Damnit.

But then it rang, a tone Katlin knew all too well.

"Damn," Katlin said when she broke the kiss. "I'm sorry, I've got to take this."

"Scrambling," Katlin said into the phone then punched a button. She looked at the display. After a few seconds, she confirmed, "Secure. Control, Lady Hawk here."

Katlin did not move away from Alex as his eyes grew large. She didn't care if Alex overheard the conversation. "The director wants to see you in his office at ten o'clock, Monday morning. Confirm please," a man on the other end ordered.

"Confirmed. What's this about?" Katlin asked. *Damn, why does the director want to see me? We're supposed to be on leave.*

"Unknown."

Fuck, this can't be good. "Who else is attending?"

"Director of Operations."

Jack, the ass, will be there, huh? Maybe, it's not as bad as I think.

"No one else?" she asked.

"Correct."

Fuck, no. Just me and Jackass. Well, we'll see about this! She looked at her watch. It was 2:30 a.m. She didn't care. If he was going to have Control call her in the middle of the night, he could get up too.

"Get Jack on the line," Katlin said with unhidden anger in her voice. Alex looked at her with raised eyebrows.

Katlin got up, took Alex's hand, and walked back into the

penthouse kitchen where she poured two cups of coffee while on hold. "I may need a witness, so I want you to hear this," she told Alex.

"Okay," was all he said as she put the phone on speaker.

A man's deep voice came on the line and chastised, "So glad you could tear yourself away from your partying to speak with your boss."

"Why the fuck have I been called into the director's office on Monday?" Katlin seethed, full of resentment as she lead Alex to the couch and sat down.

"Insubordination." The word was flat.

"To you?" This was incredulous. Although she was often irreverent and sometimes disrespectful toward the man, she was never disobedient or mutinous.

"Yes," he said with satisfaction.

"I have two words for you, Jack, page twenty-six."

"Bring it on," was his reply.

"Make this go away, Jack, or the entire after action report, including page twenty-six, will be on POTUS's desk as I hand a copy of my growing file on you to the director Monday morning." There was a long pause. Katlin knew the man on the other end was questioning how well he knew her and if she would actually give a file to the President of the United States. That one piece of paper could end his career. She would do it without hesitation. "I'm not kidding, Jack. I'll bring sexual harassment charges against you."

Katlin stared at the phone as the silence stretched for nearly a full minute.

"I'll see what I can do." Jack sounded resigned. "But you need to be in the office Monday morning."

"I'll be there, but you fix this," she demanded.

Smugly, Jack said, "Who's the man sitting next to you?"

Alex shot her a what-the-fuck look.

"None of your damn business," Katlin said quickly looking around the condo.

"You are my business. You're my wife."

She looked directly into Alex's questioning eyes and shook her head with disgust. Through clenched teeth and vibrating waves of rage, Katlin admonished, "I am not your wife. I have never been your wife. And I will never be your wife."

"You were my wife once," he insisted.

Still fuming, she calmed her voice and said, "No, I pretended to be your wife as part of an operation, that, if you will remember, did not go as planned, thanks to you. I'll never forgive you for that."

She took a deep breath and got a grip on her emotions. "I'm really getting concerned about you, Jack. I think you're confusing reality with the world of pretend we work in."

"Nita found company tonight," Jack commented, changing the subject. Katlin glanced down the hall toward the bedrooms.

"Good for her. At least someone got laid," she said and looked straight at Alex. "Do you have eyes on us? Did you wire my condo? Or do you have satellite infrared spying at us?"

Katlin crossed the room and quietly knocked on Nita's door. When no one answered, she stuck her head in and called for her. Using a combination of American Sign Language and combat signals, Katlin told Nita to sweep the apartment for bugs.

Laughing, Jack asked, "Are you nervous about what I'll see?"

Nita glanced at the phone in Katlin's hand. "What the fuck?" she mouthed then retrieved her equipment and began to look for audio and video devices.

"Jack," Katlin mouthed back.

"No, I have nothing to hide," Katlin told her boss. "I don't care if you know what I do...during working hours. I'm your employee, and that's it. My tracker is for work purposes only.

I'll add this to the growing list of my sexual harassment charges."

At that statement, Nita glanced over her shoulder at Katlin and gave her a raised eyebrow. Katlin signaled that they would talk about it later.

"You're not going to do that," Jack said confidently.

"You know what, you're right. I'm just going to shoot you if you don't back away from my private life," Katlin said as casually as though they were discussing the weather. She sat back down beside Alex, who seemed to be absorbing everything.

"Did you just threaten my life?" Jack said unconcerned.

"No, I'm a much better shot than that, and you know it. I just made you a promise that I would shoot you someday, maybe cripple you, just a little, so every time the barometric pressure changes you'll feel pain. A reminder of what an annoying long-term pain you are to me."

Nita pointed her equipment around the room and found two bugs that were sending audio and video, most likely straight to Jack's computer.

"Hi, Jack! Hope you're enjoying the show," Katlin said, holding the devices in her hand. She moved over and straddled Alex's lap, and then she kissed him passionately.

"Show's over Jack, you ass." She smashed the bugs between two sandstone coasters then pressed End on her smartphone.

"Nita, make one more sweep, please, to be sure we got them all," Katlin ordered.

Alex ran his large hands up and down her bare thighs, which were still on either side of his.

"That fucker," Nita said as she tweaked her hand-held device and pointed it in a circle around the main room of the suite. "Christ, I hate him. I'll check the bedrooms, too. I wouldn't put it beyond that ass to have bugged them."

"He knew you were *busy* earlier." At Katlin's words, Nita's head popped up.

"Really? Well, he couldn't have watched. We were at Dave's place. Unless he saw us on a sat signal. In that case, I hope he enjoyed it as much as I did," she said with a devious smile. "We're going out again tomorrow…or maybe we'll just stay in."

Nita walked into the dining area and toward the kitchen before she headed back toward the bedrooms. "I'll sweep yours first."

"Thanks, Nita." Katlin then looked at her friend, braless in a sleep tank and short shorts. "Sorry to wake you up, but—"

"Glad you did." Nita smiled and headed down the hall.

Katlin looked back at Alex, gold flecks sparking from his eyes.

"What the fuck are you involved in?" His words stung. "And where the fuck can I find this asshole Jack? I'm going to kill him for you."

CHAPTER 17

Katlin didn't know whether to be pleased at Alex's alpha tendencies or scared that he might just kill her boss. He certainly had the skills. But deep down, she wanted the pleasure of her nemesis in her crosshairs.

She glanced down the hall, confirming all the doors were closed. She'd already broken so many of her own rules tonight. What was a few more? Alex could keep a secret, that was for sure. He'd had a top-secret security clearance for years. Most importantly, Alex could be trusted with the truth, at least the part she was willing to give him.

Inhaling a long, slow breath, Katlin gazed into eyes she knew well. On a heavy sigh, she told her oldest friend, "I'll answer any question I can."

"Who do you work for?" Alex quickly asked.

She could answer that one. "The United States government."

Alex cocked his head to the side and asked, "Can you be more specific? Or let me guess, you'll have to kill me if you do?" He cupped her face in his palm and held her gaze as though he could see all the way to her soul. "You could try, but I don't think you could kill me."

She leaned in and laid her lips on his. The real her. Katlin Callahan kissed her old friend who now called himself Alex. And it felt so right as the warmth of his closed mouth gently moved against hers. She leaned back, breaking the nicest kiss she'd had in years. "No. I couldn't kill you."

She smirked. "But I have the skills to do it."

His fingers dove into her hair, and he pulled her head to his chest. "Oh, Kat, what have you gotten yourself into?"

Although she liked lying on his chest, he was treating her like a child whose problem he had to fix.

She jerked up. "Alex, this is just work shit. My problem. Not yours."

"Okay, let's talk about your work." His hands fell to her hips. She realized that she was still straddling him and tried to get off, but he held her firmly. "You're fine where you are. Now, when did you leave the Navy?"

Resolved to her position, she answered, "I'm still in the Navy…technically."

"Are you still with Naval Special Warfare Command?" Alex's question indicated he knew more than she'd thought.

"Technically."

"Does Jack work there?" Maybe Alex would hunt down her boss and kill him.

"No." She'd promised to answer his questions. Every interrogator was aware that sometimes knowing the right question to ask was more important than its answer.

With a slight nod, Alex tried a different approach. "Who does Jack work for, and what's his title?"

"He's the Director of Operations of Section 7 at Homeland Security." That just revealed so much of her job.

"They tried to recruit me when I left the Marine Corps," Alex declared. "Back then, it was a good ole boys club of former special operators and all male. I take it that has changed some?"

Not much, Katlin admitted to herself. It was still driven by testosterone, but her team was proving the value of estrogen. "Not much has changed." She needed to end this line of questioning. He already held more pieces to the puzzle than he should.

"Are you an analyst for them?" His questions were too probing.

Changing the subject, she apologized. "I'm sorry I used you to piss off Jack…but I'm not sorry I kissed you." She bent down and kissed him lightly before she lifted herself off his lap. She took his hand and stood.

"I'm sorry, Alex." She took a deep breath. "That call took the last bit of energy I had. I'm exhausted." Alex stood, and she moved into him. He simply hugged her and held her close for several minutes before he took her hand and headed toward the door.

"You do have a sexual harassment case against him," Alex admitted.

"That little exchange is nothing compared to what I have as evidence." Someday, when the time was right, she would use it too. But she loved her job, and would never allow anyone to think she was a whiny bitch who couldn't handle a little extra attention from her boss. She still couldn't be one hundred percent sure this wasn't another test. Anger management and pressure from above were often breaking points for leaders. Besides, she had two years left on her military contract, and they couldn't return her to the regular Navy until the Joint Chiefs of Staff approved of women in special operations. That wasn't going to happen anytime soon. So, in the meantime, she had to tolerate Jack the ass.

"You shouldn't threaten to shoot your boss." Alex's smile warmed her to her toes.

"I am going to shoot him," Katlin said with sincerity. She was serious and would someday do it.

"You scare me sometimes," Alex confessed.

"Good, I like to keep a man guessing." She smiled. "It keeps him interested."

Alex just slowly shook his head. "You've never needed mind games to keep me interested."

"I had a wonderful time tonight, Alex," Katlin said, standing at the door. "I hope you enjoyed dinner, even though my friends put you through the third degree about our youth. Thank you for going dancing with me and for dancing with the others. It was fun."

She looked down for a moment before meeting his eyes. "Thank you for a wonderful evening." She went up on her toes to kiss Alex on the cheek.

He slid his arms around her and pulled her close. "What are you doing tomorrow night?"

"Taking Jenny to the opera, *Pirates of Penzance*." Then she had a brilliant idea. "Why don't you go with us?"

One side of his smile quirked up. "So you're the reason I couldn't have her the whole day."

"I'm sorry." Katlin felt terrible about taking her goddaughter away from her father. "But if you go with us, you get her for the whole day and most of the night."

"Double bonus." He lightly brushed his lips over hers. "Because I get you too."

Then his lips touched hers, and she was lost. When his tongue swept across her bottom lip, she opened for him. He explored her gently, and when she kissed him back with the same moves, he pulled her to him, every inch of their bodies aligning. She couldn't miss his erection pushing into her belly and her own heat a few inches lower.

If she didn't stop now, she'd have him naked on that couch within a minute. Alex broke the kiss, turned, and opened the door. "What time is our date tonight with Jenny?"

"I usually get picked up around five in the Guardian

limousine. We do supper then the opera and dessert afterward if she can stay awake that long," Katlin called to his back.

"I'll see you tomorrow." He looked at his watch. "Actually later today," he said as he headed down the short hall to the elevator.

Katlin closed the door and flipped the deadbolt. "Wow. What am I going to do with him?" She hadn't realized that she'd said it out loud.

Nita wandered in from the hall and suggested, "Well if you don't know, I have a copy of the Kama Sutra I'll lend you."

"Thanks for the offer, but I have a copy." She hugged Nita goodnight and dragged her tired body to bed.

Katlin wrestled with her sheets and thoughts for hours. Still angered over the late-night conversation with Jack, and about the bugs he had planted in her condo, she'd felt violated. Jack was becoming a problem. He was inserting himself into her personal life, not that she'd had much of one until yesterday. She needed to finish seducing Alex, ring every ounce of pleasure out of his magnificent body, by Sunday morning since she now had to go into her fishbowl of an office on Monday.

The way Alex had kissed her she knew he'd wanted more. She'd felt his erection and thought about it far too long into the night. Was it fair to Alex to make love with him then walk away? Was it fair to him to use his body for her much-needed sexual release then leave him for what could easily be months?

Before she left Alex, there were some nagging questions that needed answers. Like why had he left her alone after the funeral. And why so many years of silence?

She was sure it had to do with her former husband. Once again, Ty stood between them just as much as he had in life. A thousand times she'd questioned her decision to marry the man. Once a cheater, always a cheater, and the lies he'd told her to cover his inability to keep his fly zipped were endless. Deep down, she believed that Ty had truly loved her and she had certainly loved him, like an idiot.

She was simply never enough for him. He obviously needed something she could never give him. What exactly that was she'd never been able to figure out. She'd tried numerous things to keep him in their bed. Every time she discovered another of his flings, he'd swear it was only one night, he'd been drunk, they'd been separated too long. He had an excuse for each and every one of them. In the end, he always came back to her, and she forgave him— often after long, heart-to-heart talks with Alex.

Damn Ty. He'd been dead more than three years and he was still controlling her. Memories of the two men who'd filled her life for fifteen years ebbed and flowed through her brain.

Maybe she was just better off without men. That had worked for the last three years, kind of. But she missed the way a man held a woman. That inner connection with someone of the opposite sex. And, damn it, she missed sex.

Then there was Alex's explosive kiss. The detonation had blasted through some of her buried feelings, and she wanted desperately, needed sex for the first time in years.

Katlin punched her pillow then stuffed a second under her head. She fell asleep just before the first streams of yellow dawn broke over the Atlantic Ocean and sifted through her bedroom's wall of blinded windows.

Nearing noon, with her second cup of coffee in hand, Katlin decided she seriously needed a run to expend some of this pent-up energy, or was it frustration? Her thoughts went to Alex and how he'd look in nothing but running shorts. She could imagine his ripped torso with well-developed pecs and abs. A light dusting of dark chest hair and a thicker line leading from his navel down to where she knew a thick mat lay at the base of his—

Katlin grabbed her phone, ready to call Alex, when she remembered he had Jenny that day. She would see them for dinner and the opera. No big deal, right?

Five hours later, her cool demeanor was shot to hell as she stood in front of the full-length mirror and evaluated the sapphire blue dress that clung to every curve through the top of her hips then flowed out to the floor.

"How do I look?" she asked the four women congregated in her bedroom. She hadn't been this nervous going to the prom with Ty, or any formal function since.

"Beautiful," Grace said and handed her the small jacket.

Katlin snaked her arms down the heavily beaded bolero that fastened in front, covering most of her cleavage. She thought of it as conservatively sexy, appropriate for the opera with a nine-year-old and yet enticing for the man she hoped she was seducing.

When her phone rang, she glanced at the diamond-jeweled watch on her wrist. It seemed foreign compared to the black diver's watch she wore during missions. They were a minute early.

She grabbed the phone, checked the caller ID, then answered, "Katlin Callahan."

"This is James, Miss Callahan. We're pulling onto the street to your condo."

"Thank you. I'll be right down." She took one last look at herself and finger combed the carefully curled hair to give it a carefree style.

Tori took a brow brush and touched up Katlin's naturally blonde eyebrows, which were darkened so they could be seen against her pale Irish skin.

"Great eyes if I do say so myself." Tori's years as a model made her a makeup genius. She had artfully arched each brow and applied the smoky eye shadow tinged in blue, which made Katlin's eyes appear bigger, brought out the blue in them, and matched the dress.

"I think the nails look perfect," Lei Lu told the women. "There's an innocence in silver that works for her." Katlin looked at the pearly silver polish on her usually bare yet buffed fingernails, and then she peered at her toenails peeking out of sparkly blue and silver sandals with a short two-inch heel.

"Thank you, ladies. I couldn't have done this without you." Katlin felt prepared and turned to leave the room.

"Wait up," Nita called. "Your necklace."

"Oh, Damnit," Katlin said and whirled around as hundred pounds of overgrown puppy bounded into the room. She bent and rubbed his head. "I couldn't leave without your male approval." As if he understood, the dog looked her up and down before he drooled.

"Oh shit." Nita scurried from the room, handing the necklace to Grace. "I forgot to feed him. Come on, Damnit." At the sound of the cabinet door opening and rustle of his dog food bag, he twirled around midair and bolted for the kitchen.

Grace stepped behind Katlin, who lifted her hair so Grace could reach around and fasten the necklace. "I believe you're as ready as you're going to get."

"Go get 'em, tiger," Lei Lu encouraged.

"Whoa, I'm not a tiger." Katlin shook her head as she started out of the bedroom, the three women trailing behind. "Your momma, on the other hand, is queen of the pride. Nor am I old enough to be a cougar, so banish those thoughts. Besides, Alex is a year older than me."

"Didn't you graduate together?" Tori asked.

"Yeah," Katlin said and put the silver chain of her purse over her shoulder before she slid her Glock into it. "But I was placed a year ahead when we moved to Miami."

"Well, weren't you Miss Smarty Pants," Nita chided, joining the others at the door.

"You're one to talk," Tori said to Nita. "Med school at twenty, two years earlier than anyone else." Nita shrugged.

"Bye, you guys. Have fun at the clubs tonight." Katlin closed the door behind her and hoped she was ready for this.

CHAPTER 18

James pulled the Guardian limousine through the iron gates and under the porte-cochere just as Katlin stepped from the elevator. She moved through the glassed-in lobby like a princess, shimmering in blues and silver, her golden hair a mass of curls floating down her back.

She was beautiful. And his for the night.

Alex gave her his hand as she approached the car and pulled her into his embrace. He had to touch her, to be sure it was really his Kat. She had been absent from his life for too long. His kiss was gentle, more than friendly, but not the I-want-to-rip-your-clothes-off-take-you-now kiss he really wanted from her. Maybe he'd get that later. He'd damn sure try.

"You look lovely," he said as he helped her into the back seat.

"Thank you. You look stunning in your tuxedo," she complimented. "Other than our high school prom, I can't remember ever seeing you in a tuxedo. For your wedding you wore Marine dress blues."

He countered, "For yours I wore my officer dress whites."

She settled into the buttery soft leather seat and asked

teasingly, "So which do you like better, the lovely opera-attending Katlin tonight or the sexy clubbing Katlin of last night?"

"It's the same person, so it doesn't matter. Just a different facet of your personality." Alex had to touch her, so he ran his finger the length of her gold necklace and touched the pendant at the bottom. It had a pale blue, full-carat, round stone in the middle with rays of gold swirls adorned with progressively darker blue stones at the outer reaches. It matched her dress perfectly with its multi-blue-colored beads on the jacket.

She shivered under his touch. Good. He wasn't the only one affected. "This is beautiful,' he said as he fingered the pendant.

"It's my favorite necklace." She watched his finger follow a swirl of blue then over the curve of her exposed breast. Shakily, she commented, "I love sapphires, even though my birthstone is emerald."

"Are these all sapphires? They're all different colors of blue," he noted.

"To answer your second question first, sapphires come in all colors of the rainbow," she explained. "When they're red, we call them rubies, but chemically they're all the same. These are all natural sapphires except the one in the middle. It's a blue diamond."

"Diamonds come in blue?" he asked and picked up the pendant for a closer look, brushing the naked part of her beast with his knuckles. "I've only seen the clear ones."

"Blue is one of the rarest colors of natural diamonds." Her voice was low and a little rough. "Daddy gave this to me on my twenty-fifth birthday."

Alex was only inches from her mouth when his gaze met hers. "I'll bet he wrote you a special note and you keep it with this necklace." Wordlessly, she nodded. Years ago Alex had seen her jewelry box, stuffed with handwritten notes. Because her father had traveled so much as military liaison to multiple embassies when she was a child, he would include a personal note with every gift, and she'd kept every one of them. "What did it say?"

As though quoting memorized prose, Katlin recited, *"This diamond is like you, Little One, all natural and very rare, and so very precious. They are the hardest rock known to man, but it sparkles from within."* She blinked rapidly as she fought back memories of her father. She missed him so much. They had been very close, especially after her mother's sudden death only nine months before Ty had been killed in action.

"Sounds like your dad." Alex had liked the man, respected him, and appreciated everything he'd done for him…until the major general had him sequestered after Ty's funeral and interrogated for hours about his son-in-law's death. All he wanted to do was be there as support for Kat. And to grieve with her. Hold her and allow her to lean on him. Ten hours later, on the orders of Kat's father, he was rushed back to Afghanistan and his SpecOps company.

He brusquely shook his head to erase those thoughts, and his gaze was filled with Kat's breasts. Oh, yes.

Alex dropped his fingers a few inches and ran them along the edge of her buttoned jacket. She grabbed his hand and held it in both of hers. Good thing she'd stopped him. A few more minutes and he would have ripped off her clothes and slid into her tight, wet heat right there in the back of the limo.

"I'm having a hard time keeping my hands off you," Alex admitted.

"Try harder," she chastised. "We're going to dinner and the opera with your daughter, my goddaughter, who thinks we are both guardian angels that swoop down and rescue her from a house filled with crying baby boys."

"But we're alone now," he pressed.

Katlin pointed out the window as the car turned the corner into a modest middle-class neighborhood, where tricycles adorned most every yard and driveways were colored in chalk.

His ex-wife, Rachelle, stood next to their little girl as the limousine pulled in front of their 1980s ranch. Jenny was a vision in her long blue gown and beaded bolero jacket, a miniature version of Katlin's.

"Doesn't she look sweet?" Katlin asked. "A few months back, Rachelle and I took Jenny out for a real girl's day. We did the spa thing, and then the three of us went shopping for Jenny while Ted cared for their boys."

"That was nice of you." Alex was sure Katlin had paid for everything. Even though he paid monthly child support well above the norm, and had secretly helped Rachelle's new husband get a better job, they weren't rolling in money…like him.

In the old days, when he'd still been married to Rachelle, she and Katlin would talk for hours, cook side by side making meals for him and Ty. The five of them spent many a weekend together roaming the exhibits at the Smithsonian because it was free and money was always tight, especially for Alex and Rachelle. Katlin would grab Jenny the moment the child whimpered and pampered their baby girl with gifts at every visit. She was apparently still doing it.

As he and Kat got out of the car, Rachelle stroked her daughter's long dark brown hair, the same color as his. Her mother had pulled some of it away from her sweet heart-shaped face and secured it with a matching blue beaded bow while the rest fell loosely down her back. Her large dark brown eyes were like the ones he saw in every mirror. Jenny looked so much older this evening, so more mature than her mere nine years. She would break the hearts of many boys all too soon. Alex was both proud of this beautiful child he and Rachelle had created and, at the same time, afraid because she was growing up too quickly. He had missed so much of her life between Marine deployments and her mother taking her to Miami and never returning to their home at Camp Lejeune, North Carolina. Even now he saw her only when he was in Miami, but they talked often. He'd given her a kid's phone for her seventh birthday with one button to call him, one to call her mother, and a third that was supposed to call the police, but he'd reprogrammed it to call the Guardian Operations Center.

Rachelle stood at the screen door in old khaki shorts and a blue t-shirt with baby throw-up on it and her hair in a green headband. She hadn't bothered with makeup to hide dark crescents from lack of sleep that shadowed her tired blue eyes.

She gave him a weak smile. "Our one-year-old is cutting molars, and I had to rock him most of the night. Then the three-year-old refused a nap this afternoon so he hates everyone at this moment. Meltdown pending," she explained, her gaze bouncing from him to Kat.

"Good thing we're going to take this one away for a few hours, then." Katlin held out her arms and scooched down to be on Jenny's level.

Alex just smiled at Rachelle and announced, "We'll have Little One back right after dessert." He'd used the nickname Katlin called Jenny, and Rachelle's eyes widened. He glanced at his daughter hugging Kat before returning his gaze to Rachelle. "She's getting so big."

"You have no idea," his ex shared.

He really didn't. It was like Kat had said. Their few hours together that afternoon at the park hadn't been enough. He'd asked what he thought were appropriate questions about school, her friends and home life with the little boys, but many of her answers were limited to one or two words. Although, she had enthusiastically told him about her upcoming birthday party listing all the girls attending, but he didn't know a single one of them, of course. He was missing so much and needed to change that, immediately.

He wanted to get to know his daughter, but there was never enough time. He had responsibilities to ten business locations, hundreds of employees, and thousands of people who had placed their trust in his company.

Katlin's movement brought him back to the present. She leaned in and hugged Rachelle, whispering something to the woman he'd called wife for a little over two years.

"Bye, Mom. Love you." Jenny slipped her hand through her father's on one side and Katlin's on the other as she pulled them to the awaiting car.

"Have fun. Love you, too," Rachelle called to their backs.

"Do you go see your Nana Rosa?" Alex asked Jenny as they waited for their meal. Katlin wondered how often Alex saw his grandmother. He'd lived with her for his last three years of high school.

"Yes, of course, she's my family," Jenny replied as though he should know these things. Katlin hid her smile behind a sip of water.

"Does your mom take you?" Alex asked as he attacked the breadbasket.

"Sometimes. Usually I go with Aunt Katlin." Alex looked across the linen-covered table at her. She just shrugged. Alex and Jenny were communicating. He was getting to know her better, and that was what she'd promised Rachelle earlier that day. Katlin had called her friend to confirm that it would be all right for Alex to join them for the opera. She was sure it would be, but Katlin always checked with Rachelle when it came to her goddaughter.

Jenny continued, "She and Nana Rosa speak Cuban. It's kinda like Spanish, but it's different. I don't always understand what they say, but they laugh a lot. I get to play with my cousins and practice my Spanish. I'm fluent in two languages now." Her face beamed.

Alex and Katlin shared a look. "That's great, Little One," Alex said in Spanish. Jenny looked up and smiled at her father, who grinned back, pride evident. The three of them finished the meal speaking elemental Spanish, helping Jenny with her pronunciation and introduced a few new words.

An hour later, they were seated and watching swashbuckling pirates bounce across the stage singing and dancing. At the intermission, Katlin announced that she was thirsty.

"Katlin Callahan," an elderly woman adorned with opera-length, cream-colored baroque pearls draped over a burgundy gown called in a gravelly voice as Katlin, Alex, and Jenny headed toward the refreshments.

Jenny turned first and dashed to the octogenarian. "Mrs. Finestead, how are you this evening?" she said and curtseyed perfectly as if she were in the presence of royalty. In Miami, the elderly philanthropist was the next best thing. The woman offered her hand, and Jenny took it lightly in hers, bobbed it once, and released it.

"Jenny, so nice to see you. I trust all is well with you." The formality of the woman's demeanor made Katlin smile as Jenny matched it, courtly phrase for phrase.

"Yes, ma'am, I am well. We're celebrating my birthday," she replied as Katlin and Alex approached. "Mrs. Finestead, may I present my father, Alejandro Lobo." Jenny rolled the "r" in the Spanish fashion while she open-handedly gestured to her father.

She'd used Alex's given name, not the Americanized version. Katlin thought it was sweet until she realized that Jenny's legal last name was Lobo. She might not even know he now went by Alex Wolf. Alex hadn't let Ted adopt his daughter, so to her, he was Alejandro Lobo.

"Good evening, ma'am. It's a pleasure to meet you," Alex

said and flashed his lady-killer smile while he held out his hand.

Mrs. Finestead delicately gave Alex her right hand. She touched Katlin's arm with her left and said sotto voce, "My dear, where have you been hiding this excellent example of manhood?" She looked at Alex with approving eyes and a smile purchased from the best dentists in West Palm Beach.

Alex took her hand and bent his head to her, but his gaze never left her eyes when he touched his lips to her spa-softened knuckles.

"You always come here with the best looking men," the elderly woman rasped. "But this one makes even my old heart jump with anticipation."

Katlin didn't come to the opera with men. She came with Jenny and, on rare occasions, Rachelle. Never with a man. Mrs. Finestead was losing it. Katlin didn't date. She glanced at Alex then remembered…her bodyguards. Yes, they were all good-looking men, and no, they didn't hold a candle to Alex in the looks department.

The older woman leaned to Katlin's ear and very quietly asked, "Is he good in the sack?" she asked with eyes that begged, "Please tell me yes."

"Earth shattering," Katlin replied on a deep exhale with a hungry look at Alex. At least he had been. She figured he'd learned more than a few new tricks since they'd been lovers.

"Thank you," the elder said and slapped manicured fingers to her chest. "My faith in youth has been restored."

The elderly woman smiled as she reviewed them. "It is so wonderful to see your whole family here together, Katlin. Give my best to your parents. Please be sure that your daughter partakes in our new Young Actor's Summer Camp." Katlin stifled saying, *but she's not my daughter.* Alex didn't correct her either. She also didn't mention that her parents had died several years ago. The older lady was losing it, for sure.

A cackling laugh a few yards away caught the attention of Mrs. Finestead, who scowled at the loud couple then said, "Forgive me, but I must depart your wonderful company. My sister seems to have had too much wine already, or she's found a new man."

"So you are now my wife?" Alex teased in her ear while they stood in the refreshment line. "Does this mean I get conjugal visiting rights?" He was so close she could feel the heat of his breath on her ear. The wife part was a joke, and they both knew it, but she was interested in the rest. Then she looked at the delightful young girl who stood in front of them and knew she needed to keep a lock on those feelings, especially now.

"Not tonight," Katlin replied so low only Alex heard.

"But that means there's hope for some other night." Optimism splashed across his angled face as desire smoldered in his eyes.

"In my life, there is always hope," Katlin said as the three stepped up to the bar, where Alex ordered two glasses of white wine, a soda, and snacks.

By ten o'clock, Jenny had fallen asleep on the way to dessert, so James took them to Rachelle's home. Alex carried his sleeping daughter up the steps, and Katlin knocked quietly.

Rachelle answered the door with a yawn. "I'm sorry. I'm simply exhausted, and tonight isn't going to be much better than last night. Baby molars suck the life out of parents."

Although she felt sorry for her friend, Katlin had no point of reference. She'd never been around babies, and since she couldn't have any herself, she normally avoided the subject.

"May I tuck her in?" Alex asked.

Rachelle's brows flew up, but she nodded and pointed down the hall. Alex headed that direction.

Quietly, Katlin asked, "What's up? You look surprised."

"Alex has never asked for that before. He usually hands

over our tired or sleeping daughter and he leaves with very few words," Rachelle explained.

"On the left," Rachelle said from behind him. She opened the door to Jenny's room, where she slipped their daughter into a purple-flowered granny nightgown while Alex slipped the dressy sandals from her tiny feet. He laid her on the sheets, tenderly covered her, and kissed her forehead. Rachelle stared at Alex.

From the bedroom door, Katlin watched as her two friends peered down at the child they had created together.

"Thank you, Rachelle." Just above a whisper, Alex admitted, "It was one of the best nights of my life."

Katlin heard the sincerity in his voice, and it tugged at her heart.

"Sorry, Rachelle, but she's going to want the dessert she missed tonight for breakfast," Katlin cautioned once they'd reached the foyer. All three laughed quietly.

"Well, that isn't going to happen. She'll be on a sugar high most of the day with twelve nine-year-old little girls invading our home starting at ten o'clock."

"Thanks for letting her come out tonight," Katlin said then hugged her friend good-night.

"Thanks again, Rachelle." Alex gave her a small smile and turned to leave, placing a hand on Katlin's back.

Katlin forced in a breath. She was going to be alone with Alex, and the night was young.

Seduction time.

CHAPTER 19

In the limo on the way to Miami Beach, Alex took Katlin's hand. "You're really good with Jenny." She'd kept the conversation going all evening and included everyone in the discussion. He'd had a great time and gotten to know his daughter so much better than ever before. Kat had made it easy.

"She's the only child I will ever be able to spoil," Katlin said with a slight sadness in her voice.

What the hell?

"What do you mean? You'll have children of your own someday." The idea of Kat having a baby both excited and scared Alex. His baby, yes. That would be fine. Maybe even better than fine. But the idea of her carrying someone else's child within her body riled him to the core.

Katlin took a deep, slow breath and stared straight ahead into the dark depths of the long car. She finally spoke. "No, I can't have children." There was a slight break in her quiet voice.

"What? Why not? You're just turning thirty next month. That's plenty young enough to have kids." At least he thought it was.

Katlin was silent so long he wasn't sure she was going to answer. Then she explained, "During my induction physical for Section 7, they discovered ovarian cysts and operated. The doctor ended up harvesting my eggs."

Alex's throat closed, and his chest pulled tight. "You didn't give him permission to do that, did you?"

"Certainly not knowingly. He used a clause within the permission paperwork," Katlin said forcefully. "The doctor explained that by removing the eggs I wouldn't get any more ovarian cysts. He placed them in an egg bank for me for later. Lots of military women are doing that before they leave for an overseas or dangerous duty. Men are leaving their sperm for the same reason, in case they don't make it back. But the storage facility conveniently lost my eggs."

Now totally outraged, Alex all but shouted, "Lost them?"

"That's what they claimed." Kat shrugged. "I believe that they sold them."

Sold? "Who buys human eggs?" The idea was absurd.

Katlin looked at him as if he was the most stupid man on the planet. "Well, here's a news flash for you, Alex. Designer babies are here. Do you have any idea what the eggs of a five-foot-seven, natural blonde with blue eyes, athletic body, and genius IQ go for?"

Alex was too appalled to speak. He stared at her.

"At least $10,000… each… and they can go as high as $100,000 depending on how desperate and rich the parents-to-be are." Alex watched her jaw set. Katlin wasn't ready to cry. She was too angry.

"I guess I'm lucky, though," she continued. "He left my ovaries to control my hormones, but I have to be on the pill for Section 7 anyway."

"Why? What does Section 7 have to do with your personal birth control?" He wondered if the organization mandated men use condoms. He always did, but some men liked it bareback enough they'd take chances.

Repeating her how-can-you-be-so-dumb look, Katlin clarified, "Having a period in the middle of an op would create problems."

"Yeah, but you're an analyst. You don't work in the field." Alex was extremely thankful she was safe behind a desk in D.C. and not in some Godforsaken Third World country where bleeding from a bullet was a much bigger concern than whether she had enough tampons. He hadn't had to worry about a woman's menstrual cycle in years, probably since he and Rachelle separated.

He had to worry only if a woman missed her period, and he was very, very careful about contraception and protection. He had always used a condom, even after Rachelle had given birth to Jenny. She'd been so afraid to get pregnant again yet couldn't tolerate the pill, so they'd used condoms in conjunction with her IUD. When they had sex, which hadn't been often after the birth of their daughter. His wife hadn't seemed in the least interested.

Turning to Katlin, Alex asked what he thought should be an obvious question. "Well, there are other ways of having… getting children, aren't there?"

"Get real. With my job? No adoption agency would ever let me have a child." She paused, and he watched her gain her composure, "Besides, I'm selfish. I'd want my own. For me, that would require a husband anyway. Mine is buried in Arlington."

At that moment, James pulled through the gates to her condo. It was obvious that Katlin was agitated, upset by the topic. She turned to face him. "Thank you for a wonderful evening. I really enjoyed it, but I am very tired. I almost fell asleep when Jenny did."

Alex saw it for the lie it was. "Can I carry you to your bed, too, and tuck you in?" he teased. She looked so beautiful, bathed in the exterior lights of the condominium. He wanted to kiss her, touch her everywhere. He wanted to know the ecstasy of pushing inside her once again and find his own release as she shuddered under him.

The smile she gave him was forced. He saw only pain in her pretty blue eyes. She didn't need a lover tonight; she needed a friend. Alex brought her to his chest. He just held her and consoled her. He liked the feel of his arms around her so he hugged her harder. He wasn't sure what to say, nor could he change the past.

She looked up at him and kissed him affectionately on the lips. When she withdrew, he felt her pull more than just her head away. She was going to flee.

Oh no she wasn't. He wouldn't allow her to run from him ever again. He pulled her to him and took her mouth. Holding back at first, showing her tenderness, he nipped at her lips. "Where are your friends tonight?"

Breathlessly, she told him, "Clubbing." She wove her arms around his neck and rolled into his lap before capturing his mouth. She opened for him immediately, and their tongues tangled in an old, familiar dance.

"Invite me in," Alex all but begged. Making out in the back of the limousine with his employee behind the wheel, albeit behind the privacy window, wasn't a good idea.

"Let's go." Katlin moved off him and grabbed his hand as she opened the back door. He signaled to James to leave as they walked hand-in-hand to her condo.

As soon as the elevator doors closed, he pushed Kat against the wall and shoved his hands into her hair, picking up the kiss. He rocked his erection into her as he thrust his tongue into her mouth. He wanted her with a ferocity he hadn't felt in years.

Too soon, the doors opened again. Out of habit, he glanced around the hall, and this time, he noticed the small camera. "Do we handle your security?"

She unlocked the door with a button on her key fob, an upgraded version of the one used for his Guardian apartments. Glancing over her shoulder, she said, "Of course." He wondered if the men in his control room were watching. Shrugging off the thought, he followed Kat in and heard the automatic click of the lock.

"Would you like someth—"

Alex grabbed Kat and plastered his mouth to hers. He dove in, taking what he needed, giving to her whatever she accepted. She gave as good as she got, exploring his mouth as he retreated. He slid his hand to her breast, but it was covered by the thick, jeweled jacket with only a small hint of her rounded breast peeking from the top. He wanted to feel the weight of them in his hands, the soft smooth skin on his palm.

He broke the kiss and ordered, "Take it off."

She looked dazed. "What?"

"The jacket," he explained. "Take it off."

She quickly unhooked the front, and as she started to shrug out of it, he placed his hands over hers.

Smiling down at her, he offered, "Let me help you." He slid his hands under the jacket at her shoulders and kissed every inch of revealed skin starting at her neck. When his fingers stumbled over the dress straps and the navy blue bra she wore underneath, he slipped both off with the jacket. He bared Kat's shoulders, then stopped when the cloth reached her elbows, binding her arms behind her back. The position thrust her breasts toward him, her softly rounded mounds straining against the material.

With his tongue, he traced the satin edge of the low-cut dress as she watched, her eyes turning a deep sapphire, her chest rising and lowering rapidly. He wanted to suck her hardened nipples then make his way down her naked body and taste her wetness once again.

He shoved the jacket off her arms and tried to push the dress down.

"Stop." Katlin's word froze every muscle in his body. He slowly forced his eyes to meet hers. Did she want to stop what they were doing? Or going to do? Her smile was small. "It doesn't come off that way. You'll rip it."

She turned her back to him. "There's a hook at the top of the zipper."

She swept her long curls to one side, leaving him with a view of her half-naked back. He deftly slid the tiny metal hook from the eye on the other side and slid the narrow zipper down her spine. When he laid an open-mouthed kiss on her newly revealed back, her whole body shivered. He uncovered a pretty, navy blue lace bra, and with the flick of his fingers, he unsnapped all three hooks at once.

He stopped unzipping at her waistline and ran his hands over her ribs, around the front. Using his fingertips, he lifted the bottom of the bra and cupped both breasts. They were heavy as his hands encircled them, gently massaging. He laid his lips on the top of her spine and kissed his way to her ear.

She dropped her head on his shoulder and whispered his name on a slow sigh. "Oh, Alex."

"Yes, sweetheart?" He kissed her just below her ear and rolled her peaked nipples between his thumbs and forefingers. He wasn't sure if the sound she made was a moan or a mewl, but his Kat purred as he dropped his hand over her flat stomach.

Alex burrowed his hand under the dress that now lay folded at her small waist. His fingertips touched soft lace. He'd bet his next bonus check her panties matched that pretty bra. But they didn't stop him from what he wanted. An inch lower, he raked through a strip of hair then found her wet folds.

Oh, yes. She was ready for more. As he parted her, he skimmed his middle finger over her hardened clit then returned to the button of nerves, slowly drawing circles around it. She pushed her tight little ass back into his cock, and it was his turn to moan.

Christ, he wanted to bend her over and slide into her slick

heat until they both screamed.

"Spread your legs." He whispered the order into her ear then bit the lobe. She widened her stance, and he dropped down farther until he found her entrance and thrust in a finger. He felt her inner walls clamp around it. Christ, the way it would feel when she grabbed his cock and held it within her body was going to be heaven. Using the heel of his hand, he pressed on her clit and pumped his finger in and out.

"Alex," Kat gasped.

"What do you need, babe?" He pinched the nipple he'd been playing with using his other hand.

On a cry, she begged, "More."

He slid a second finger inside her and rubbed her clit with his thumb.

She screamed as she fell apart in his arms, her whole body shaking with her release. She went limp, and Alex quickly scooped her up and carried her to the couch, sitting down with Kat curled on his lap. Her body quivered with an aftershock, the kind he liked to be inside a woman for just before he made her come again.

He slid his hand back under her dress to start round two.

Female voices filled the outer foyer.

Kat's eyes flew open. She glanced down at her naked breasts and jumped off him. "Don't leave," she called as she sprinted down the hall toward the bedrooms as the voices became louder.

His fingers were wet with her essence. He quickly shoved them in his mouth, the long-forgotten flavor of Kat exploding on every taste bud. Next time he would savor her as she came on his tongue.

Alex shifted his hips to relieve the pressure from his pounding cock. He lifted his ankle to rest on his knee as he got his body under control.

The door opened, and Grace and Tori stepped in, deep in conversation.

CHAPTER 20

Alex hadn't slept well, angry with some unknown doctor who four years ago had stolen Katlin's eggs, robbed her of her future as a mother. He poured his first cup of coffee and wondered if he wanted more children. Jenny was great, but she was more like a beloved niece than a real daughter.

When she'd been born, he was too wrapped up in trying to graduate from college on time, tutoring to earn enough money to pay the rent and feed his new family. While they lived at Quantico, Jenny was often asleep when he got home from a long day at TBS. Then, shortly after they'd moved to Camp Lejeune, Rachelle had taken her from him. What was supposed to have been a trip home for their two-year-old to get some grandparent time became a permanent move.

Rachelle had been right to leave him. He hadn't been a good father or a decent husband.

He'd always believed that children needed to be around the house, under foot, where parents could keep an eye on them and know what they were getting into. Like the home where he'd grown up. His parents had not only loved him, but they'd also cared about him, his brother, and sister. They'd been concerned about their friends as well. There was always a hot meal on his mother's table, and friends were always welcome to eat.

After his father died, his mother loved him enough to see when his group of friends changed and his grades fell. She'd sent him to Miami, to her mother's home, so he could finish high school away from the gangs that threatened to overtake his life.

He thought about a future home with a couple of children where he would constantly give them hugs and kisses and tell them that he loved them. They would know he really, truly loved them, unconditionally.

That hadn't worked for him and Rachelle, though. Maybe they'd married too young. Maybe it just wasn't meant to be. His job had gotten in the way. Rachelle had hated the military life. His life now was even worse since he traveled between the ten Guardian Security Centers, always on the road, in the air, on the move. He had a multimillion-dollar business to run. It was hard enough finding a few hours during his visits to Miami to see Jenny. It wouldn't be any more fair to a child now than it had been nine years ago for Jenny.

He loved his daughter with all his heart. Their time together last night had been so special. Jenny was animated, relaxed, and fun to be with. Kat had helped with that. Maybe he'd bring Jenny home with him for a week that summer.

Home. He suddenly realized he didn't have a home. He had ten apartments that all looked exactly alike so he felt comfortable no matter where he was. The company owned several safe houses he could use whenever he wanted, but he didn't own a house. He didn't have a place to call home.

He'd grown up in D.C. and his mom and stepdad were there, in a new house he'd bought for them in a better neighborhood. But that wasn't a home he'd ever lived in. Miami felt like home, too, because Jenny and Nana Rosa lived there.

He had plenty of money to buy a house for himself and

Jenny. But where? The better question was, why? He had what he needed in the apartments scattered across the U.S.A., and he would have her for only a week, two at most. Maybe she'd like to travel with him, see part of this great nation. He could arrange for a tour guide in each city. Something to consider. He didn't need a home.

He stepped back from his thoughts and asked himself why he was thinking about a home filled with children. It had been the sad look on Katlin's face from the previous night. He thought about bouncing, blonde-haired little girls with blue-on-blue eyes that ran into the open arms of their mother. Unfortunately, that mother was not Katlin. It never could be.

Anger welled from deep inside him as he felt the loss. Her loss.

His loss.

The idea of him and Kat and children shook him to his core.

His cell phone buzzed in his pocket. He glanced at the screen to see it was Barry and swiped to accept the call. "What the fuck is going on in Dallas? I heard those sons of bitches made bail, with stolen money most likely."

"Well, hello, Alex. I'm doing fine. Thank you for asking," Barry said, while Alex harnessed his emotions.

"Sorry, man," Alex apologized. "It's been a rough few days." But also some of best days…ever.

"What's up besides the situation in Dallas?" Barry had become a great sounding board in the past few years, although most of the conversations had been business related.

Alex smiled as he remembered Thursday. "I got into Miami early and was held at gunpoint by a naked woman who had been sleeping in my bed."

"Whoa, some bitch you'd slept with pulled a gun on you?" Barry had moved into lawyer mode.

"No," Alex explained. "I found Katlin Callahan in my apartment, and she pulled a gun on me."

Barry laughed. "And she was naked?"

"Yes." His tone was low and rough at the mental picture of her days ago.

"Guess I'm not surprised she pulled a gun on you." Barry chuckled. "Are you okay?"

"Yeah." Alex wasn't sure it was the truth. Kat had turned his world around to the point that he thought about her night and day, but he was good enough to talk business with the company's CFO.

"In that case, I can answer the initial question." Barry continued, but Alex didn't miss that his friend moved the conversation away from Kat. "Yes, they made bail, but the judge took their passports because the prosecutor convinced him they were a flight risk. If they bolt, they'll lose their homes since that's what the douche bags used to secure the bonds. I'm on top of it."

"Good. Stay that way."

"Hey, if you're in town for a few days, can you carve out some time to meet with me? We have some business to go over. You free for lunch?"

"No, I can't today. I'm swamped here." Alex shuffled the papers on his desk. "How about supper?" Maybe Katlin would join them. He really wanted to see her tonight.

Barry hedged. "I'm actually having supper with Katlin. Since she didn't shoot you, I take it you left on friendly terms?"

"You could say that." Alex had left Katlin with more than a friendly kiss last night. After their evening had been abruptly interrupted by her friends, she had changed her clothes and walked him out to meet his ride from Guardian Security. In the elevator, she had rubbed her hand over his crotch as she apologized for not taking care of him. He'd almost come like a virginal teenager when she'd tightened her grip on his slacks-covered cock.

"How about I call and talk with Katlin?" Barry suggested. "Just to be sure it's okay with her if you join us."

"Sure. I'll plan to see you tonight. Text me if she has a problem with it. Later, man." Alex ended the call.

Alex poured another cup of coffee before he headed to his office to review quarterly reports.

He wandered into the Miami Control Center later that morning, third cup of coffee in hand, and asked, "Any messages for me? Anything I need to know?"

"Yes, sir." Rick spoke up. "You have a car scheduled at seven for your dinner with the C.F.O. at seven thirty at the University Club. Miss Katlin will be joining you there."

"She's not riding over with me?" Alex asked.

"No, sir. Miss Katlin will be picked up by her bodyguard at four thirty and taken to five o'clock mass." Alex had forgotten just how religious she was. He wanted to spend more time with her and knew that she had to be in D.C. Monday morning, which meant that she'd fly out tomorrow.

"Change in plans," Alex announced. "I'll go with the limo to pick up Katlin at four thirty and take her to mass. Then we can go together to supper with Barry. Since I'll be there, she won't need a bodyguard." No one else needed to overhear their conversations or know what he did with a woman, especially Kat. Besides, he wasn't sure why she even needed personal protection. She was just an analyst.

"Yes, sir," Rick replied and started typing on the computer keyboard.

At four twenty-five James drove under the porte-cochere at Katlin's condo. "I called and she's on her way down now, sir."

"Thank you, James. I know you've driven us around a lot this week, and I truly appreciate it. We'll all be leaving tomorrow so you'll be back on open duty again," Alex said and made a mental note to put a little extra in his paycheck. Alex stepped out of the car to greet Katlin.

"Hello," Katlin said with a smile and look of surprise on her face. "I thought I'd meet you at the restaurant."

"I thought it would be a good idea to go to mass together then to dinner." He wanted to spend time with her, and if that meant attending mass, he'd go to church. The last time he'd been in a church, Ty's coffin-draped body had been positioned in front of the altar. He didn't think the building would fall down because his sin-riddled soul entered a house of God for the first time in more than three years. He hadn't been to confession since he joined the Marine Corps. He didn't think any Miami priest could forgive him for the things he'd done for his country and the list would be long.

Don't go there. Concentrate on the beautiful woman in front of you.

A pleased smile crossed Katlin's face as she stepped into the Guardian limo once again. Alex slid onto the seat beside her and took her hand. He slowly lifted it to his lips and pressed a kiss into her palm.

"I've missed you today," Alex admitted. "What have you been up to?"

"Cooking. I was in the kitchen at Guardian all day so Sara could have the day off and she and Louis could celebrate their twenty-fifth anniversary tonight." Katlin then told Alex all about the excellent Italian meal she'd prepared for his men.

Damn. She'd been a floor away all day, and he hadn't known it. He could have popped in to see her, touch her, taste her kiss.

He smiled as he remembered all the meals she'd cooked for him over the past fifteen years. The mini-meals in college made from whatever she could scrounge from her tiny dorm fridge, the impromptu dinners after tutoring for hours, the fantastic suppers she'd cook for the four of them in his and Rachelle's D.C. apartment, and the delectable Sunday suppers at Quantico. Katlin could cook, and she enjoyed it.

All too soon, the limo stopped. Saint Kieran's was very modern, white stucco and angular with natural wood beams. The service was more contemporary than Alex remembered. He followed along as though he did this every week. As a child he'd attended parochial school until he'd been suspended so many times as a high school freshman his mother wasn't sure he would pass that grade.

After the mass, Katlin entered the confessional and spoke for several minutes. As the minutes ticked by, he wondered how many sins could she have. Alex wandered over and lit a candle to the Virgin Mary, offering a prayer for the woman who was leaving him all too soon.

When Kat and the priest emerged, Alex watched them as they went to the altar. She knelt, and the priest blessed her. That was sweet.

Once outside in the warm Florida sunlight, Alex took Katlin's hand. "What was the special blessing all about?"

As though it were nothing, Katlin replied, "The Rites of Shriven."

What the fuck? Was she terminally ill and hadn't told him?

Alex stopped and spun her to face him. "The priest just gave you last rites?"

She nodded and placed fisted hands on her hips. "Yes. I have a priest perform them every time before I leave, or at least I try. If I die on unholy ground or before a priest can get to me, I'm covered."

"Are you—" He couldn't say the words. The thought of losing her so soon after he'd found her again was too much. He pulled her to him and simply held her as he harnessed his emotions. A fist squeezed his throat, but he managed to ask, "Are you…sick?"

She stepped out of his arms and studied his face for a long minute. "No. I'm very healthy."

"Then why?" Alex asked with incredulity.

She glanced at the limousine waiting at the curb. "My soul

is important to me." Katlin looked back at him and said in a stern voice, "I take my faith seriously." She paused as though deciding exactly what to say. "No one knows what's going to happen from one minute to the next." She said something so quietly he wasn't sure he'd heard correctly.

She turned and walked toward the car.

Frozen in place, Alex tried to understand. He wasn't sure he'd heard the words spoken under her breath. *I tempt fate far too often.*

That couldn't be right. She wasn't in any danger as an analyst. Unless she thought her ass of a boss would kill her. Maybe that's why she needed a bodyguard. Was she really that afraid of the man? Or was it something else?

At the request of his company's chaplain, a very devout priest, Alex and several of his men had Rites of Shriven performed just before they left for a sure-to-be-ugly mission in Iraq. It had been a very private, almost secretive, ceremony performed mere hours before they boarded the plane. They'd been headed into the heart of ISIS and thankfully, they'd all returned unharmed. But that had been a completely different situation.

As he slid into the seat beside her, she had transformed back into his Kat. "It's only six, and we aren't expected for supper until seven thirty. What would you like to do?" She smiled expectantly.

"I don't care," he admitted.

"I have an idea, then." She pressed the button to talk to the driver. "James, take me to my usual Sunday location."

"Yes, ma'am. With pleasure." The driver pulled the big car away from the curb.

Alex didn't care where they were headed. He was in the back, alone with Katlin. Her light perfume was citrusy with a hint of spice. He never liked women who drenched themselves in flower scents or, worse yet, musk.

He took her hand, and she interlaced their fingers as they

talked amiably about Guardian, the Miami office in particular, during the short ride. When the car came to a stop at a curb, Alex finally looked out the window. He was shocked to see he was in Little Havana, in front of his Nana Rosa's house.

Where he'd lived for three years.

Where his life had changed.

From the outside, most would think the Spanish-style building was a multiplex with more than four separate apartments. In truth, it was a single home with four bedrooms, three with separate outside entrances. The one in the back had been his.

The freshly painted white, spiked six-foot fence caught Alex's eye, and he regarded it with the humor of a thirty year old. The first week he'd arrived in Miami, he had broken Nana Rosa's well-defined rules, and his punishment had been to hand paint the fence that ran all four sides of the manicured quarter-acre property. He'd cursed that old lady with every brush stroke but now realized what she'd taught him.

The limo created quite a bit of neighborhood attention, so Alex asked James to come back and get them in thirty minutes. As an afterthought, he gave him some instructions while Katlin opened the ornate iron gate and walked through the high Spanish-style arches to the front door.

"Nana Rosa, may we come in? It's Katlin and Alex. I mean Alejandro." Katlin spoke in the Cuban dialect of Spanish used by everyone who entered this house. A small square woman with thick white hair trundled toward her with open arms, chattering away in the same language.

Alex came through the familiar door and realized the place he'd once called home had changed little in the past fifteen years. More pictures of baby faces adorned every inch of the hallway, but the place was spotless, just as it had been in his teens.

How long since he'd been there? Alex was desperate to

remember. How could he forget to find time to visit this wonderful woman who'd taught him so much about life?

Alex looked into the first room on the right. It may have been called a living room, but it was not for living. It was for serving the priest Cuban coffee, heavily laced with rum, during his weekly visit. Every inch of solid surface was covered with a white starched doily under framed photos of children, grandchildren, and great-grandchildren at all stages of life. No picture ever got thrown out. He smiled as he looked around at his vast extended family.

In the center of it all sat Nana's throne, the ornately hand-carved rocker that Alex's grandfather had bought her days before their first child was born. He'd purchased it from a family friend and carried it onto the U.S. Naval Base at Guantanamo Bay, Cuba. Every child in his family had heard the story too many times, along with how Papa had swept her off her feet, literally and figuratively, when she taught salsa dancing to the sailors at the U.S.O.

His eyes fell to the table next to the well-worn chair where a solitary picture sat, as if his grandfather were still by her side. Alex picked up the framed photograph with reverence. The colors had blanched, so the old photograph looked almost sepia, the wooden frame bright from Nana Rosa's fingers where she'd held it daily for more than twenty years. His grandfather looked so young in his Marine Corps dress blues with lance corporal stripes on the sleeve.

At the sniff, he turned and found his grandmother at his side. She lovingly ran a finger down the face behind the glass.

"I miss him." Her voice was soft and filled with love. "You look like him you know." She reached up to cup his face in her thickly padded hand. "You have his eyes and, thank goodness, his height. Do you remember your papa?"

"Bits and pieces." He recalled, "I used to sit in the backyard and listen to his war stories for hours."

"Yes. You told us then that you wanted to be a Marine."

She picked up the picture of Alex in his officer dress blues from another table. His captain's bars shone bright on the epaulettes. Side by side, they both wore the same no-nonsense expression, except eyes that had seen far too much looked back at him from his photograph.

He'd made the right decision to leave the Corps. Eventually, those eyes would have solidified into unyielding granite, along with his soul. The only future he had in the military was more of the same, missions he couldn't talk about and a progression of shiny officer pins that laid heavily on his shoulders as the eagle, globe, and anchor dug into his neck, and his life. He was in the right place, now.

"You grew up good, Alejandro." He smiled into the rounded face of one of best women he'd ever known. She'd been tough on his young ass, but he'd learned about people and business from her. True leadership was taught by example.

He set the picture of his grandfather back in the exact place he'd found it and hugged her. "Because of you, Nana. It's all because of you." He gave her a smacking kiss on the forehead. He knew he'd better get her out of there. She would pick up every frame and tell the backstory of each person in the picture. They'd never escape before midnight.

"What do I smell?" Alex asked, diverting her attention.

"Oh, dear," she blustered and stepped out of his arms.

He followed her into the kitchen where Nana Rosa always held court with a worn wooden spoon in her hand that she waved like a scepter. Something was continuously cooking on the stove and made the room smell like the best home he'd ever known. He meandered over to the sparkling clean stove and stuck a spoon into every pot to taste. Damn that woman could cook. The nearly ninety-year-old smacked her grandson on the hand and swore at him in Cuban.

"My Alejandro, about time you stopped in to see your Nana Rosa. You are a big man now, too busy for old ladies, huh?" she chastised him. He planted a big kiss on her cheek, "Oh, men."

He glanced at the well-used kitchen table, where Katlin sat casually drinking Cuban coffee. She grinned at the both of them. In his beloved grandmother's kitchen, he'd become a teenager again.

For half an hour, they chatted about relatives, the warehouse business, which she still checked, concerning everyone and everything, daily, and bantered like only family can.

When his phone buzzed with a text message from James, Katlin rose and placed her empty cup in the sink after rinsing it. They started moving toward the front door.

From the long buffet, Nana Rosa grabbed a picture and shoved it in front of Alex's face. "See this? This is my family home in Cuba."

"Nana, this looks new. Where did you get it?" The crisp photo was framed well, as if taken by a professional photographer.

The family matriarch rattled on. "A friend took it for me while visiting Cuba. Found my father's sister and her family who lives in the house I grew up in. I will never see it again., I have this other picture, taken from the front door looking at the ocean. Isn't it beautiful?"

A friend? Who did she know who could travel to Cuba? It was banned from the U.S.A. for all but dignitaries and those establishing a new relationship with the country. Nana had always had strong ties to her homeland, and he'd often thought she was involved in smuggling relatives into the country. "Are you harboring illegals? Are you helping people escape from Cuba?"

"No, no. I just have this friend who went there recently and took these pictures." She pointed to a whole stack. Alex picked them up and rifled through. The photography was wonderful, but it was the subject matter that worried him.

"Nana, it's dangerous for you to be associated with anyone who travels to Cuba," he insisted. Nana looked at Katlin with concern all over her face, but Katlin just smiled at her and winked. Alex saw it all and suddenly knew his grandmother's friend. He felt better about the older woman but began to worry about Katlin's work.

Katlin literally shoved Alex to the front door. She turned and hugged the older woman and spoke several sentences in Cuban so fast that Alex caught only a few words. He gave his grandmother a big hug and picked her up off the floor as he gave her another smacking kiss on the cheek. She swatted at him with the big wooden spoon she still carried.

Once back in the car and headed to supper, Alex turned to Katlin and pinned her with his gaze. "Did you take those pictures of my distant cousins in Cuba?" he pressed.

"Yes," Katlin admitted without hesitation. "I love Nana Rosa like a grandmother. She and I have talked for hours about Cuba, and she'd really hoped that someday she could return to her home there. That's never going to happen now, even though Castro is dead."

"Are you sure he's dead?"

"Yes. Confirmed," Katlin said with finality. "So I took those pictures while I was there. It was something I could do for her that made her happy."

Alex bent and kissed Katlin, gently at first, but as she leaned into him and kissed him back, it grew much more intense and deeper. Coming up for air, he simply said, "Thank you."

"For which? The kiss? The pictures? Or the trip to Nana Rosa's?"

"Yes. Yes. And yes." He kissed her between each word.

CHAPTER 21

Alex took Katlin's hand as he helped her out of the limousine and kissed the palm again before they walked into the exclusive club. He smiled at her reddened lips and slightly flushed cheeks. She was gorgeous. And he wanted more.

As they started into the private club, the hairs on the back of Alex's neck bristled. He suddenly felt as though he was in someone's crosshairs. As covertly as possible, he scanned the area and dropped Katlin's hand, in case he needed to get to his guns fast.

She was already reaching into her purse. He was afraid she'd pull out a gun but, instead, removed a mirror and played with the hair around her face. "He's behind the huge azalea bush across the street."

What? She wasn't primping. "You can see him?" he asked.

"Yeah. Paparazzi." Her voice was low so it wouldn't carry. "Happens often at this club. Sports celebrities show up all the time. We're nobody important to him."

Alex turned his head and gave the man a threatening glare.

Katlin excused herself immediately inside the door to check her makeup in the ladies' lounge. Alex also availed himself and slid into the men's room. Damn how Kat could make his blood boil. He pressed cold paper towels to his face but wished he could stuff them into his khaki dress slacks. He was very thankful for his suit jacket, which he casually buttoned to cover his prominent erection.

For the third night in a row, they were having dinner together…with other people. And she was leaving tomorrow. He needed to be alone with Kat for more than half an hour in the back of the limo. When he took her home tonight, he'd suggest a long walk on the beach.

He had to wait in the lavish lobby only a minute for her emerge. She had repaired her light makeup and maintained an inner glow that he found irresistible. He wanted to grab her away from their commitment and hide until her flight the next day.

"Ms. Callahan," the maître d' called as he approached. "Mr. Wolf." He nodded to Alex. "Mr. and Mrs. Howell are this way." He gestured, and Katlin led the way into the posh dining room.

The sooner they got started with this evening, the sooner they'd be able to leave. And he'd have Kat naked and under him as quickly as possible.

Dinner with Barry and his wife, Sherri, was just what it was, four high school classmates together again after many, many years. Stories and laughter bounced around the table, years of who-did-what-to-whom catch-up and delicious food, all mixed with great wine. Alex had truly had a great time.

As they finished the last morsels of dessert, Sherri asked, "Alex, I heard that you played Goldilocks and the Three Bears when you arrived. You found a blonde asleep in your bed."

He slid a glance at Kat, who blushed. "Not exactly. Yes, she'd slept in my bed, but she discovered me and thought I was an intruder. She held me at gunpoint."

Sherri clapped her napkin to her lips to hold in her final bite of chocolate mousse. "No kidding." She high-fived

Katlin. "I can just imagine Mr. Macho here with his hands up in the air."

Katlin just smiled.

"What were you doing in his bed? Or dare I ask?" Sherri ventured.

"I was sleeping, and had been for nearly thirty-two hours," Kat explained.

"Why weren't you at your beach condo or one of your other houses?" Sherri pressed. Alex wanted to know the real answer to that, too.

"I often sleep at Guardian." Katlin sipped her Amaretto-laced coffee. "It's quiet."

"Well, I suppose you can. You own the company." Sherri picked up her coffee cup.

Alex gulped the hot coffee. "What?" He glanced at Kat for her reaction. Had he heard Sherri right? No. He, along with TLM Investments, owned the company.

Katlin closed her eyes.

Barry's gaze shot daggers at his wife. "What did I do?" she asked in innocence.

Katlin opened her eyes and laid a gentle hand over Sherri's. "Alex doesn't...I mean didn't...know."

Dread washed over Sherri's face. She looked back and forth among the three. "I'm sorry. I didn't know it was a secret. You two...you're together again...aren't you? You're here. I...I thought he knew." Her eyes pleaded for forgiveness.

Katlin grimaced with resignation. "Well, he does now." She then gave Sherri a reassuring smile. "It's all right. He had to find out sometime."

Barry looked nervously at Katlin. She nodded.

"Listen, Alex, I want you to know that, personally, I'm glad to get everything out into the open," Barry began. "It's been tough. You've pinned me with questions that I could not legally answer.

I'm still an attorney you know, even though I'm your chief financial officer. What you don't know is that Katlin has been my client for years since right after I passed the bar. She swore me to secrecy about the angel money for starting Guardian Security."

"Angel money?" Sherri asked.

"Yes, it's what they call it when venture capitalists invest in a long-shot company," Barry explained. "Start-up money is extremely hard to come by. Most banks and investors want to see years of experience in that business and require solid collateral, but sometimes they are willing to take a chance. In Katlin's case, it's paid off well."

"So it's true? Kat is one of my business partners?" Alex asked, his gaze never leaving Kat's. She'd closed down. He couldn't read her face.

"You and Katlin are equal partners." Barry looked at the napkin in his lap and confessed. "I own three percent." He lifted his head and glared across the table at Katlin. "At her insistence."

Alex shot a glance to one of his oldest friends then back to Kat.

"You mean...you own TLM Investments?" Alex's tone was accusatory, but he couldn't help it. Betrayal sliced through him like a butcher knife, one solid move straight to his bones. She'd been his silent partner for two years. She hadn't spoken to him since Ty had died three years ago. In all that time, not one fucking word. Yet, she'd given him the money to start Guardian Security when no one else would.

"Yes." Her reply was barely audible.

"You know, I looked several times, and I could never find TLM Investments." Confusion clouded Alex's mind. He didn't know whether to be grateful or hurt.

Barry looked at Katlin, who nodded acquiescence. "You couldn't find it because we incorporated overseas. It's a shell company to cover...certain investments."

To hide from me? She hated me so much she felt she needed to hide? The blade in his gut twisted.

"Why?" The single word was all Alex could manage.

"Why TLM Investments?" Barry tried to clarify.

Yeah, he wanted to know that too. Unable to speak, Alex nodded.

"Tyler Lee Malone," Barry explained. "It was Ty's insurance money."

Katlin sat still as a statue, her eyes flicking from Barry to Alex then back again.

All Alex could do was shift his stare from Kat to Barry.

Barry threw him a beseeching look that begged for understanding. "Katlin didn't want to touch the money. She treated it like it was poison, so she had me invest it." His friend's words didn't make sense. They couldn't explain the duplicity of their actions.

"Remember when I wanted a security system for my new law office?" Barry asked with patience in his voice. "You had just gotten out of the Marine Corps and were getting started in the security business. I saw Katlin a few days later and mentioned it to her. She said it was the best place for that money."

Barry reached and took Katlin's hand. "She really wanted you to have it."

It hit Alex like a shot to the chest. Katlin had taken the life insurance money when Ty died and given it to him. The three of them were still tangled together. His mind flashed to holding Ty on the packed sand half a world away. He couldn't save Ty, but Katlin had made sure that Ty gave him a future. A very prosperous future.

Alex glanced down as if checking the time on his Rolex diving watch to give himself a moment to regroup. "Who was it that insisted that I hire Top Cooper for the D.C. office?" Alex stared at Barry. "You said it was a mandate from the investors. Don't get me wrong. He was a great choice. His knowledge of the personal protection business has been extremely profitable."

"I did," Katlin said. "Top had been my bodyguard since I was four years old. He followed Daddy from embassy to embassy most of his Marine career until we came back stateside. That's when I came to high school here in Miami, and Top went to teach at the Embassy Guard School in Quantico. He saved my life, and I owed him. I wanted him to have a good life after the Marine Corps."

"Glad to hear you like him. He's a character," Barry added. Yes, he was. Never once had he ever indicated that he knew Kat, but then again, her name had never come up.

Alex attempted to wrap his mind around the sheer magnitude of this revelation as he asked, "So it's just the two of us that own this whole company?" The last balance sheet had two commas before the decimal point.

"Yes, but you're the managing partner. It's your show," Katlin tried to assure him. "I have my government job and don't want to be involved." After a moment she added, "Unless there are really big decisions that mean we'll have to move money around."

"Last year when I wanted to expand to the West Coast, it was your money that bought out the San Francisco firm?"

"Yes."

"Is that why it took so long to make a decision?" Alex continued his inquisition.

Barry jumped in defensively. "As you know, Katlin spends a lot of time outside the U.S.A., and there are times I can't reach her for days, even weeks." Barry sent Kat an imploring glance.

Alex stared at Kat.

No. He had no idea she ever left Washington, D.C. No analyst he ever knew traveled unless it was for pleasure. Maybe she took a lot of international vacations.

Barry tried to explain. "She's given me very specific limitations, and that one was beyond my pay grade."

Sherri tilted her head and mouthed to Katlin, "I'm so sorry."

Alex was beginning to wrap his mind around it all, now. "When you asked me a few years ago if the investors could stay in the apartments when I wasn't using them, it was really Kat who wanted to stay there, right?"

"Smart boy. Hey, maybe that's why you got to join the rest of us brainiacs at a Miami magnet high school," Barry teased in an attempt to lighten the situation.

"Yes, sometimes I prefer to sleep in the Guardian apartments." Kat met his gaze, but he could tell she wasn't about to say anything more.

That brought a small grin to Alex's face as he thought about Kat, asleep, naked, in the king-sized bed in the apartment, with him holding her with the look of satisfied woman he had put on her face more than once. In *their* bed. In their apartment. In their company.

Everyone sat quietly and gave Alex time to digest all this new information and the ramifications. He finally spoke. "Barry, thank you. I'm sure I'll have more questions, but it's a lot to think about right now."

Katlin reached across the table and patted her friend's hand. "Sherri, don't worry about it. I'd planned to tell him tonight, anyway."

"I'm so sorry." Sherri bit her bottom lip.

"Barry, I believe you have some papers for me to sign?" Katlin changed the direction of the conversation. "I know what all these basically say, and as long as you made the revisions I asked for this morning, we're good."

Barry opened his briefcase, which had been hidden under the table, and handed Kat a stack of papers. She flipped through a couple of documents to specific pages and read parts carefully then signed where Barry pointed.

He slid them in front of Sherri and said in his best attorney voice, "You are only witnessing that Katlin signed these papers, and that this is really Katlin Callahan. I'm sure you don't need to see her ID."

"I know, Barry, I do this all the time for you," she castigated him.

"I know, dear, but I have to say it each and every time." He pecked his wife of eight years on the cheek. Their love was so evident in every caress he'd given her throughout the meal, every time she'd playfully smacked his still bulky bicep when he'd teased her. Alex wondered if he and Rachelle would ever have become this close had they stayed together.

A veil of blonde hair shielding the contents as Katlin bowed over long legal papers, Alex looked at his best friend in the world and instantly knew that he and Kat already had that kind of relationship.

Friends.

Yes, Barry and Sherri were married, but they were also friends and had been for years before they dated and fell in love. Maybe that was where he'd gone wrong with Rachelle. They'd been brief lovers then a married couple with a baby on the way, and then their lives had been consumed with their love of Jenny. He and Rachelle had never been friends.

He was thankful for his friendship with Kat and had been since the first day in bio lab. He wondered, not for the first time, if she'd become his lover again. He'd try damn hard tonight because just watching her do something as mundane as read over documents made him hard. He could almost feel her fine hair trickle heat over his bare stomach, her warm breath on every taut muscle as she kissed her way down to his—

"Got any more questions?" Barry interrupted his mental movie. "I know you have some. Discovering Katlin was your business partner was a shock, I'm sure. But, Alex, she made me promise not to tell you. It was legally privileged information."

Alex looked directly at Kat and said, "My questions are personal, and only Kat can answer them."

Her eyes popped up to meet his. The flash of silver fear surprised him. He didn't ever want Kat afraid of him. He slid his arm around her and gave her what he hoped was a comforting hug before he placed a chaste kiss on her temple.

"Almost done." Kat's smile reassured him but didn't reach her eyes.

Ten minutes later in the lobby, Katlin declared, "Barry, this has been a wonderful evening. Thank you for everything." She turned to Sherri and Alex. "I apologize that Barry and I had legal work to finish tonight. I don't get down here as often as I'd like, so when I am, we take what we can get."

After hugs and kisses, more apologies and reassurances, Kat and Alex climbed into the limo.

CHAPTER 22

Katlin situated herself on the back seat and glanced over to the side, where a bottle of champagne chilled in an ice bucket next to two flutes. Then she saw the three yellow roses in a small vase, and her heart melted a little. Alex leaned over and poured the bubbly wine while James started toward Miami Beach.

"This definitely looks like a seduction," Katlin said with a warm smile. "Even yellow roses." *He went to a lot of trouble for all this. For me.*

"I was told that you prefer yellow roses. That's why the staff puts them on the tables when you stay in the penthouse. I'd never noticed it before, but now I'll know you've been there."

"Do you know why I like yellow roses rather than red ones?" She accepted the filled flute with a smile and fell into his rich brown eyes.

"I have no idea." He smiled expectantly.

"Because of you."

"I'm lost here," he said, then sipped the fine champagne.

"When we were seniors, that last month in high school, when we were together, remember?" She looked into his eyes.

"You sent me a dozen roses for my birthday. No one had ever given me roses before. When they arrived, they were yellow and so beautiful, bright, and cheerful. I kept them in my bedroom so they were the first thing I saw in the morning and the last thing at night." They had brightened her life from that day on.

"Those were your first flowers?" he asked.

She nodded. "The day after they were delivered I got a call from the florist who said they'd made a mistake. They were supposed to deliver red roses. The woman said that's the color boyfriends are supposed to give girlfriends, but since Mother's Day had been the weekend before, they'd run out of red roses so a helper had substituted the yellow ones." She was lost in those days so long ago. She could still picture the yellow roses sitting on the desk in her bedroom. Damn, that had been nearly thirteen years ago. She'd come so far since then. Much further than she'd ever imagined.

"The next day they delivered a dozen red ones, but they were dark, not happy and cheerful like the yellow ones." Katlin sipped her bubbly wine. "I left those downstairs. I really liked the yellow ones, my first roses. I think I liked them most because they were from you."

She leaned over and kissed him. The instant their lips met, the now familiar zing reverberated through her whole body. She wanted more. She opened her mouth and slid her tongue over his. He tasted of champagne and passion.

She didn't know when, but he'd taken her glass and set it aside. Alex pulled her tighter to him and kissed her harder and deeper until they were both lost in the kiss. His hands dove into her hair, and he pulled her closer still, devouring her. She raked her nails at the back of his skull and felt him shiver in response. At a sharp right turn, they broke apart, breathless.

The car had turned into the condo driveway. Katlin didn't want to leave Alex. She had to fly to D.C. the next day and didn't know when she'd see him again. "Let's go for a walk on the beach," she suggested.

"Great minds think alike." With a smile, Alex grabbed the bottle and glasses then stepped out of the limo. He spoke to James for a minute before James drove away.

The sun-warmed sand slowly surrendered its heat to the moonless night sky and felt wonderful on her bare feet, the only way to walk on a beach. They'd left their shoes on the condo steps and taken the champagne with them.

Alex broke their silence. "Do you remember walking on Onslow Beach at Camp Lejeune?"

"Yes, at Thanksgiving. What were we, twenty-three or twenty-four?" Katlin asked as she sniffed the rose she'd brought with her.

"Something like that," Alex said.

"Daddy had taken over as the base commander that summer, so I was twenty-three, and that makes you twenty-four at the time. I was stationed at Norfolk at the time, and Mom didn't want me to be alone for the holiday, so I came down to North Carolina. I think she was the one who didn't want to be alone." It always surprised her how she kept track of the years. Since she'd moved so many times as a child, where they lived was the reference point, not the numerical year. Same went as an adult, college in D.C., Norfolk for a year, then to a whirlwind of bases for the secret training. Then Ty died. The next years were a blur, because time hadn't mattered. She'd lived in the present and had left the past behind her.

"Rachelle had already left me, and Ty was on a ship somewhere," Alex added.

"Yeah, after another affair. I think that one was with some lonely wife of a submariner."

"This isn't such a pleasant walk through memory lane," Alex admitted.

"No," Katlin admitted. "But after we wade through all the

past pain, what I remember best is when you and I found that huge black shark's tooth. It was as big as my palm. Then we sat on the beach and dug for little ones."

"Yes, it was right after a big storm, and hundreds of the fossils had been tossed up from that manganese pit just off shore. We sat in the sand for hours as we sifted through and looked for those tiny black teeth…and talked," Alex now said with a small smile.

"I still have them, you know."

"Really?"

"Yeah, and more. Every time I came to visit Mom and Daddy after that, I spent hours on base beach hunting million-year-old sharks' teeth. I put them inside my Mom's Stiffel cut-glass lamps," Katlin said, laughing. "They're in storage right now, but someday I'm going to have my own home, and I'll put them in my living room."

"You already have a house, several from what Sherri said."

"Yes, but I don't live in any of those. Someday I'm going to have a real home I live in, all the time, just me. I'll go to work and come *home*." She emphasized the last word.

She had mentally designed this house over and over again. "It'll have a great kitchen with a big six-burner gas stove and commercial grade oven and huge dishwasher. I'll need a double freezer, too, and plenty of granite counters. You can never have enough counter space. And I can cook and bake and throw great parties. Or I'll just curl up in a big overstuffed chair with a lusty romance novel in my living room, next to a lamp filled with million-year-old sharks' teeth." She loved talking with Alex this way, about dreams, the future.

"What about your husband?" he asked.

Had Alex lost his mind?

"He's dead." *What the hell is he thinking? He was there when Ty died. He was there when we buried him.*

"No, I mean, you'll get married again, won't you? Won't he live in this house, too?"

Oh, I hadn't thought about that. She'd never pictured a man in that house with her. Her dog, Dammit, would be curled up in front of the crackling fireplace while she read a novel. Very Norman Rockwell. But never a man. Never a husband. She wondered why not a husband.

"I guess he can live there, if I ever get married again," Katlin said, resolved.

"Do you want to get married again?" Alex asked without inflection. Without looking at her.

"I don't know. The first time didn't work out too well, as you know." For years she had thought her marriage with Ty was good. They'd been busy with their own careers. Not perfect, but certainly not bad. Then she'd been given the video, just before he'd left.

"For me either," Alex admitted as he stared ahead at the slight curve of beach that seemed to vanish into the darkness. Room lights in the beach hotels flickered off, but the outdoor spots washed the gleaming walls with light that shone on the beach.

"It would have to be someone who believed in wedding vows and that marriage is forever. I'll never tolerate infidelity again. He'll have to love me and only me. Sleep with me and *only* me." She'd already gone the other route once, and never again would she endure unfaithfulness. She wouldn't cheat, and he hadn't better either.

Maybe it was easier not to trust a man with her heart ever again. She knew there were good men out there, like her father, like Top Cooper, like Sara's husband. She just didn't attract those men. It was her fault. She didn't bother looking anymore. She had her job, the Ladies of Black Swan, and a lot of business concerns that kept her completely busy. She didn't need the complications of a man in her life. As a friend, yes. As a lover, maybe. Forever, probably never again. Since Alex had never remarried, she wondered if he felt the same way. "What about you?"

"Sometimes I feel like Rachelle and I were never really married. It seems like we played house while I went to school, first at George Washington, then at TBS in Quantico, then all the Special Operations schools I attended. Rachelle had left me before I became a company commander, so all she ever knew of me was school and studying. We never made it to the 'work and go home part,'" Alex admitted.

"So, answer the question. Do you want to get married again?" Katlin pressed.

"Are you proposing?" Alex teased and threw an arm around her shoulders.

"No, and quit answering my question with a question," she demanded.

Alex said nothing, just stared at the blackened Atlantic Ocean as it rushed to the sand beneath their feet.

"Well?" Katlin persisted.

"Yes, I think I'd like to get married at some point. I like your dream of going home to a comfortable house and someone I love. Someone I can talk to over dinner, someone who doesn't feel the need to fill every minute of the silence with mindless chatter, someone who doesn't bitch at me all the time. Then we go to bed and have great sex all night long." With this last line, he stopped and turned to Katlin.

She simply rolled her eyes. "Good luck with that. Fantasies are wonderful, aren't they?" She chuckled.

Katlin held out her flute, and Alex filled both of them. They walked in silence for a long time as they listened to the waves and sipped champagne. He took Katlin's hand and intertwined his fingers with hers. Palm to palm, his gentle warmth flowed through her, soothing, rather than the usual flame-inducing heat.

Finally, he broke the amiable silence. "Why did you lend me the money to start Guardian Security?"

"Because you needed it," she said simply.

Alex stopped and faced her. "You lent me hundreds of thousands of dollars of your money, money you may need someday. Most new businesses fail in the first year, and all your money would have been gone." Anger seethed through his voice. "What the hell were you thinking?"

Why was he mad at her? She'd always hoped he'd be pleased that it was her who'd given him the money.

"You don't know how to fail. I knew you were going to succeed. And you did. Look at all you've built in just two years. You've made Guardian highly successful in such a short time. You're an excellent manager, able to see and seize an opportunity. You've always had the drive to succeed. That made you a good Marine and a great SpecOps commander. I knew you'd be good at anything you put your mind to."

"You still haven't told me why." He was insistent.

No. She didn't want to tell him. Yet, he deserved the truth. She took a deep breath and let it out slowly, controlling the pain in her heart.

"The money was just sitting there. When I got the checks, the life insurance money, I just handed them to Barry and told him to invest it. I didn't feel right taking it." Maybe he'd accept that answer. It was the truth. Just not the whole truth.

"What do you mean you didn't feel right spending it?" Alex pressed. "You were his wife. It was meant for you to build a new life."

"I shouldn't have been his wife," she blurted out. Another truth.

"What the hell are you talking about?" Alex grabbed her shoulders.

"I had asked Ty for a divorce." She looked down and buried her bare feet in the sand. "We should have been divorced by then."

Alex just stared down at her, but she couldn't meet his eyes. She didn't want to see the unspoken accusations.

"The Kat I know believed in her wedding vows." He gently lifted her chin up so she would look at him. "That Kat would never have even considered divorce."

She held his gaze. "I had the papers all drawn up."

"You asked Ty for a divorce?" Alex enunciated every word.

"Yes, the night before he left for the Middle East. I had the separation papers all ready for his signature. My plan was that, by the time he came back, we would've been divorced," Katlin explained. Why didn't Alex understand? She was sure he and Ty had talked about this. They talked about everything. So why did he look surprised?

The warm ocean breeze swept over them as Alex stared at her for a long moment, his gaze searching her face for an answer she didn't have. To fill the silence, Kat went on, "I left him that night, sitting at the dining room table with the legal papers—"

She closed her eyes to gather her resolve, to go on, to tell him the whole truth. "I had a video playing on the TV in the living room, of him…taken just hours before…in bed with his Lieutenant JG's wife." His betrayal, once again, pierced her heart and squeezed all the way up her throat. She would never let another man do that to her again.

Alex clenched his hands on her shoulders, as if signaling her to continue.

"He never signed them. When I came back home the next day, he was gone, headed to the ship. The papers were where I'd left them…with a big FUCK NO scribbled across them."

Now angered, Katlin continued, "That *sonofabitch* was still controlling me…from the grave." She drew in a ragged breath. "I didn't want him in my life anymore when he was alive, so I sure as hell wasn't going to use his money to build a new life for myself after he was dead. No matter what I bought with that money, it would be a constant reminder of him and his betrayals." *Telling me relentlessly that I wasn't enough woman to make him happy, to keep him in my bed and only my bed.* She couldn't say those words out loud but felt them rip another gash into her heart. God damn Ty. He was dead, but he continued to hurt her.

She forced a slow, deep breath and told Alex the rest. "He loved you. You were his best friend, the brother he chose."

"Oh, babe. I know Ty loved you." Alex caressed her arm. "The two of you put me in the middle all too often with your confidences about each other. And, no, I always kept your secrets from him." He answered her question before she was able to ask.

"Then why did he cheat on me? And not just once." She ranted on, fighting the twist in her heart, not sure she wanted to hear the answer. "Why was it necessary for him to share his body with other women? I would never have done that to him. We were married. We'd taken vows before God pledging ourselves only to each other."

Alex looked at rolling tide then back into her eyes. "What the fuck...he's dead and can't beat the shit out of me for telling you this." He brought her a step closer to him. "Katlin, you blew into our lives larger than life. You'd been all over the world, spoke several languages, knew real fucking princes and princesses, and called them your friends. You could shoot guns and knew martial arts. Hell, you could kick our asses. Neither of us had ever known anyone like you, least of all a girl."

Alex swept away the strand of hair that had blown across her face and secured it behind her ear. "Ty wanted to claim you, as his, from the first day he met you. He was obsessed with you belonging to him. But you also scared the shit out of him. You were this badass wrapped in a deceptive package of big boobs and a sweet smile with that perfect little ass of yours."

He smiled. "Which, by the way, that package has definitely improved with age." He sucked in a short breath. "I think Ty went into the SEALs so he could be better than you. Maybe then he'd be worthy of that unconditional love you gave him."

Damn. Then she'd gone and one-upped him once again by being selected for the secret special operations training program. With approval from her commander, she'd excitedly told Ty about the pilot project. He'd acted happy for her. Was it an act? Had he really resented her success?

Alex's voice interrupted her memory of that night. "He told me once that he had to fuck a normal woman now and again to prove he was still a man."

The knife that pierced her heart threatened to rip it out of her chest. The wonderful champagne threatened to reappear. Through the tears that filled her eyes, she managed to ask, "So I'm abnormal? Gee, thanks for that revelation."

Alex cupped her face and brushed a thumb over her cheek. "Oh, yes, sweetheart. You most certainly are. You are the most unique woman I've ever had the pleasure to know. And I can tell you from experience, you are a tiger in bed, and not many men can tame a wild Kat. You can be intimidating, but you know that. Personally, I prefer a woman who knows what she wants and isn't afraid to ask for it."

Alex had always seemed to inherently know what she needed, physically and emotionally. She'd never had to ask him for anything.

"But he loved you...and only you." Alex's words were reassuring, just not enough for Katlin to forgive the man who'd shattered her heart.

"He certainly had a strange way of showing it." Her voice broke as she held back tears. "He never cheated on you. He never stabbed you to your very soul." She refused to cry over that bastard.

Alex pulled her to him and surrounded her with his

friendship, just like he'd done so often over the years. He was such a great friend. She needed him to hold her and tell her she'd be all right.

"I'm sorry he hurt you. He could be such an idiot." Alex stroked her hair, crown to back, over and over again.

She laid her cheek on his chest and listened to his short, shallow breaths. She'd thrown a lot at him and knew it would take him time to process. But that wasn't all of it. Not by a long shot.

Finish the money part. It's the good part. The rest will wait. "So, back to Guardian. When Barry told me that you were getting out of the Marine Corps and wanted to start this security business, I gave you the money so you could start a new life. It was Barry's idea for me to maintain a percentage of the corporation, but I made him promise that he'd never tell you where the money came from. To be sure he didn't, I gave him a small percentage too."

Alex hugged her tighter. "I couldn't have done it without you. You believed in me when no one else would." They stood on the beach warmed by the sand and ocean breeze.

Finally, Alex continued, "I had painstakingly written a business plan and showed it to bank after bank, and half a dozen venture capitalists, all with the same result…no."

"I knew you were a good investment, and you've made a lot of money for me in the past two years. A hell of a lot more than I would have made in the stock market." Katlin pulled back from him so she could see his face. "But more than that, it was the right thing to do. You've made a new life for yourself, and that's what insurance money is for."

Alex jerked her to his hard chest and rocked her in his arms. "Thank you. Thank you." He whispered the words over and over again into the top of her head as they stood as one surrounded by darkness.

Katlin drew in a steadier breath. "I think I also did it as a way to keep you in my life. I've watched you grow this idea of yours into a multimillion-dollar company. It makes me feel so good to know that I could help you reach that goal. I hope it made you happy."

"No, it didn't make me happy." Alex lifted her chin up. "It made me successful. But I am happy now that you are back in my life." Alex bent down and kissed her, ever so gently. She let him take her mouth, kissing him back. When she opened for him, he swept in, taking her, possessing her, thanking her.

They finally ended the kiss, and Kat stepped back. "I have to fly to D.C. tomorrow, so I'd better head back to the condo and get some rest. Where are you headed next?"

"Actually," Alex said as the two walked back up the beach, his arm around her shoulders, hers at his waist, "I need to check the D.C. office. Maybe we're on the same flight."

Katlin knew better. Then she had a brilliant idea. She turned to look up at him and smiled, "Do you want to fly with me?"

"Sure. Maybe I can get on the same flight." He then added, "What time do you leave?"

"Whenever I want." She grinned ear to ear.

Alex looked at her with questions in his eyes, and she explained. "We have our own plane. We call her Black Swan. I'm the pilot tomorrow. You can fly with us to D.C. Top Cooper picks us up so he can take you to Guardian Security's D.C. office."

"You are a pilot?" Alex asked.

Her smile broadened. "There's a lot about me you don't know."

"Obviously. But I'd like to find out," Alex said as he bent to kiss her again, now that they were back to the steps of her condo.

Katlin grimaced. He might not like some of the things he found out. Like her real job.

Holding her against his chest, he said, "I don't want to lose you again. You've just come back into my life."

"Not really. I've been here all along. You just didn't realize it." Katlin buried her hands in his long, soft hair and pulled him against her lips. When she broke the kiss, she bent to pick up her shoes and roses and then handed him the champagne flute. "I'll call you tomorrow morning and let you know exactly when to be at F.B.O. at Miami International." She glanced at her watch. "Since it's twelve hours bottle to throttle, we'll leave around one o'clock."

He stepped in so close her hardened nipples scraped across his chest with every breath. "Come back to Guardian with me," Alex begged. "Spend the night with me." He chuckled. "In *our* bed."

It was so damned tempting. But they were now going to see each other in D.C. starting tomorrow. He was going to see her in her element as a very capable pilot. She had time to finish her goal of using Alex as a launch pad to dating.

Tonight they both had needed a friend, and that was exactly what they had been for each other. Although well aware of the hard-on he sported, she hadn't drawn that friends-with-benefits line yet. She needed to set the parameters of their relationship, but tonight wasn't the right time for that discussion. She'd put it off until they were in D.C.

"I had a wonderful time tonight, Alex." She stroked the side of his face. "Tonight, we needed to be friends, not fuck buddies. There would be too many people in that bed if we made love right now." She shuddered. "I don't know about you, but I need to shake off Ty's ghost before we go there."

She ran her hand the length of his erection then gave it a squeeze. "Because when we make love, and I assure you we will, soon, it's only going to be you and me."

She went on tiptoes and laid her lips on his.

"Tomorrow, Alex."

CHAPTER 23

"So, you've brought Katlin and her friends here before?" Alex asked as they approached the Miami International Airport. He wondered what kind of plane Katlin flew, maybe a little six-seat Cessna or a King Air. He didn't revel in sitting for hours in a small plane, but Kat had invited him and he wasn't going to say no.

"Yeah," Griffin said and pulled into the Fixed Base Operations side of the Miami airport, where private planes loaded and deplaned, filed flight plans, refueled, and had maintenance performed. Huge hangars scattered alongside the runways stored several planes each. From single-propeller two-seaters to multimillion-dollar, supersonic business jets, F.B.O. handled them all through an elegant terminal where jets pulled under a porte-cochere to load passengers and baggage. Usually.

Griffin drove around to a white hangar that looked like any other...except for the Marines armed to the teeth patrolling the exterior.

What the fuck? Alex glanced toward his friend, who shrugged at the unasked question.

"No idea. But I'm not allowed out of the vehicle." Griffin

nodded to the door guarded by a Marine with an M4 carbine rifle pointed at them. "Miss Katlin warned me the Marines have orders to shoot."

I'm here, Alex texted Kat.

The door opened, and Grace flashed her badge as she talked to the Marine, who eventually lowered his rifle. She smiled and waved then pointed to Alex and gestured for him to come.

"Thanks for the ride, Griffin." Alex shook his hand and jumped out of the Guardian SUV. "I'll see you in a month or so." He grabbed his duffel from the back seat and followed Grace into the hangar.

And stopped.

Katlin had called their plane Black Swan. It was as elegant as its namesake. Ninety-feet of shiny black jet sat as the sole inhabitant of the bright hangar. A silver stripe ran from its pointed nose below the oval windows and the twin engines mounted at the rear just before the tail.

"Beautiful, isn't she?" Grace peered up at Alex then started walking toward the stairs. "Black Swan is a Gulfstream 550, which is technically an all-weather, long-range business jet. She has two Rolls-Royce turbofan engines with thrust reversers. Cruising speed for us is about 500 knots —that's 575 miles an hour—with a range just over 4,000 miles."

"Impressive," Alex admitted. "Whose plane is it?" He knew Kat had friends who could easily afford a jet like this. Maybe that Jordanian prince he'd met while they dated in college had lent it to her…or some other royal she'd grown up with. Christ, he was out of his class with her if this was what she used as private transportation these days.

But she deserved this luxurious lifestyle. She was meant to be pampered and coddled by a good man. God knew he wasn't a good man, not after all he'd done. Now, his job was to keep people like Kat safe from the evil that lurked everywhere in the world.

Grace changed the subject. "Come on up into the cabin. Katlin is prepping the flight. She's flying in the pilot seat today." Grace bounded up the steps. "Make yourself comfortable. I need to check in up front and see how we're doing since I'm second seat for this flight." She glanced down the aisle. "Hey, Nita, will you stow Alex's bag in the hold, please?"

With a smile, Nita replied, "Got it." Before Alex could offer, the dark-haired cutie had grabbed his duffel and was out the door.

"Tori, Lei Lu, will one of you get Alex something to eat and drink, please?" Grace asked then ducked into the cockpit.

Damnit bounced toward him. The large dog stopped at his feet and sniffed before he licked Alex's extended hand. "Hello, boy." He scratched the large dog's ears. Satisfied, the pup returned to his bed in the back of the plane watching everything and everyone.

"Hi, Alex." Lei Lu waved from the galley. "Welcome to the Black Swan. Sit anywhere. We'll be a few minutes yet."

"Alex, do you need a table to get some work done? Or a computer? They're in the wall cabinets." Tori slid a table out from the side wall.

Lei Lu popped appetizers into the microwave. "Want a beer? Wine? Soda?"

"I'll take a beer," Alex said as he nestled into the soft leather seat the size of a recliner.

"Make that two," Tori called. Lei Lu opened the mini-fridge and pulled out two imported beers then retrieved two frozen pilsner glasses from the freezer.

"I could get used to this lifestyle," Alex admitted as he accepted the beer from Lei Lu.

Tori glanced around the cabin. "It's home. We spend a lot

of time on this bird." She and Lei Lu glided into the seats across from him.

So, Kat and her friends traveled together often. Must be nice. He wondered if her gorgeous friends were daughters with daddies who had more money than brains and were willing to indulge their children with wealth. Although Kat had said they worked together. He could see these women in cubicles next to Kat's as they analyzed data from all over the world. They were extremely smart. Perhaps they spent every dime of their hard-earned money on travel and partying. He'd met lots of women like that in the past two years. All were looking for a sugar daddy so they could maintain their lavish lifestyle. These women weren't at all as self-consumed as those jetsetters.

Katlin appeared from the cockpit wearing casual slacks and an aqua t-shirt, along with a warm smile. "I'm so glad you could fly with us today."

Alex stood, and she walked straight into his arms. "Me too." Her body against his felt wonderful. Perfect. Right. She lifted her mouth to his and kissed him, in front of her friends. If she didn't care, he certainly didn't. She kept it sweet, just long enough for him to want more.

"Hi," he said and gave her a small kiss before he stepped back.

Katlin grabbed the front of Alex's dress shirt and pulled him to her. "Hi, to you, too." Then she kissed him soundly. His body had gone from *it's good to see you* to *I want you naked...now...* in a single heartbeat. How could she do that to him? With one simple kiss? They *had* to act on this attraction. Soon. That was the word she'd used last night on the beach.

But if he didn't take his mouth off her right then, he'd have them both on the floor, or in one of the luxurious chairs with her riding him. By her actions and heavy breathing, she wanted him as much as he wanted her.

Enough. That was just a teaser. Or a promise.

He broke the kiss and stared into her deep blue eyes. She gently stepped away, released his shirt, and then smoothed it with the palm of her hand. His pectoral muscles twitched under her touch, and his abs tightened when he inhaled sharply as her hand dropped down his body. It rested just above his belt.

Breathlessly, she said, "I need to get this bird off the ground. We'll have plenty of time to talk in D.C." She glanced back at him as he hitched his slacks, readjusting himself before he sat down. Both Lei Lu and Tori wore grins.

To take the attention away from him and Kat, Alex asked, "Why is your plane called Black Swan? Because it's black? Or did you paint it that color?"

Tori smiled. "Actually, our team was named Black Swan when it was formed, long before we got this plane. And, no, we didn't paint it this color. It was black when we got it. The name seemed to fit the plane better than the team."

Nita took up the explanation. "A few years back there was a book about the Black Swan Theory, which refers to unexpected events that basically change the world and become historical turning points. A Black Swan event has to meet three criteria. First, the event has to be a surprise to almost everyone around the world. Second, it has to have a major impact that changes the direction of history. Third, in hindsight, it is rationalized as if it had been expected. The September eleventh attack is a great example."

Alex had read the book and understood its principles as applied to Wall Street and international markets. This application was new, yet logical.

"Our team tries to prevent Black Swan events," Lei Lu claimed. "Section 7 studies threats all over the world and determines possible outcomes of a large magnitude that could create devastating consequences, and then we eliminate that threat to mankind."

Made sense, especially since they were analysts.

Tori tried to explain more simplistically. "Using the 9/11 event, intelligence reports about how dangerous a man Osama bin Laden had been started hitting the CIA and other intelligence desks in Washington nearly ten years before the attack. Had they been compiled, examined, and projections made—then confirmed over time—the terrorists could have been eliminated and most likely the Twin Towers would still be standing today."

"I understand." Alex studied each woman. "You take information gathered from across the planet by hundreds of sources and decide who is the greatest threat. I'm not sure I like the government making those kinds of life-and-death decisions, but I'm sure you're good at your jobs." That was when he realized why the five beautiful women on Kat's team needed security. They held the power of life and death for some of the most influential men on the planet.

All three women exchanged a smile. Nita spoke first. "Yeah. We're fucking good at our job. Best in the whole department."

Katlin softly set Black Swan down onto the short landing strip at Marine Corps Base Quantico, Virginia, just south of Washington, D.C. She taxied toward the signalman then straight into a non-descript drab green hangar with all the windows blacked out. As soon as the engines wound down, the huge doors shut. A Marine ran to the bottom of the steps as Nita descended to the polished concrete floor.

"Afternoon, ma'am," the Marine said as he nodded in salute.

"Good afternoon, sergeant," she replied. Lei Lu and Tori came down the steps and headed to the exterior hold door. Alex followed a few steps behind. He didn't bother to hide the fact that he carried two pistols in his shoulder holster. The

Marine looked at him warily and stared at his guns for several heartbeats then at his long hair. Alex remembered those days of quickly assessing every person in the room for threat level. One corner of his mouth kicked up.

He figured the Marines in the hangar wouldn't know that his slacks were custom tailored of the finest wool and his jacket cost more than they make in three months. He was sure they had their orders: assist whoever exits that plane, guard the plane with your weapon and your life, and assure no unauthorized persons enter the hangar. If he was their CO, those were the orders he would have given.

"Good afternoon, sir."

Alex looked at the Marine's rank insignia and name embroidered over his pocket and said, "Good afternoon, Sergeant Hayword."

Right then Top Cooper walked up to the plane and declared, "Last time I met you here I was calling you Captain Lobo and you were in Dress Blues. Now you look like a millionaire CEO. You been back to Quantico since?" Out of the corner of his eye, Alex watched the sergeant reassess him. *Yeah, I was a Marine, and once a Marine, always a Marine.*

"No, but it hasn't changed that much since I landed in a KC130 about a thousand feet that way." Alex nodded to where he'd brought Ty's body three years earlier. "A lot has changed for me since that day, Top. You now call me boss, and neither of us will ever have to wear those damn high collars on Dress Blues again. This uniform is much more comfortable, especially the shoes." Both men laughed.

"So who landed her today? It was perfect." The retired master gunnery sergeant ran his hand over silver hair that was barely there in its high-and-tight regulation Marine cut.

"Kat."

"So our little lady had the stick?"

"Yes," Alex said as he scanned the growing pile of black duffel bags. Tori reached into the hold for the next and handed it to Nita, who set it to her right. The following bag went on her left side. Each rectangular, soft-sided bag looked exactly like the last with a dozen black-zippered pockets and a shiny black swan embroidered on its side.

Katlin followed Grace down the steps. "Top," she called, a huge smile on her face, and walked quickly over to hug the forty-five-year-old block of a man who lifted her off the ground.

"You look great," he said and gave her another quick little hug. "Welcome home, Little One."

She kissed his cheek. "Good to see you."

A shot of jealousy coursed through his veins. There was so much there he didn't know. Secrets both had kept from him. Anger chased the green monster away.

Alex forced his gaze to the floor of the hangar where ten identical black bags lay in what could be construed as some kind of an order. "How can you tell which belongs to who?"

"Our code name is on each of our bags," Nita explained, pointing to a small hawk in flight. "Lady Kite is Lei Lu, so this bag is hers with the Asian Kite on it. I'm Lady Harrier, and this one is mine. This one is Katlin's because her code name is Lady Hawk."

That handle resonated deep within him. He'd heard it before, but it had been far outside this bright setting, and he couldn't capture the memory enough to concentrate on it. Then he felt her beside him. "How did you get the name Lady Hawk?"

"You." She bent and picked up two bags. "Ask me later when we're alone," she replied in almost a whisper.

Katlin turned to the other ladies and spoke in what Alex thought was Portuguese. They carried on a brief conversation, changing languages several times, then she hugged each woman and kissed them on the cheek.

She turned to Top then asked, "Is there a bodyguard and car for the ladies outside?"

"Of course," he said taken aback, as if he hadn't done his job. "Wherever they want to go."

Katlin took a few steps.

Stopped.

She stood completely still. Her face went blank. The ladies halted all movement. No one moved or spoke. Alex wondered what the hell she was doing but felt her tension ramp to the point that he was looking around, trying to see what she saw.

Her eyes swept the entire hangar as though she were hunting for something. She seemed to absorb everything within the large open space filled with Marine guards, her team, Alex, Top, and Black Swan.

Alex felt it then, too. Something was off. Wrong. Bad.

Katlin's eyebrows lowered, head cocked, lips pursed as wariness washed across her face. Katlin spoke again to the ladies, this time in Chinese. All five reached into their go bags, shrugged into their holsters, checked their guns, and slipped them into place. The Marines took notice, and the tension in the large hangar escalated to a palpable, almost living entity. Anyone who'd ever served in combat knew that feeling, as every sense, especially the sixth one, came to full alert.

"I have to double check on the arrangements for the plane," Katlin said loud enough for everyone in the hangar to hear. To Top and Alex, she suggested, "Why don't you come with me?"

Hell yes, he was going with her. He wouldn't leave her alone in a time like this.

With small hand signals that Alex almost missed, the women spread out. Nita and Lei Lu slowly walked the hangar while Grace and Tori examined every surface of Black Swan.

"Just a feeling," she told them as they followed her into the office, where she gave the staff sergeant on duty specific instructions, beginning with an order to immediately change the guards.

The instant they emerged from the office, they were met by the other four women. Grace spoke for the rest, "Clear, but Nita's scalp is itching."

"I felt it too. Something's off, but I can't pinpoint it." Katlin took a deep breath. "Let's go home. We'll deal with it when it happens."

The ladies all nodded, said good bye to Alex and Top, then left by the small door at the rear of the building.

CHAPTER 24

Alex sat with Kat in the back seat of the Guardian Security Land Rover. He needed to be close to her. Almost immediately after they pulled from the parking lot, she dialed her cell phone. To his surprise, she put it on speaker. "Go back to the hangar in a few hours under the guise that you'd forgotten something and sweep the plane for bugs."

Tori piped in, "Grace and I'll check over the plane late tonight after the guard is changed again."

"Thanks, ladies. I'm glad it wasn't just me. Call me after your sweep, but let's give it a few hours." When she disconnected the call, Alex took her hand.

"I felt it too. I learned a long time ago to listen to my sixth sense. It kept me alive more than once. Did you feel like we were being watched? Do you have cameras in the hangar?" Alex asked.

"It wasn't so much being watched. We get that from the Marines every time we land. They're curious about us. A black jet that's quickly moved into a protected hangar, and then five women disembark?" Katlin explained.

"Five absolutely gorgeous women," Top threw in. Katlin blushed. "They're young men. They're going to notice."

"Thanks, Top. My ego needed that lift today." She lovingly patted his big shoulder. After Ty's secret had been revealed last night, Alex had no doubt her femininity had been bruised.

"No, this was different. It hit the bottom of my stomach, which usually means something's wrong. Ominous. But I couldn't put my finger on it." She shrugged. "Fresh eyes tonight from Tori and Grace will help. They'll take care of it."

She took a deep breath and, obviously feeling the situation was now under control, Katlin said, "Top, I need to talk to Daddy." He turned off Interstate 395 toward Arlington.

Alex didn't say much in the car. He wasn't sure how much he wanted Top Cooper to know about his relationship with Katlin. He didn't pay much attention to where Top was going until the car passed the Old Post Chapel headed into Arlington National Cemetery. When they pulled to a stop, they all got out and Katlin walked toward her father's grave.

Alex started to follow her, but Top grabbed him. "This is private for her."

"You're very protective of Kat." Alex couldn't hide the irritation in his voice.

"I've safeguarded her since she was a kid." The former Marine walked around the SUV to keep her in sight. "I followed her family around the world. I've killed for that little lady, and I've been shot for her."

"When?" Curious about Katlin's early life, Alex was also interested in his D.C. Center's manager and his real relationship with Kat.

"She was four years old." Top settled as he leaned into the Land Rover's fender. "I was usually her bodyguard when I wasn't on duty at the embassy. Her father knew that she was a target for kidnap so he'd hire off-duty Marines for protection. She was this precocious little blonde with a brilliant mind and sharp tongue. Sometimes I'd forget that she was so young." Alex had seen pictures of Kat at that age, white-blonde with a glint of mischief in her riveting blue eyes.

"One day a new guard was with them when she and her mother went into the city market. He was distracted for just a second, and someone grabbed her. Mrs. Callahan went crazy, tore apart the open-air stalls, screamed and cried. Within an hour the ransom demand was delivered to the embassy. They wanted just over a million in U.S. dollars."

"Holy hell," was all Alex could manage. He couldn't imagine what her parents had gone through but had a good idea when he thought about someone, especially in a Third World country, kidnapping his daughter. He'd be killing people. Or at least torturing them until someone fessed up with viable information.

"The Callahan family didn't have money like that, and we both know that the United States doesn't negotiate with terrorists. Everyone from the ambassador on down was trying to get the money when the local police got a tip." Top stared at Kat's back as she knelt in front of a white stone, the cool April breeze lifting strands of her long blonde hair as thought her father was playing with it.

"I put together several Marines, and with the local police, we went to this falling-down, one-room stone house on a narrow back street in the slimy section of the city. By the time we got to her, she'd been gone over fourteen hours." He glanced at Alex then quickly away, but not fast enough. Alex saw the self-recrimination in Top's eyes. "I'll be honest with you. We were scared what we were going to find." The remembered fear reverberated in his voice.

"We scoped the room from every angle we could establish and identified three men." Top swallowed hard. "I saw her on a pallet bed in the corner, just sitting there. She looked so small. Her usually perfect blonde hair was all mussed up. Her face was dirty, but I didn't see any tear streaks. She played with the torn pieces of her dress and just watched her captors.

She studied them. I could see it in her eyes. I've seen that look several times since."

He considered for a minute. "She had that look in the hangar."

Top returned to the story. "We broke in the door, guns blazing and killed the three bastards, right in front of her. I'd never killed a man before or been around a dead person other than in a funeral parlor." Top sighed and closed his eyes.

"I ran over and scooped her up in my arms. She wasn't in shock; she wasn't bawling or screaming. She just hugged me and told me she was a big girl. She hadn't cried. Then she repeated the words I'd heard her father say so many times to us. 'Assess the situation, define your objectives.'"

Alex joined in with the familiar phrase. "Develop an action plan and do it." He'd heard the general say those words more often than he could count. "She really said that?"

"Yeah." One side of Top's mouth quirked up. "She used to follow her dad around the embassy like a puppy. She was a sponge, absorbing everything."

Top looked at Alex. "Later, I asked her what her plan was, and she told me she was going to wait till the bad men all fell asleep and run away."

That was his Kat. She always had an exit plan.

"She about broke my heart when she asked why it took me so long to come get her." He choked out a small laugh. "She asked to be put down. I remember watching the blood pool around the dead douchebags and looking at her tiny white sandals. I didn't want the blood to touch her, but it was too late. She was spattered head to feet."

His big hand washed over his leathery face. "She put her tiny hands on my face and made me look at her, and once again said she wanted down, so I did. That little child walked over to one of the dead guys, made the sign of the cross, and said, 'Go with God.'" He took a deep breath and washed his face with his both hands. "She repeated it with the next man."

He huffed a chuckle and smiled. "But at the third, Katlin hauled off and kicked him then said, 'You can go to the devil.' She kicked him again and said, 'That's for making me eat peanut butter sandwiches.' Then she kicked him again and said, 'That's for not letting me play outside.'" A full smile danced across the tough Marine's face as he slowly shook his head.

"You've been around the newly dead so you know the body relieves itself from every orifice. Well, with that third kick, it released all the air in the lungs. Katlin got this really scared look on her face. Those powerful blue eyes of hers got so big, and then she said to us, 'I think I let all the air out of him.' Well, I'm about to burst out laughing when she says, 'Can I go now? I think he pooped his pants.' We all lost it at that point. Between the adrenaline and the relief of getting her back safe, we were all laughing as we took her out to her father. We'd made him wait outside a few hundred feet back, out of range." Top took a minute to regroup.

"A fourth man was captured within hours. It was the custom of that country that the offended party got to decide the fate of the criminal, so here's our little lady, a four-year-old *goddamnit*, who had to decide if this last man lived or died. Fucker said some pretty ugly things to her, but she just stood there and held the judge's hand. Her father was ready to kill the sonofabitch with his bare hands when Katlin said, 'He's a bad man. He should go to the devil.'" At this revelation, Top shook his head slowly, side to side.

Alex was riveted. He had no idea what she'd gone through as such a small child. She'd never told him she'd been kidnapped, and he'd never envisioned anything like that. Top's deep voice brought him away from his thoughts

"The judge looked at her then nodded to the police chief, who shot the guy, right there in front of her. Mrs. Callahan went into shock; she just shook and mumbled. I think it was her first dead body. Katlin's father was terrified as to the effects the whole ordeal would have on her." He looked at Alex. "Did you know she still sees that shrink they got her way back then? The woman now works for Homeland."

"I had no idea," Alex admitted. "But a kidnapping would fuck up anyone, not to mention having four men shot in front of you."

Top resumed his story. "Our little lady walked over and began to comfort her mother, who was hysterical by then. She patted her on the back and told her mother that he was bad and God sent him down to the devil."

Alex closed his eyes as he absorbed the events from long ago that had formed the woman he cared about so much. She'd seen such brutal deaths at a young age; it would affect anyone. Even at four years old she was administering death to bad men. It was no wonder she was so damn good at her job. She'd literally been sentencing men to death all her life. Only now, she did it from a distance behind a computer. Alex was thankful she didn't have to face the blood and gore he'd seen as a special operator. Or the bullets flying back at her.

The two men leaned against the SUV, thick arms woven across massive chests, and watched as Kat spoke quietly and pulled long grass from the base of the headstone.

"There were other attempts on her life?" Alex finally asked.

"Twice more. I took a bullet the next time protecting her." Top rubbed his thigh. "She was probably seven or eight. After I recovered, I taught her how to shoot. She learned extremely fast and was a natural. She's very good."

"I know. I watched her practice in Miami." Alex said, and shifted so he leaned on the hood with one forearm. "So, there was another time?"

"Yes, when she was twelve, we were all caught in a coup in Central America. Banditos had taken over the capital and governmental palace, and they were attacking the embassies. Her father and I had gathered the children from all the embassies and put them in her parents' quarters. It was the easiest to defend, and we never imagined that anyone could get to them. Her mother had an Uzi, and I gave Katlin the H&K MP5 mini sub-machine gun that I'd taught her to use." He smiled, and Alex watched him relive that incident.

"The banditos heard where we'd put the kids and broke down the door. Mrs. Callahan's Uzi jammed after a few shots, and Katlin stepped up beside her mother and started mowing them down in perfect spurts of five before they could get off a shot."

He stopped and shot Alex a glance. "You've met some of Katlin's friends. Ever meet Miguel Sanchez? He married her roommate, Solange. Big guy, played football for Georgetown."

Alex had to think back to Kat's college days. He remembered a bed that was too small for the two of them and making love to her for hours. "Of course I remember Solange and Mike. He'd Americanized his name for college. Wasn't his dad the Colombian ambassador to the U.S.? I knew he'd met Kat years before that, but I had no idea it was in Panama."

"Yes. Exactly. Miguel was there, too, and stood right beside her with another MP5. They'd killed seven men before we came up from the rear and took the rest out. Those two were amazing. Cool. Focused. And not even teenagers yet," Top said as the two men watched the twenty-nine-year-old version carry on a quiet conversation with a tombstone.

"When did the general pass away?" Alex asked with as much reverence as he could. Top had obviously had a special relationship with Kat's father. Alex hadn't known the general was gone.

"About four months after we buried Ty. Heart attack, in his office at the Pentagon. It was a rough year for our little lady," Top said with compassion.

Fuck. He should have been there for Kat. He'd been in

Afghanistan, finishing his final tour seven thousand miles away, when it happened. The Marine Corps wouldn't have let him come home unless the funeral had been for one of his immediate family members. Although the general had been a father figure to him, that wouldn't have counted.

"Daniel was there for her, wasn't he?" Alex felt sure her brother had been there, although he hadn't come for Ty's funeral. But that was no surprise. Daniel had openly despised Katlin's husband.

"No. Right after their mother died, he took a deep cover assignment overseas and has been under ever since. Katlin doesn't talk about him. I'm not sure if he's even alive."

"Damn." Alex cursed under his breath and wondered who had been there to hold Kat. Help her through the days, and nights, after her father's death. He wished he'd been there for her. She and her father had always been close and to lose him so suddenly must have devastated her. Alex had lost his father to a work-related accident when he was fourteen. It had changed his life, and not for the better.

He'd make it up to Kat, somehow. He owed her that much, and more.

Top's voice broke through, as if he could read Alex's thoughts.

"I sat with her in the front row, her Uncle Tom on the other side. Her Uncle Francis performed the ceremony, of course. Then we both walked with her behind her father's casket. I guess I'm the closest thing she has to family now, besides her uncles." Top confessed, "I love that young lady like she was my own child. I've watched her grow up into the beautiful woman she is today." They watched as Kat gracefully rose, kissed her fingers, and touched the top of the sturdy white stone.

When Katlin walked back to the two men, Top asked, "Do you want to go—"

"No!" Katlin snapped emphatically. She closed her eyes,

took a deep breath, then said, "I'm sorry for being so abrupt and inconsiderate. Top, would you please take Alex over there if he wants to go."

Go? Go where? Then it dawned on him. To Ty's grave.

Alex quickly submitted. "There is nothing there for me." No. Unlike Kat, he believed that, once you were dead, you were gone. He'd never understood visiting someone's grave, but it apparently gave Kat some degree of comfort.

The three walked silently to the Old Post Chapel, where Katlin anointed herself with Holy Water upon entering, as did Alex. She walked to the familiar rows of candles and lit three before she kneeled to pray. Top seated himself in a pew twenty feet away. Alex followed Katlin and lit a candle before he kneeled beside her. He crossed himself and prayed silently.

The old saying was true; when bullets fly at you, there are no atheists on a battlefield. He'd prayed and been saved from the clasp of death more than once and would always be thankful to God for that and more. Alex prayed for his friend Kat and that the saints would watch over his daughter, so she'd never experience one-tenth the hell Kat had lived through as a child.

Lost in his silent talk with God, he asked him to protect her. Alex reached to touch her, connect with her.

She was gone. He whipped his head to the place she'd been mere seconds ago.

Vacant space.

The instant emptiness resounded in his soul as his eyes focused on the flickering candle he'd lit for her. It seemed to warm him within, with confidence that she was all right and nearby. He twisted around and saw her, waiting for him, hands demurely folded in front.

She smiled at him, and his world became a brighter place. His heart lightened. He wanted to run to her, tell her she was important to him. Hold that little girl inside her who'd been kidnapped, the teenager who'd been shot at, and tell her what a special woman she'd become.

But her smile said she understood, all of it, without the words he knew he'd screw up.

Alex rose and walked to her.

"Ready?" Kat asked him with understanding in those amazing blue eyes.

Alex took her hand. "I am now."

On the way to the car, he held Katlin back for a minute. "I'm so sorry I wasn't there for you," he said with a crack in his voice.

"You haven't been there for me in a long time. I've learned to cope. I'm just glad you're here with me now," Katlin replied quietly and pressed her lips to his cheek. They walked silently to the car, hand in hand. Alex needed that firm connection. He wasn't sure of anything else except that he'd try his best to make up for all the times he'd failed her, and there were many.

"Top, would you please take me to my condo?" Katlin asked.

"Certainly, little lady." Top's smile was filled with familial love. "Do you need a bodyguard tonight? Are you and the Ladies going out dancing or to dinner?"

"No, I have a dinner date with Alex." She smiled at him, and he remembered the hot kiss on the plane. "I'll be fine with him protecting me."

"Are you sure you don't need protection *from* him?" Top teased.

"I'm sure. I never need to protect myself from Alex, and he sure as hell doesn't need to protect himself from me." She smiled and leaned over to press a kiss to his cheek.

The warmth of her touch traveled to his heart. He squeezed her hand and smiled. He couldn't wait till supper... and he wanted her for dessert.

CHAPTER 25

When her cell phone rang, Katlin expected to hear Alex's voice, but it was Bret Reed, the computer expert for all of Guardian Security. He announced that he was waiting for her downstairs.

She checked herself in the foyer mirror, happy she'd decided to wear her hair down in soft curls that contrasted nicely against the royal blue wraparound dress that brought out the color of her eyes. The neckline wasn't revealing, but the folds of cloth that moved as she walked teased a man's imagination. Cinched at the waist, she looked curvaceous and very feminine. Her strappy blue high-heeled sandals made her legs look even longer. She needed to feel like a woman, not the camo-wearing, gun-toting Lady Hawk.

Katlin wanted Alex to desire her tonight because she sure as hell wanted him. Preferably touching her, everywhere. Tonight was the end of her celibacy. She pressed the button for the elevator with a confidence she hoped she could hold on to.

Alex now knew some of her secrets and seemed to be fine with the fact that she could never have children of her own. He knew that she'd asked Ty for a divorce the night before he left for the Middle East. There was more to that secret, but she wasn't ready to share. Not yet. Maybe she'd never tell him. That was history.

Then there was her biggest secret. Her real job. She had misled her friend to believe the Ladies of Black Swan were analysts. If her relationship continued with Alex, she'd tell him. Then he'd never want to have anything to do with her. The idea of having her best friend back in her life, then him rejecting her because of her job, would break her heart all over again.

The elevator doors opened, and she stepped in.

She had lived without Alex, or any man, for the past three years. She could do it again. But next time she'd be having regular sex with lots of men. Use them for her body's needs then move on. She could be like everyone else in her covert world…no one got too close. Relationships could get you killed.

Tonight was all about seduction…and sex.

She wanted to be desired and loved as a good friend, maybe even more. She could be a friend with benefits, and it'd been far too long since she'd had any male benefits. The thought of Alex touching her skin sent ripples of desire through her. She could practically feel his lips kissing down her neck and sucking a nipple into his mouth.

She glanced at her reflection in the mirrored walls. Thank goodness the folds of her dress hid her peaked nipples.

Bret met her at the door with an approving all-male expression he couldn't hide, although in his professionalism, he tried. Obviously, she'd hit the mark with her dress choice.

"Miss Callahan, it's a pleasure to meet you." Bret offered his hand, and she took it with a firm shake.

"Please, call me Katlin." She smiled at the man who had spent time behind bars for his outstanding hacking skills, glad to have him as a Guardian employee. The day might come when she needed those abilities to work on Section 7 computers.

"As you wish, Katlin." He was such a contradiction. He looked like a surfer with sun-bleached spiky hair and golden brown skin, but spoke like the highly-educated man she knew him to be. Obviously he'd spent his prison time at Club Fed on the Florida panhandle. These days, he spent more time behind a keyboard than on a surfboard.

Bret escorted her to the back door and took her hand as she stepped up into the SUV. The back seat was empty.

"Bret, where's Alex?" she asked as he buckled in. Maybe Alex been tied up at work.

"I have my instructions, Katlin, sorry," Bret said as he merged onto DuPont Circle.

"Which are?" she demanded.

"I was to pick you up at your condo and bring you to Guardian Security."

"That's it?" This was weird.

"That's it," he said.

Katlin sat back to enjoy the ride to the eleven-story, black-glass and chrome building that was the Guardian Security D.C. Center. Bret pulled into the underground garage, and the iron gates rolled closed behind him. He came around to the back seat and assisted Katlin out of the car. Her dress rode high on her thigh as she stepped down, but he kept his eyes on hers. The two walked to the elevator together, where Bret pushed number five, the Control Center level, and eleven, the apartment.

"Am I to meet Alex upstairs?" Curious and a bit intriguing.

"Just following orders. I'll log you in," Bret said as he exited on the fifth floor with a knowing smile. "Have a nice evening, Katlin."

"Thank you," she managed before the doors were completely shut.

When she stepped from the elevator on the top floor, she could smell onions and peppers mixed with some interesting spices. Her mouth watered as she inhaled and tried to identify each scent; garlic, basil, olive oil, and a few others that were too diverse to separate.

She walked to the apartment door and knocked rather than use her electronic master key button to let herself in. Alex answered, wearing a yellow polo shirt and faded blue jeans with a green spattered apron overtop.

He was barefoot.

Katlin burst out laughing. He looked good enough to eat. All hard angles. Very male. The short sleeves stretched over well-developed biceps. Damn. She had a thing for big, defined biceps. During their time in Miami, he'd never worn jeans. These were soft and faded from use, worn in all the right places.

Bare feet. But the spattered apron did her in. She could love this man, who, she knew, was all man.

"Do I look that funny?" Alex asked as he took her hand and pulled her into the apartment. He closed the door to control room eyes.

She felt his eyes drop over her from her head to the pink toenails peeking through laced sandals. Her skin tingled as though he'd touched her everywhere his eyes had roamed. A slow smile grew when his gaze met hers. She watched as the gold flecks in his eyes dimmed and heat darkened his expanding irises.

He backed her up till she was against the foyer wall. With one hand on each side of her head, he leaned in to kiss her. Before he touched her lips, he said, "I don't want to get anything on that beautiful dress, but I have to kiss you," and his full soft lips brushed over hers.

She grabbed his face and pulled it to hers, kissing him back hard and long. That was exactly what she needed right then. It was a perfect way to start a perfect evening.

When they finally ended the kiss, Alex came back for a quick one. He pushed off the wall and took Katlin by the hand to the kitchen.

"Something smells wonderful." She inhaled deeply. "Are you cooking?" She had no idea the man could do more than reheat pizza in a microwave.

"Yes. I didn't want to share you tonight," he explained. "We've spent so much time with other people and in vehicles in the past four days that I want you all to myself tonight."

"So you decided to cook for me rather than go out to dinner?" That was really sweet of him. "I had no idea you knew how to cook. What did you make?"

"Cuban pork with mango chutney, Spanish rice, and seared squash." Alex proudly announced the menu as he poured two glasses of an excellent Chardonnay then handed her one.

"I'm impressed. How long did you have to marinate the pork?" Katlin said then sipped the wine.

"Two days," Alex answered with guilt written all over his face.

"Wait one." Katlin caught the expression. "Where did you get the pork?"

"I went to see my mom, and this is what she was going to cook for dinner. We had a long talk about you, and she said you liked home-cooked meals...so we traded. She and my stepfather should be having their salad right about now at that great steak house over on H Street. We get Cuban pork, rice, and veggies," Alex said with satisfaction.

"You stole your mother's dinner? You bastard!" She accused.

"Hey, I sent them out to a great dinner in the company limousine on my credit card. They're having the time of their life." Alex smiled back and then took another sip.

"I love your mother, and she deserves tonight out on the town." Katlin leaned in and gave him a quick kiss. "You are forgiven, only because this means that I get to eat your mom's pork roast without having to put up with your gangsta-wannabe brother."

He looked at her with incredulity. "My Mom seems to know a lot about you. Exactly how often do you eat at my mother's house?"

"Sometimes," Katlin said sheepishly then hid behind a sip of wine. "She has the pictures of Nana Rosa's childhood home, too, by the way. I also brought her pictures of Jenny since you don't."

Alex took a deep breath and, on a sigh, said, "I forgot. I'm busy, you know, running ten offices and flying all over the United States."

"Business is more important than family?" Katlin raised her voice a little more than she should have, and she suddenly realized the subject was stirring her own shortcomings.

Alex took a drink of wine and looked into the glass as he swirled the golden liquid. "I guess I've let business rule my life for the past three years. I think I was trying to fill every hour with work so I didn't have to think about…other things."

"I resemble that remark," Katlin said with honesty, in a softer voice. "After Daddy…." She slammed her eyes closed. The pain of his death still hit her hard. It was a long second before she went on. "After he was gone, all I had was my work. Daniel went undercover in some godforsaken country right after Mom died, but he couldn't get away for Daddy's funeral. I found him, though, a few months later." Her grin was sarcastic. "I'm good at finding men who are hiding." She took a long drink and rolled the delicious wine on her tongue to sweeten her mood.

"I dressed as a hooker and picked him up in a grimy bar in Nicaragua." Katlin watched Alex's eyes pop wide. "Daniel was so surprised it was me but went along with it. I took him back to my hotel suite, and we spent the night talking about Mom and Daddy. He told me later that, when he returned the next day to the militia camp looking exhausted, the men all thought differently of our night together. So when I'm in the area, I always go see him."

"You were dressed as a hooker in a fucking Nicaraguan bar? Do you have any idea how dangerous that was? You could have been kidnapped, or killed." Alex's voice sounded almost angry.

"Yeah. That first time. I really wanted to see him." She shrugged and continued. "We, Daniel and I, inherited a small hotel in Costa Rica. It's really more like a bed and breakfast with only ten suites. It'd been an income-generating property for Mom and Daddy. We decided to make the Costa Rica compound for family only. We both needed a safe place to go or hide sometimes. If paying guests were there, they'd be in danger. So, now when my team is in that area of the world, we always stop in and see Daniel. Each of the Ladies takes a turn picking him up in a bar and bringing him to the compound. Section 7 doesn't know about him, and never will if I have my way."

"I'm glad you found him," Alex acknowledged as he sprinkled spices onto the squash that sizzled in the fry pan.

"Me too," Katlin admitted. She was truly grateful for maintaining some contact with her only sibling. "I was a little pissed at Uncle Tom for not telling me where he was or that Daniel worked for him in the CIA. You know what he had the gall to say? That I didn't ask the right question. Damn him." She took the last sip of her wine and refilled both hers and Alex's glasses.

"I think these are done so let's eat," Alex proclaimed with pride in his voice. Katlin turned toward the table and saw that he'd set it elegantly with a white linen tablecloth, tapered candles, and yellow napkins edged in white to match the yellow roses in the centerpiece.

Yellow roses. Her heart leapt. *He did this for me. He cooked for me. He knows me like no other man ever has.* She picked up the plates and brought them to the kitchen to make serving easier.

They took their time savoring each bite as they talked about his day and Guardian business. They finished the bottle of wine and opened a second and laughed at stories of events that each had missed in the past three years. Just two old friends catching up.

"I am so full I can't eat another bite. I hope you didn't make dessert because I have no room for it," Katlin said as she pushed her chair back from the table. "You cooked, so I'll clean up."

"It'll go faster if we both do it." Alex got up and reached for her. She stepped to him, and he couldn't wait any longer. He kissed her. She was so pretty in the candlelight. Her eyes sparkled like sunshine reflected on the deep blue of the ocean hundreds of miles from land. Her laughter warmed him to his soul where nothing but darkness and death, illuminated by tracer bullets, had touched him in years.

Katlin pulled back and asked, "Do you want dishes or leftovers?"

What he really wanted was for someone else to handle the mess so he and Kat could continue what they'd been doing. But the right thing to do was to clean up. "I'll handle the leftovers if you can grab the plates."

The two worked efficiently, as though they'd done this together for years. She looked so right working beside him in his kitchen. He had to touch her. Alex slid his hand over the small of her back as he passed behind her. When he slipped a pan into the sink for rinsing, Katlin hip checked him. Yes. That was the playful Kat he'd known for so many years.

Everything was completed within minutes. Alex refilled their wine glasses and headed to the tan microfiber and chrome couch in the ultra-modern living room. He propped his legs up on the dark brown leather ottoman that was the size of a love seat, grabbed the remote, and turned on classical music, which immediately surrounded them.

Stage set, he watched Kat carefully for clues as to where the evening would go. She'd been friendly but not overtly seductive, although that dress kept hinting at her rounded breasts. Maybe he'd start there.

But he'd learned long ago to let her set the pace. She'd always needed to be in charge, but someday she'd have to let it go and share the responsibility of her life. He could wait. He'd already waited a lifetime.

Katlin sat down beside him, kicked off her high-heeled sandals, and stretched her long shapely legs out next to Alex's on the ottoman. He wanted to feel those naked tight calves under his hands or, better yet, wrapped across his back as she pulled him into her.

Alex slid his arm around her shoulders and pulled her in. Having her body close to his warmed him inside like no other woman ever had, or could.

When she laid her head on his shoulder, he closed his eyes, thankful for small steps. He'd missed her more than he'd realized. Sitting beside Kat, thigh to thigh, hip to hip, Alex lazily ran his fingers up and down her arm as he told another story about his Marines onboard ship and the ridiculous competitions they held to stay in shape while crossing the ocean.

"Are you glad you got out of the Marines?" He knew Katlin tried to keep the topics neutral as Mozart filled the air.

"Yes. I wouldn't be living like this if I were still in. I'd be sleeping in those decrepit old barracks on Onslow Beach or in a tent in Afghanistan or Iraq or God knows where. I would never make this kind of money. I'm thirty years old and make more money than the Commandant of the Marine Corps with a hell of a lot less responsibility," he said. *And nobody dies on my watch.*

"I'm glad you like your new life," Katlin said with satisfaction. He still found it hard to believe she'd played such an important part in making his dream come true. How could he ever repay her for that generosity and trust? He'd find a way.

"It could be better though." Alex gazed down at her.

"How?" She looked up at him with anticipation. He bent and kissed her, gently at first, but the moment she nipped his bottom lip, he felt a bolt of desire shoot through every nerve in his body and merge in his lap. The erection he'd fought to keep under control all evening refused to listen any longer.

With such unleashed intensity, he could no longer hold back. He pulled her tight against him and dove into her welcoming open mouth. She responded in kind, meeting his need to be inside her. She tasted of good wine and spicy Caribbean food...and Kat. Their tongues tangled, and her essence awoke appetites that had lain dormant for many years. He was suddenly a starving man, and only she could feed him.

He wanted her. All of her. He wanted to push into her until they both shuddered in ecstasy. But she had to willingly share her whole body with him. He couldn't move too fast. She had to set the pace. Holding back took every ounce of control he had.

When he broke the kiss, Alex said, "I'm so glad you're here." He kissed her hard again, running his hand up and down her entire side, sliding over her silky hair, the soft skin that covered strong shoulders, her rounded hips, and down bare legs to naked feet. Tchaikovsky did nothing to soothe the deep desire to roll her back onto the couch and strip her bare, tasting every inch of her.

This time when they broke, breathlessly Katlin told him,

"I'm right here." She took his face in her hands and held him tight as she kissed him deeply, exploring his mouth with her tongue. The assault was an invitation he couldn't miss. She wanted to be as much a part of him as he wanted into her body.

He ran his fingers down the loose folds of the soft dress and cupped her breast with his hand then gently massaged it before he ran his thumb over her nipple. On a trip back across, she'd hardened to his touch. Her low moan of pleasure made his erection throb with every heartbeat.

He moved his hand under the fabric and traced the lace on her bra while he kissed his way down her throat. Her pulse rushed at the side of her throat and made his lips tingle. He touched the spot with the tip of his tongue, reassured the heated blood that hurried millimeters away matched his own.

Yes. She wanted him. He ran the tip of his tongue to the dip of her collarbone and licked. Her swift intake of breath made him smile deep inside.

Alex found the front clasp on her bra and had it opened with a flick. His hand moved to her bare breast to feel the firm curve, and her hardened nipple responded to his touch, peaking as he circled it lightly with one finger. She gasped as he continued kissing his way to her other breast. Her hands dove into his hair, and for just a millisecond, he feared she'd pull him away. Instead, she pressed him against her large mound. Relieved and reassured they both wanted this, he sucked the nipple into his mouth as his fingers pulled at the other pebbled tip.

CHAPTER 26

Hot waves slammed through Katlin and drenched her panties as Alex sucked first one nipple then the other, drawing them deep into his warm mouth. She could hardly breathe. The connected nerves felt as if he was sucking her between her legs, and she would explode if he'd only touch her there.

"Alex." She moaned his name and arched into him, offering him more. She hadn't let a man touch her like this in years. She hadn't wanted any man to. But tonight she needed Alex. She trusted him to reintroduce her to the pleasures of the body she'd denied herself far too long. Tonight, she'd prove to herself that she wasn't the frigid bitch the men at Section 7 thought. Or, worse yet, a man's sensibilities in a woman's body.

"Agh." The strangled noise escaped from her throat as he lightly pinched her nipple, and she automatically squeezed her legs together. She was so close.

Alex rocked his erection into her belly as he rolled onto his side, aligning his body with hers.

See. She was a woman. A woman who a man wanted, desired, not just as a female, as herself. Alex Wolf wanted

Katlin Callahan for who she was, not just an orifice for pleasure.

"Alex," she managed to say.

"Right here, babe." He looked up at her with eyes so dark brown all the gold flecks had melted in his heat.

"Please," she groaned in a whisper.

His hands stilled.

No. No. Alex's kisses, his hands, the warmth of his body against hers had stimulated the passion that had lain dormant for more than three years.

"Please...what?" His gaze held hers.

She needed him to touch her, remind her that she was a woman. Show her what it meant to be ravished once again. "Please, don't stop. I want you. Now."

Heat flared in his eyes, and relief washed over his face. He dragged his body over hers and ground his hips into hers. She couldn't miss his full, hard erection. Kiss-swollen lips met hers softly, and he took her bottom lip between his teeth.

"We'll get there." He rolled to the side and adjusted her the way he wanted then kissed her tenderly. Once again, he started down her throat to her breasts.

He moved his hand down her rib cage and gave her hip a not-so-gentle squeeze before he touched her bare leg. He dragged his fingers over her outer thigh and back down again to her calf. Slowly, he started back up again, this time on the inside of her leg, passing over her lace panties and pressing down in just the right spot before he moved over to the other leg. Had he done that a moment ago, she'd be flying right now.

She felt his hand move down the inside of her leg, sparking each nerve ending, slowly lighting the fires that made her burn. Up the outside of her leg then back down again. His hands were in constant motion, one hand attended to her breast while his mouth devoured the other. His right hand stroked her legs. In this position, all she could do was enjoy his every touch.

He finally stopped when he reached the apex and cupped her, pulling his long fingers slowly over her sex, lace panties the only barrier.

"Christ, I can feel your heat." His breath was short and shallow. "Tell me what you want, Kat." He smiled up at her with a fiendish grin and lightly ran his teeth across her over-sensitized nipple.

"Oh," was all that came out of her mouth. Her hips thrust against his hands, and all the muscles in her legs clenched as she rode the edge. It had been so long for her she couldn't remember her last man-induced orgasm.

His whole body stilled. She wasn't going to have one now either. *Goddammit.*

He kissed her between her breasts and just watched her as she regained her breath.

"Tell me, Kat. Tell me exactly what you want."

"You. I want you. Inside me. Now." The words came out between pants of breath.

He lunged for her and captured her mouth with his. When she opened this time, he thrust his tongue in and out. It was the way she wanted the rest of him. He lifted his face off hers only a few centimeters.

"I thought you'd never ask." His voice was deep and raspy, filled with need…for her.

She smiled and grabbed the back of his head, bringing his lips to hers. He gave her a quick kiss then leaned back.

"Not here. Not on a couch. I feel enough like a teenager as it is." He scooped her up and started to carry her the few feet to the bedroom. "I want you in my bed."

"Alex, put me down. I can walk." She hung on to his shoulders and wriggled.

"No. You might change your mind and walk away." Before she could say anything more, he covered her mouth with his. She was lost in his warmth, his strength, his wanton kiss.

He let her feet drop to the floor next to the bed but held her hips tight to him. She could feel his erection pressing into her belly.

"I've wished for this every minute since I saw you naked in the Miami apartment." He kissed her neck, just below her ear. "Just hearing your voice was enough to make me hard."

"I'm sure being held at gunpoint and the adrenaline letdown afterwards had something to do with it." She ran her hands up and down his back and kissed his cheek, the only thing she could reach. If he'd wanted her so badly, why hadn't he acted on it? *Because I wasn't ready, and he'd known it. He knows me all too well. But he's right in front of me now. And mine for the taking.*

He nipped her collarbone, and lust dropped straight to the knotted nerves between her legs.

He stepped back and removed her wide belt. At the same time, she reached for his and unfastened it.

She ran her hand the length of his zipper. Damn he was big.

Alex sucked in a short breath. "You can sleep in my bed anytime, but I prefer that I'm in it with you." He cupped her face with both hands and kissed her softly, as if to seal the request. His hands fell to her shoulders, and he started to shove her dress off them.

"No. This way." She tugged the hem up from the bottom and over her head.

Alex just stood and stared. His gaze started at her eyes and unhurriedly dropped as he studied her body. No one had ever looked at her that way. Ever. She worried that she didn't even come close to the starlets he'd been dating. They had perfect bodies, and hers was hard with muscles she kept strong through daily workouts, and she bore the scars of her profession. Katlin shifted her feet.

"You're so much more beautiful now." Alex was such a liar.

She immediately lowered her eyes and touched her scars. He grabbed her hands and pulled them behind her, cuffing them with one of his.

"No, they're beautiful too. They're so much a part of who you are." He tilted her chin up to meet his eyes. "You never need to be embarrassed about them. I'm so sorry I wasn't there to protect you." He kissed her, long and slow and sweet.

When he released her hands, she found the bottom of his shirt and dove her hands underneath. She wanted to touch his skin. Her fingers found rock-hard abs, and she traveled up to run her palms over his sprinkling of chest hair. His small male nipples fascinated her when they puckered like hers. She shoved his shirt up to his shoulders, and he broke their kiss to help her remove it then shucked out of his slacks, taking his boxers with them.

Katlin couldn't help herself. She gawked as his erection sprang free. She didn't remember him being that large. But it had been nearly four years since she'd seen an erection that close, over ten years since she'd seen his. Had her memories really faded, or was this a different man than he'd been before? She was certainly not the same woman he'd known in college.

"Nothing you haven't seen before, but I like the way you look at me."

"How's that?" Heat rushed to her cheeks. Oh, damn. She'd blushed.

"Hungry. Like you're starving and I just uncovered your favorite meal." He stepped to her, gently smoothing his arms around her and removing her bra at the same time. He kissed each breast and reminded her nipples of his previous ministrations.

Katlin spun up immediately, as if the last several minutes were long forgotten and he'd never stopped nurturing her body. Alex ran his hands to her hips, snagged the tiny strings of her thong, and guided them leisurely over her hips and down her legs.

Kneeling in front of her, he leaned in and buried his nose in the strip of blonde curls. He inhaled deeply. His fingertips dug into her hips, and he remained completely still for a long minute.

Abruptly, he was on his feet and had swept back the covers and placed her on the cool tan sheets. Alex stretched out beside Kat and stared into her eyes. Glints of gold had returned, and his face was now serious.

"Kat, are you sure about this?" Leave it to Alex to give her an out.

Oh, hell yes she was sure. "Are you trying to talk me out of it?"

"Christ, no. I want you more than I've ever wanted anyone." He glanced at his cock. "There's no hiding how much I want you. But I want to be sure it's right for you."

Katlin rolled on her side, face to face with Alex. His hand automatically landed on her hip.

She brushed a kiss across his lips before she took his hand and placed it on her mound. His lids lowered, and he sucked in a breath. Boldly, she guided his middle finger over her slick engorged nerves down to her opening. Without further encouragement, he slipped one finger inside her.

Katlin could hardly inhale. Each breath shuddered as she dragged it in. Assured he was now aware of just how ready she was, she told him, "This is right for us."

CHAPTER 27

Alex slipped two fingers into her, stretching her. Damn she was tight.

Katlin gasped.

"Am I hurting you, Kat?" He started to withdraw his fingers, and she caught his wrist.

Her gaze met his, and she begged, "No, please don't stop."

Thank God. He wanted her, no, needed her.

With his thumb, he encircled her point of passion and felt it harden as muscles within her grabbed his fingers and squeezed. It would be good, damn good.

He slipped his hand away and reached for his slacks. He always carried a condom in his wallet, usually two or three. There were none in the side table because he never brought women to the Guardian apartment. But Kat in his bed seemed right on so many levels.

Foil package in hand, he rolled back over.

Katlin froze.

"No." It was a command.

He saw no give in her stern face and hard eyes. Was she calling a stop?

"Alex, you don't ever have to protect yourself from me, and unless you know something that isn't in your Guardian medical file, you have nothing to give me except yourself."

"I've never—"

"That's obviously not true. You have a daughter."

"Damn thing broke. I was a poor college kid and bought cheap ones. Rachelle always insisted, even while pregnant. I've never had sex without one."

"I want the real you and the real me. You know I can't get pregnant." That might be true, but there were a lot of other worse things out there. Did he trust her? Was she as clean as he was? He had no idea where she'd been—there were parts of the world that had diseases without cures—and he had no idea who'd she been with in the past three years.

Plus, Ty had been unfaithful, at least once according to Kat. Probably more than that, given his record. Could he have inadvertently given Kat—

No. He would not go there. Not now. Not with Kat hot and so very wet next to him.

She was still in the Navy, and that meant she had to be tested constantly for disease, and it'd been well over three years since they'd buried Ty. Besides, Ty had always been adamant about protection. Once, he'd said he was scared Kat would cut off his dick if he gave her an STD. She probably would have done it too.

Alex took in the curves of Kat's soft body, her pebbled nipples that begged to be tasted again, and knew she was just waiting for him.

The condom package crinkled between his fingers.

He'd wanted her for more years than he cared to remember, or would admit. But he'd never....

Kat's eyes softened, and then she lowered them for a full second. When she opened them, they glistened in the low light of the bedroom.

Her voice was husky, but steady. "I'm still two men away

from virginity. One has been dead for more than three years, and the other is naked in this bed."

Alex wasn't sure how to respond to that new information. Kat had never taken a lover. He and Ty were the only men she had ever had. A major part of him liked that thought. He was the only man alive who had ever been inside this beautiful woman. There was something very comforting in that.

"No condom?" he asked.

"None needed," she assured him.

With his thumb, he flicked it over the side of the bed. Alex kissed her with all the gentleness and caring he had within him. She kept surprising him. Damn, what a woman. His woman. Bareback.

She changed the kiss and opened her mouth to him. When she dug her hands into his hair and pulled him to her, hard, he felt her desire. He ran his hands down the length of her again several times before he reached for her feminine softness. She was ready for him and rocked into his hand as he slipped first one then a second finger inside her.

"I want *you* deep inside of me, not your fingers," Kat said.

Alex settled between her parted legs and watched her. His eyes never left hers as he slid into her, just a little at first; she hadn't had a lover in a long time. Damn, she was tight. It felt wonderful. He held still and savored the feel of being surrounded by Kat and nothing else.

She studied him with frightened eyes. "What's the matter? Did I do something wrong?"

In a hoarse, breathless voice, he said, "Christ, no, Kat. You're unbelievably tight and so very hot, yet it's so soft. I've never felt anything like this before." He pulled out and glided back in easily, no lubricated condom between them, just him and Kat. It was incredible. Then he buried himself deeper into her, and it got even better. He held back, not wanting to hurt her, well aware he was a big man.

"More," she demanded and arched her hips, capturing

more of his length. He let out a sigh of relief as he withdrew slightly then buried himself entirely into her.

When her small whimper escaped, he stopped. "Give yourself a minute to adjust. It's been a while."

"Hell, no."

She raised her knees and levered her hips upward. *Oh, Jesus.* It was almost over before he got started when all her internal muscles grabbed him. A pleasure he'd never experienced before shook him to his very core. It wasn't merely her body that surrounded him. It was the unleashed essence of Kat. Christ, what this woman could do to him.

He moved within her and found his stroke as she rocked in counter balance. He bent to kiss her. "You are so perfect."

She smiled up at him, pleased with what he'd said or what he was doing, he wasn't sure. Her smile encircled his heart, which intensified every nerve ending. It was like coming home, but to a new home.

Vivaldi's *The Four Seasons* wafted throughout the apartment, violins amassing the tempo as if a planned accompaniment.

Alex wasn't going to last much longer, so he slid his hand between them and massaged her clit. Her whole body tightened in an instant, and she vibrated in ecstasy. Her internal muscles grabbed and took him milliseconds later. They fell together into blackness, both their bodies shaking in unison.

Still locked inside her, Alex rolled to the side, taking his weight from her, but held on to Kat as the waves of aftershocks rocked her world. Too exhausted to even speak, they fell asleep.

Katlin's satiated brain stirred when she heard a moan and felt warmth on her naked breasts. A cool breeze chilled her nipple. Had she fallen asleep on the beach in Costa Rica again? She listened for her teammates, the jungle birds, or the rakish monkeys but heard nothing, not even the lapping of the Caribbean Ocean as it licked the beach in front of her home.

She felt lips and kisses on her stomach, and heat jettisoned to liquefy between her legs. A scratchy five-o'clock shadow brushed her sensitive belly, and she could smell Alex. Spicy. Sweat. All male. Sex. She could smell the two of them.

She smiled as she opened her eyes.

"You still here?" She looked down her body at messy brown hair that she'd raked fingers through several times. Deep brown eyes appeared from between her breasts. God, she liked the way he looked, all disheveled, tousled, by her.

"The only place I'm going is right here." He lowered his head and licked the most intimate spot on her body. Her hips automatically thrust upward, and she gasped. Using tongue and fingers, he had her on the edge almost immediately.

Breathlessly, wanting to hold out for him, she called his name. "Alex."

"No, babe, this is all for you. Come for me." He rolled his fingers over and brushed across that magical spot. She fell uncontrollably as her eyes closed once more.

Before she could completely catch her breath, he was stroking her clit. "Once again. This time with me."

"I can't. Give me a minute," she managed between breaths. "Actually, I'll need a few."

He slid into her, all the way to the hilt, with one smooth stroke. He braced his forearms next to her head. "You can do this. You want this as much as I do."

She opened her mouth to beg for another minute to recoup, and his tongue slid in and out, in rhythm to his hips. The double assault stimulated her instantly, and then she was there, with him. As he slammed into her, she neared the edge again.

He lifted his head and stared at her with melted chocolate eyes. "There you are. Take us both. Now." She closed her eyes and concentrated on the tension he'd built within her.

"Oh no you don't. Look at me, Kat. Look at me and take me with you. We go together." His pace increased. How it was possible she didn't know, but he went even deeper. She wanted so much to just close her eyes and fall. But she couldn't.

His jaw clenched as he held back. "Kat...I..." He huffed. "I..." His eyes flashed golden at whatever he was going to say.

"Alex..." she cried out and tumbled into the longest orgasm she'd ever had in her life. She'd kept her eyes open long enough to see him arch and stiffen as he growled her name. She felt her body buck and every muscle clench and release, totally out of her control.

She was out of control...and didn't care. She was safe with Alex. Her body was anyway. Her heart was safe from any man because it was still in shattered pieces encased within a wall of ice.

Katlin felt him roll onto his back and pull her on top of him, still locked together. She was too exhausted to hang on and sprawled, her knees next to his hips, her arms surrounding his head. He kissed her temple and pulled the soft sheet and blankets over them both.

His heartbeat slowed, and she curled into his chest, her long hair draping them both. Alex brushed several strands away from her face and enveloped her in his arms.

"I'll never get enough of you." His whispered promise cradled her as Chopin's nocturnes accompanied them into sleep.

Exhausted from the best evening of her life, she lightly dozed with her ear an inch from Alex's slowly beating heart, lulling her into sleep. Katlin heard the music change to Wagner's *Ride of the Valkyries*. It sounded terrible, and somewhere in the distant realms of her barely-functioning brain, she wondered where he'd gotten such a horrible download. It was very mechanical, hollow in a way, not a chorus of symphonic instruments. The single word "important" screamed through Katlin's mind.

Fuck! It was her cell phone, and that was the emergency ring. One of the Ladies was in trouble…big trouble.

"Alex, I have to get that." She shot naked out of bed and dashed toward the living room, where her dress lay pooled on the floor. She patted the pockets then twisted to search the couch as Wagner played on. She reached deep into the seat cushions and finally found her phone. She swiped the screen.

"What?" she said too sternly.

"Katlin, I'm so sorry," Grace began. "I guess you're with Alex. I'm sorry,"

Another voice was heard in the background. "Give me that damn thing."

At full volume, Nita said, "Katlin, get your ass down here. Some fucker planted a bomb on Black Swan."

Snapping fully to her senses, Katlin repeated, "A bomb?"

CHAPTER 28

Alex leaped out of bed and stood close to Katlin, hoping to hear the conversation.

"A bomb?" he tried, unsuccessfully, to control his initial shock.

"Are you safe?" Katlin calmly asked into the phone. She glanced up at him and answered his question before he could ask. "I'm talking with Nita. She and the team found a bomb on Black Swan. I knew something was wrong." She held the phone so he could hear.

"Yes, it's molded C-4 wired in, on a timer to go off twenty minutes after you turn the Master switch on," Nita explained.

"Sonofabitch." Katlin hissed through clenched teeth. "I'm leaving Guardian now. Wait, I'll have to change. Don't touch anything. No telling who did it. I'll have to bring the HMX1 Wing Commander in on this. Keep it tight. No one in or out until I get there."

"Already locked down. And you're right. We're not real popular with a lot of people these days, especially those in South America...and Iraq...and Syria...well, shit, we've pissed off a fucking lot of people," Nita admitted.

"I'll call you from the car. Keep the lid on this one so tight a mosquito couldn't get in that hangar." Katlin disconnected.

Turning to Alex, she snapped, "You are now officially my bodyguard. We need a bulletproof vehicle with all the toys, now. We both need to change into black ops," she instructed as she slid her dress over her naked body and headed for the door.

Alex wasn't used to taking orders, but Katlin seemed to be in control of the situation. It was her plane, but he was livid that someone would try to kill Kat and her team.

"Where are you going?" Alex asked as he sprinted into the suite closet for the black clothes that were always there for him.

"Basement. I have clothes there," she yelled back.

She does? He'd never seen her clothes anywhere in the building.

"What? Wait a minute and I'll go with you," he said while grabbing black cargo pants, a black long-sleeve T-shirt, black boots and socks. "You have clothes in the basement?" he asked from inside the huge closet.

Katlin yelled back from what sounded far away, "I'll hold the elevator but hurry."

Alex slipped into black boxer briefs and carried an armful of black clothes and boots as he dashed to the door. He grabbed his holster, evenly weighted down by the two weapons, and slung it over one bare shoulder.

The elevator doors opened, and they stepped in. Katlin punched the S2 button, and the doors closed. Alex jabbed another button on the elevator panel and gave the control room instructions while he stepped into the black cargo pants. He was just glad the men had no idea how little she was wearing. And didn't that thought wake up his cock again.

The elevator doors opened into a cool, darkened concrete space. Katlin flipped on the overhead fluorescent lights and strode to a wall of storage lockers. She opened a small cabinet and pressed a board inside, which popped back to reveal a lighted keypad. Katlin punched buttons.

Well, damn. When was that installed? More secrets she kept from me. He didn't care that she was an owner of this company, he should have been told about this—

The whole wall moved open, and lights came on automatically within the large hidden room.

What the fuck?

Alex followed Kat into a brightly lit walk-in closet the size of the master bedroom upstairs. He was sure this hadn't been on the architectural drawings he'd approved when they renovated the building.

Formal dresses hung to the floor on one side, dozens and dozens of them in all colors. Along another side were short, club-style dresses and business suits with matching skirts and tailored slacks next to assorted silk blouses. Shelves with neatly folded cargo pants in black, green, white, gray, solids and camouflage patterns sat ready in one corner. Matching shirts were stacked above them, and small military boots lined the floor. Another wall contained women's shoes of every style and color. *Who needs that many shoes?*

Katlin quickly stripped off the dress, shook it, and hung it on a padded hanger with the clubbing dresses. Alex stopped to look at her bare backside as she reached for a sturdy black bra and wick-away panties. He wanted to cry as she covered the rounded breasts that he'd suckled and teased to hardened points. He'd intended to give them even more of his attention in the next round of lovemaking. When she bent to step into the panties, he couldn't stop himself. He strode up behind her and grabbed her hips. Katlin froze.

"Oh, God. I don't want our night to end." Alex ran a line of kisses down her back. "Promise me, if we can deal with this quickly, you'll come back here with me?"

Still bent over, she pulled up her panties, wiggling her delicious butt cheeks against his solid erection. He gritted his teeth to control the urge to free himself and push into her one more time. It would be so tight given this position, so fast on his part.

Kat stood, one vertebrate at a time, before she turned to him. She ran her hand over his hardened shaft then looked at him. "We'll do that, and yes, we'll do that, too." Had she read his mind, or had he read hers when she taunted him? Hell, he didn't care, as long as he got to slide into her again and again. Any position and way she wanted it.

"Let me take care of the bomb first. Then I promise I'll take care of this." She stroked him one more time then gently squeezed.

Bomb. The word screamed through his brain. Someone was trying to kill her. His Kat. No. Not after what they'd just shared. Not since she was back in his life. He'd kill the fucker who'd planted a bomb on her plane.

Alex cupped her cheek and placed a forceful kiss on her smiling lips. "We'll get him." He stepped back and sat on a white padded bench to put on his boots.

Katlin took the sandals she'd carried down from the apartment and placed them on a shelf next to others. Within seconds she grabbed black pants and stepped into them as she moved toward a stack of black shirts, where she picked the one off the top. She slid it over her head and stuffed her arms down the long sleeves then picked up socks and boots.

Barefoot, she padded to a numeric panel next to the door, where she entered a code. The door to a large black gun vault opened, and she took out a black shoulder holster before she picked out a handgun with two extra ammunition magazines.

She turned to Alex, who was fully dressed in black, with his shoulder holster stretched in place. "You ready? Need another gun?" She pointed to the gun safe.

"I'm good. There are more in the car if we need them." As

he followed her out, Alex gave the room one last perusal. He wondered if every Guardian Center had one of these. Katlin stopped briefly to enter a code that shut the doors.

Minutes later, Alex maneuvered though the light D.C. traffic toward Virginia in the customized Mercedes SUV. Katlin slid on black socks and twisted her long blonde hair covering it with a black watch cap. Multitasking, she punched in numbers on her phone and laid it on the console between them as she pulled on silent-soled military boots. "I've got to get ahold of Colonel Bower, HMX1 Commander," she explained. He nodded and changed lanes.

The man answered on the second ring and identified himself in a festive voice. She'd interrupted a party.

"Is this a secure line, sir?" Katlin asked without introduction.

Alex had watched the complete transition of his friend, and lover, Kat, into this completely other person, code name Lady Hawk. When she'd slipped out of that sexy dress and into black baggy cargo pants and a loose-fitting black shirt, she'd wholly transformed into a federal agent. Her body language had changed, and she'd become authoritative and decisive. But he knew that underneath the dark clothes she was still filled with him. They hadn't had time to shower, although he'd heard her in the bathroom.

"Well, no, it's my cell phone," the colonel said pensively over the phone's speaker.

"Hold on." Katlin pressed several buttons and watched for a green light as she speed-laced her boots. "We are now secure. Colonel, listen very carefully, code name Black Swan."

"Yes, ma'am," he said as if coming to attention. Alex grinned as he considered that Kat commanded the respect of a Marine colonel.

"We have a problem. Meet me there in twenty minutes." She disconnected the line.

Holy shit. Kat just hung up on a senior officer who wears eagles on his shoulders. Who the hell is this woman? He was beginning to doubt she was just an analyst.

Alex barely listened as Katlin talked at length with Tori and Nita about the bomb while Grace and Lei Lu went over every inch of Black Swan. Fortunately, no other troubles had been found.

He pulled into the small parking lot at the ugly green hangar on MCB Quantico. She had badged them through the main gate with only three words, priority one alpha. The headlights caught Colonel Bower and a lieutenant colonel, both dressed in Marine desert camouflage, as they impatiently waited outside the door to the hangar. A young Marine guard pointed his M4 at the senior officers. *Good for him for holding his post.*

"I'll be right back," Katlin told him as she got out. Without a word, she approached the Marines, put her finger to her lips, and shook her head. She pointed to her fingertips and to her touch phone, signaling Colonel Bower to lay his fingers on the display area. When he did, it scanned his fingerprints.

That's a cool app. Alex waited patiently in the running vehicle and watched his woman in command mode.

Katlin looked at the display then nodded and pointed to the SUV. Both men wordlessly got in the back as Katlin slid into the shotgun seat. She held up her index finger to signal silence until she had pressed a few numbers on her phone's keypad.

She finally spoke, "This vehicle is now soundproof in case someone is listening with a directional dish mic. We are emitting lots of white noise outward, but we still need to keep our voices quiet," she explained as she looked around the car at all three men. *Another cool app. She has lots of new toys. I wonder how we could use that technology for Guardian.*

"I am Lady Hawk, and he's with me," she said, nodding toward Alex. "I don't know who the hell you are, Lieutenant Colonel, but from this moment on, Colonel Bower is responsible for everything you hear. What you already know can get you killed. Neither of you two have the security clearance to even see the plane in that hangar, but we have a problem, and I mean *we*," she said as her gaze swept the vehicle.

She continued, "Some sonofabitch put a bomb on board our plane and wired it to blow twenty minutes after the Master switch is turned on." Alex winced at the picture that truth painted.

"My team has gone over every inch of the plane and found nothing else. Understand this, gentlemen. Someone put a bomb on a top-secret jet less than a thousand feet away from the presidential helicopters. All of which are guarded by your men. *We* have a problem." The Marines stiffened their backs and carefully listened as Katlin continued to explain the situation.

"We landed here less than twelve hours ago. I had a bad feeling as we were leaving the hangar. I had the senior NCO, a staff sergeant, rotate the guards, but that obviously didn't take care of it. We need to keep a tight lid on this because none of us can afford for this information to get out until we've identified the perpetrators. I want you to interrogate every person who walked within thirty feet of this hangar today. You need to give to Alex the social security numbers of every one of them." Kat looked directly at Alex and gave him a decisive nod.

He now knew his role in this. He texted Top Cooper to assemble men and get them to the hangar ASAP.

It was now obvious Kat didn't want Section 7 to know about the bomb. So did she suspect them? Shit. She could be in more jeopardy than he'd ever considered. An enemy from within was so much more dangerous than an outside source.

Turning to Alex, Kat ordered, "Run them through like an employee, especially finances. Money changed hands here. Look deep. Somebody turned and decided to become a terrorist against the U.S. government." The Marines looked at each other with intensity. Katlin caught the exchange.

"Colonel, I don't know if I can even trust you, but I have to right now. There's a possibility that my own agency did this, perhaps to test all of us, but more likely it was meant to kill my team. We are the only ones who fly this plane." She finally took a deep breath and exhaled slowly.

"Colonel, I need you to find the bastard who planted that bomb. Then I can find the sonofabitch who hired him. I need EOD to get it off our plane, now."

She turned toward Alex. "I want the plane fingerprinted by your men and run through Guardian. Use as few people as possible. Every person we add to this circle endangers all our lives exponentially."

Katlin looked from one man to another. "We need to find this asshole and right now. Understood?"

"Yes, ma'am," both Marines replied.

Alex sent another text to Top outlining the added assignment.

Katlin reached for the door handle, hesitated, then turned to the Marines in the back seat and warned, "By the way, all my team are women. Be smart men and never let their looks fool you." She opened the passenger door and led the way to the hangar, where she flashed her badge, which was simply a metallic black swan. The young Marine opened the door for her.

Colonel Bower took obvious pleasure as he ordered the Marine who'd held him at gunpoint. "Follow me, Marine."

The lieutenant colonel gathered all the Marines in and around the building and lined them up to begin the interrogation.

"Lady Harrier, you go with Colonel Bower. Lady Falcon, you're with the lieutenant colonel," Katlin ordered. "Find someplace to interrogate the guards. Hostile if necessary. Find this fucker and everyone who helped him."

Twenty minutes later, the door opened, and Top Cooper strode in wearing the authority he'd perfected while serving as both a master gunnery sergeant and a sergeant major. Behind him stepped several heavily armed Guardian men, who took up positions at the entrances while others attacked Black Swan with fine florescent powder to find fingerprints.

Bret sauntered in with a long-haired-surfer-dude attitude and a laptop under each arm. "Katlin, I hope you were able to enjoy most of your evening. Mr. Wolf, where do you want me to set up?"

"This is her show," Alex said and looked to her for direction. "I'm just here for personal protection for Lady Hawk." He emphasized her code name, hoping no one had overheard Bret.

"Lady Hawk, where can I set up?" Bret raised his eyebrows as he spoke.

She held up one finger to him and called, "Lady Kite." Lei Lu jogged over to their location. "Lady Kite, I'd like you to meet Bret, Guardian's computer guru. I need you two to run everybody. Go deep and wide. Find the money."

They soon had a scarred table filled with computer equipment. The two geeks worked totally in sync, speaking in the language of computers. Alex had initially been concerned when Top had suggested Bret because he wasn't former military, but he spoke the language of code and flirted with Lei Lu as his fingers flew over the keyboard. Lady Kite, Alex mentally corrected himself. We're in theater here.

Grace was busy with the EOD officer, who had arrived within an hour to remove the bomb.

Excellent, Alex thought as he took in the orderly chaos.

It was after three in the morning when the first confession was made.

"Lance Corporal Patterson said he'd been approached around seventeen hundred hours by a white male with short dark hair wearing a black suit, pressed white shirt, and black tie in aviator sunglasses. The man produced a Homeland Security badge and showed him orders to plant a fictitious bomb onboard your plane as a test," Col Bower reported to Katlin, Alex by her side. "The suit claimed he would return the tomorrow at zero-nine-thirty with bomb-sniffing dogs and handlers for a training exercise. LCpl Patterson checked with the Non-Commissioned Officer In Charge, a Staff Sergeant Johnson, who seemed to know all about it." The colonel took a deep breath and washed his face with his hand before he continued.

"Ma'am, I don't have a SSgt Johnson," he confessed, shaking his head. "Staff Sergeant Stein, who is now on duty, had replaced Johnson at nineteen hundred hours, the normal time. Stein didn't know Johnson. but per SOP," he looked at Katlin and unneededly explained, "Standard Operating Procedure, we move people around every few months and have new men cycling in all the time. Stein gave a detailed description of the man, though. He also said the turnover went as usual. Stein's a good man. He's been with me for over a year." The colonel sounded sincere in his trust of this man.

"Upon questioning SSgt Stein, he showed me the faxed orders in the log book concerning the Homeland Security bomb training. Your teammate, Lady Harrier, is damn good. She looked over the fax and caught it for the forgery it was. My men aren't trained to look for falsified documents, but they will be now." The colonel sounded apologetic and humbled.

"Col Bower, could SSgt Stein work with our computer team to create a picture of this Johnson?"

"Certainly." Loudly, the colonel called, "Stein, front and center."

By five in the morning, the bomb was headed to The Basic School range, where new Marine officers and FBI agents in training would get a rare look at a chunk of C-4 being exploded. Katlin let the colonel decide the fate of LCpl Patterson and Johnson, if found.

"Colonel," Katlin said, "Guardian Security will continue to protect our plane until it's discovered who planted the bomb."

"Understood," the colonel said with a nod. "We've fingerprinted and questioned every man here and on the earlier shift, except of course the mysterious SSgt Johnson. Guardian Security has all the pertinent information. I've put everyone on lockdown till further notice. Is there anything else?"

"I think we've got everything covered," she said. "Thank you, Colonel. I'd appreciate it if you'd go home and sleep before you file any reports. I'll know more by noon and contact you then."

"It's your bird and your call." The Colonel rubbed his tired eyes then shifted his gaze to Katlin. "It may sit in my hangar, but ultimately, I report to you on this. Since you called me, I've had teams going over every inch of each helicopter we designate as Marine One. They've found nothing, so it looks like your team may have been the only target."

That reality stung Alex to his core. Someone wanted Kat's team dead. Somewhere in the recesses of his mind, he'd known that Kat was a target. His greeting at gunpoint in Miami was proof that she knew it and lived with it daily. But to hear Col Bower say it seemed to make it real. Damn. Alex wanted to sweep her out of there and wrap her in the protection of Guardian and his arms in the penthouse apartment. He wanted—no, needed— to keep her safe.

Lei Lu staggered over. "Lady Hawk, we need some sleep. My eyes are blurring, and my mind is fading. Bret and I are going to crawl into Black Swan and curl up for a few hours. The computers are running a facial recognition search right now based on the drawing SSgt Stein and LCpl Patterson gave us, so we have a few hours. It'll beep us if it finds anything. You look tired, too."

"I am." Suddenly she sounded exhausted. "I'll catch a power nap before facing the director in a few hours."

Fuck. She had to go into the office…and meet with Jack-ass. Alex couldn't protect her from her boss, either.

Grace walked up as Lei Lu left. "I want to go over the plane one more time with the Section 7 mechanic who just now showed up. I called him in under the guise that we had an electrical problem on the flight from Miami. He's agreed not to report any findings until after noon. That should give you enough time to determine if this was a Section 7 test. It would be just like those jerks to pull something like this on us."

"Yeah, but it doesn't feel like them." Katlin yawned. "Finish up as quickly as you can then get some sleep."

"Sure thing." Grace scanned Kat's face. "You headed home for some shuteye?"

"Yes. I have to face Jack-ass and charges of insubordination in four hours." Kat shrugged.

"It'll be okay," her friend reassured her as she slid both arms around her and hugged her tight. "Jack's just jerking you around." She gave her one last squeeze and trotted off to the steps to Black Swan.

In the parade of final reports, Top Cooper strode up to Katlin and Alex. "Smith will take Tori and Nita back to D.C. Alex, if you'll get Katlin to her condo, I'd appreciate it. I'll stay here and see that everything is secure through the next shift change then take Grace home, Lei Lu, too, if she's ready."

"Sounds like a plan," Katlin agreed as she hugged him. "Thanks for everything. Tell Gina I'm sorry to take you away for the night."

"No problem. She was exhausted from work today and crashed as soon as she got home. The intensive care unit was overflowing and had her hopping for a full twelve hours."

"Then you didn't miss much," she kidded as she poked him in the ribs.

"Probably not. I'd have been here to take care of you, even if she was ready, willing, and able." He pecked her on the cheek.

It was six in the morning when Alex pulled into Kat's parking space at the rear of the building.

"I need to sleep for the next two hours before I go to the office this morning. You're dead on your feet. Come on up. We are just going to sleep, though." Katlin's invitation was sweet, but he was exhausted before they'd left Guardian.

Alex got out and threw a very tired arm around her shoulders. She slipped her arm around his waist, and they leaned into each other as they managed the trek to her apartment.

Too tired to even talk, they took off their boots at the door and stumbled to her bed, where Katlin and Alex fell onto the comforter. She pulled up the extra blanket she kept folded on the end of the bed to cover them, and they quickly fell asleep in each other's arms.

CHAPTER 29

Katlin stared at her desk, which was hidden under piles of files, a small stack of mail, and a dozen pink call notes.

I should really come here more often and take care of this crap.

She'd just picked up her second envelope when Jack Ashworth, Director of Operations and her nemesis, walked by. "My office. Now."

Fuck. She rose and followed him past a line of mostly empty, glassed-in offices designated for team leaders to the solid oak door of the corner office.

Dressed in his thousand-dollar gray wool suit, starched white Italian shirt, and burgundy silk power tie, Jack moved with the authority he wielded. At forty, he was one of the most powerful men inside the Beltway and one of the most attractive on all levels. With Jack's natural good looks, gym-toned body, international influence, and inherited money, women begged to run their fingers through his hundred-dollar haircut and kiss his square jaw line.

But not Katlin.

He had once used his six-foot two-inch frame, and position as her boss, in an attempt to rape her, *in the nature of the mission.* He'd claimed sex with her was essential to maintain their cover.

Bullshit.

It was against agency rules and could have gotten her fired. Not him though. No one dared touch the golden boy who knew more international secrets than any one man should hide. Besides, he was a card-carrying member of the Section 7 men's club. Katlin was nothing more than a test subject in an experiment that could fail so easily and set women's equality back decades. She needed to protect not only her job, and those of her team members, but to shatter the glass ceiling set by Congress. And Jack held all the power over her and he wasn't afraid to use it.

She had known for some months, before that appalling night, of his desire for her as a woman, the way no boss should. She'd always discouraged his advances, but when he'd assigned himself to the mission, she had no choice but to pretend to be his wife.

Jack had openly enjoyed playing house, sparring verbally with her. He'd told her later that he loved her quick mind as well as her sharp tongue then suggested some things she could do with that tongue. He'd told her, more than once, that he loved that she cooked for them while under cover. She did it because she liked to cook, and it went with the good-little-Stepford-wife role she played during that op. He had used the L word far too often for Katlin's comfort in a boss/employee relationship.

Every minute of their interaction on that op had been watched by both sides, and she played her role very well. Maybe too well, a consideration she'd had dozens of times afterwards. She'd actually enjoyed the quiet evenings in their pretend living room as they read and watched the news. She could see herself living that life—not with him of course—but sharing a home with someone she loved.

She'd almost had that life with Ty, but she was never sure

of his unconditional love. She also questioned his fidelity, which turned out to be right. He had been a lying cheating bastard. Never would she live like that, again. She'd live alone forever before she'd trust a man with her heart again.

She knew Jack had enjoyed sharing a bed with her most of all, but per standard operating procedure, she drew the line at sex, as a good agent should. Besides, the entire house had lots of eyes and ears everywhere, except the master bedroom and bathrooms. Section 7 was watching as closely as the bad guys who had wired in their own audio and video. It was a dangerous game they played as a very select audience watched.

The operation ended badly when a wrong move by Jack forced Katlin to take collateral damage. She had been forced to shoot an innocent man in order for the two of them to escape. That act tore at her soul, although she had confessed her sin and done penance prescribed by the priest. God may have forgiven her, but she hadn't forgiven herself. She would never forgive Jack.

She'd written the truth in her After Action Report, but Jack had removed page twenty-six, the incriminating information, before he filed it. Thankfully, Katlin had always kept copies of everything. She held the page over his head as blackmail and was, honestly, insubordinate on a regular basis.

As she closed the door behind her, Jack started in on her.

"Who the hell were you with in Miami and again here in D.C. last night?" Jack demanded as he placed his coffee cup on his oversized mahogany desk that contained only a phone, three computer screens, a leather desk pad, and a pen set.

"How do you keep this desk so clean?" Katlin asked, remembering her own pile a foot high and ignoring his question.

"Who were you with?" he repeated with impatience.

"That's none of your goddamn business," she snapped

with no tolerance whatsoever and anger fueled by lack of sleep.

"It is my business. You are my business," he insisted.

"Is this business, or is it personal, Jack?" Katlin asked, leaning over his desk, looking him directly in the face. He was such a practiced liar, but his eyes often gave him away.

Changing the subject, slightly, Katlin asked, "Did you make this insubordination accusation go away, or do I need to make sure POTUS gets page twenty-six in the next hour?" To protect herself, she'd set things in motion, a plan that, with the click of her phone, ensured the President of the United States would receive her official resignation, a sexual harassment complaint with all the supporting documents, and a viable threat to post everything about Black Swan to the Internet if he didn't fire Jack immediately.

Yeah. She virtually had the man in front of her by the balls. And he knew it.

He stared back at her for a long three seconds before glancing away. "The director still wants to see us. We're going to get a little lecture about working together. Nothing gets written up in our folders."

Ah. So he was in trouble for this too.

She inwardly smiled but allowed only a stern look on her face. "Jack, I'm warning you. You have crossed the line several times in the past few months, and I won't tolerate it. Stay the hell out of my private life. You do not have any claim on me except to assign me as part of the Black Swan Team to agency operations. You are my boss and *nothing* more," Katlin said as controlled as she could make her voice while seething with resentment.

Jack's intercom beeped, and his executive assistant said, "The director wishes to see you now."

Katlin shut her eyes, composed herself, and followed Jack through a connecting side door into the director's office.

Seventeen minutes later—after a speech on how important

it was for the two of them to work together and try to get along—Katlin's hands were sore from squeezing them together. She'd been bitched out before, and the director didn't get any cherry this time, but he'd had his say, and it was now over. They'd move on, business as usual. She did her job, very well. No one could complain about that.

As they rose to leave, the director said, almost in passing, "I heard you found a bomb on your plane."

Katlin spun to face him and said with fury, "Yes. Did you have it put there?"

Resentment sparked in the senior civil servant's eyes. "Certainly not. Why would we do that?"

"To test us." She threw the accusation at him.

"I don't need to test you with a bomb on your plane." His face tightened. "I test you every time I sign the order to send you out."

True. She was glad he saw it that way.

"And we have never failed an operation," Katlin said proudly. "Do you have any idea who planted that bomb?"

"Not yet but we're working on it," Jack answered for his boss, letting everyone know that he was on top of the situation.

"Katlin," the director said as she and Jack were at the door, "get your desk cleaned up and sleep. The Ladies of Black Swan fly back to the sandbox tonight, whether we know exactly who planted that bomb or not. We're sure it's related to your assassination of al Jamil."

"Yes, sir," she replied and walked out of his office, back into Jack's.

As soon as the door closed, Katlin grabbed Jack's arm and said, "How did you know about the bomb?"

A sly smile crossed his too-handsome face. "I know everything that happens with you."

"Fine, then, who planted it?" she demanded.

He stared at her a long minute before answering. "Your

next assignment. We're confirming Intel right now, but my bet is on Turhan al Jamil, brother of Nassar. We tracked two of his lieutenants coming across the Peace Bridge at the Canadian border six hours after you landed on U.S. soil and have been watching them every minute. They spend a lot of time on their cell phones, which are encrypted so we don't have ears on them. We think they bought some local talent here in D.C., mercenaries, who posed as Homeland Security and that Marine staff sergeant."

Katlin was awed by how much Jack knew and wondered if the hangar was bugged. Of course it was. Jack had eyes and ears everywhere.. *I should have thought of that before. I'll have Nita check it out and tap into it for us.*

Jack tried to put his arms around her. She abruptly pushed him away and took a step backward to increase the distance between them.

"Katlin, I wouldn't let them get to you. We were already scrambling other teams to take control of the hangar when your Ladies showed up last night."

He looked at her intently. "I would go crazy if anything happened to you. You know how I feel. I will do anything within my means to protect you."

"As my employer, I would expect that." Katlin also knew Jack would go much further than his governmental position allowed to watch her…and yes, to keep her. "But that doesn't give you permission to invade my private life. I have a life outside of Section 7 that does not include you, Jack. When, and if, my personal life and my professional life clash, you're not going to like my decisions. If you ever interfere with my personal life again, I'll shoot you, without hesitation."

"Are you fucking Alex Wolf?" Jack went straight to the point.

So, his earlier question about who she'd been with in Miami and last night had been a test. "My relationship with Alex is none of your business." Thank God they had been in the Guardian apartment last night, or Jack would have gotten a first-hand look at her doing exactly that. She'd have Nita sweep her D.C. condo for Jack's bugs as soon as she could send a text.

"He was at the hangar last night," Jack accused. "You used his civilian corporation for Homeland Security business. How do you know Wolf didn't plant that bomb? He was on the Black Swan from Miami."

"First of all, I own that civilian corporation." After the words left her mouth, she regretted telling him.

Jack looked startled. This was obviously news to him.

"And secondly, Alex would never do anything to hurt me. I trust him implicitly, which is more than I do you." Katlin turned and walked from the room.

"The file is on your computer. You heard the director. Wheels up at midnight," Jack said to her back.

At her desk, Katlin carefully read the entire mission file, memorizing it and organizing her operational plan. Then it took two hours to clean off her desk and another to handle the missed phone calls. Several of her male counterparts dropped in to say hello and discuss business and pleasure. She kindly turned down two offers for lunch and another for supper.

Midafternoon Jack walked by and looked at her through the glass then turned and came into her office. "You look exhausted. I know you had a rough night, and this morning was no joy. Go home. Get some sleep," he said with real compassion in his voice. "Let Grace and Tori fly tonight. They've been asleep for the past few hours."

Katlin looked at him wondering how he knew that. "Trackers," was all he said as he exited her office. Every agency employee who worked in the field had a tracking beacon implanted in an artery, which was powered by his or her own heart. A computer in Bio Ops recorded every heartbeat as a tech watched the feed from dozens of agents recording their activity. All this information was available to Jack at his fingertips.

"Thanks for letting me get out of here early, Jack," she said to his back. He turned and smiled at her warmly with brilliant white, perfect teeth. He was gorgeous, and that smile usually got him whatever he wanted, especially from women. But not her. Ever.

"You're a field operator." He stared at her, as though taking a mental photograph of her sitting behind her desk. It didn't happen often, that was for sure. "I know how much your type hates desk duty."

Twenty minutes later Katlin grabbed her briefcase, stuffed papers she deemed important and essential mission information into it, and headed for the agency car that would take her home.

Disappointment washed over her as she walked through the maze of offices on her way out. She'd hoped to spend more time with Alex, especially in bed. She had thoroughly enjoyed her re-indoctrination into sex last night and had been looking forward to more fantastic orgasms at the hand, mouth, and cock of her new lover.

Exiting the oppressive building, she scanned the lot for her ride home and saw the man of her thoughts.

Alex stepped out of a Guardian SUV parked at the curb. The way his cargo pants pulled across that tight ass of his was enough to make her panties wet, wanting her hands on those naked buns as he pushed into her. His gray polo shirt hugged powerful biceps and covered a chest she knew to be sprinkled with hair that had abraded her oversensitive nipples each time he'd slid into her.

A huge smile broke out at the sight of him. Maybe she could have a few more hours in his arms. She had been ordered to go to bed.

CHAPTER 30

Alex had been having a mellow morning, satisfied by the best sex he'd had in years. Even all the shit that had rained down afterward, and through the long night, couldn't dampen his mood. He'd made love with Katlin Callahan, and if he died in the next minute, he'd die happy.

"Excuse me, Mr. Wolf." Brett interrupted his thoughts with a knock on his door. "I...I remembered but couldn't put my finger on it...I knew I'd seen that name before..."

"Brett, just spit it out." Alex had never seen his computer geek flustered like this before.

"She...Miss Katlin..." Brett shook his head. "I can't believe that the gorgeous woman of yours is Lady Hawk. But last night, seeing her in action..."

Alex smiled. "Yeah, wasn't she something?" She'd been fucking awesome. In command mode, his Kat had been a lioness hooked on a scent last night, and her pride of women were equal to her every move. Damn they were magnificent to watch. Kat's Navy officer training shone through as she analyzed each element of the situation and came to her conclusions.

Brett looked at him with wide-eyed shock. "Mr. Wolf,

she's a fucking assassin with a confirmed kill count of sixty-eight. And those friends of hers aren't far behind." He jabbed at the paper in his hand. "Lei Lu, that tiny piece of Asian delight that I fantasized about all night, has over twelve kills...with her bare hands. I dreamed about those hands—"

Alex cut him off. "I don't want to know. Take a deep breath. What the hell are you talking about? Assassins? Kill counts? What the fuck, Brett?"

The casual surfer-dude persona was gone, and a frightened twenty-five-year-old man stood in Alex's office. Vibrating.

He dragged in a dramatic breath and, on an exhale, explained. "I knew I'd seen the name, Lady Hawk, before, when I was hacking around buried government files. I thought it was a cool name, and it stuck in the back of my mind."

"Close the door and sit down," Alex ordered. He thought it was a cool handle, too, then remembered Kat had said she got it because of him. He couldn't imagine why though.

As soon as Brett's ass was in the chair, he bounced up and started to pace. "So, when Miss Katlin used that code name last night, and I knew we weren't supposed to say their real names in front of the Marines, I had to go find it again."

Oh fuck. "Whose top-secret files did you hack last night, and is there any way they can trace you to Guardian?" Alex had to protect what was his, his company and his men.

Brett stopped in his tracks and smiled. "I used Lei Lu's computer when she was asleep. It was running that facial recognition program through some impressive data bases and...well...I was able to jump off in places and run a quick search here and there."

Alex let out a long, slow breath. "So, Lei Lu will be arrested, not you." How the hell was he going to explain that to Kat?

"No, that's the thing." Brett started pacing again. "She had access to all kinds of cool places and secret files at all levels. It was easy. I didn't have to—" He glanced at Alex. "I just mostly looked around at what was there in front of me."

"And…" Alex encouraged.

Brett took a deep breath. "Black Swan is the code name for a team of female assassins. Your girlfriend, Katlin, is their leader, and Lei Lu is their computer expert and spotter for the snipers in the group. She's also the expert in hand-to-hand as well as a pilot, and she's smart as hell. Like Mensa smart. They all are."

Brett laid the paper on Alex's desk. "Mr. Wolf, do you think they're being friendly with you because you are their next target?"

Alex burst out laughing. "No, Brett. I can assure you I'm not a target, and neither are you."

"Then what do they want with Guardian Security?" Brett's eyes darted around the room as though looking for a spy in every corner.

Alex hesitated, but the truth would come out soon anyway. "Miss Katlin, and I, own Guardian Security, Inc. She's my silent partner." Alex wondered if he should tell others about Kat's ownership. Every employee should know who she is on sight and treat her with the same respect he receives. He put that memo on his mental To Do list.

"She's my boss?" Brett's jaw dropped.

"No, I'm your boss. I'm the managing partner." Alex hoped that clarified things for him, and for anyone else Brett would discuss this with. Sometimes his men were bigger gossips than women.

"Did you know all this?" Brett jabbed at the papers on Alex's desk.

Alex wasn't about to admit that Katlin had lied to him. Continuously. According to the information in front of him, she was not an analyst for Homeland Security. She was a fucking international assassin, doing their dirty work in the bowels of the world. Not a place he wanted her to even know about and certainly never go there, to deal with the dregs of the world, interact with those animals. She should be safe in her D.C. condo, protected by Guardian Security…and by him.

Alex looked up at Brett. "You don't breathe a word of this to anyone. This kind of information in the wrong hands can get them killed." And the thought of Kat as a target was devastating. But someone had found their plane and tried to blow it up. How much of a target was she? If his computer geek could track down their identity, others could too.

He needed to talk to Kat. Right now.

"Brett," Alex ordered, "find out where Section 7 is located."

Thirty minutes later Alex pulled to the curb in front a nondescript, governmental-looking brick building with no outward indication of which alphabet agency was inside. His plan was to go in there and find Katlin. Then he could get some answers. Maybe what Brett had shown him was misinformation. The government was good at spreading lies to cover truths. Perhaps Section 7 had used Katlin and her friends as decoys, and that was why they needed his men as bodyguards.

Deep down, though, Alex knew better. Either way, he needed to hear it from her lips.

Fortune was on his side. As he slid out of the vehicle, he watched Kat step through the front door and purposefully stride down the long walkway. He could tell the instant she saw him. Her whole face lit up.

An internal battle waged. He did not want to be pleased with her reaction, but she stirred him. She brightened his whole world. Made him feel things he'd forgotten long ago. But if she had lied to him…

As soon as she was close enough to hear him, he accused her. "You are not an analyst."

Kat stopped four feet from him. Her enticing smile

disappeared. "I never told you I was, but it is part of what I do. I analyze people, situations, so yes, I'm an analyst."

"That may be, but it's not your primary job." The fury Alex felt deep inside permeated every word. "Tell me the truth, Kat. What do you do for them?" He jutted his chin toward the building behind her.

A man in a custom-made suit stepped beside Katlin. "So, you really don't know." He threw his arm around her shoulders and gave her a hug. "Good job keeping our secret."

A smirk crossed his clean-shaven face. "Not that it's any of your business, Mr. Wolf, but Katlin has a *special* job with us, special operations. She is the leader of Black Swan, a team of lethal female operatives."

Katlin's jaw dropped, and she gaped at the man beside her. "Thanks, Jack. So much for operational security." She quickly searched the area and lowered her voice. "Want to announce it to the world? Like I don't already have a big enough target on my back."

At the man's name, every protective muscle in Alex's body tensed. This was her asshole boss.

Jack grinned at him as he pulled her closer. "And she's mine."

Katlin growled and shrugged out from under his arm then took a wide step away from her boss. "Like hell I'm yours. I belong to no man." Her eyes shot daggers into Jack.

Jack continued his assault on Alex. "You should have taken the job when we offered it to you, Alejandro Lobo." No one missed the use of Alex's given name. "You could be working side-by-side with Katlin."

"No, he couldn't." She looked at Jack as though he'd claimed the earth was flat. "I have a team of all women, and I can guarantee you Alex is all man."

Jack glanced at Katlin and smiled before returning his gaze to Alex. "I've paired you up with men before." Watching Alex for his reaction, he added, "Including me."

"I didn't take the job because I didn't want it." Alex had needed out of the shadow world. He'd sought to build rather than destroy. "I much prefer my current position." He loved his job and the company he'd created.

Jack sneered. "I'll bet you do. Good move, sleeping with the boss." He yanked Katlin back to him and slid his arm around her waist this time. Even though she stood stiff as a board, Jack pulled her to him until they were hip to hip, but Jack's eyes never left Alex's face. "We know all about sleeping with the boss, don't we, darling?"

Alex wanted to smash in the man's too-handsome face for the way he was manhandling her. Even if Alex wasn't positive about Katlin's feelings toward Jack, her body language screamed disdain, edging on revulsion. Alex was about to step in and free her from the inappropriate embrace when Katlin wiggled away, fury blazing from every pore.

She glanced at Alex. Turning her head back toward the man who controlled her work life, she gave him a gotcha smile. "There's a *big* difference between sleeping in the same bed with another operative during a mission and the way I fucked Alex's lights out last night. I would have gladly stayed in his bed for hours of repeat performances, but we were rudely interrupted by my job."

A Cheshire-Cat smile crossed Alex's face while Jack pinched his features and his whole body stiffened, withholding the rage mounting in his eyes. In a flash, it was gone, replaced by calculation.

Jack Ashworth could be a dangerous opponent, especially given the control he had over Katlin. Alex had to protect her from that man's clutches, and any other man on the earth who wanted to harm her.

"You know I had a team on its way to handle the situation." Jack edged toward her, and she backed away from him. "I would never let anyone hurt you."

"You knew about the bomb?" Alex accused and balled his

fists. "And you allowed Kat and her team to be in danger? What kind of man are you?"

Jack's gaze slid to Alex. "I'm her boss. I'm the man controls her every move. Where she goes and when. And I was the man who allowed her to handle the situation, her way, because Lady Hawk can handle anything I throw at her." Then the ass laughed. "She's in danger almost daily and loves the adrenaline rush of it. Katlin has volunteered for the most hazardous assignments we have, ones some of my fiercest men considered suicide missions, and yet this beautiful woman accomplished the operation with great success. She's the most remarkable woman I know."

Jack stared at Katlin for a heartbeat, and then his face softened… into a loving smile. "As I said, she's mine."

Alex knew that was a lie. Kat was his. At least she had been last night, and he had no reason to believe she wasn't still, given her smile just minutes earlier. But did he really want a woman like her in his life? She had lied to him. Kind of. It had been a lie of omission, which was still a lie. He wasn't sure if he could handle a relationship with her jetting off in that black plane into danger whenever the ass in front of him ordered her team on another mission.

"Jack, you are delusional." Kat glanced at Alex then back to her boss. "You're just trying to piss Alex off, aren't you?"

Alex took in the infuriated, gorgeous woman in the navy blue pantsuit with light blue blouse, which brought out every color of her stunning eyes. Although her soft blonde hair was tied in a tight bun at the back of her neck, he had relished the way it felt on his naked chest. And her perfectly rounded breasts had felt so right in his hands when he had tortured her nipples into peaks. Nothing could ever compare to the ecstasy of sliding into her bareback.

He would do anything to have her back in his bed again. And in his life, even if it meant he had men on her personal protection duty every day. "You may control her at work, but

Kat is mine the rest of the time and under my protection. I know I can keep her safe. Can you make that same guarantee?"

Katlin stepped away from both men, glancing back and forth between them. "You know what, you two are perfect examples of the sexism that still exists against women in combat roles. I'm perfectly capable of taking care of myself, whether it's bullets flying at me or fists. You two are living proof that I don't need a man in my life. I don't want anything to do with either of you, on a personal level, ever again."

She turned and faced Alex. "I appreciate the re-initiation back into the dating world that you've given me these last few days...and nights." She spun to face Jack. "And thank you for demonstrating everything I *don't* want in a life partner. I'm not even sure I want you as my boss anymore."

Katlin took two steps backwards. "In case you two missed it, I am the Alpha bitch in this pack. Thanks to my *special* CIA training...and the vagina I was born with...I can have any man I want, anytime, anywhere. Right now, though, Lady Hawk has new prey to seek out and kill. Goodbye, gentlemen."

She turned her back on both of them and hopped into the waiting company car, leaving as the two men snarled at each other.

Jack spoke as Alex started toward the SUV. "Can't handle an Alpha female? Very few men in this world can. They have to be more dominant than she is. An uber Alpha who has more courage and bravery than she does. Obviously, you're not man enough to handle her and what she does for a living. When she's done slumming with the hired help, she knows where to find a real man who can handle her every need and desire."

Alex stopped and stared across the hood at a man who considered himself above everyone else. The asshole needed to be knocked down a few notches. A corner of Alex's mouth kicked up. "You heard Kat. I filled her every need and desire last night and she wanted more of me. You will never feel the ecstasy of sliding into that sweet-tasting, tight body of hers. But I have…and will again. And as for slumming, I paid more in taxes last year than you made as a government employee. Your financial portfolio is probably bigger than mine, but that's because yours was given to you by your rich daddy and even richer mother. I've earned every dime of my investments. That's more than you'll ever be able to say." Alex then gave Jack a shit-eating grin. "And I'm so Alpha my name is Wolf."

Leaving Jack to chew on that, Alex climbed into the SUV and pointed it toward Katlin's condo. He was going after his woman.

CHAPTER 31

Spaghetti.

It was the first coherent thought that went through Katlin's sleep-deprived brain as she grabbed to turn off her cell phone alarm.

Mmmmmm. *One of the Ladies of Black Swan must be cooking.* They often carbed up before a mission. Their work drained them physically as well as emotionally and mentally.

As her eyes began to focus, she dragged in deeper and deeper breaths. Alex's aftershave drifted in and lit up every nerve ending. She snuggled the comforter to her nose, trying to find where he'd slept hours ago, leaving his scent. She wasn't finding it because someone was pulling the covers away from her.

"No," Katlin managed to mumble. "Not yet." She was not a morning person, and it was morning no matter what time of day she woke up. Except when she was in theater. She was always so wired when on a mission, she rarely slept, and when she did, it was lightly. A change in her teammate's breathing would instantly awaken her. But when she was home, she crashed.

"Come on, sleepy head, you have a plane to catch," Alex

whispered as he brushed her ear with his lips then kissed that special spot an inch below.

"How did you get in here?" Katlin wasn't sure if she wanted to scream at him for being an overprotective, misogynist ass, or offer him half her portfolio to make her come one last time.

"Nita answered the door and invited me in." Alex placed gentle kisses down the artery in her neck that pulsed faster matching her growing desire for this man.

Her body came to full alert, begging for him to touch her more and to soothe the growing ache between her legs. She opened her eyes, and his face filled her world.

"So you don't want anything to do with me anymore?" Alex asked and ran a hand between her bare breasts, over her stomach, and straight down her moist slit. He tweaked her hard clit before he shoved two fingers into her soaked channel. "That's not what your body says."

He pushed his fingers in and out, pressing the heel of his hand on her clit.

Katlin wanted to come. But she was mad at him, at all men, especially the two domineering, testosterone-enriched men currently in her life. She didn't need a man controlling every aspect of her life, day in and day out…but she wanted this one…at least his body. And right now.

She looked up and smiled at Alex then pulled him down on the bed beside her. "Well, my inner bitch is horny and wants you deep inside me. The intelligent woman is still mad at you for trying to be a controlling ass." Then she kissed him. In sync with his fingers thrusting inside her, she stroked his erection through the khaki pants as she took his mouth with her tongue.

Alex broke away and looked down at her. "Damn I want you. All of you, but right now I want your body."

Given permission, Katlin unbuckled his belt and unzipped

his pants. "You're overdressed for this party," she teased and grabbed the bottom of his shirt.

He rolled to his back and stripped off his slacks, taking his boxer briefs with them and removing his shoes and socks on the way. Tossing them beside her bed, he pulled off his shirt. "Now, where were we?"

Katlin pinned him on his back and straddled his thighs. "Where we were doesn't matter. This is where we're going." She hadn't done this in a long time but couldn't resist as she licked the liquid pearl that had escaped the broad tip of his cock. The salty essence of him awoke every ounce of passion that had gone unseen for years.

Alex moaned and lifted his hips as he wove his fingers through her hair. "You're killing me, Kat."

She laughed around his long erection as she took him deeper into her mouth. Then she dragged her bottom teeth along the underside of his shaft. "If I wanted to kill you, you'd be dead." She smiled at him. "I prefer to torture you first then take my pleasure." She cupped his balls in her hand.

An alarm sounded on her phone.

Damn. She had to get a move on.

She kissed her way up his sculpted body and captured his mouth with hers. As she thrust her tongue in his mouth, she lowered her body onto his cock in one smooth downward plunge. She moaned into his mouth then pulled her lips from his as she sat up and closed her eyes, enjoying the way he filled her in that position.

God, he stretched her in every direction possible. She took a deep breath and let it out slowly, releasing all the tension in her body.

When she opened her eyes, Alex stared up at her. "I love that pleased look on your face."

Heat filled her from the top of her head to the bottoms of her feet. She knew she was blushing. The perils of being a natural blonde.

"Ride me, babe." Alex thrust his hips up, burying his cock even deeper.

She needed this. She tightened her butt cheeks and Kegels as she rose up. When Alex's eyes went wide, all she could do was smile and do it again. She'd forgotten how much she enjoyed sex. It was the interaction with men that had kept her celibate for years, but now she had a man who physically gave her what she wanted. She rode him hard, teasing them both with a fast pace then slowing things down.

"You little vixen." Alex sat up and took a nipple into his mouth and sucked on it. Hard. But she wanted this to last. The sensations of Alex sharing his body with her, filling her completely, physically and emotionally, would have to last her a long time.

Earlier today she had vowed to date, a lot, when she returned from this mission. She was almost thirty years old and only had a few more years as Lady Hawk. Then she'd fold up her wings and leave the game. It was time for Katlin Callahan to have the life she'd always wanted.

But Alex Wolf, and tonight, would set the bar all other men would be measured against. They weren't right for each other forever, but they were damn good together right now. There were too many differences for anything more than sex and immediate satisfaction. But Katlin would take what she could get and use the experience to move on.

The man beneath her lightly bit her nipple, and her whole body tightened. He grinned up at her. "There's more where that came from." He moved the hand massaging her other breast down her body and rubbed her clit with his thumb.

"Alex." She huffed out his name on a short exhale.

"I know, babe." He licked the nipple he'd bitten with the flat of his tongue and moved to the other side as he circled her clit with his thumb. "I'll take care of you. Always." He then sucked her other nipple deep, abrading the oversensitive peak with the tip of his tongue.

She loved that. Sometimes she thought her nipples were directly attached to her clit. Her internal muscles quivered, and Alex gasped.

"I can't hold out much longer, Kat," Alex warned through clenched teeth. "You feel too good."

Then he bit her nipple. She lost all semblance of sanity as her world exploded into bright colors around her and tore through her body.

When she opened her eyes, his head was in his hand, arm cocked, and he was staring down at her.

"I like waking up with you beside me," Kat told him and kissed his nose.

"I would have liked that, too, this morning, but you were gone when I woke up." He kissed her neck and worked his way down her jaw.

"You were sound asleep, and I just couldn't bring myself to wake you." She shrugged. "It was bad enough that I had to be up." *And go to work and get my ass chewed.*

"Waking up alone in your bed wasn't exactly what I had in mind when I thought about sleeping with you. I wanted to start our morning right." His wet lips dragged kisses down toward her collarbone.

"Like we used to?" She ran her hands over his bare back down to his butt and squeezed.

He stopped kissing her to look into her drowsy eyes. "No. Not exactly. We're different people now. We certainly aren't the same Kat and Alejandro we were ten years ago," he said as he bent to kiss her, taking her in his arms.

She buried her head on his shoulder. They lay wrapped in each other for what seemed like a long time to Katlin.

Then her alarm went off again.

She rolled her head to see the clock and said regretfully, "I need a shower and to grab some food, and then I've got to get to Quantico."

He hugged her tighter when she tried to get off the bed. "I know you do, but I like you just like this."

"Me, too. But I have to go." She brushed a kiss over his lips.

"You shower, and I'll finish supper," he suggested and released her from his powerful hold.

She crawled off the bed. "I thought one of the Ladies was cooking." Kat headed for the bathroom.

"They left about an hour ago." Alex shoved his legs into his underwear and slacks. "I think they wanted to give us some privacy. Do they all live here?"

"No, not exactly," she called from the bathroom as she turned on the hot water. "They often stay here because I have five bedrooms, each with its own bathroom. Tori bought the unit next door, and she has three bedrooms. Lei Lu has an apartment in Crystal City, but she's rarely there. I think her family has all but moved into the place, and she tolerates them in tiny doses." Katlin stepped into blissful, pulsating heat.

In less than ten minutes, Katlin emerged dressed in a black flight suit, wearing no makeup. From across the table, Alex noticed the bruised half-circles from lack of restful sleep under her eyes. She pushed herself too hard. She'd been through a lot in the past twenty-four hours.

"So did the director write you up?" Alex asked.

Katlin told him the whole lecture and the surprise at the end that both the director and Jack-ass knew about the bomb. "We're headed out to deal with the bomber now."

"So when will you be back?" He really wanted to see her again. Soon.

"We never know. As long as it takes." She sipped her water. "Can I call you when I get back to the U.S.A.?"

"No," Alex said quickly.

Katlin stopped with a forkful of spaghetti halfway to her mouth.

He smiled and continued, "You can call me the minute you head toward home so we can figure out where to meet to celebrate your thirtieth birthday."

"It's a date," she agreed and smiled warmly.

"Now eat your spaghetti. You'll thank me for those carbs tomorrow. I'll take you to Quantico. I want to check the men we left there and make sure every trace of Guardian disappears when you lift off."

"Alex, I want to thank you for helping us out last night. Guardian really came through for us." He heard the sincerity in her voice. Guardian was her company, too, but he'd do anything and everything he could to protect her and keep her safe.

"I'm sure we'll eventually find the guys who planted the bomb, but we are going to take out the man who ordered the hit. Hopefully, we'll have verified Intel by the time we reach the Middle East." Kat twirled the last of the noodles around her fork. She looked up at him. "I'm not excited about going back to Iraq. Although I'm rather sure no one is looking for five women, they obviously know our plane."

"Is this why you always have a bodyguard?" Alex asked. "Because there are men hunting you?" The thought of Katlin, on the run constantly, fearing for her life, in that state of hyperawareness, made his stomach clench.

"No." Katlin looked down at her plate. "I had a bodyguard my whole life until we moved to Miami. I was so scared of going to school without an armed escort, and shopping with Mom at the mall without a six-foot tall Marine in uniform with a gun. It took me years to be comfortable doing what every American girl grows up doing without a second thought, but I never really felt safe." She twirled long thick noodles around a fork cuddled inside a tablespoon.

She went on. "One night we flew into Miami very late, and I really needed to sleep, but the hotel had a loud convention going on. I met with Barry the next day, and he said that you were in D.C. and headed to Chicago. He suggested that I stay in the Guardian apartment because it would be quiet. That day he got your okay for the owners to stay there. I crawled into your bed that night and had the best sleep in years." She looked into his eyes. "Years, Alex. I felt safe for the first time since I was fourteen, living behind twelve-foot walls with concertina wire on top, surrounding an embassy overseas."

She slipped the spaghetti into her mouth, and he watched her as she chewed. How could chewing be sexy? The way Katlin did it, it was.

He said nothing, waiting for her to continue.

"Once I left the Guardian building, I got the same edgy feeling again, like I had to be aware of everything and everyone. Our company was making money for me so I decided to reinvest it in bodyguards, giving you back the money."

Shock registered as he realized what Kat had done.

"I really enjoy the company of the Guardian men, maybe too much. I'm quite familiar with them, like I was with my bodyguards growing up. Besides, I'm not their boss; you are," Katlin reminded him. "They give me male company and make me feel safe. To be truthful, if it ever came to a shoot-out, I'd be the one protecting them. Not that they're poor shots, but I wouldn't let them take a bullet for me. I'd kill every sonofabitch shooting at us."

"I'm sure you would," Alex said with new understanding. Changing the subject, he said, "My spaghetti must be pretty good, or you were starved. You ate the whole plate. Want more?" She looked at her empty plate, and he had to laugh out loud. Damn, he liked just being with her.

Together they quickly cleaned up the kitchen and started

the dishwasher. Kat glanced down at the manly black dive watch on her wrist. Alex had worn an almost identical one during his years as a Marine. It reminded him what she was and where she was headed.

"I need to go. I'm actually late, but I don't care." She wrapped her arms around his neck. "I thoroughly enjoyed my reason for being delayed." She popped him a kiss.

"Yes, we need to get a move on." He pulled her tight to him.

"I'm sorry we were rushed." She brushed her lips over his. "We'll do it better next time. I promise."

"If we do it any better, you'll kill me." He kissed her with reserved passion. *Damn she feels so good in my arms again. I don't want to let her go, but she has to leave now.* The dread, not knowing what she faced, but realizing it was highly dangerous and she might not survive, sent cold chills through him.

CHAPTER 32

On the ride to Quantico, Katlin was in Lady Hawk mode as she got updated Intel from Command Central, spoke with her team members, and checked maps on her tablet. She practically ignored Alex, but not on purpose. She had a lot to do as team leader before any mission.

When they pulled up to the ugly hangar, Alex reached over and lifted her across the center console and onto his lap. "I don't want to let you go," he said, hugging her very tight to his broad chest. She loved the way he'd simply picked her up and put her where he'd wanted her. No one manhandled her like that and lived, except Alex. "I just got you back in my life."

"Not really. I've been here all along. You just didn't realize it." Because she hadn't wanted him to know. There was still so much she had to confess to him, including that she wasn't interested in anything except sex. She hadn't found the right time for that discussion.

"Well, I realize it now, and I don't want to lose you again." He kissed her hard and long. Once again, she memorized and savored every moment. This might be all she ever got, and it was times like these that would carry her through the long days, and even longer nights, ahead.

Her phone alarm beeped.

"We need to go in. Black Swan has to be wheels up in twenty minutes. I should be on board now." Katlin kissed him again, quickly, and scrambled onto the passenger's seat and out the door.

They went their separate ways at the hangar, Katlin throwing her go bag into the hold and trotting up the steps to the cabin. The big runway-side doors opened, as Katlin buckled in. Her phone rang. Without looking at the caller ID, she answered and said with a smile and anticipation, "Did you call to say good-bye?"

"As a matter of fact, yes," Jack's baritone voice answered. "Glad to see you made it in time." Katlin's blood ran instantly cold.

She snapped, "Plenty of time. I have complete faith in my team to prep the plane."

"Make sure Wolf gets all his men and equipment out of there before I have him arrested for trespassing on government property."

"You'd better remember everything I said, Jack. Stay the hell out of my personal life." *Damn him! What is it going to take to get him out of my life?*

There was a long pause before Jack quipped, "Good luck. Stay safe. I'll see you when you get back." The line went dead.

Katlin was shaking with rage as her phone rang again. This time she looked and saw it was Alex, but she couldn't hide the lingering rage in her voice. "I'm so glad you called."

"I tried to call a minute ago, and it just rang and rang. Are you okay?" She heard the unmistakable concern in his voice.

"It'll just ring if I'm on a scrambled line. I'm sorry. Jack called. He wanted to be sure you got all your equipment out ASAP. He's not happy I brought Guardian in on the bomb incident. Actually, he's more unhappy that I brought you into my life, both personally and professionally," Katlin explained.

"He'll just have to get over that because I'm not leaving." Alex sounded so positive, but Katlin wasn't as sure. "You and I are tied together in so many ways. I don't think we could ever cut those ties if we wanted to, and I sure as hell don't want to."

"That puts it into perspective. You don't just see the big picture; you see the mural. I love that about you." Yeah, she'd used the L word, but she did love Alex. He was a friend, and she loved her friends. She'd also loved those added benefits the past few days. She had missed sex.

There was a long pause before Alex said, "Call me when you're headed back to the U.S.A. I don't know which coast I'll be on, but we have a special birthday to celebrate. Stay safe, Kat." There was a long silence before he added, "Come back to me."

"I will, always." Katlin said and stared out the window into the darkness as Black Swan sped down the runway.

All Alex could think about on the drive back to Guardian Security was the unknown danger Kat was headed into at the speed of sound. He felt helpless for the first time in his life. He had an irrepressible need to follow her and make sure she was safe.

"Fuck!" he shouted at no one and pounded his fist on the steering wheel.

"Alex, what's wrong?" Top asked from the shotgun seat. Alex had been so deep in his personal thoughts he'd forgotten he had a car full of Guardian men. They'd packed up every ounce of gear owned by his company and had been off the base five minutes after Black Swan went wheels up.

"I've never been on this side of a—" Dare Alex call what

he and Kat now had a relationship? Did a few dates and a couple hours of sex qualify as anything more than a casual connection? Nothing he and Kat ever had, was casual. Volatile, often. Tumultuous, usually. She kept him on edge all too frequently.

And he loved it.

He loved her…as a friend…with benefits. And damn those bennies. He'd fucked a lot of women in his life, but nothing compared to the sex he'd had with Kat. Recently or in the past. No, they hadn't just had sex; they'd made love. It was the way they were together. They shared not only their bodies but also their souls when they brought each other to the edge then fell together, trusting one another throughout the fall.

Could he trust her now to keep herself safe?

And did he really want the men in the SUV to know what she meant to him?

Alex admitted, "I've never had to say goodbye to someone who might not come back."

"Sucks, doesn't it?" Top agreed. "Ever since she joined the Navy I've worried about our little one. Then when she went to work for Homeland…it scares the shit out of me every time I hug her goodbye. Tears me apart that it might be the last time." He shook his head. "I don't know how my wife did it all those years."

Alex slid a look at his D.C. Center manager. "You know what she does for them?"

The smile on the old Marine's face was almost a grimace. "Yeah. She discussed it with me when they sent her over to Homeland. Why do you think I come and pick them up no matter what time of day or night? I have to be sure my girl is okay."

Alex totally understood the man's feelings. "I'm worried about her. They tried to kill her a few days ago."

No," Top corrected. "They tried to kill the people on that black plane. You haven't followed the news, have you?"

"What are you talking about?" Alex had been too busy to watch the international news. He religiously checked the stock markets and kept up with his industry, but the further he got away from the military, the less attention he paid to the broadcasts about the wars and the happenings in the Middle East.

"The death of Nassar al-Jamil?" Top asked.

From the back seat, William "Wild Bill" Lancing piped in. "That was an Army Special Forces team out of Fort Bragg. He was some high-ranking fucker in the Islamic State. I haven't heard which team of my buddies actually got him, but it wasn't any damn SEALs this time. Hoorah."

The cloudy night chose that moment to flash as though in punctuation. Seconds later, a deluge of water dumped on the ten-lane interstate and traffic slowed to just above a crawl. Raindrops on the roof made conversation nearly impossible, and idiots on the road demanded Alex's full attention.

When they pulled into the underground garage at Guardian, Alex breathed a sigh of relief. Katlin and her team had gotten off the ground long before the storm hit so they'd be far above any thunderheads by then.

Top hand signaled to Alex to hold. "We'll catch up with you guys in a few," their manager announced, dismissing the men in the back seat.

Alex glanced over at Top. who moved his head ever so slightly back and forth. "That wasn't any green berets who took out al-Jamil."

Fuck. Katlin and her team did that? "Are you sure?" Alex quietly asked Top, who shrugged one shoulder.

"Timing." Then the man who had known Katlin most of her life added, "I think that's how they protect the girls." He chuckled. "No one would believe the truth anyway. Especially over there."

Hell, Alex was having a hard time believing it.

After the rear doors were closed, Top asked, "How much do you know about Katlin's training?"

Alex thought about that a short minute then answered, "She had the standard naval officer training, I'm sure. How the hell that qualifies her to go after leaders of the Islamic State I have no idea." Then he reasoned, "They probably gave her some training at Section 7."

Top's smirk belied Alex's statements. "This goes no further than you." Top turned in his seat to face him. "Katlin was one of a hundred women selected from all the services to be secretly trained in special operations. All the women on the Black Swan team were. It was a test program long before the Army allowed those women into Ranger training, which the media made such a big deal about."

Top scanned the garage before returning his gaze to Alex. "The initial pilot program sent them through SEAL training in a secret location but used the Coronado staff. More than half washed out, but nowhere near the numbers of men who start BUDs and never finish. It surprised the hell out of everybody."

"No shit?" Alex thought back to what Ty had gone through. "Swimming, jump school, sniper training?" Alex had also been through a similar hell at Marine Special Operations training.

"And more," Top continued. "So the powers that be, and I'm talking the Joint Chiefs, said the women could never handle Army Special Forces training so next they went to Fort Bragg. A few more dropped out before they sent them to Camp Lejeune for Force Recon and SpecOps, Marine Corps style."

"Kat was in Camp Lejeune while I was there?" Shit. When the hell was that? They could have gotten together.

"No, you were deployed." Top smiled. "In the end, about ten passed everything the military threw at them."

"So why are they at Homeland and not back in their respective services?" Alex questioned.

"Because the Joint Chiefs *still* have not opened all combat roles to women." Top glanced at the elevator when it opened, and two men in the Guardian uniform of the day strode toward one of the fleet vehicles.

"But there's only five on Kat's team," Alex noted. "Does Homeland have another all-female team?"

"Not that I know about," Top admitted. "Have you met Harper Tambini, Katlin's neighbor here in D.C.?"

"No."

"She lives across the hall next door to Tori," Top explained. "She's an explosives expert so they sent her TDY to the International Explosives Team at the ATF. Good kid. Smart as hell."

"And the others?" Alex wanted to know how many lethal women were running around out there.

"I have no clue." Top shrugged.

"So what you're telling me is that I have nothing to worry about? She's more trained for these missions than I was?" He wondered if that was possible. He'd been through dozens of advanced training schools. And this was his Kat. That soft body, as she rode him mere hours ago, was now headed to face some ruthless IS leader. The protective Alpha within him wanted her safe and in his bed. But if she'd been trained like him, maybe she could handle it. She'd always been a daredevil, but he and Ty had her back during high school. Who was protecting her six now?

"Yeah, I suppose." Then Top looked away, as though gathering his thoughts. When his gaze returned to Alex, the older man's worn face was tight with tension. "I just have a bad feeling about this one. My brain tells me to trust her skills"—he pounded a fist over his chest— "but my heart says she's in for trouble."

"I thought it was just me since it's my first time." Alex

could practically feel an invisible fist clench around his heart. "What do you want to do about it?"

"If I were fifteen years younger, I'd follow her. Just to be sure she was safe." Top shook his head. "But this old body doesn't like sleeping in the dirt and eating sand anymore. My knees aren't what they once were." His gaze met Alex's. "But that doesn't mean I can't be a great manager for Guardian."

Alex smiled. "Don't worry, *old man*. You're doing a wonderful job here. The men are happy, the clients are satisfied, and we're making money." Besides, Katlin would have a fit if he ever fired her long-time friend without a damn good cause.

"Have you ever followed her before?" A plan started to form in Alex's mind.

"No," Top said. "Never had this ache in my gut like I do this time. I had the same feeling about her just before the coup in Central America and when I let that new Marine take Mrs. Callahan and Katlin to the market just before she was kidnapped."

After a moment of consideration, Alex had made his decision. "Well, I am fifteen years younger, and I'm going after her."

When Alex reached for the door handle, Top laid a hand on his other arm. "Do you think that's a good idea? If she catches you there, she won't be happy."

"Top, I worked covert ops for years. She won't even see me unless I want her to." *Unless I think she needs me.*

Top sighed. "You can't go there alone. You'll need a team."

Alex was two steps ahead. "I have an entire company filled with former SEALs, SpecOps, and Special Forces. I'll pull together a team before dawn and be less than twenty-four hours behind her."

"You know where she went?" Top looked excited and nervous.

"I know she's after Nassar al-Jamil's brother." Alex

smiled. "And I have a world-class hacker who can find the man for me, maybe before Kat finds him."

"Okay then." Top nodded. "What can I do to help?"

"I'll need a command center, and you're the man who's going to run it for me." Alex felt the plan come together. "My office, five minutes. I've got to make some calls and get men in the air so we can leave here tomorrow."

As he reached for the door handle, the old mission excitement stirred. It had been several years since he'd planned an operation like this, and it felt great. He was going back to the sand box to protect his woman.

Top looked across the hood at Alex. "If Jack Ashworth finds out you're there, he could come after you. He's a dangerous man, Alex, with a reach far deeper than most people realize. I don't imagine he's happy about you and Katlin to begin with, but this could throw the wrath of Section 7 after you."

Alex huffed. "I met Jack-ass this afternoon. It wasn't a cordial meeting, but I don't think he'll bother me and Kat again." Alex mentally added one more thing to his to-do list.

CHAPTER 33

Under the protection of his front porch, Jack shook the droplets off his raincoat. The gray weather matched his mood.

It had been one hell of a day…then there had been his fight with Katlin. At least he'd gotten to hear her voice before she'd taken off. He hated arguing with her, but she would eventually come to her senses. Wolf would fuck up soon enough, and she'd bury her sorrow in her work.

Jack knew from the man's profile that he'd not only let Katlin go Wolf would push her away. When he did, Jack would be there to catch all her broken pieces and put her back together, the way he wanted her. This time his plan would work, especially since her interfering father was out of the way now.

Water dripped off his oversized umbrella as he tapped it on the concrete in a failed attempt to leave the evening rain and dismal day behind him.

He unlocked the heavy door to his Georgetown home and stepped onto the marble foyer. After stuffing the umbrella into the brass stand, Jack shrugged out of his overcoat and hung it on the antique hall tree. He removed his woolen suit jacket and folded it precisely before he laid it over the back of the couch. He slipped off his shoulder holster rig, and it went on the hook next to the coat, gun butt out in case it was needed. The terrible day and lousy weather was behind him as he flipped the locks and set the alarm for HOME.

He loosened his burgundy silk tie as he crossed the wide-planked oak floor toward the kitchen. He needed scotch. No, what he needed was his woman to do what she was told. With his next breath, he caught traces of her scent.

"Welcome home, Jack." Her voice was smooth as eighteen-year-old whisky and had the same burning sensation as it went down.

"Glad you got my message." His eyes met her light blue ones. She was gorgeous as she emerged from his bedroom. Long blonde hair spilled over the hip-length mink coat he'd bought her.

"I love my new gift." Red-tipped fingers stroked the soft fur over her breasts as she strutted down the hallway in red stilettos, crossing her bare shapely legs as though she was on a runway.

"Just a little something to wrap around you and keep you warm when I can't." Jack knew she needed smooth lines and lots of gifts to get what he wanted. "But it's our secret, right?"

"Oh, yes." Her husky voice shot to his cock. "Remember? I'm good at keeping secrets."

"I know you are. You're one of my best agents." A lie but she needed to hear those words.

"I know you had a bad day, darling. I'm sorry for that." Her blonde eyebrows rose as she dropped the mink to the floor. Her high, rounded breasts barely moved as she strode toward him...naked, except for the strappy spiked heels. Christ, she was stunningly beautiful. His cock hardened and pulsed with every step she took.

"Yes, but I think it just got much better." He slid the top button of his starched white shirt through the hole and moved to the next. Before he reached the third, she brushed his hands away and took over the task.

He cupped her face in his hands and stroked her cheeks. She wore a little too much makeup tonight. He gently pressed his lips to hers as she pulled the shirt from his slacks and finished with the buttons. She kept moving down and unbuckled his belt, unfastened his pants, and unzipped. She ran her fingers down the length of his pounding erection through the silk of his boxers.

"Oh, my naughty little kitty ca—" His breath caught as she squeezed his cock and forced her tongue into his mouth.

"Ka—" he managed between short breaths, just before he took her mouth with an uncontrollable hunger. "Were you followed?"

"Not hardly. You know how good I am. I think we have everyone at Section 7 fooled." She arched her neck as he kissed his way to her collarbone. "That nosey secretary of yours made me knock on your door."

"This has to remain our secret," he said between kisses. When he took her breast into his mouth and sucked hard, her breath quickened and he thought she'd come right then. She was so responsive to him, but he'd learned how to control the woman in his arms.

Her hands hadn't stopped moving, and she had his slacks and boxers pooling around his ankles when she broke the kiss. She knelt before him, blonde hair tickling his thighs as she took him in her mouth. From this angle, she was perfect. She licked the tip and pumped his shaft, just the way he liked it. She surrounded the head with her warm mouth, and Jack closed his eyes and thought his dreams had come true.

He was about to explode when he pulled her bobbing head away from his body. "Kat—"

"I like it when you call me by that nickname," she purred.

He pulled her to standing and attacked her lips. When he shoved his tongue into her mouth, he tasted himself and her.

The heady mixture almost threw him over the edge. "I want to be inside you when I come."

"Anything you want, boss." He took her by the hand and led her to his bedroom, where he made her obey his every wish for the rest of the evening.

Hours later, Jack's sated brain and body startled awake. He thought he'd heard an unfamiliar tick. He slid his hand under his pillow, reaching for his gun, and listened. All he heard was smooth breathing beside him. He felt the warmth of the woman who sprawled in the bed next to him. Her blonde hair fanned across the pillow, her body replete from hours of mindless sex.

His brain sleep-muddled, he almost called out, "Katlin."

She turned and reached for him.

No.

Katrina.

Why the hell was she still in his bed? He examined the woman next to him. She was beautiful, but she was no Katlin. Katrina's nose was too narrow and a little too long.

Katlin's breasts were more rounded, at least one cup size larger. Not that he'd ever touched her breasts, held them in his hands the way he stroked Katrina's now.

His hands moved over Katrina's hard stomach, the same as Katlin's. They were both his agents and had to maintain peak conditioning. Once, during that special mission, he'd stepped behind Katlin and slid his hands around her middle. Later, when they were alone, she'd read him the riot act, but it hadn't mattered. He'd held her from behind, the way he'd wanted to bend her over and take her. The way he'd taken Katrina a few hours ago.

Jack slid his hand lower to Katrina's mound and parted her folds. When he'd licked inside her several hours ago, he'd been so pleased that she'd dyed her hair blonde there. Katlin was a natural blonde, and although he'd never seen for himself, he was sure she was blonde there as well.

Katlin's angry words came back to him from earlier that day. He'd lied when he agreed that it was over for them. No, it would never be over for the two of them until it was her in this bed beside him, not Katrina. With Katlin's image in his mind, he reached for another condom and slid into Katrina once again. With the fantasy rolling in his head like a future vision, it didn't take long.

Spent, Jack rolled off Katrina and tucked the sheets around her. He wasn't sure if she'd even been awake that time. He didn't really care. In his mind, he'd been with someone else.

He padded into his bathroom, lit by a small nightlight, to remove the condom. He started taking a piss.

A large hand came over his mouth and the cold steel of a knife pricked at his throat, its point at his carotid artery. He felt the heat of the man's breath on his ear.

"Keep your hands on your cock, or I might get the idea to cut it off," the man ordered in a low tone, barely above a whisper.

"Who are you?" Jack demanded through the man's tight grasp, but it came out as a jumble of vowels.

"Shut up and listen. You will leave Katlin and me to our private lives."

Fucking Wolf. He should have known his security system wouldn't stop any man with Wolf's training. The bastard should be dead and buried next to Katlin's husband.

Jack shifted his weight ever so slightly as he tried to roll to the balls of his feet.

"Don't try it." Wolf's quiet voice promised retribution as the knife dug in.

Pain shot from his neck to his balls as they drew up and tried to crawl into his body.

Jack felt the warmth of his own blood trickle down his neck. Damn. There seemed to be a lot of it. He swallowed back the bile that had risen and threatened to choke him.

"You're one sick fuck, you know that. You'd better keep fucking the lookalike in your bed because you'll never have Katlin. She's mine, now and forever. If you do anything to her outside the purview of her job, I'll hunt you down and kill you. If you touch her, speak to her in any way other than professionally, you're a dead man. Nod if you understand."

Jack nodded…then saw stars.

Can't breathe. Knocked out? Dead? Those were his final thoughts as his world went black.

Jack was cold as he awoke. The bathroom tile was cool on his naked body, and his muscles had tightened from all the night's activities. What the hell? Had he slipped and fallen? He did an internal body check, and except for the pain in his throat, he was fine. He touched the small slit on his throat. It was wet. In the darkness of the large bathroom, he couldn't see but knew it was blood.

No, he hadn't been asleep. He'd been knocked out. Fucking Wolf.

Jack strained to peer into the shadows. Was he still there? His gun was under the pillow, fifteen feet away, next to the sleeping woman. He listened carefully, but a trickle of blood moved over his collarbone. Panicked, he jumped up and flipped on a light, then quickly searched the room.

Jack was sure the man was gone.

Jack stared in the long mirror over the sink, stretching his neck to get a good look at the cut. He pulled his shaving mirror close. It was really small, less than a quarter-inch, perfectly positioned over his artery. His pounding blood had broken through the thin scab.

God. Damn. Alex Wolf. How the hell had he gotten in?

Jack stomped into the bedroom and looked at the woman's makeup-smeared face. The woman of his dreams was not the one in his bed. No. Katlin was on her way to Iraq, but she'd recently been in Alex Wolf's bed.

Jack yelled, "Katrina."

The woman bolted to a sitting position and quartered the room with her gaze. "What is it?"

"Time to go." One-handed, he grabbed the pile of her clothes next to the furrier's box and threw them on the bed next to her hand.

No, Katlin isn't mine…yet, but she isn't yours either, Wolf.

CHAPTER 34

Katlin lay on her stomach and pointed the directional microphone and video receiver toward the large house inside the manufacturing compound five hundred feet away. Damn, it was hot. At two in the morning the temps were still in the nineties. Hollow voices came over her ear bud.

"My home was burned, and they...they...killed my husband." Lady Harrier's voice shook appropriately through the crackly connection. She was doing great, and her Iraqi Arabic dialect was excellent in Katlin's opinion. She tweaked the device's position a fraction of an inch, and video appeared on the small plastic square she wore over the corner of her right eye.

"I think we've got it," Lei Lu exclaimed from the second-floor room they'd established as the communications center. "Video and sound coming in clear."

Katlin couldn't see much of the woman in front of Lady Harrier, who been introduced as one of Turhan's many wives and head of the household when the door had been answered. The double-veiled niqab hid much, but the woman's attitude came through loud and clear when she asked, "Who?"

Lady Harrier sniffed as though she were holding back tears. "The...the men. Shiites. We had been told that there was work here in Tarmiyah. I will work hard for you. I can cook."

Lei Lu sniped, "That alone will kill off half of them."

Katlin chuckled. Her friend had many skills, but few were found in a kitchen. "You're doing great, Lady Harrier. Keep it up. You're desperate and scared." Through her eyepiece, she watched the woman soften then glance down.

"Are those cooking herbs?" the gatekeeper asked.

"Some." Lady Harrier admitted the truth. Hidden in the reed basket were also pretty purple mountain flowers, readily found a hundred miles north, which would be used to kill Turhan. Since autopsies were not allowed by his Muslim faith, no one would ever know the alkaloid toxin extracted from the roots would make it seem as though Turhan had died of a heart attack.

"Are you a healer?" The hope in the housewife's voice couldn't be missed.

"Tell her yes," Katlin ordered. They hadn't expected that question, but her team was great on the fly.

In the humble persona Lady Harrier had established, she answered, "I know a little. My grandmother was teaching me." In truth, Nita had suddenly quit med school and blown her way through to becoming a physician's assistant specializing in emergency medicine to fulfill her Navy contract, which had paid for her education.

"Come in, quickly. We are in great need. So many men are ill." The woman reached out, but Lady Harrier stepped back.

"No, no men." Lady Harrier shook, making the video move side to side.

"All will be well." The woman ran a hand down Lady Harrier's arm. "You will stay in the house with us. The only men here are Turhan and his guards, but they sleep in the barracks, not here."

Good to know. That'll make it easier for Lady Harrier to get to the target.

The woman moved in slowly, gently encouraging Lady Harrier into the house. "Allah has sent you to us."

Her teammate responded with what could have been "I'm in" or "amen," and the video dimmed to interior lighting as the two women walked slowly through the house, speaking in low tones.

As Lady Harrier touched the corners of walls placing miniature audio-visual equipment, Lady Kite announced from their operation center, "Inside video coming in now. Pinging audio. Record on."

Katlin breathed a sigh of relief. Stage one, complete. Out of habit, she surveyed the neighborhood of square, block homes that surrounded the deactivated electromagnetic isotope separation plant, which had been used to enrich uranium for nuclear weapons before NATO inspectors shut it down in the early 1990s. The extremely modern facility had rivaled any clean room in the Western Hemisphere and had included a chemical wash facility to recover uranium after the initial enrichment process. Because almost no trace had been released into the atmosphere, international overseers had missed the hidden operation for years. Now the gigantic buildings supposedly made generators so dedicated Sunnis could work round the clock in support of the Islamic State.

Katlin was relatively sure power generators weren't being made there, but that wasn't her mission. Although they'd been trained in reconnaissance, their focus had always been on watching a single target, always male, followed by an up-close kill. Of course, they would report anything they found significant about the plant. Perhaps USSOCOM, the special operations command under which Section 7 ultimately operated, would assign Black Swan's backup team to deal with whatever was happening inside the mammoth building. The men, led by Vic Viceroy, were on standby forty-two miles away in Baghdad. Somewhere in the area was a SEAL team, which was his backup. Command layered teams just in case an op went to hell—like it had with her husband three years ago—but Jack always made sure the Ladies were covered, even though they'd never needed it.

The plan was for the mission to last a week, two at the most. Nita's curly dark hair and brown eyes would help her blend with the locals when out of her traditional garb. They'd spray tanned her naturally olive-colored skin so it more closely matched the women in the area. She had been selected for this mission because of her medical expertise and the delicate handling necessary of the dangerous poison.

Katlin brought her rifle to her shoulder and flipped the scope to infrared. Orange and red blurs moved inside the massive building that hummed in the dark of night. Hundreds of people worked inside, and a huge heat source bloomed in the center of the room. She'd add that to the report she was about to file.

She spied Tori and Grace as they entered on the street level of the two-story house they had sequestered. Lady Falcon and Lady Eagle had been on perimeter patrol. To the untrained eye, the women seemed to move at a natural pace, but Katlin knew that something was wrong by the way they carried their bodies. The problems they'd had with communications now solved, the women would never leave again without their comm units. Turhan had been running jammers, but Lady Kite had found a way to work around them. Katlin scanned the area to assure they hadn't been followed. All clear.

"Lady Hawk, where are you? You're not going to fucking believe this!" Lady Falcon's voice came through Katlin's comm piece via Lady Kite's microphone. These were awesome new communication units they were testing for Section 7.

"Tell them I'm on the roof, but I'll be right down," Katlin

ordered Lei Lu. "It's more important we get eyes and ears on Lady Harrier right now. Lady Kite, run it through its operations. Let's test this baby." The arm holding the tiny modified microphone and camera moved in several directions. It pointed from one side of the house to the other and up and down.

"All set, Lady Hawk. We've got it." Relief gushed in Lady Kite's voice.

"On my way." As Katlin dropped down through the roof access hole to the second story floor, she heard Lady Falcon on the steps, Lady Eagle right behind her.

Through her earpiece, and echoing up the stairwell, Katlin heard Lady Eagle exclaim in stereo, "They're here."

Katlin pulled the tiny comm unit out of her ear and stood at the top of the stairs. "Who's here?"

Lady Eagle flipped back the niqab and shoveled her red hair from under her abaya. "Griffin."

Katlin froze. *Griffin is in Tarmiyah? Why? Is he taking military jobs off the books? Did he quit Guardian?* "Did I hear you right? Did you say Griffin is here?"

"Yes." Lady Falcon flipped her entire black garb off and rolled it into a ball. "And so is Alex."

Fear ran through Katlin's veins. This small Iraqi city was a dangerous place. Turhan was a powerful leader in the IS rebellion. Even though Alex was black ops trained, he'd been out of the game for years. She worried for the man who had been inside her body a few short days ago. If anything happened to him—

Then anger shot through her. Why the hell was he even there? She digested the words as her gaze slowly found its way to her tall friend's Bambi-beautiful eyes. "What the fuck?"

Lady Eagle, who became klutzy when flustered by a man, fought with the tiny buttons that ran down the front of her abaya. "They're kitty-corner from us, facing the east side of the compound."

Katlin's mind spun. *Is Alex back into black ops? Did he ever really leave? Is there something else going on that we don't know about? Did someone send Alex here?*

Lady Falcon crossed her arms over the ball of black cloth mandatory in this part of the world. Formally reporting to her superior officer, she explained, "Lady Eagle and I were on patrol when we saw Griffin, and someone who looked familiar, walking down the street coming right toward us."

Finally free of the cloak-like garb, Lady Eagle continued the story. "Of course they didn't recognize us under all this." She carefully folded the yards of cloth into a neat square and set it on a small hall table before she led the way to what they'd transformed into a war room. Pointing to a house on the wall map of the town, she said, "They're here. We checked for external security cameras, and when we didn't see any, we peeked in the windows. Bold as day, there was Alex and several men we recognized as Guardian employees, although I can't remember their names. Some were from the D.C. office and some from Miami. I'm not sure about the others." Lady Eagle looked nervously into Katlin's eyes. "Lady Hawk, Griffin is here."

"Understood." Katlin nodded. She saw the same concern in her friend's eyes that she felt for Alex. These men could be in danger, and that added another burden to their own situation. She glanced to Lady Falcon. "What's your assessment?"

"Looks to me as though they just got here and are getting set up." The former model lifted her hair off the back of her long neck. "Some kind of surveillance would be my guess."

"Any idea what they're looking for?" Katlin glanced back and forth between the two women. They both shook their heads.

"We trailed them on what seemed to be a perimeter

check." Lady Eagle pointed to the satellite map once again. "They followed a standard pattern surveillance of the immediate area. We shadowed them for about two blocks on the south end. My initial reaction would be they are setting up to observe the compound, but there's a strong possibility that they are here to find us."

Lady Falcon added, "The property they're in is one we looked at and rejected, but it does have a direct line of sight to the house where Lady Harrier is located."

"So they might be here to work an op for the government." That idea pissed Katlin off. She thought she'd known what Alex had been up to the past three years but had no idea he might be taking black ops jobs, but for who? Any number of alphabet agencies would want a man with his skills. Then there were the Beltway bandits, which were little more than organized mercenaries. It didn't matter. Alex and his team presented a major problem for the Ladies of Black Swan. They knew who her team was and could fuck up their op all too easily.

Then Katlin worried that Alex and his men might get blamed for Turhan's death, although the SEALs who would take "credit" for the kill were close by. Jack flashed through her brain and the way he had taunted Alex a few days ago. Had her boss hired her lover to be in Tarmiyah to take the backlash for the IS leader's death? Would Jack do that to eliminate Alex from her life?

Hell yes. Jack the ass had no limits when it came to his pursuit of her. Now she was even more concerned about one of her oldest friends. And she might have been the one to put him directly in the line of fire. She had to break off any kind of relationship she might have with Alex, to keep him safe.

After a brief internal debate, Katlin announced, "Let's watch them for twenty-four hours and see what they're up to. This whole mission may be over by then and we can deal with those men." She shrugged. "Or not. We'll simply bug out of here and leave them to do whatever it was they were sent here to do." And she would deal with Alex Wolf on her own, back on U.S. soil.

"Lady Harrier is down for the night," Lady Kite announced and removed the headphones. "System is set on alarm. I need to get some sleep too."

"I slept earlier. I'll take first watch," Lady Eagle offered.

Five hours later, Katlin, Tori, and Lei Lu stood in front of the largest computer screen in the ops center.

Lady Harrier whispered, "Are you seeing this?"

"Yeah," Katlin replied. "What the hell happened to them?"

"Radiation poisoning would be my guess." As Lady Harrier slowly moved her head as though to scan the open room, she shared what she saw with her team. Red-eyed men heaved blood into buckets placed beside bed pallets, noses oozed, and moans filled room. "They've divided the room into severity. The ones over there aren't going to make it, and I have nothing here to ease their pain."

"Are you in danger of exposure?" Katlin asked and wondered what they could use to test her.

"I don't think so. They all mentioned an accident a few days ago." Lady Harrier sucked in a breath. "Christ, it stinks in here."

She moved to an open door and stepped out as though to get some fresh air. "The doctor is wearing a hospital badge like we had during my residency. There's a Gray counter on the back, which records how much radiation the wearer has been exposed to over his life. I'll grab his and check it as soon as I can."

As soon as she returned to the sick room, her gaze went to the men on the far side, the ones worst off. "Hey, Lady Hawk, if I have any toxin left—"

"Absolutely." Katlin hated seeing anyone in that kind of pain.

On a smaller screen, she watched Alex and Griffin leave

their house. "Lady Kite, it looks like they're doing a perimeter check every two hours." *What the hell is he up to?*

Dread washed over her whole body as she watched Alex in a flowing white thaub turn the corner. That was it. She was done. "We're going over there tonight and talk to them." She glanced at the women around her. "We'll take them out one at a time. Since they have a height and weight advantage, we'll go in pairs. Stun them if you have to, but dead weight is a bitch. I'd much rather truss them up and talk to them together. I've got Alex, though. I can handle him by myself. We'll leave shortly after midnight."

CHAPTER 35

Four large men sat on their knees in nothing but their underpants and blindfolds, hands tied behind their backs to their ankles then the rope looped around their neck. Uncomfortable, for sure, but effective. The Ladies of Black Swan had silently taken each man by surprise in a gag-and-bag move before he could see their faces or even realize a female had captured them and stuffed a balled cloth in his mouth.

Lady Falcon leaned against the kitchen counter four feet away with her H&K MP7A1 submachine gun pointed at them. She'd never shoot them, but a few shots always intimidated a sightless man. In a deep voice, she spoke broken American English laced with a heavy Arabic accent. More than once, Lady Falcon had pulled off sounding as though she was an Arab man stumbling with the English language. They all just hoped none of Alex's men recognized her voice. "Not one sound out of any of you or you're all dead."

Using American Sign Language, Lei Lu signaled, *Answers the boxers or briefs question. No tighty whities here.* The petite

Asian woman grinned as she perused the line of muscled men.

When Katlin's own gaze fell upon Griffin, she was glad she'd stationed Lady Eagle outside on exterior watch. If her friend, Grace, had seen the amazing body of the man who protected them most often in Miami, she'd be a bundle of nerves. Guardian's Miami Center manager wore boxer briefs that hid nothing of his remarkable package. The former SEAL had a lot to be proud of.

Lady Falcon pointed to one of the buff men none of them recognized and licked her lips. He'd popped an impressive combat boner that tried to peek out of his Ranger panties.

Katlin smirked. She loved these women. Using their self-designed hand signals, she indicated she was headed upstairs to the bedrooms…and Alex. Although they'd already swept the rooms on the first floor, and infrared indicated there was only one person, prone, on the second floor, Lei Lu followed her to double check the other rooms.

Heart pounding, rifle nestled into her shoulder, Katlin slid on silent feet into the room as she stared into the scope in night vision mode. She could smell the familiar spicy scent of Alex and fought the instinct to ease her focus as she swept the room. His gun lay on the nightstand, but that didn't mean there wasn't another under his pillow. She hid weapons all over her bedroom.

His breathing never changed as she approached the side of the bed. Damn, he was beautiful, and her heart kicked in a totally different way from the mission adrenaline that had pumped through her since the team had left their base house. Part of her wanted to crawl under those sheets and touch every inch of that amazing body before she allowed him to take her where only he could. The way he made her come was addicting.

The other part, the sane part of her brain, was so angry

with this man that she could have shot him right there and then. His mere presence endangered her team.

She rolled her rifle to her back and pulled out her pistol before she bent down and brushed her lips over his. "Fancy meeting you here, Alex."

He breathed out a long, slow exhale and snaked his arms around her neck. When he tried to pull her down onto the bed, she laid the cold barrel of her gun against his temple.

"Get the fuck out of that bed, now." Her tone was ice.

He twitched.

She jumped back out of his reach, snatching the gun from the side table., He'd stretched for it a second too late.

As he stood beside the bed, she scraped her gaze down his body, searching for a weapon.

Of course he was naked…with an outstanding erection pointed at her girl parts, which instantly saturated.

The arrogant bastard had the audacity to grin. "Once again, you're holding a gun on me."

"Yeah." She smiled. "But this time you're naked."

"You could be too," Alex suggested and stepped toward her.

"Not happening." After tonight, she would never again have the pleasure of his hands and mouth on her body. She had to end whatever it was that they had between them. Something she had never dared define before. Friends? Friends with benefits? Lovers?

All the above? Probably.

Soul mate? Yes.

And damn, wasn't this a hell of a time to realize that she not only loved Alex but that she was *in* love with the naked man before her? Yet, for his protection, she needed to cut ties and run far, far away. It was the only way to keep him safe. He had to leave Tarmiyah right now. The clock was ticking, and Turhan would be dead soon. She raised the pistol to chest level.

Alex stopped in his tracks. He glanced at the gun in her hand then back to her eyes. "You wouldn't shoot me."

What a cocky bastard. "Are you willing to bet your life on that?" she asked through clenched teeth. "I'm so fucking pissed at you right now, shooting you would solve several problems. I don't know what the hell you're doing here or who sent you, but I'm not happy you're here. But that doesn't matter. You're leaving. Now."

"Top sent me."

At those three words, Katlin's entire body went on alert. The man who had been her bodyguard since she was a child was still looking out for her.

Well fuck.

Alex pushed on. "He had a bad feeling about this mission. He said to mention Panama to you."

As though of its own free will, the hand holding the gun dropped to her side.

Over fifteen years ago, Top had revealed to her father his gut feeling a day before the Panamanian coup. Had her dad not paid attention to his Marine's warning, her whole family would have been kidnapped and publically executed by the banditos who wanted to take over the Panama Canal and the country. Because of Top's twitchy stomach, her father immediately began preparations. By the time shooting broke out in the palace and governmental buildings, the American Marines had already rounded up all the children from the embassies and hidden all of them on the main level of her parents' large brick home inside the U.S. embassy walls. Katlin and the other teenagers had placed mattresses against the windows, secured the doors, and stood ready, guns in hand.

She had killed that day, for the first time. When the bad guys busted through the front door of her family's home, the need to protect the innocent had taken up residence in every cell in her body. That moment had changed her life forever.

She was no longer a helpless child. She had the power to stand between good and evil and shield those who couldn't protect themselves. Safeguarding the young children who had lived in the surrounding embassies had morphed into protecting an entire country by the time she'd finished college.

"Babe." Alex's voice brought her back to his darkened bedroom. She needed to protect him too. "Are you okay?"

"No." Katlin wondered why Top hadn't contacted her but then realized she'd never made arrangements for her old friend to get in touch with her while on a mission. It could have been a fatal error.

She'd correct that as soon as this op was over. "So you came all the way to the boonies of Iraq to give me Top's message that his infamous gut is twisting?"

"No, sweetheart." He took a step closer to her. "I'm here to watch your six."

Kat about lost it. "I've been a field operative for more years than you were. I've got this. We have plans in motion, and our backup plans have backup plans. Thanks so much for playing, but you can take your toys and you can take your boys and get the hell out of here before you fuck up my mission."

"I'm not leaving. I have a man inside." Alex jammed his fists on his naked hips.

She refused to allow her eyes to go there. "Lady Harrier..." Katlin's brain was in Lady Hawk mode, and Alex wouldn't know her teammate's handle, so she added, "Nita is inside that house and will complete her mission within twenty-four hours."

"Chase is in there to help her." Alex must have seen the flash of fury as her whole face tensed because he quickly added, "If she needs it."

"She's not going to need him." Kat took a different approach, hoping the man she loved would understand.

"Alex, when Turhan dies, they're going to look for a scapegoat. Your man, being the newest, will be suspect number one." And that could lead to Alex, and he could get killed.

"He's not the newest recruit. Matter of fact, he's with Turhan's lieutenants, right now, in Baghdad shanghaiing men to work in the plant." Alex glanced in the direction of the facility that looked empty from the outside but bustled with activity. "Chase said so many of the men are sick, Turhan is taking anyone who shows and kidnapping dozens every night from the larger cities. When Chase showed up with his own gun, they immediately made him a guard. The way the workers described it, the deaths were ugly and painful. They are slaves, working for food and a roof over their head. We can help you destroy the factory."

Katlin shook her head. "That's not our mission."

Alex raised an eyebrow. "Do you know what they're making in there?"

"I'm well aware it used to be a nuclear processing facility, and I'm sure there's residual radiation, but it is not our concern. That building is not my mission, not my focus, and not my job. We're here to eliminate Turhan. He'll be dead shortly after the sun sets, and we'll be in the sky before it rises the next day. You have to pull your man out of there. If he blows Nita's cover—or if Lady Harrier gets hurt or, worse, she—" Katlin couldn't say the word. She sucked in a shaky breath. "I swear to God I'll kill every fucking one of you."

Alex stepped closer. "Now, Kat…"

She raised the gun, pointing at his crotch. "Maybe I won't kill you, but I'll make you regret the day you decided to interfere in my work."

"What are you going to do?" There he went with that big bad Alpha attitude again.

Katlin smirked. "I'm just going to blow your balls off. I

believe taking away your manhood will do more to damage Alex Wolf than anything else could."

"Kat, you'd never do that. You enjoy my body too much."

Argh! Men.

Katlin smiled as she replied, "Oh, I most certainly do, but you'd still have a mouth and fingers. I can still enjoy your body. You just couldn't."

Fear flashed through his eyes a brief second before he dropped his hands over his shrinking cock. "Fine. What do you want?"

Finally, he was taking her seriously. "Are you sure you weren't sent here by some government agency?" Katlin stared at him warily. He'd given in too fast. "Are you taking black ops missions? Have you become a mercenary?"

"Fuck no," Alex burst out. "What I am is a man who wants to protect his woman and make sure she's safe."

His woman? Hell no. Katlin Callahan belonged to no man. And never would. She was not property to be bought, sold, and traded like too many misfortunate others in the world. She was an American female and could make her own decisions. Stay or leave at will. She clarified, "First of all, I'm not your woman, and second—"

"Oh, yes you are," he interrupted. "You always have been. I just don't think either of us wanted to believe it." He lunged forward and grabbed her shoulders. "Katlin, you know I have always loved you."

Oh, no. This could not happen. Not here. Not now. Not ever. She had to break this off. That was the plan. Execute the plan. "Alex, I love you too. You've been my friend—"

"No, Kat. I'm *in* love with you, but it's okay if you can't say the words back to me." He lowered his head to stare into her eyes. "I know you love me. You show me all the time. You could have killed us all in our sleep. But you didn't. Before you left to fly here, that wasn't just a quick fuck to relieve stress. We. Made. Love, Kat. We always have."

The truth of his words filled her fractured heart. "Goddamnit, Alex, why are you doing this to me? My head has got to be in this mission. Especially now that Top has put me on hyper alert. The shit is about to hit the fan. And here you stand, telling me that you're in love with me. We've only been together for a few days." A few absolutely wonderful days in her opinion, not to mention the fantastic nights.

"This time," he reminded her. His face inches from hers, he softly said, "Kat, I think I've been in love with you since tenth grade bio lab." He tenderly laid his lips on hers.

Jolts of passion coursed through her body as her hips rocked against his and she lost herself to the man who had taken a piece of her heart and filled it with love.

"Lady Hawk, comm check." Lady Eagle's voice sounded through her ear bud.

"Yeah, Lady Hawk," Lady Falcon sniped. "I, for one, have really enjoyed this trip down your memory lane, and obviously the man has it bad for you, but I have four men hogtied here in the kitchen and at least one now knows who I am. Permission to release the prisoners."

Alex had heard every word. He swept the hair back from her ear and growled. "Untie my men."

"Sorry, Alex, you're not the boss of me," Lady Falcon informed him. "Lady Hawk, I repeat, permission to free the prisoners?"

"Granted," Katlin said on a sigh. Refocused on their mission, she tried to explain, "Your timing couldn't be any worse. I need you to leave now. We'll talk about this other … thing…when I get back home. Promise me, Alex, that you'll pack up and be far away from here before nightfall. We have a mission to complete, and your presence here has exponentially endangered all of us."

He must have seen the desperation in her eyes. "Fine. We'll leave."

"Yet tonight?" she pressed.

He shook his head. "No, but as soon as I can get Chase out safely."

Katlin stepped closer. "Thank you." *Then he'll be safe.*

She cupped his face with her hand and pressed a gentle, ever so tender, kiss on his lips.

Alex tried to deepen the kiss, but she wouldn't allow it. Even though she'd like nothing more than to strip off her clothes and crawl into his bed to show him how much he meant to her, she couldn't.

She had a mission to finish.

CHAPTER 36

Alex watched the monitor connected to the tiny camera attached to Chase's collar as Turhan clutched his chest and screamed in an Arabic dialect Alex didn't understand, but the man's eyes told the story.

The lieutenant dove toward the bed and started administering CPR. "Get the doctor. He's in the infirmary on the other side of the compound. Hurry."

Chase bolted from the room, and Alex instructed, "Find Nita and the two of you get the hell out of there."

"That's the plan," Chase confirmed. He turned down the hall to her bedroom to find several women gathered, laughing. With those damned abayas covering every inch of their bodies, he couldn't tell if Nita was there. "Turhan is in pain. He needs a nurse."

The women scattered, two of them rushing past him, the others escaping toward their rooms.

"Is the new one, the healer, here?" Chase asked.

One of the women, head bowed, answered, "No, she's in the hospital. It's her shift."

"Fuck." Alex ordered, "Go get her." But Chase was already running.

When his man reached the makeshift hospital, he yelled for the doctor to go take care of Turhan. The room passed before Alex as Chase scanned for Nita. "Any idea which one she is?" he whispered.

Hell no. Alex then remembered her handle. "You're leaving anyway, say in English, 'The harrier needs to fly,' and let's see what happens."

As soon as the words were out of Chase's mouth, a woman bustled over to him.

In local Arabic, she said loudly, "I can help him, soldier of Allah, but you must show me the way."

Once out the door, he motioned to the shadows. "Nita?" He didn't waste words.

"Yes, but who the hell are you?" She continued to shoot questions at him. "And why are you here? This wasn't the plan for my extraction. Is my team in trouble?" She then cocked her head as though listening to something.

Probably her team, Alex thought. He watched her face ease. Not talking to Chase, she answered, "Got it." Facing his man, she smiled. "You're Alex's inside man."

Alex ordered, "Tell her Turhan is dead and you're going to get her out, right now." At Chase's repeated words, Nita sprinted toward the house.

When she stopped to open the door, Chase demanded, "No, this way."

Flinging the door open, barely missing him, she explained, "I have to grab my gear from my room." Scooting through the house, she whispered but even Alex heard, "He wasn't supposed to die so soon. It should have taken at least four more hours." There was a short pause. "A congenital heart defect. Maybe he'd been exposed to radiation. It attacks the weakest organs, and combined with the poison, his heart gave out sooner than I expected."

The women's wing was empty as Chase followed Nita to her room. "What can I do to help?"

"Watch the door," she suggested and efficiently collected hidden weapons and stuffed them under her abaya. "Ready."

Alex was glued to the nineteen-inch screen, seeing everything in real time that his inside man did. Nita's abaya flowed around her as she casually walked out of her room and down the hall. At the corner, they turned toward the back door and faced the lieutenant's men.

"We got them." The Arabic words filled the air and clearly traveled over the channel to Alex and his team. When Chase turned to check his six, more men moved up from behind.

Alex walked into the safe house the Ladies of Black Swan had established as their base to find Katlin pacing as she talked on a satellite phone.

She glared at him. "Don't you say a word," she warned. "Just sit down. I'll get to you."

Less than a minute after Chase and Nita had been captured, Tori and Grace arrived at the door of the house he and his men occupied. They'd been summoned by Katlin and instructed to tear down their operation. With the help of the women, it took ten minutes to load out and get to her team's safe house.

Alex shook his head. He'd fucked up. Kat had warned him, and he hadn't pulled Chase out. The terrorist had immediately accused his man of working with Nita, making her carry his weapons as they failed to escape. Alex had watched the initial interrogation. They had asked Chase who else he was working with. When his man wouldn't tell them, Alex had witnessed the first punches. At least they hadn't beat Nita. Yet. But Turhan's men had found her with loaded weapons and communication buds, and, of course, their fiber optic cameras.

Alex had let Katlin down. He'd let his men down. He

pledged he'd make this right as he watched Katlin in full Lady Hawk mode pace their war room.

"What do you mean Vic and his team are gone?" Katlin's controlled voice belied her tense body . "Fine. Where are the SEALs?"

Griffin's gaze whipped to Alex, but he shook his head before his friends could say anything.

"So what you're telling me is that we're on our own in rescuing Lady Harrier." Alex watched Katlin's back stiffen. "Yes, sir. We've got this. I'll call you back in ten with our op plan. Black Swan out." She jabbed a button on the phone before tossing it onto the large table in the middle of he room.

Ignoring the men who lined the walls, she motioned, and all the women grabbed a seat. Katlin leaned her hands on the back of the chair at the head of the table and announced, "USSOCOM pulled our Section 7 backup team, headed by Vic, and the SEALs backing them up, off to Ramadi. The Islamic State bombed several Shia locations there last night. Bottom line, our nearest safety net is seventy-five miles away."

Although he loved watching her in command mode, Alex pushed off the wall. "Your safety net is right here." He strode toward the woman he'd die for and asked, "What do you need us to do?"

"We need a distraction," Tori suggested. "Let's blow something up. That should pull all the men out of the house so we can sneak in and grab Lady Harrier."

"We really need Harper." Grace looked at Katlin. "Let's call her and see if she can jump in here with some explosives. Chaz would be awesome."

Katlin pulled another sat phone from her pocket and dialed as Alex asked, "Who's Harper and Chaz?"

Grace answered as Katlin laid the ringing phone onto a device in the center of the table. "Harper trained with us and lives down the hall from Katlin and Tori in D.C. and Chaz is a what, not a who. It's the most lethal, non-nuclear bomb on the planet. Harper helped develop it."

The phone on the table continued to ring.

Tori picked up the explanation. "It's the newest and coolest shit you'll ever work with. A cup could level this entire block, but you can bake it into cake and eat it, pound it with a hammer and nothing will happen."

The phone continued to ring, the annoying sound filling the room. The women glanced at it then each other. Katlin picked up and dialed again.

Lei Lu, who'd been digging in a bag, pulled out a detonator. "But connect Chaz to one of these babies, and it goes boom."

After five rings, the phone stopped, and there was a long single tone. Katlin leaned over and entered a code. The phone rang twice more, and a man answered, "Good, bad, or ugly?"

"Fugly," Katlin replied.

"What do you need, Little One?" The voice sounded familiar to Alex, but he couldn't place it. Definitely an older man and the nickname was one Top used for her. Family?

"Do you know where Harper Tambini is? I just tried to call her, and she didn't answer." Katlin stared at the triangular fixture in the middle of the table.

There was a long pause, and the silent black speaker drew everyone's attention.

"Uncle Tom? You still there?" Katlin asked.

Ah, Alex thought. Her uncle was the deputy director of the CIA. Interesting that he was able to help her and understandable that he'd be willing. The man had never been married long enough to have children, and Katlin was close to her family, what was left of it.

"Harper is tied up in Colombia, but we're all working on getting her out safely." There were obviously underlying codes in that sentence.

All the women stiffened and glanced from one to another

then at Katlin. She nodded once. "As soon as we're done here, we'll fly to South America."

A chair creaked in the background before the number two man in the spook world said, "We'll make that decision after you get Lady Harrier out of there."

The other sat phone rang. Lei Lu picked it up and mouthed, "Ops."

Katlin nodded in acknowledgement.

"Thanks for the inside scoop, Uncle Tom. Gotta go. I love you." Katlin's face was soft as she smiled.

"We all love you, Uncle Tom," a chorus of female voices rang out.

"Take care, Ladies. I'll see you all out at the farm when you get home." The affection he had for the women in the room was undeniable.

"Yes, sir," was repeated by each woman.

"DD CIA out." Alex took that opportunity to glance at his men. Each face sported raised eyebrows and a slacked jaw. He smiled inside but schooled his face. These women were well connected.

Grace leaned over and picked up the phone to click off the line before she handed it to Katlin, who slid it into her pocket. With a nod from her leader, Lei Lu depressed a button on the other sat phone and laid it on the speaker.

"Black Swan here," Katlin announced. "You're on speaker with the entire team." She looked at Alex then down the line of men. She shook her head and pressed her index finger to her lips.

"Ops Director here, Ladies," Jack announced. "I know you've been trained to handle a raid and rescue, but I'm not comfortable having you go in there without backup."

"We're not leaving Lady Harrier behind, and we're not waiting." Katlin's voice was fierce.

"You do not have permiss—"

Katlin overrode Jack's protest. She looked directly at Alex

and asked, "Do I have permission to hire American mercenaries?"

"Lady Hawk, I've already looked into that possibility, and we don't have any contractors in the area." Jack sounded as though he were talking with a petulant teenager.

"I know of some," she insisted. "How much can I offer them?"

"Do you trust these men?" Concern wove through every word.

Staring at Alex, she smiled and ran her gaze down the line of his men. "Absolutely. With my life."

"Control here," another male voice interrupted. "I have SOCOM on the line, and they want to talk to the boots on the ground."

Jack ordered, "Patch him in."

"Director SOCOM here." The male voice was deep and commanding. "We've been listening in."

"Shit." Jack's word was just above a breath, but everyone heard it.

The number one man in special operations for the U.S.A never missed a beat. "Lady Hawk, we've been following your progress and are aware that you've never done an R and R before, but we have complete confidence that you can do this. But there is another mission that could assist yours. What nation do these mercs claim?"

"They are all former U.S. military officers, SpecOps, SEALs and Special Forces."

"We didn't know anyone was operating in that area," SOCOM insisted. "Who are they? I need names before I'll allow you to hire them."

"Sir," Jack interjected.

"Ladies, you work for Jack, but your lives are ultimately my responsibility." The man who'd once been head of the Joint Chiefs of Staff had just put Jack in his place. Alex grinned.

Katlin raised an eyebrow and stared at Alex. With his nod, she informed everyone on the line, "They are led by former Marine Captain Alejandro Lobo."

The sound of clicking keys was interrupted by Jack's exclamation, "What the fuck is he doing there?"

Katlin popped back with, "Well, I certainly didn't invite him."

Jack huffed. "I'm not happy about this turn of events. We'll discuss his presence there when you get back."

The former five-star general spoke over Jack's chastising. "Jack, you don't have to worry about him. I'll hire him. Given the Intel Black Swan provided on that factory, we want it leveled. It'll make an excellent distraction so her team can extract Lady Harrier. SOCOM out. "

Alex's phone rang, but before he was able to leave the room, he heard Jack say, "Lady Hawk, your mission is still the same. Get Lady Harrier out of that house and then get the hell out of Iraq."

"Yes, sir. Black Swan out." She hung up on her boss before he could say anything else.

Alex stepped into the hallway and answered his phone. "Alex Wolf speaking." He wandered down to the living area, followed by his men.

"Captain Lobo, this is General Peterson. We've worked together before when you were serving active duty in the Marines. I understand you are in Iraq, near Baghdad, and might be able to lend assistance in a little situation we have in Tarmiyah."

Alex had played this game from the other side, hiring local mercs to help him. "Maybe. If the price is right." But he'd do it anyway because it was Katlin's life on the line, and she would go in after Nita alone if he didn't help.

The price quoted was better than right—it was almost insane—although Alex knew better than to instantly agree. He'd never wanted to be back in the shadow world, putting his life, and those of his men, on the line every minute of every day. But Kat needed him, and he'd do anything for her, even die for her. This was a slippery slope he'd stepped on, agreeing to work for the government again. It had to be on his terms.

"Do we have a deal, Mr. Lobo?" the director of SOCOM asked.

"I'll call you back on this number in five minutes." So many thoughts ran through his mind. He had to get them all straight before he committed to anything. "I need to talk with my men."

As soon as Alex disconnected the call, every man in front of him agreed they'd do it for free because, seriously, who didn't like blowing shit up? Besides, they were already there. SOCOM just sanctioned them. The money was a bonus.

Money. What to do with the money? Alex was a good businessman and would never leave money on the table unless it involved something illegal, and this mission had been endorsed by the top man himself. He called his CFO.

"Hello, Alex. You in town? Want to grab a beer?" Barry offered.

"Maybe when I get back. This is a dry country, and a beer sounds really good," Alex admitted. "Hey, man, but I need your help. Where can I send half a million dollars?"

"To my account," Barry cajoled.

"No, my friend, I'm serious." Alex hoped his desperation sounded real because it was. His five minutes were dwindling fast. "How hard is it to set up an overseas account?"

"Katlin uses a bank in Grand Turk," Barry explained. "That should be good enough for you. Ready for the number of your new account?"

Two minutes later, Alex gave the string of numbers to someone at USSOCOM.

"Sir, I've been instructed to transfer you to Ops Center." *Here it comes.* Alex dreaded the next lecture.

"Ops Center here, Mr. Lobo." The woman's voice was pleasant and a true surprise. "I've been ordered to support you in any way we can. Do you need a food or water drop?"

Shock passed through Alex. They'd never had such service when he was active duty. "No, ma'am. I think we're good."

"Very well then, what explosives do you want?" she asked. "I have RDX, and some HRDX in your area, reachable to you within four hours. Oh, and I have some CMX-3 five hours away."

Alex suddenly remembered Katlin's conversation. "Can I get some Chaz?"

"One minute, please," she replied.

The director of SOCOM came on the line. "Mr. Lobo, what do you know about Chaz?"

Well, damn. Next to nothing, but it was what Kat's team really wanted. "The women mentioned it as their preferred explosive." That was true and accurate.

He heard the former Army general exhale a long, deep breath. "Excellent thinking on their part. It might work better and help contain any unprocessed nuclear materials. They'll have to—" The man cut off his thought verbalization. "Mr. Lobo, change in plans. Your team will have to integrate with the Ladies of Black Swan. Only Lady Falcon is certified in handling Chaz, which means someone from your team will have to replace her and accompany Black Swan inside to rescue Lady Harrier. This changes our deal, and you have the option to back out because Lady Hawk is now in charge of both teams. Tell me right now if you have a problem following orders from a woman."

"No, sir. We can do that." Especially if it meant saving Nita and destroying the Islamic State's means to nuclear weapons that would be used against Americans.

"I need to talk with Lady Hawk to be sure she's okay with

this idea." The man then ordered Alex to continue with what he needed to successfully accomplish the job.

The drop size increased as Alex considered all alternative situations. He wouldn't take any chances with the safety of Katlin and her team. Alex felt like a kid in a candy store. Anything he wanted was his for the asking.

"Sir, I'm to inform you that you are to report to Lady Hawk immediately for further instructions," the woman at USSOCOM informed him when they'd finalized the list of provisions and weapons.

"Do you always handle the Ladies of Black Swan missions?" Alex asked the young-sounding woman.

"No, sir." She lowered her voice to just above a whisper. "I didn't even believe they were real until ten minutes ago when I got to talk with Lady Hawk herself. They're like an urban legend among the women here, and the men would never believe it in a million years. Maybe now that I know about them, the brass will let me handle them all the time." She sounded so excited about the possibility. "So, you know Lady Hawk?"

Oh, yes. He knew her. In ways that would probably make the young woman blush on the other end of the line. "Thanks for all your help." Alex cut off the conversation. It might be a test, knowing those fucking bureaucrats.

He needed to get back to Kat and her team. "Wolf out."

CHAPTER 37

Katlin crouched next to Alex in the deep shadows, around the corner from the back door to the house where Nita and Chase were being held. She was on point. Lady Eagle had the opposite side of the large home and would follow her and Alex inside, guarding their six.

They had a pretty good idea where the terrorists had taken their team members, but since Lady Harrier had never been allowed in that part of the house, they'd had no eyes and ears there. Fortunately, the devices she'd planted on the walls elsewhere had allowed them to eliminate those areas. Unfortunately, they worked well enough to overhear the beating someone had taken. Katlin hoped Lady Harrier had been spared most of the brutality, not that she wanted Chase beaten senseless.

With no air conditioning and temps that had reached over one hundred that day, infrared was relatively worthless. Even the external walls registered as body temperature, though it was past midnight.

"Number one set," Lady Falcon announced over their comm units. She had been put in charge of bringing down the nuclear processing operation with the Chaz air dropped to them by SOCOM. Two of Alex's men were positioned in sniper hides, and one was with her, protecting her as she armed the dangerous explosive.

Sweat dripped down Katlin's back as she silently took a knee, constantly scanning the area through her night vision goggles.

"Two men approaching, east side, carrying weapons," Lady Kite stated. She was on the roof of their safe house covering Alex and Katlin. "No worries. They're talking and sharing a cigarette."

Twenty minutes ticked by slowly. With every breath, Katlin had inhaled the scent of Alex. Her heart had been beating so fast from the mission, not his nearness. That was what she had told herself over and over again. It was going to break her heart, especially since he'd claimed he was in love with her, but she had to end things with him. On the other hand, now that he'd seen her in combat, he wouldn't want her. He'd made it perfectly clear that women didn't belong in theater and should never be allowed in Special Operations. Hell, he was there because he didn't think she could handle a situation like this. She'd show him, and then he'd probably dump her before she even had the chance.

"Last one in place." Lady Falcon's words signaled the end of phase one.

"Flipper, you have a go," Katlin ordered.

"For the record, I fucking hate that handle," Griffin mumbled and strode into the factory as though he belonged there. Seconds later, a deafening horn blast filled the air. Like ants leaving a colony, men shoved into the night when doors on every side of the metal building flew open. They didn't hang around either. Most sprinted for the nearest gate and disappeared into darkness.

The house door near Katlin banged open and bounced back on the next man. Arabic expletives and yells of confusion surrounded her as she waited patiently, counting the soldiers running toward the factory.

"That's eight," Alex noted. "That leaves at least four more inside. You ready?"

This was her op, and she wouldn't allow Alex to take over just because he had a Y chromosome. She had twice as many X's as him, and that made her twice as good. "Just wait," she insisted. He probably didn't know that two of the guards regularly banged several of the women inside. She was willing to reduce the number of encounters through patience. Sure enough, a half-dressed soldier ran out with untied boots while jabbing his arms into his shirt.

A deep voice inside the house called out that he'd stay and protect the women.

Damn. He was close to the door.

Didn't matter. It was time. "Bravo headed in." Katlin peeped around the corner. "Lady Eagle, move in." Both women rounded to the back of the house at the same time. They breached the door, Katlin going high and immediately spotting the half-dressed man. She double tapped him in the head and started moving before his body hit the floor. The shot report bounced down the hall, even though she had a silencer.

Lady Eagle and Wolf peeled off to quickly check the rooms behind her. Not the conventional way to clear a house, but Katlin was worried they'd kill Lady Harrier and Chase as soon as the house fighting began.

She came to what should be a basement door and an open padlock hung through the latch. Someone laid a big hand on her left shoulder and gave it a squeeze. She smelled Alex's sweat. Memories of their naked bodies in bed streaked through her mind before she chased them away. There was no time for those thoughts.

She cracked the door and glanced down a set of stairs into a barely lit dirt hole. "On three."

With trained precision, as though they'd been working together for years, Alex followed her quietly down the steps…into hell.

Lady Harrier lay naked, chained on a pallet bed in one corner. Her face was a dirty, bloody mess, her eyes swollen closed. Katlin could hear her short, labored breaths.

She finally tore her gaze from her battered friend, Nita, and quickly scanned the room.

Chase seemed to float out of a darkened corner,

All her training and muscle memory instantly returned as she raised her gun to shoot the terrorist holding Alex's man as a human shield.

She was half a second too late. She had gazed too long at her teammate.

The terrorist had gotten off a shot, but it wasn't at her.

Katlin fired, and the man's hand disappeared in a mist of red blood. His gun went flying, and he dropped Chase, who slid to the hard-packed floor. She drilled two shots into the bad guy's chest and another into his head as her aim followed him to the floor. Yeah, it was overkill. Kill being the important part of that term.

Looking through the sights of her pistol, she swept the room, searching for more bad guys. Finally, she said, "We're clear down here."

She turned and saw Alex checking Chase and Lady Eagle at Lady Harrier's side. "We need to move," Katlin demanded. "Wolf, can you carry him?" She went to the dead guy, seemingly the only guard in the basement, and searched his pockets for the keys to Lady Harrier's chains.

"Yeah." Alex glanced over at Lady Harrier. "I can get her too."

"No need," both Lady Eagle and Lady Hawk replied at the same time.

"We practice this all the time," Katlin explained. She looked at Lady Eagle, who had wound Lady Harrier's discarded abaya around her battered body. "I've got point until we're out of the house." She and Grace would switch off then.

Katlin cautiously topped the stairs and looked both ways before giving the signal for them to follow. She hadn't made it two steps when the world shook.

Kaboom.

She turned to see Alex shove Lady Eagle through the door, and then her friend fell to her knees and laid Lady Harrier on the floor as gently as possible.

Alex tossed Chase on the floor…then disappeared as though an elevator had swept him down while gray and tan dust plumed where Alex had stood seconds ago.

Katlin ran toward the doorway and slid to her knees. The stairs were gone, and she couldn't see a fucking thing.

Her ears rang from the explosion. "Alex," she screamed into the tiny particles of dirt.

Lady Eagle knelt beside her and stared into the darkness.

Chatter filled Katlin's comm unit as others reported activity outside, but all her energy was focused on the man she loved who was in the hole in front of her. She snatched a chem stick from her pocket, cracked it to release its luminosity, then tossed it into the hole. Was it her imagination, or was that basement deeper than before?

A slight movement caught her eye as dust swirled. "Alex, are you okay?"

"Fuck." He coughed and sat up then pulled his shirt over his nose and face to act as a filter. "Give me a minute."

The house creaked and white stucco-like material sprinkled from the ceiling.

"We don't have a minute," Grace noted and stared at a large crack above her head.

Alex tried to stand up and swore again.

"Where are you injured?" Katlin asked. To Grace, she ordered, "Rope."

"On it." Grace started searching the area. When Lady Harrier moaned, Grace bent and reassured their teammate.

"It's my knee again." He hobbled toward the opening as the dust settled around his feet. When Alex reached toward the open door above him, he winced. "Jesus Christ."

"Shoulder? Arm? Did you break something?" Katlin questioned.

"No. The fucker shot me in the bicep." He looked at the tear in his shirt. "I thought he'd just grazed me, but I think it might be a through and through."

"Lady Eagle," Katlin called. When her friend stepped beside her, Katlin jumped into the basement. "Alex, I want you to stiffen your whole body as straight as possible."

"What the hell are you going to do?" Alex's eyes were so wide she could see the whites surrounding his big brown irises.

"Lift you." She slammed her fists on her hips. "Do exactly as I say. Raise your arms as high as you can and try to get your elbows over the lip of the door.

He stood there, gawking at her.

A loud cracking noise saturated the basement.

"Now," she shouted and bent her knees on the outside of his legs. She clasped her arms around his knees. "Hold your body stiff as a board." The second she felt him tighten, she thrust upward.

Lady Eagle caught his forearms and pulled him through the doorway. She rolled him away and lay on her stomach, arms reaching down. Katlin leaped and grabbed her teammate's arms close to the elbows. She held her body rigid as Lady Eagle scooted backwards until Katlin could grab the edge. In one swift move, she was sitting on the main floor again.

"Eagle. Hawk. Can you hear me?" Flipper called over the comm. "Are you ladies all right? Answer me."

"We've been a little busy here." Lady Eagle's voice was terse. She exhaled a long, slow breath.

"Need some help?" several male voices asked.

"Nope." Katlin high-fived Grace as they rose to their feet. "We got this." Then she looked at Alex, who was ignoring his own pain and checking for broken bones on Chase. "We could use a tall shoulder to help Alex limp to the extraction site, though."

"Lady Hawk, ETA one minute," Lady Falcon announced. "Wait till you see this ride. Look for the big black Chevy SUV. Somebody here likes American vehicles, or they stole it from our guys. It's bulletproof."

Jack slammed the phone back into the cradle and stared at the row of blinking lights, all waiting for him. He had hundreds of operatives all over the world, senators and congressmen who thought he worked for them, and over a thousand people who reported to him, but there was only one he truly cared about. And damn her, she occupied way too many of his thoughts. He'd been ready to kill someone over at USSOCOM when he'd been informed Lady Hawk's backup team had been pulled off and she was vulnerable.

An annoying bleep preceded his secretary's voice. "Sir, you have several calls waiting, and it's nearly six thirty. They all claim to be urgent, but shall I pass them on to someone else? I'll be leaving within ten minutes."

Fuck them. Fuck them all.

"Yes, do that." He shoved his chair back and stomped to the large window. "I'll be leaving shortly myself."

"Very well, sir. I'll see you tomorrow." The older woman who guarded access to him disconnected the line.

Jack stared at a beautiful setting sun but saw nothing. Fucking Wolf. SOCOM had given permission for Black Swan to fly the bastard and his team out of Iraq. He was on the jet right now…with *his* Katlin. Jack hadn't even flown in their jet. He wondered if Wolf and Katlin would join the mile high club on the way back to the U.S.A.? Just the thought of Alex fucking his woman made him furious. She'd spread those soft, smooth legs apart for him, and she'd be drenched with need.

Jack closed his eyes and licked his tight lips as though he were tasting her passion himself. He inhaled slowly, remembering the smell of the little pink panties he'd stolen from the laundry while they'd shared a house during their one and only op together.

His cock had instantly hardened and now pulsed as another fantasy of making love to Katlin had taken over every cell in his busy brain. He ran his hand up and down his erection, pretending it was her small fist tightening around him.

Fuck. He opened his eyes and saw his reflection in the glass. He should be happy that Lady Harrier was alive. Although she'd been beaten badly, she had only bruises, no broken bones. What thrilled him was that she'd be forced to recuperate for at least a week so the Ladies of Black Swan would be grounded until Lady Harrier had been cleared for duty. That meant he'd have Katlin near as the ladies trained. He'd see her every day. She'd be in the office some, too. He had a greater chance to be with her. And more opportunities for Wolf to fuck things up so she'd come running to him.

If Wolf went to work for SOCOM, Jack could dispose of the man so easily during a mission. He had done it before. Men died on the battlefield every day.

Jack would never let Wolf keep her.

She's mine, and I won't ever let her go.

The dream of Katlin being his, forever, made him smile. He'd rush home from this office and the worries of the world, to find her cooking him supper. She'd greet him at the door in her apron...and nothing else. After a passionate kiss in the foyer, she'd turn, and he'd watch that beautiful ass of hers move away until he couldn't stand it another second. He'd throw his coat on the floor and rip off his shirt, sending buttons like bullets in every direction. He'd chase her toward the living room and bend her over the back of the couch, driving his cock into her wet heat until she screamed his name. Only then would he release himself into her, planting a child that would grow within her, tying her to him with tighter bonds.

He was hard as a rock and ready to come for a woman who wouldn't land for another six hours. Even then, she wouldn't take care of his hard-on. But he could do something about that. Jack grabbed his burner phone and dialed a familiar number. The sexy voice that answered asked, "Where and when?"

"Thirty minutes, my house." Jack glanced at his desk, knowing he had reports to read, but he wouldn't get to them tonight. "Wear the apron." He had plans for her.

Forty minutes later, Jack unlocked the door to his Georgetown brownstone home where he slept in at least three days a week. He smelled her perfume, Katlin's favorite, as soon as he stepped inside. A glance toward the kitchen assured him she'd followed his instructions. An apron covered her luscious breasts, showing just a hint of cleavage. She shook her long blonde hair, and it fell forward when she leaned against the island that separated the two rooms. His cock pounded on his zipper, begging for freedom and the woman thirty feet away.

She looked good enough to eat. His mouth watered at the remembered fantasy from less than an hour ago. Maybe he'd hoist her bare ass to the cold granite counter and slide his tongue down the slit that protected her moist center. He could practically taste her creamy desire for him.

He slid out of his jacket and folded it neatly. When he

passed the couch in the formal living room, he carefully laid it over the back. His gaze never left hers as he closed the distance. She would be his to do with what he pleased for next several hours.

"We need to talk, Jack." The Deputy Secretary of Homeland Security stepped in front of him. Rodolfo "Rod" Santiago had been hidden in the shadows of the bookcase.

What the fuck is he doing here?

His boss looked at the beautiful woman standing in his kitchen. "Thank you, Agent Chernakov. This mission is complete. I expect your final report on my desk by noon tomorrow."

Mission? Was *he* a mission? What the fuck was going on?

When Kat—no, Katrina...no, her name was Nikkole Katrina Chernakov—came around the corner of the island, she had already untied the apron. She was in a low-cut tank top and slacks. Not naked.

"Thank you, sir." She nodded as she passed the number two man at the agency. Her face was totally unreadable when she looked directly into Jack's eyes. Then her gaze dropped to his crotch, where his dick was shrinking by the second. He swore the corner of her mouth twitched as she walked by.

With the closing of the front door, his boss gestured to the silk brocade furniture. "Have a seat, Jack. This will only take a few minutes."

Jack sat on the century-old couch that had been in his grandparents' home his entire childhood. It had been uncomfortable during the mandatory Sunday visits and hadn't improved with age. He never used this room, favoring the overstuffed leather sectional upstairs in front of his big screen television. The old feeling of parental inspection overwhelmed him.

Rod leaned forward and rested his elbows on his knees. "There's nothing I hate more than having USSOCOM call me and tell me I have a problem." He nodded toward the door. "Especially one I already knew about."

Jack had been in the civil service all his adult life and knew how to play the game. They'd sent Nikkole to test him. "Sir, I have never revealed any state secrets to her or anyone else," Jack stated emphatically. He gave a self-deprecating smile. "We've been having consensual sex. Stress relief. She's not in my department." Yet. She had done all kinds of things to persuade Jack to request for her to transfer to operations. He knew what lines he could cross and which to step back from.

Dark brown eyes the color of cola stared at him. "This has to end, Jack."

"No problem, sir." Jack sounded convincing even to himself. "I'll break off the affair—"

"You misunderstand, Ashworth." His boss's tone showed the man's impatience. "This comes straight from SOCOM… leave Katlin Callahan alone. We can replace you much easier than we can her."

CHAPTER 38

Katlin held the tablet over Lady Harrier's forearm. "What do you think, Doc?" She spoke through her comm unit to an orthopedic surgeon at Walter Reed National Military Medical Center just outside D.C. who was looking at the mobile x-ray via satellite.

"I can't tell for sure, but she may have a slight fracture." The doctor hummed. "Looks like someone twisted her arm. This new gadget is good, but for such a fine break, I'll need to see it with our equipment."

"What do we have?" Alex's quiet voice distracted Katlin. She looked across Chase's battered body to where her lover stood beside Reed, who'd been a medic with Army Special Forces. The careful stitches on Chase's face told a different story. This man had training far beyond that offered by the military to field medics.

"A few broken ribs but the pneumothorax, that's a punctured lung, is doing better. There's a possible cranial fracture if that amazing toy of theirs is accurate." Reed nodded to the tablet in Katlin's hand. "I didn't find any internal bleeding, but there could be a slow leak somewhere."

Reed looked around the back of their jet, which had been

turned into a flying hospital. Plastic sheets covered the walls and floor. The comfortable chairs had been lifted and pronated before they were draped in thick synthetic then surgical sheets. "This is beyond amazing." He glanced through the clear wall to where the others slept, ate, or played computer games. "I didn't know our government owned anything like this."

Katlin smiled. "They don't. Not exactly." She diverted his attention back to Chase. "What else do you need? We're still five hours from D.C."

"I can handle these two patients." He gave her an assessing once-over. "I understand you'll be flying the last leg. Why don't you try to catch an hour or so of sleep? Doctor's orders."

Alex moved to wrap his good arm around her shoulders. "Come on. Reed will call us if anything changes here." He guided her to the cabin, where one of the men moved so she and Alex could sit side by side. She slid into the seat to his left since his right arm was bandaged.

She called over her shoulder into the cockpit, where Lady Eagle flew pilot and Lady Kite handled the second chair. "How's it look?"

"We're two hours out from refueling, and they're ready for us," Grace explained. "It'll be a fast turn and burn."

"Excellent." Katlin was too wound up to relax just yet, and she couldn't have a glass of wine because she had to fly the plane soon. She turned to Alex. "I heard you on the phone with SOCOM. Were they pleased with the mission?"

"Yeah." Alex took her hand and squeezed. "Too fucking happy. They asked me if we'd be interested in more missions."

Well, that was interesting, but probably not unexpected. "What was your answer?"

"I left the Marines because I didn't want to do this anymore." He rubbed his forehead then looked into her eyes.

"I love my job running Guardian Security, making sure when grandmothers fall down there's an ambulance to help her within minutes, protecting CEOs, and monitoring people's homes and businesses." He glanced at the back of the plane where Reed checked the monitors connected to Nita and Chase. "Nobody gets hurt on a regular basis, and I've never had anyone die on my watch since I left the Marine Corps."

Katlin shrugged. "Then tell them no."

Alex bounced their joined hands on his knee. "I want to be there for you. I want to be your backup. Things can go to hell in seconds and..." His gaze wandered to where their injured teammates lay in drug-induced sleep. "Things could have been a lot worse for Nita if we hadn't gotten her out when we did."

Katlin let out a long sigh as she stared at her friend. "I know that, all too well." She was sickened by what they'd done to Nita. Her breasts were black and purple with bruising that matched her swollen face. She had open striations on her butt cheeks where something like a whip had ripped her skin. Her wrists and ankles were abraded from the chains they'd used to tie her to the platform bed. Thankfully, she hadn't been raped. She'd still be seeing the Section 7 shrink for months over this one.

Alex grabbed Katlin's chin and forced her to look at him. "That could have been you." His voice broke on the heartfelt words.

She stared into concerned eyes and shot back, "And you could be the one lying in that bed in the back with a lung punctured by your own rib. Or worse."

She placed her palm on his beard-roughened cheek. "In all the missions I've been on in the past three years, and there have been a lot of them, this was the very first time my agency backup and the military backup were pulled off before we were wheels up."

"But it happened and could happen again," Alex insisted.

"I worry about you...when you're out. I don't want you hurt."

"If our roles were reversed, I'd worry about you, too." That was very true. "We're trained for this, and we are damn good at it."

Why was she fighting to keep this relationship? She wanted him to walk away...didn't she? So he wouldn't end up on a bed like Chase. This was her opportunity to shove him out of her life. The fact that her heart might never get over it when he dropped it into a million pieces, well, that was her burden to bear. At least Alex would be safe, protecting grandmothers and families in the United States.

"Alex, this is my life." She had to say it. "If you can't accept what I do for a living, then there's no reason for us to go on. We'll just end up hurting each other."

"No!" His voice was a bit too loud, and several gazes shot their way. Quieter, he claimed, "I love you. I hate it every time I have to say goodbye. It's your job, and I understand that part better than anyone else. You've made a commitment, and I'm sure you're still under contract to the military or government or whatever. But I can't let you leave my life again."

He had to let her go. It was the only way to be sure he was safe.

Alex brushed his lips over hers then stared into her eyes. They widened as though he'd just realized something.

"You didn't think you'd get rid of me that easily, did you?" Alex smiled.

Had he read her mind? How the hell did he know?

"You don't have to protect me. Your job doesn't frighten me. I've seen you and your team in action. I'm proud as hell that I know you and these awesome women who work with you." He exhaled heavily. "Section 7 terrifies the fuck out of me, and if it's that Jack-ass making life-and-death decisions, especially where you're concerned, I don't like it at all."

Alex brought their joined hands to his lips and pressed a

kiss on the back of her hand. "I have to talk with the others, but I think I'm going to tell SOCOM I'm willing to take jobs now and then, especially if we're going to be the ones backing you up."

He smiled. "The money is insane, and to think I used to do the same thing for a captain's pay. Besides, Guardian wouldn't be the first security company to run black ops out the back door."

Katlin wasn't sure how she felt about Alex back in the shadow world, but it was his choice. He'd been there before and was well trained. As far as backing her up, well, if he were close, she could protect him.

"I'm not letting you out of my life so just let that crazy thought go," Alex insisted. "Promise that you will always come back to me at the end of every mission...and only me. When you left me standing in the hangar at Quantico, you took my heart with you."

She brushed her lips over his. "I left my heart in your hands that night, too."

"You know I love you, Kat."

"I've always loved you." She could admit that now. "Life has taken us on unrelenting, intertwining paths that I've tried to ignore. I'm tired of fighting it. This is right, you and me."

"Through all those years, as I watched you with Ty..." Alex glanced away then returned his gaze to Kat. "It tore my heart apart because, even then, part of me knew you belonged with me."

Katlin nodded. "How do think I felt when you married Rachelle?"

"You know I had to do that," Alex shot back.

"Yes." Katlin admitted, "And it made me love you even more that you and Rachelle have shared your daughter with me, allowing me to love a child. I'll never have that for myself."

Alex pulled her to him. "We'll do whatever it takes if you want kids. We'll figure out a way."

Katlin sniffed back tears of hope. "I can't go there right now."

When she buried her face in his neck, Alex rubbed his cheek over the crown of her head. "Everything will work out." He ran his hand up and down her back. "You need to go to sleep so you can fly us safely home."

She sighed deeply, melting into his loving warmth. "I don't have a home," she admitted.

Alex kissed her temple. "Yes, you do. This is home. Wherever we're together. You in my arms."

EPILOGUE

The humid heat and aqua-blue water of the indoor pool at The Basic School on Marine Corps Base Quantico reminded Katlin of Costa Rica. A vacation sounded wonderful, and needed. Warm sand, Caribbean breeze, clear water, and Rosita's cooking. And sleep.

She was hoping to take off a week, maybe two, and go to Central America to see her brother. Daniel was undercover in Nicaragua but he'd sneak away to see her. He too could use some fun in the sun. They all could. Her teammates would go with her. They loved the Callahan compound.

Katlin wondered if Alex might be able to join her. They'd only been able to spend a few nights together since returning from Iraq. He was behind in his office rotation and had flown out to the Guardian Security Los Angeles Center. Although they talked almost every night, she missed him. Since he was guarding a starlet that night at some red-carpet event—stepping in for one of the many out sick with the flu—they wouldn't get to talk later. Alex had been the woman's bodyguard before, which would make it easier on him, but he'd complained that she was a nightcrawler, not his favorite nighttime activity. Still, maybe he'd call.

"So, ladies, what you think?" Marine Corps Brigadier General Ava Standish asked the Black Swan team members sitting in the bleachers at the Ramer Hall Aquatic Training Center.

"This place still looks the same, and smells like chlorine and sweaty men." Nita started to lean back against the bleacher behind her, but when her cast bumped, she winced and repositioned her butt on the metal bench.

"I hated jumping off that platform." Tori glared at the set of double stairs leading to the narrow bridge fifteen feet in the air where Joint All-Female Special Operations School trainees stood waiting their turn to step off. They were completely dressed in a camouflage uniform, jumping boots-first into the water below. "I'm fine once I'm in the water, but that first step still gives me the heebie-jeebies."

"I'd rather drop off a fast boat with tanks and fins and swim five miles in the dark ocean than take that leap of faith again." Lei Lu shuddered. Her gaze shot to Brigadier General Janet Nichols. "We don't have to requalify, do we, ma'am?"

"Not today," the highest-ranking woman in the Air Force replied. "Since your team isn't mission-ready at the moment, we decided to give you a break from busywork at Homeland Security. Your team has been out in the field for a couple years. You know what's required of you. We're curious as to what you think of this group."

Army Major General Nancy Burkhoff scowled. "The Joint Chiefs of Staff didn't allow us to create a second group for the pilot program until you proved yourselves."

All four women wearing stars on their shoulders turned and smiled at the Ladies of Black Swan.

"We're so Goddamn proud of you." General Standish started to move her hand toward Katlin but quickly withdrew it. Aunt Ava, as she'd been called for most of her life, had a habit of patting her on the knee, but she was in general mode and couldn't show any affection. Katlin gave her an understanding smile.

"We certainly are." Admiral Willet smiled ear to ear.

"Thank you for proving us right." General Nichols nodded to each woman on Katlin's team. "So, what do you think about these recruits?"

Everyone shifted their gaze to the water.

Katlin scanned the forty-five women in and around the pool. "I think you have some good possibilities in this class. Several look to be strong swimmers. I haven't seen any that I would really consider weak. That'll come in handy when they move to SEAL training."

"We added solid swimming skills as a requirement for application to the program," General Nichols interjected. "In your group, over a dozen Dropped On Request during the swimming portion of Phase I. We beefed up several other conditions as well."

"We're almost a month into training and only five have DORd." The satisfied grin on Army Major General Nancy Burkhoff's face said it all. "We've had two injured who will not be able to complete the course. Hopefully, we'll be allowed to have a third group start as soon as this one completes the program. Anyone injured will be given first choice to join the new class."

"Have you had them out in the ocean yet?" Katlin asked.

"No. We'll ship them out to Camp Lejeune, North Carolina, next week. You remember how often we moved your class. It helps maintain the secrecy of the program, as well as keeping recruits on the edge," General Standish explained. "They'll spend a lot of time in the gritty sand and Atlantic Ocean on Onslow Beach, just like their soon-to-be counterparts at MARSOC."

Since Alex had been a company commanding officer at the Marine Special Operations Command at the same time her father had been base commander, Katlin had spent a great deal of time on that particular beach. Her training class had gone to a private beach with former SEAL instructors.

Admiral Betsy Willet tracked a recruit as she rapidly performed a perfect breaststroke to the shallow end. "That's Piper Knight. She swam for Florida State. She shocked her parents, and her coaches, when she announced at graduation that she was joining the Navy rather than try out for the Olympics. She probably would've made it. Her brother is a SEAL, East Coast, lieutenant."

"What kind of relationship does she have with him?" Katlin had been thinking a lot about Daniel. She needed to see for herself that he was okay. Since they were grounded while Nita's fractured arm healed, Costa Rica sounded awesome.

"He's seven years older than her. Although they were never together in high school or college, Piper seemed to follow in his footsteps. Her brother was also on the swim team. He never won as many medals as she did, nor was as competitive." Admiral Willet smiled. "She seems bound and determined to beat his records, as though she has to prove herself better than her brother."

"That's why she jumped on this opportunity." Lei Lu downed half of her water bottle. "We all had our reasons."

Short bursts from a whistle echoed around the aquatic center.

The women lined the pool edge, standing in the water. Every time the whistle blew, they pulled themselves out of the water, held for five seconds then went back in, immersing their shoulders. They repeated this ten times.

The Ladies of Black Swan knew what was next. Treading water. Sore shoulders made the torture even worse.

"Anyone want to give them a pep talk?" General Burkhoff asked after five minutes of watching fully-clothed women peddling their booted feet and slowly moving their arms around her body to keep their heads above water.

To Katlin's surprise, Lei Lu jumped up. "I've got this."

After a moment's whispered discussion with the lead trainer, he smiled as he held out the megaphone. When she waved it off, his eyebrows rose.

"Ladies," she called out in a clear, concise voice. For such a small-framed woman, Lei Lu had the command voice of a Marine drill sergeant. The dual silver bars on her collar glistened under the bright lights. "Do you know why you're here?"

"Ma'am, yes ma'am." The chorus of female voices filled the white block building.

"I doubt that's true." Lei Lu paced the edge of the water, her gaze never leaving the wet women. "You're here because we want to keep you alive. Water is the great equalizer. It doesn't give a shit who you are, where you came from, whether you're male or female, or if you live or die. It doesn't care how *special* you are." She rounded the far end of the pool, moving silently and gracefully as she spoke. "If you can't handle yourself in the water, you're going to die there."

Katlin wasn't sure if anyone else saw the furtive glance Lei Lu gave the group of male instructors gathered ten feet away. The biggest one, who had to be six foot three inches and go at least two twenty-five, had the audacity to roll his eyes.

"That was a fucking big mistake." Nita leaned forward.

"This ought to be good." Tori stood to get a better view, then whipped out her phone. "She's going to want to see this on video, again and again."

Brigadier General Janet Nichols's gaze darted around the pool. "What's going on?"

General Standish chuckled. "I believe that big Marine over there is about to get schooled."

"You're going to have to make life-and-death decisions, in and around the water," Lei Lu explained as she stepped closer to the men.

The big guy leaned toward the man next to him and whispered, "Yeah, like she'd know anything about that."

Big mistake. Every woman on her team could read lips. Katlin simply smiled and crossed her arms over her chest, waiting for the show to start.

"Oh, you fucking idiot. Now you've gone and done it." Nita shook her head.

Tori giggled. "I love watching her kick ass."

"And you never know when you're going to be attacked and be forced to fight in the water." Lei Lu bent her knees and launched her body into the air, roundhouse kicking the large Marine in the head. He fell into the water and she followed him.

A few women squealed in surprise as they all backed away. Katlin and her teammates couldn't see much because of the bubbles made by their thrashing in the deep water. The fight went on for nearly a minute.

"Do something," one of the recruits yelled to the instructors who simply watched.

"No one needs saving," the lead instructor yelled from across the pool.

Lei Lu's head appeared first. In the crook of her arm she dragged the unconscious Marine to the edge next to his fellow instructors. "Somebody might need to revive him, but it sure as hell isn't going to be me."

The other men lifted Lei Lu's victim out of the pool and began resuscitation.

"You could have killed him," accused one recruit.

Lei Lu pulled herself out of the water and she jumped to a standing position. Fists on hips she glared at the woman. Then she smiled. "Yes, I could have. And by the time you've finished this program, you'll also be able to."

As she strode past the lead instructor, he threw her a towel. "Why him?"

She didn't even slow down. "I didn't like the way he looked at the women. He has a bad attitude." Her strong voice carried across the water, so everyone heard. She pulled the tie from the uniform bun at the back of her neck and let her long black hair drop to her waist, towel drying it before twisting it into a turban. Stripping out of her clothes as she walked away, she stood in front of the generals in nothing but a green tank top and black lace panties.

Admiral Burkhoff offered her another towel. "Ma'am, I want them to see how little I am. I want the smallest woman amongst them to know that she can do what I just did, on land and in the water. I want every one of those women to understand they don't have to tolerate sexual innuendos."

Brigadier General Ava Standish handed her another towel. "Are you all right, Lei Lu?"

"Yes, ma'am." She glanced across the pool to where the big Marine was coughing and spitting up water. "I'm in a lot better shape than he is. Since I couldn't kick him underwater, I grabbed his balls and squeezed. I don't think he'll be having sex anytime soon."

General Standish winced. "He's off this assignment." She smiled up at Tori. "Send me a copy of the video. Like everyone involved in the program, he signed a nondisclosure agreement. If he decides to talk about what happened, we'll see how fast this video can go viral. As far as the Marine Corps is concerned, he was hurt during a training exercise."

"Misogynistic asshole." Admiral Willet threw her arm around General Standish's shoulders. "I like the way you think."

"Ladies, I think we've caused enough mayhem here today." General Nichols glanced at Lei Lu. "I'm impressed. We'll see you tomorrow at the range."

Major General Burkhoff looked at each member of Katlin's team. "Don't get any ideas and decide to shoot someone tomorrow to prove a point. And by the way, these recruits believe they're the first to go through the program. Please, help us keep that secret."

"Are you ever going to tell them the truth?" Grace asked.

"At graduation. When they're ready for the field. They might run into you, or one of the others." General Standish's face went serious. "Until they join your ranks, their knowledge of you is a direct threat to you, and your missions. We can't allow that."

"Understood," Katlin said for all her team. "And thank you for that."

"By the way," Grace asked as they left the aquatic center. "How are the others doing?"

"Several who graduated with you have been added to other agencies depending on their area of expertise," General Burkhoff noted. "We've had a few injuries. I know you keep in touch with Bailey Conrad and Ryleigh Davenport. There have been a few others, very few. Everyone else is doing well in their positions."

"Has there been any word on Harper Tambini?" Tori slowed her long stride to match the others. "Is it true that her ATF team ran into trouble in Columbia?"

All four generals exchanged a glance.

General Burkhoff grimaced. "We're not exactly sure of the parameters of the situation."

That meant they didn't know shit. Not only was Harper a good friend, but she also lived next door. Katlin decided to place a call to Uncle Tom and see if he would give her any information.

The next morning, as Katlin showered after her morning run, her cell phone rang. It was Alex's ring tone. She stepped out of the hot water and wrapped a towel around herself, smiling, glad Alex had called. "Hello."

Katlin was not a morning person. She loved her sleep, especially when they were home.

"Kat, I'm glad you're up." He hesitated.

She sat down on the edge of the bed, fully on alert. "What's wrong? Are you okay?"

"Yeah, I'm fine." He paused again. "I just want to be sure *we* are. That's really why I called."

"Alejandro, what the hell is going on?" Katlin started to worry.

"I love you, and nothing is going to change that." His insistent voice put her on edge.

Ty used to say things like that. "What the hell did you do?" The nightmare of her life with her husband flashed through her brain. The lies. The cheating.

"Nothing." Alex rushed to say. "Absolutely nothing, except my job."

Katlin scooted so her back was against the headboard. "Explain." She had to control the tense muscles in her body. This was Alex. Not Ty.

"I can tell you haven't seen the pictures that are all over the Internet." Alex sounded worried and tired. He blew out a long breath. "Last night, I was escorting Jaemie Jones. Well, with her, I'm as much her date as I am her bodyguard. She wants it to look that way." He huffed out a breath. "Like I told you yesterday, I've played this part before with Jae."

Katlin didn't miss his familiarity and shortened name for her. The envy monster began to climb up her throat once again. *No. Alex wouldn't do this to me.*

"Jae got drunk at the premier's after party. She was a supporting actress in this movie and got in the face of the lead actress bragging how she has the lead in her next movie." He paused. "So...I... She was about to fuck up her entire career in front of everyone at that party. So, I grabbed her by the hand and practically dragged her out of the room. When she screamed at me to go back, I literally picked her up and carried her out the front door. That's when she...she threw her arms around my neck and kissed me."

He hurried on to say, "Kat. I wasn't kissing her. I was more concerned about getting her into the limo and home. The paparazzi were everywhere, though."

Well, that was different. Katlin was used to hearing about Tyler's affairs secondhand or third. With Alex, there was photographic proof.

"By the time I got her home, she was puking." He sighed once again, as though this was difficult for him to say. "It was too late to call her friends and I couldn't leave her alone. She was so sick. Crying."

"So, you stayed." Katlin loved that he was that thoughtful but couldn't help wondering if it was a lie.

"Yeah. And when I left in my tuxedo an hour ago, paparazzi were throwing questions at me right and left. There's no telling what headlines they're going to put with those pictures. Please, Kat," his tone had changed to pleading. "Ignore anything you see and hear about me associated with Jaemie Jones. It's not true. You know I love you."

Katlin was well aware of the celebrity rags. Tori loved to read those magazines and websites. Deep in her heart, she knew that Alex loved her. Possibly for the first time in her life, she was *in* love. Alex was nothing like Ty. She had to let go of her past if she wanted Alex in her future, and she wanted him more than anything else in the world.

"I trust you." She said the words, she realized they were true.

"Thank Christ." Relief left him on another sigh.

He'd been worried. That thought made her smile as her heart warmed a little more.

"Listen to me, Kat. Hear me. I haven't even wanted another woman since you appeared—naked, might I remind you—in my Miami apartment." He was so sincere. "You're the only woman I want in my bed and in my life."

"I've missed you, too." At that moment, all she wanted to do was hold him and reassure him that she loved him. But they were separated by thousands of miles. She had to tell him, though, how she felt. "I'm sure I'll get a little upset when

I see those pictures of you with her, or any another woman. But we never agreed to be exclusive."

"Bullshit. I meant it when I said that I don't want any other woman in my bed. Let's just agree right now, we're exclusive. No other men in your life, in your bed, in your body. You're mine."

"I'm yours? That sounds very possessive, as if you own me," she bristled.

"I don't own you; you agree to be mine. Just as I agree to be only with you." He was insistent and she loved it. "Say it, Kat, we're exclusive. Monogamous. Right?"

"Yes. I don't want any other man, because I'm in love with you." And, maybe, she had been for years. "You're mine. I'm yours. Exclusively." She had an idea. "How do you feel about Costa Rica?"

"Kat, I'll meet you anywhere in the world. Anytime. Just let me know the mission and what color camo to bring."

Damn, she loved this man!

"No camouflage." She laughed. "A bathing suit is a good idea. Let's get away for a week and enjoy the Caribbean Sea."

"That's the best idea I've heard in weeks." He chuckled. "Sure we need bathing suits?"

The End

Continue reading for a Sneak Peek at **Uncaged Love,** the next novel in the Black Swan series

SNEAK PEEK - UNCAGED LOVE

Harper Tambini ignored the tingling that nipped and niggled at the back of her neck. She blamed the cool breeze sweeping down from the snow-topped Andes Mountains and automatically looked that direction even though she couldn't see them in the dark of night.

"Who'd believe spring this close to the equator would be so chilly?" She rubbed her bare arms and considered digging a windbreaker out of the bag slung over her shoulder.

"We'll be on the jet soon enough," her teammate, Marcus Hernandez, reassured her. "The cold wind sure cuts right through."

"What do you expect?" Robert Sanchez flipped up the collar on his nylon jacket and hunkered into what little warmth the lightweight material offered. "We're at almost nine-thousand feet."

"Yeah, I know." She scoffed at herself. *Tambini, you're getting soft.* After some of the most rigorous training in the world, including a month in Alaska for cold-weather drills, this night breeze shouldn't bother her as much as it did. For a fleeting second, she considered the chill might not be the external temperature, but her internal sixth sense. She brushed the possibility aside, but glanced around the poorly-lit parking lot as they made their way to the hangar on the private aircraft side of Bogota's international airport.

She didn't see anything unexpected for two o'clock in the morning. Besides, she could handle whatever came up. Like an overprotective big sister, she scanned the five men she'd lived and traveled with for the past three weeks. They were all capable agents for the United States Bureau of Alcohol, Tobacco, Firearms, and Explosives, but none had intensive special operative training like hers.

Three years ago, Harper had been selected for a top-secret program to prove women could be as effective as men in the clandestine world of SpecOps. Out of one hundred candidates, less than half had successfully completed the same testing of mind, body, and soul the military puts Army Special Forces, Navy SEALs, Air Force PJs, and the Marine Corps' Raiders through. She'd been designated as an elite special operator for the United States government before additional training with the CIA. Even her boss on this task force had no idea of her extensive skills.

"I can't wait to get home and hug my wife and kids," Senior Special Agent Mike Estes told his team. "I feel like I've been gone for months rather than a few weeks."

Harper moved the long strap on her duffel bag to her other shoulder. "I'm just glad we didn't find anyone who could make Chaz." While working on her master's degree, she'd been instrumental in the development of the most lethal, nonnuclear explosive on the planet. The unique process was supposed to be classified, as was her involvement in the DOD research. "I'm still pissed that scientific magazine published an article, including major portions of the formula, then referenced our research in the damned footnotes."

What scared her more than anything else, was her name was included as a member of the development team. For her protection, when she entered the special operative training program, her identity had been scrubbed from social media and flagged with any reference to her military service. No one had thought to redact her name from a research project she'd worked on during college, even though technically she was still on active duty.

Robert Finch chuckled as he walked beside her. "Like the bad guys don't read English or smart people magazines."

"Y'all can just thank the Freedom of Information Act for our *vacation* in Columbia," her mission boss said from her other side, his Tennessee accent creeping in as it often did when he was tired. "I'll be happy when we touch down on U.S. soil once again. This has been one hell of a trip. I despise Third World hotel rooms."

Harper glanced over her shoulder to watch their local CIA contact pull his beat up brown van through a gate in the chain-link fence and disappear into the obscurity of the country's largest city. Keeping up with the conversation, she noted, "I can't wait to sleep in my own bed. I swear the hotels put rocks in the mattresses."

It had been a brutal mission. For three intense weeks, from one end of Colombia to the other, Harper had constantly been on edge. More than once, she'd felt as though someone was watching her, which was to be expected. At five-feet ten inches, she was tall by American standards. She was gigantic compared to most South Americans. Then, there was the fact she traveled with five men. Her unease went far beyond the furtive glances she received almost everywhere. The whole trip, she'd felt as though she were in the crosshairs of an expert sniper. The hyperawareness had emotionally drained her. She was more than ready to go home.

"At least you get to go home to a nice place," Marcus said. "I'm still bunking in with Robert in the bachelor pad that always seems to look like Thursday morning after a hump day party."

Robert laughed. "Hump day is right. You're still just jealous both those twins ended up in my bed, and you slept alone."

"TMI, gentlemen." Harper dramatically stuck her index fingers into her ears. With a grin of satisfaction she gazed at her complaining teammate. "I can't believe I was able to find such an awesome apartment."

"Do you think your friend, Katlin, can find one for me?" Marcus flashed her a lady-killer smile. "How about I move in with you? Didn't you say your place has two bedrooms?"

"Not only no, but hell no." Harper threw him a look that she hoped he interpreted correctly. There was no fucking way she was going to allow him to even visit her new place. She was well aware of his hound dog reputation. A thought crossed her mind, and she didn't bother to hold back the evil grin. Her girlfriends would eat him up and spit him out. She might invite him to one of their clubbing nights just to watch that happen.

Harper was excited about her new beautiful apartment in Washington, D.C. Finding such an awesome place down the hall from the women she had covertly trained with for over a year, was a godsend. Sweat and blood created an unbreakable bond only those who had endured the journey together could understand. She couldn't wait to get back home and tell her friends about this latest mission. Because they all held one of the highest security clearances in the United States, they never worried about comparing adventures.

She couldn't wait to see the faces of Katlin, Grace, Nita, Tori, and Lei Lu when she told them about going undercover in a Cartagena bar on a Caribbean beach to seduce a drug lord wannabe. As their CIA training had predicted, within a few hours, and a few chemically laced cocktails, Harper had been able to get the man alone by making him believe he was God's gift to American women. The corners of her mouth turned up as she remembered him, naked, tied spread eagle to the four-poster bed.

By the time she was finished with her interrogation, she was sure he'd legally purchased the CL-20, a key ingredient in Chaz. Fortunately, the inebriated idiot didn't have the HMX which was needed to complete the formula. He also didn't seem interested in purchasing the popular explosive. His plan was to sell the CL-20 in its solid state to the Revolutionary Armed Forces of Colombia, better known as FARC. Her team had quietly speculated the purchase was one of the CIA's means of supporting the subversive guerrillas when after they reported their findings, they had been ordered to follow up several leads on HMX smuggling.

For nearly two weeks, the six members of the International Explosives Task Force chased a gunrunner who'd smuggled the HMX explosives into the country and was holed up in the far western regions. There was no way to ferret him out. It didn't matter since no connection could be found between him and the hopeful drug lord. Harper had personally confirmed neither had the technology—or brains —to complete the complicated process.

Mission accomplished, they were headed home, and none too soon in her opinion. She was tired of beige hotel rooms that wouldn't get a one-star rating in the United States and restaurant food that was either tasteless or so spicy her mouth burned for hours. Harper longed to slide between the soft yellow sheets of her own bed in her new condo. She'd fall asleep, the monuments around the National Mall in D.C. as her personal nightlights, and refuse to wake up for a week.

"Someone get the hangar doors," Estes called to the team.

Jarred from thoughts of home, Harper yelled back, "I've got it." She trotted to the exterior control panel and reached for the button to power open the gigantic hangar doors facing the tarmac.

Huge rough fingers gripped her wrist and squeezed. For a

nanosecond, she stared in confusion at the sun-browned hand and an arm covered in night camouflage utilities as the man tried to pry her hand away from the red button. His acrid body odor nearly turned her stomach before training took over.

She whirled and brought the heel of her free hand to the tip of the man's nose and jammed it upward with complete focus on her immediate duty to silently take out her aggressor so she could then stealthily assist other team members. The crunch of cartilage and the hiss of his breath through clenched teeth gave her temporary satisfaction.

She continued her spin to bring her knee up. He must've anticipated the move because she contacted his thigh instead of his groin.

He still had her wrist and pulled it behind her back, drawing her closer to his body to reduce the impact of any more of her moves. He caught her arm just before her arrowed knuckles connected to the windpipe-crushing spot above his prominent Adam's apple. He stepped between her legs and pinned her against the cool metal sheeting of the hangar. His huge hand covered her mouth and pinched her nose.

She couldn't breathe. Her rapid heartbeat was using up what little oxygen was left in her lungs.

Harper glared into the shadowed eyes of her enormous attacker as she twisted, seeking any advantage.

She instantly stilled when the cold steel barrel of a gun was pressed into her temple.

"Move and you're dead, *perra*." The gunman growled with a thick Spanish accent.

He was right to call her a bitch. She was one, especially when her life was threatened. But she wouldn't acknowledge his intended insult with as much as a twitch of a muscle.

"I take my hand away. Scream if you want." The glint in

her attacker's eyes said he'd like to hear her beg. "Do you no good. Your team is—"

"Shut up, fool," the gunman snapped in Spanish and sneered.

As if in a dance move, she was yanked from the building and spun around so her back was to him. She sucked in a much-needed breath, replenishing her dazed brain. He had her wrists secured with flex-cuffs within a second. Before she could fight free, another set of large male hands had grabbed her at the hips and bound her kicking legs with strong arms and they'd placed plastic restraints on her ankles.

Once she was secured, the gun returned to her head. She furtively scanned the area. She hadn't heard gunshots, but that didn't mean her team was still alive.

The minimal light from the crescent moon revealed only shades of black, but Harper observed movement everywhere around her. Well-camouflaged men rushed about like ants before a rain, purposeful and under time constraints. *Sicarios*, if she had to guess. These were a drug cartel's armed men who carried out assassinations, theft, extortion, and kidnappings.

Had they been targeted simply because they were Americans? Or had her ATF team angered a capo to the point he wanted retribution before they left the country?

Harper ignored her attackers as they patted her down, choosing to scan the area for her team. The *sicarios* brutalized her breasts and buttocks, then roughly rubbed between her bound legs. They wanted to humiliate her, but she'd been trained by the best in the world. Their hands on her body meant nothing, and neither did their crude suggestions and taunts. They removed all her communication devices and weapons—even the knife hidden in her ankle boot.

She found the rest of her team.

Relief washed over her. They were alive. Distinguished by their casual American traveling clothes of jeans and polo shirts, they stood bound, side by side, guns to their heads. In the diminished light, she still caught the glances they shot her way. *Damn.* She hated when they checked on her because she was female.

This was her fault. She'd let her guard down, eager to get home. They had been minutes away from boarding their jet that would whisk them away to freedom.

She twisted and turned the plastic ties on her wrists, but they only cut deeper into her tender flesh. She was flexible enough to slip her tied hands to the front, but the pistol at her temple kept her from trying more.

What do they possibly want with us? Good luck if it's money they're after. They obviously don't understand government jobs don't pay very well. As team leader, Mike Estes carried cash in both U.S. and Colombian currencies, but they'd gone through a lot of money between living expenses and bribes. Harper vaguely wondered how much he still had left.

～

This concludes your Sneak Peek at Uncaged Love.
Available in all formats
Uncaged Love: **Harper & Rafe** (Black Swan Book #2)
The jungle isn't the only thing that's hot while escaping a Colombian cartel.

She couldn't lose another sick baby…then he brought her his dying daughter.

Choosing Love: Grace & Griffin (A Black Swan novella #4.5)

Hard choices have to be made when parents interfere in a growing relationship.

Unbeatable Love: Lady Falcon (Tori) & Marcus (Black Swan novel #5)

Scarred outside and in, why would his beautiful friend ever want more with him?

GUARDIAN ELITE SERIES

Former special operators, these men work for Guardian Security (from the Black Swan Series) protecting families in their homes and executives on the road, but they can't always protect their hearts.

Double Jeopardy(Novella #1 Guardian Elite series crossover with Hildie McQueen's Indulgences series)

Guarding a billionaire and his wife isn't easy when you can't keep your eyes off your bikini wearing, gun carrying partner who is lethal in stilettos.

Justice for Gwen (Novella #2 Guardian Elite series crossover with Susan Stoker's Special Forces World)

She's not what she seems. Neither is he. But the terrorist threat is real. So is the desire that smolders between them.

Rescuing Melina (Novella #3 Guardian Elite series crossover with Susan Stoker's Special Forces World)

When Jacin awoke stateside, he remembered nothing about his escape from the Colombian cartel or his torture. He was sure of only one thing, his love of Melina, his handler. When she disappears, neither bruises nor the CIA will keep him from rescuing her.

Snow SEAL (Novella #4 Guardian Elite series crossover with Elle James Brotherhood Protectors World)

Terrorists want her…but so does he. The chase isn't the only thing that heats up when the flint of the former SEAL strikes against the steel of the woman warrior.

Securing Willow (Novella #5 Guardian Elite series crossover with Susan Stoker's Special Forces World)

Guarding her wasn't his job, but he couldn't let her die…even before she stole his heart. When he discovers the temptingly beautiful foreign service officer is being threatened, his protective instincts take over.

SEAL in a Storm (Novel #5 is part of the Suspense Sisters new wave of connected books, Silver SEALs featuring a seasoned hero and heroine, second chances, and edge of your seat suspense.)

With a hurricane bearing down on the tiny island, they only have days to find and rescue ten kidnapped young girls and their chaperones…and keep their hands off each other.

CANCUN SERIES

Follow the Girard family —along with their friends, former SEALs and active duty female Navy pilots— as they hunt Mayan antiquities, terrorists and Mexican cartels in what most would call paradise. Tropical nights aren't the only thing HOT in Cancun.

Christmas in Cancun (Cancun Series Book #1)

Can the former SEAL keep his libido in check and his family safe when the quest for ancient Mayan idols turns murderous?

Conquered in Cancun (Cancun Series Novella #1.5)

A helicopter pilot's second chance at love walks into a Cancun nightclub, but she's a jet fighter pilot with reinforced walls around her heart.

Captivated in Cancun (Cancun Series Book #2)

His job is tracking down terrorists so he's not interested in a family. She wants him short-term, then needs him when their worlds collide.

Claimed by a SEAL (Cancun Series crossover Novella #2.5 with Cat Johnson's Hot SEALs)

How far will the Homeland Security agent go to assure mission success when forced undercover for a second time with an irresistible SEAL?

Never Series

The mission brought the five of them together, disaster nearly tore them apart, a mystery and killer reunited them forever.

A Love Never Forgotten (Never Series novel #1)

Dreams or nightmares. Truth or lies. He can't tell them apart. Then he discovers the woman who has haunted his dreams is real. Is she his future? Or his past?

A Promise Never Forgotten (Never Series novel #2)

As a Marine Lieutenant Colonel, he could take on any mission and succeed. Raising his two godchildren…with her…just might kill him.

A Moment Never Forgotten (Never Series novel #3)

The moment he realized she was in serious danger…he couldn't protect her.

KaLyn Cooper is a USA Today Bestselling author whose romances blend fact and fiction with blazing heat and heart-pounding suspense. Life as a military wife has shown KaLyn the world, and thirty years in PR taught her that fact can be stranger than fiction. She leaves it up to the reader to separate truth from imagination. She, her husband, and Little Bear (Alaskan Malamute) live in Tennessee on a micro-plantation filled with gardens, cattle, and quail. When she's not writing, she's at the shooting range or paddling on the river.

For the latest on works in progress and future releases, check out KaLyn Cooper's website www.KaLynCooper.com
http://www.kalyncooper.com/

Follow KaLyn Cooper on Facebook for promotions and giveaways https://www.
facebook.com/KaLynCooper1Author/

Sign up for exclusive promotions and special offers only available in KaLyn's newsletter https://kalyncooper.com/kalyn-cooper-newsletter

facebook.com/kalyn.cooper.52
twitter.com/KaLynCooperbooks
instagram.com/kalyncooper
bookbub.com/authors/kalyn-cooper

www.ingramcontent.com/pod-product-compliance
Lightning Source LLC
Chambersburg PA
CBHW072006190726
48293CB00001B/178